"Street deals and deals, fias .... ⅃aⅅ೦, subterfuge, high technology, and a story that rises to the top of the political foodchain...gripping thriller...satisfyingly hard to put down."

—Midwest Book Review: Diane Donovan, Senior Reviewer

"Futuristic and mind-bending elements...The ending is...sheer genius, as is the plot twist.... This novel has all the makings of a blockbuster film...."

—Ms. Beth Bruno, past president of CT Author and Publishers Association

"An electrifying, whip-smart reading experience about a rogue scientist whose lethal creations place the world at the brink of collapse.... You'll find yourself thoroughly riveted, as well as truly terrified."

—Bestthrillers.com: Bella G. Wright, Editor

"Marshall Chamberlain has lived a thrilling life; now he's writing damn good thrillers.... He's lived it, which is how he can write thrillers with a depth and realism that few can match."

—Featured author in *Foreword Reviews* November 20, 2014,
Foreword This Week issue

"...potent concoction of driven characters, grand-scale mayhem, and a...bit of paranormal."

—Alex Stoddard, an avid Goodreads reviewer

The

Apothecary

ALSO BY

Marshall Chamberlain

The Gruesome Foursome, a Terrorist Senario (Short Story: 2014)

The Owl (Short Story: 2014)

A Mayan Vision Quest (Short Story: 2014)

The Ice Cap and the Rift (2014: Book II of the Ancestor Series-Second Edition)

The Mountain Place of Knowledge (2013: Book I of the Ancestor Series-Second Edition)

Creative Self-Publishing in the World Marketplace (2004)

The Apothecary

A Novel by

Marshall
Chamberlain

THE GRACE PUBLISHING GROUP
Pensacola, Florida

GRACE BOOKS
Published by
The Grace Publishing Group
428 Childers Street, # 24550
Pensacola, FL 32534
www.gracepublishing.org

The Library of Congress Control Number: 2015907691

ISBN: 978-1517154752

Book Design by Marshall Chamberlain

Printed in the United States of America

First Edition: September, 2015

10 9 8 7 6 5 4 3 2 1

To my mother, Rita Ruth Chamberlain, who made her transition in August, 2012. She was always a warrior—focused, resilient and appropriate.

Acknowledgements

To my primary developmental editor, Beth Bruno, past president of CT Authors and Publishers Association: her competence, as well as her insightful notes of encouragement and suggested improvements filled me with renewed vigor.

To my principal copy editor, Alex Stoddard, and my diligent proofing editor, Al Bagdonas, who both helped keep my punctuation consistent and provided perspectives on word use when awkward or incomplete expression might slow the read.

Gratitude and love to my busy middle daughter, Jessica Kenfield. With four kids, a Mary Kay business, a house to run, and sports to keep up with, I don't know how she was able to finish a critical read, picking up errors and questioning anything that might interrupt a reader from the raging river of action—a major objective of my writing style.

"In any conflict the boundaries of behavior are defined
by those who value morality the least."
—Tomlinson, Author Randy Wayne White:
Doc Ford's transcendental friend

The

Apothecary

Part I

The Rogue

 Prologue

Seven Years Ago

"HERE HE COMES. I still can't believe he always wears such old-fashioned clothes. Just look at him all gussied up." Mallory Driscoll stood from the table and waved. "This was such a good idea. I'm going to miss him."

Ryan McKenzie and Mallory's twin sister, Reagan, repositioned their high-backed Elizabethan chairs, slid a huge potted floor-plant farther from the table to make room, and rose to greet the approaching elderly man dressed in a black, tailcoat tuxedo.

In the heart of Atlanta's quaint Virginia Highlands residential area, Phaedra's Grill was about three miles from Emory University in the suburb of Decatur. It occupied the downstairs of a converted, Victorian-style mansion originally built in the 1920s.

On this wintery Monday night, less than half of the eighteen tables in the charming little restaurant were occupied. A fire crackled in the stone fireplace, and the spicy fragrances of authentic Mediterranean cuisine permeated every nook and cranny. It was Professor Barius VonMitton's favorite hideaway during his many years of teaching and research at Emory. The professor had been invited to his own lair to say goodbye to three of his favorite graduating students: the Driscoll twins—Mallory graduating from

Emory Law School and Reagan from its medical school—and Ryan McKenzie, also graduating from the law school.

"Please, sit, sit. You'll cause a ruckus," VonMitton gently reproached, taking the last seat at the table. "It *was* very perceptive of you to choose this special establishment. For many years I have so enjoyed patronizing this place." He adjusted himself to accommodate his long legs and admired the formal table settings, the white linen tablecloth, and the small vase of fresh flowers.

Mallory remembered the labels students had given the professor over the years. He was tall, angular, with feline facial features, lending him a stately appearance. His infamous prancing-like movements and English wit espoused at the front of Emory's great lecture halls conjured an image of a virile cat and a personality likened to a cross between Winston Churchill and Alfred Hitchcock.

For the most part academically retired, the professor had managed to keep trim and appeared vibrantly alive. His gray-brown hair draped over his ears and thick curly strands were cut at shoulder length.

He had arrived in Chicago from the U.K. at the age of fifteen, the only son of a couple lured to academic positions at Northwestern University. He was forever English.

"We are so happy you were able to arrange your busy schedule to be with us." Mallory smiled, tears forming.

The three students retook their seats. McKenzie busied himself opening a bottle of iced-down KJ Chardonnay hidden at his side next to Mallory in a waist-high bucket.

"It is certainly my pleasure. I am honored you would invest your time dithering with an old man.... But do tell me of your plans. I am curious and I know these are exciting times for each of you. Who will take the lead?"

"I will, but first the wine." Mallory glanced at McKenzie. "Ready, Rymac?"

McKenzie rose, and very professionally held the napkin-wrapped bottle, moving to the right of each person, pouring the goblets half-full. He nestled the bottle back in the ice chips and sat down as Reagan lifted her glass.

"A toast," she said and waited until all the glasses were hoisted. "To our favorite professor and mentor, whom we adore."

"Hear hear," McKenzie chimed, and they reached across the table, gently clinking the fine crystal.

While they set their glasses down and got comfortable, a casually dressed waiter arrived to check on the wine. In advance of the professor's arrival, Reagan had instructed the waiter to keep the glasses topped off at the halfway mark. She'd also queried Mallory and McKenzie and pre-ordered their meals. VonMitton would be having a surprise feast of Tunisian roast duck, his absolute favorite.

"Well, it's my turn," Mallory said.

"I must say, you Driscolls look magnificent tonight," Professor VonMitton said. "Your bright faces are reflections of a long, hard journey. I do so congratulate you all on your accomplishments. Ryan, I needn't give you any further compliments. First in your law class and the quiet rogue—I apologize. Do go on, my dear Mallory."

"I'll keep it short. I took the Assistant District Attorney's job with Cook County in Chicago. I decided I'd get my feet wet in the criminal arena—absorb the lay of the land and learn the players...see if I like the big city. You know I want my own practice, but I figured the first step was to get solid street experience."

"I tried to talk her into staying in Atlanta," Reagan said. "She had big-money offers from two major firms here, but we all know how she is." Reagan scowled and then smiled, picking up her wine glass. "But seriously, Mal, I'm happy for you and wish you success at whatever you do. You know I'm here for you. Of course, I realize you don't need my advice. You're the best, and I already feel sorry for your adversaries in Chicago. To you, girl." She raised her wine glass.

"I second that," McKenzie put in. Mallory didn't look his way.

"I'm sure you will find Chicago fascinating," Professor VonMitton said, his eyes sparkling as a parade of memories flashed across his mental screen. "I spent considerable time in that city in the '70s after graduating from Northwestern and working for Pike and Pike on the side of the defense."

"Why didn't you continue with it?" Ryan asked in surprise. To his knowledge, the professor had never shared his past with any of the three.

"To be candid, I am much too shy for the courtroom. Procedures and accepted practices were too cut-and-dried, not like real life—and then I fell in love with the medical field and teaching. But enough of me. What about you, Reagan?"

Reagan flushed and canted her head to one side, caramel-blond curls flopping over one shoulder and splaying down her high-collared white blouse, an involuntary tic she shared with her sister. "I was offered the Deputy Director's position of Pharmco Corp's Computer Programming Department here in Atlanta." She beamed. "The Masters in computer technology and MD in neurology were the tickets. I'll be in charge of developing a three-dimensional body map and plotting functional locations in the brain, and they want me to create software applications for use in medical nanotechnology." She squinted briefly at Professor VonMitton. "You may remember Corey Parnevik, Professor. He was the team leader of a nano project I participated in at Georgia Tech during my Master's program. He's been Pharmco's Nano-

Engineering Department Head for over a year now. We'll be working together at the head office in Dunwoody."

"Yes, Parnevik...quiet, always in a secret rage about something. He never stopped to smell the roses, so to speak. As I recall, you both were in my advanced neurology class." VonMitton lifted his wineglass and held it under his prominent nose, admiring the bouquet and momentarily casting his gaze over the rim at each of his cherished students. Something about Reagan was bothering him, but he couldn't quite put a finger on it.

Since the mid-1980s, VonMitton had experienced over a dozen similar episodes, always characterized by anxiety from an unidentifiable source. Then, typically as time went on, a sense of peril would seep into his consciousness. Each time, the incidents had been harbingers for the same strange and unwelcome event.

It had been some time since he'd experienced a full-blown episode. The thought of it sent a cold chill down his spine. He'd been unsuccessful in his search for answers from a variety of clinicians and had even experimented with hypnotic and regressive therapies. When the phenomena manifested, another entity usurped his mental faculties and took over his body, often for days at a time. During those periods, the professor took on the persona of Dickerson Phelps, a private investigator with a paranormal gift he volunteered to agencies of law enforcement. He aggressively pursued an agenda of crime solving, specifically tracking down horrific serial killers.

Poor Mrs. Livingston, his faithful housekeeper and friend over many decades, had to deal with the personality change and the difficulties of learning how to coax and coerce the entity into releasing the professor from its control.

Peering through the wine glass's distorted image of Reagan Driscoll, VonMitton felt a sense of menace, a possible premonition of a coming episode. All he could do was wait and hope for its dissipation. He pushed the disturbance away and raised his eyebrows. "And last but not least…Ryan?"

McKenzie steadied himself, recalling his trepidation during the professor's oral grilling as his academic advisor during the last phase of Emory's law program. "You know I've always been attracted to the enforcement side of the law. I'm uncomfortable selling anything. I'm not interested in running after the buck. I like to figure things out and work as close as I can to the truth—to make a tangible contribution." He took a moment to sip his wine. "Anyway, the law degree and my three-year stint in the Marine Corps got me accepted by the DEA. After six months of training in DC, I'll be assigned to a regional office, preparing cases against the bad guys."

***

An hour and a half trickled by. The dinner was exquisite and the puff pastry was deserving of royalty. Satiated, one-by-one they lay down their dessert forks, napkins dabbing at any lingering evidence. In the silence of the moment, Reagan gazed at her glass of port. "So I guess this is goodbye for now." Their glasses met again over the middle of the table but more slowly this time. "We promise to be together again very soon," she declared.

"*Salud*" was the overwhelming cry as they returned the glasses to the tabletop, no dry cheeks among them.

Reagan and McKenzie took care of the bill, and ten minutes later, the three escorted the professor out to his car, duly querying his condition to drive and each lining up for a parting hug.

Watching the professor cautiously pull out of the parking area and drive away, the devotees stood mutely waving. As he ranged out of sight, Reagan bid the other two a goodnight. Mallory and McKenzie drifted to the small alcove bar serving as Phaedra's waiting area.

They slid up on padded high-backed stools.

"It's not goodbye," McKenzie said. He turned to face her and scooted his stool closer to hers. "We're just going in different directions to test the waters and settle on what we want professionally."

Mallory sensed his awkwardness. "We've been through this already," she said, gently looking into his eyes and moving her stool still closer. "I even ignored you tonight so I wouldn't have to be reminded. I'm sorry, but I just don't like the idea of you not being around."

"I'm as close as the phone. We can Skype each other.... I just wanted you to know I'm good with it. We're both *type-A* personalities. Maybe when we slow down."

"Who knows?" Mallory said, trying not to grimace.

The moment abruptly turned pregnant. The little, eight-seat waiting-bar was dimly lit and empty. One couple remained at a far dinner table, and the bartender had evidently taken a break, but Mallory suddenly felt confined. They were alone in the soft glow of the round candles lined at intervals on top of the bar. McKenzie cut the moment short by reaching an arm across Mallory's shoulders. His other hand slowly, gently cupped Mallory's chin. He leaned in and lightly kissed her lips. "This can't possibly be goodbye."

 One

Six Months Ago

"MRS. MATHEWS, ARE you up, dear?" The nurse cracked open the apartment door and tapped.

It was shortly after the resident had returned from dinner. She was sitting in her black wheelchair, glued to the TV in the far corner of the small living room.

"How are you, Eloise?" the nurse inquired, slowly walking into the resident's peripheral vision.

The hobbled old woman craned her head and smiled sweetly. She was wrapped in her favorite quilt, supple and faded from years of wear and washings. Her short white hair was fluffed in round curls, and her gnarled hands lay flaccid in her lap. "I fine," she croaked.

"I have your new *Coumadin* prescription." The nurse pulled out a bottle of capsules from the pocket of her white smock. "It was just delivered. I'll add them to your pill tray and take out the old ones."

"I no know. My huthban—I mean dotor, no tell me."

"Don't you worry. His name is on the bottle."

Brightview was a total life-care facility nestled along the murmuring waters of Atlanta's Chattahoochee River near the I-75 crossing of the Interstate 285 perimeter. All the residents had separate apartments in the four-floor structure with 24-hour, on-call care, physiotherapy, a full service dining facility, library, and recreation and prayer rooms. It was expensive to live there, but Brightview had a long waiting list. The organization was well respected, and the staff catered with courtesy and respect to the special needs of every resident.

Many Brightview residents, like Mrs. Mathews, were stroke victims and had lost their ability to communicate. Mrs. Mathews had difficulty sorting her words. When she selected one, something else would come out. To make things worse, her mouth wouldn't form the words the way she wanted. It was frustrating for her. All her thoughts seemed to pile up behind a face reflecting grim acceptance of her personal prison.

"I'm sorry I interrupted you," the nurse said. "I'll put the new bottle in the bathroom cabinet with your others."

"No—yes. Thankoo."

"Have a nice evening."

The nurse added the bottle, shut the cabinet and bathroom doors, and backed out of the apartment, listening for the faint click as the door closed and locked.

When Mrs. Mathews heard the latch on the apartment door click shut, she wheeled over to the table where she read her mail, magazines, and books. She was feeling more fatigued than usual and decided to take her evening meds and watch one episode of her favorite program, *Law and Order*, before she went to bed.

She fingered out the pills from the compartment marked for bedtime and carefully washed each down with sips of bottled water.

Halfway through *Law and Order*, strange feelings began pulling at her mind and coursing through her body—waves of long-forgotten desire. The face of her deceased husband morphed onto one of the characters on the TV screen. He was suddenly young and handsome again, and she stirred in her wheel-chair...remembering past lovemaking. In confused anguish, she reached to her private parts. The memories rushed her to a beautiful pinnacle of release, her body knotting in rigidity. The tautness slowly dissipated. A thin film of perspiration clung across her forehead, and she smiled sweetly as the TV and the room faded into blackness.

***

The next day, Brightview had an unusual visitor.

"Please inform the administrator that a representative from the Association for Humane Treatment of the Disabled is here."

The middle-aged receptionist stared over the monitor in front of her and took in the handsome young man standing on the other side of the sign-in counter: a well-creased charcoal suit, modest red and black striped tie, pencil-thin mustache, fashionably-long light-brown hair all slicked back, and wire-rimmed spectacles. He had an air of professionalism.

After mumbling into the intercom for a few moments, she said, "He'll see you, but his secretary told me to make you aware he can only give you a few minutes."

"I'm sure that will be adequate." The young man smiled, gritting his teeth, thinking she was a stiff bitch.

"His office is down the hall to the right and through the administration doors on the left."

Striding down the sterile corridor, the young man's nose involuntarily scrunched in response to the crisp institutional air-conditioning and the scent of disinfectant.

***

"Thank you for seeing me on such short notice, Doctor. I'm sure you know these visits have to be conducted without warning."

Attempting a cordial smile, Dr. Massey rose from his desk and took the AHTD representative's offered card, motioning him to an innocuous, gray metal chair in front of his desk. He'd have to let his next appointment simmer until he could dispose of this man. "What can I do for you, Mister Stanton?"

"You know the routine, sir." Stanton zipped open his black leather briefcase and handed over a sheet of paper. "According to our standard procedure, the room numbers were selected at random. As you can see, we are also requesting yesterday's videos of the halls and activity rooms."

Dr. Massey read over the request, grimacing. "I presume you are not in a hurry, Mister Stanton. Nathan Marley, our technician, should be able to save the video files to a DVD disc for you by sometime tomorrow. I'll have him call you when it's ready. You are probably unaware, but the resident in room 319 passed away suddenly yesterday evening. We discovered her body this morning, a Mrs. Mathews. A convulsion due to cerebral hemorrhage is suspected. Over the years, she'd become frail and physically humbled from multiple strokes."

"I'm sorry about your patient, but please include the video from *her* room as well. The monitoring must remain random and complete." Mr. Stanton rose from the chair and offered his hand. "And please inform Mister Marley he needn't call. If you would kindly direct him to leave the disc at the reception desk, I will personally pick it up tomorrow at 3:00 p.m."

Dr. Corey Parnevik left Brightview and drove to the Paramount Condominiums on Stratford in the heart of Buckhead. He had lived on the 34th floor of the luxury high-rise for four years. Peeling off the mustache on the way and pocketing the glasses, he ran a hand through his hair. He hoped he would never again have to wear a hot, uncomfortable suit and choking necktie.

He parked in his assigned spot in underground parking and sat in the quiet, pondering the unfortunate old woman's death, concluding she was simply expendable; all cultures should be searching for ways to purge unproductive life.

These thoughts lingered as he rode the elevator to his floor. His father would have understood the concept. Perhaps on his next trip to Europe he would try to track him down. It would be difficult. He hadn't had contact since his father disappeared shortly after his mother's death when he was a teenager, and Neo-Nazis weren't popular in Germany.

Two

Corey Parnevik: Today

PERCHED ON A metal swivel-stool in his private Pharmco lab, Corey Parnevik was engulfed in euphoric reflection, thinking back over the last two years since a Saturday meeting at Fat Cat's Bar with Reagan Driscoll. All along, he'd anticipated her reactions.

He'd known back then she would never partner with him, even if the offer had been strictly on the up-and-up. She was much too straight, by the book, and loyal to the company; but it had been worth putting it on the table and watching her squirm in confusion. Since that Saturday, she'd never once mentioned it. She knew that Pharmco would be nothing without his genius. She must have come to realize he could ruin her career unless she collaborated, and collaborate she had.

***

"How can you sit there with that judgmental scowl? I've spent the last five years with this, night and day. You've been equally as dedicated." Parnevik glared and started tapping the tabletop. Until now, he'd never needed anything from anybody. He downed his beer and smacked the heavy mug on the table. The beer splashed out. "Sorry." The smirk on his face said otherwise.

Reagan gasped at the sound and looked around to see if anyone had noticed. Creases formed across her forehead as she cast her gaze back to Parnevik. To the average person, he probably would have been considered relatively good looking, if arrogance weren't permanently etched into his facial features. He kept his brown hair in a kind of pageboy, a little like a Roman Centurion, and he dressed impeccably in the latest casual fashions of the twenty-somethings. "You're telling me you stole nanites from the lab?" She was glaring at him in disbelief.

Recently promoted to Director of Computer Operations at Pharmco Corp, Reagan Driscoll's new responsibilities included programming nanite movements within the human body.

"Borrowed—and keep it down." Parnevik looked around, seemingly taken back at Reagan's severe tone.

Fat Cat's Bar was the largest sports hangout in Atlanta. At this time of year, Saturday-afternoon football games filled high-definition TV screens in every corner of the place. It was packed, peanut shells scattered on the floor, the bar area crammed with fans sitting on stools and around small round tables. The blended aromas of pizza, wings, and beer permeated the air. Parnevik needn't have worried about being overheard; the hooting and table pounding more than covered their conversation.

"I wanted to experiment in directions the company wouldn't sanction."

"Does anybody at Georgia Tech know what you're doing?"

"I shouldn't think so." Parnevik's eyes twinkled, lips pursed.

For the last three years, he'd enjoyed the research benefits of a post-graduate working assistantship with Dr. Edward Sarcorcee, the Director of the Georgia Tech Nanotechnology Research Center.

Though Parnevik was certifiably a genius, Reagan hated the way he brandished his conceit. She wasn't aware of any friendships he had outside the workplace, and everyone at Pharmco tried to avoid him. His calm demeanor in the face of felony theft was scaring her.

Thoughts of her career raced through her mind: she was professionally tied to a freaky loner who didn't seem to have a conscience. She didn't want anything to do with him. Putting up with him in the labs was torture enough. Why had she agreed to meet him? How could he possibly think he could get away with experimenting outside using stolen, top-secret materials?

She was frightened and felt helpless. Her vision had narrowed and adrenaline was bringing her close to rage. All she saw when she looked across the table were his black eyes.

"Professor Sarcorcee doesn't care what I do in the labs as long as I keep his research progressing. It's been pathetic watching him create journal articles from insight I provided, for which the conniving deadhead never gave me a line of credit."

"What happened to the pig?"

"It died." Parnevik looked away. "I used a *bulimic* nanite for the test. The electrical stimulus was too high. It ate itself to death."

"Shit, Corey, why couldn't you just stay within the system?" Reagan's stomach was churning. Suddenly the thought of wings and blue cheese dressing brought on nausea.

"They're moving too slow. I was bored. It's time to move on. I have ideas of my own."

"You signed non-compete agreements and patent right covenants just like I did." A shiver of trepidation ran across her shoulders. "I don't think you're seeing this clearly."

"Look, I created the delivery vehicle—and I only signed away selected patent rights to Pharmco. I'm rebuilding the nanite structure using new components. It's completely different, and the applications I have in mind won't compete. I've checked it out with a patent attorney and a major Atlanta law firm."

Reagan was shocked at the blatant disregard for professional ethics. "You didn't even attempt to get approval to test the bulimics on swine?"

"I was testing the effects of varying the electrical charge using my redesigned nanite, and I did it at Georgia Tech. Pharmco's sitting on its hands, and I'm sitting around with nothing to do. They won't let me go any further. They're waiting for patent-pending status. And then there's the FDA approval process. Hell, it'll be five years before any human testing."

Reagan sat on the edge of her stool, revolted by his complaining.

"And I wanted to determine the accuracy of your targeting program."

Reagan pushed off the high-topped seat. She stood staring at him, long, curled, caramel-brown hair dropping in heaps over both her shoulders. "I'm going to the ladies' room," she said. If she was going to keep her cool, she needed to regroup and towel her face off with cold water. He had all but admitted he'd been using her body-map program outside of Pharmco, another direct breach of Pharmco's top-secret government contract.

Parnevik saw their server coming. "Here come the wings. Let's get another pitcher," he said gleefully as she walked away.

Reagan turned around, gritted her teeth, stunned he was back to upbeat and cheerful. "When I get back, maybe you can tell me why you *really* asked me here."

"Come on, Reagan. With your roommate out of town, I thought you'd like the company."

"Sure," she scoffed. "We're not even friends, Corey." She turned away before he could comment.

Parnevik watched her bustle through the maze of tables toward the restrooms. He hadn't noticed before, but she'd put on weight since college, and she used to wear her curly hair much longer, dress in Levis, tight sweaters, and spiked boots like her twin sister Mallory. The hippie look hadn't fit in with conservative corporate culture, and in his opinion Reagan's allure had suffered.

During his seven years at Pharmco Corp, Corey Parnevik's stellar career had taken him to the head of the Nanotechnology Research Department. He'd first worked briefly with Reagan years ago on a project at Georgia Tech when she was completing her Masters in computer science and he was just beginning a PhD in nano engineering.

Over the last two years at Pharmco, they had combined talents, developing test nanites that delivered electrical charges to specific locations in the brain, theoretically stimulating the brain's natural capabilities to repair dysfunctional motor and memory synapses.

The research had spread out, encompassing areas in the brain processing sensory perception and influencing a variety of behavior disorders. Theoretically, the research would become a viable avenue for healing the blind, deaf, and disabled and help the mentally incompetent toward healthy and rational functioning.

Parnevik didn't wait for Reagan. He liked his wings hot, and he devoured half-a-dozen with gusto, including the crisp bone ends, washing them down with ice-cold draft.

He caught sight of her returning to the table as she passed the reception station at the front of Fat Cat's. She weaved her way among the tightly packed bar tables, smiling, fending off comments from boisterous football aficionados, pulling her sweater over the top of her skirt, and flicking away bunches of long hair falling over her face. She always came across as poised and appropriate. Abruptly, he realized he'd never really liked her.

"Okay," she said, mounting her stool. She had noticed him watching her navigate back to the table, sitting there with a half-baked grin, gobbling the wings, dressed like a college kid, probably to humiliate her. "Why did you ask me here? We see each other almost every day." She had resolved to stay calm, hide her anger and contempt. She'd think through what to do about the situation later. All she wanted now was to get out of Fat Cat's as fast as possible.

"Lighten up, Reagan." He ripped paper towels from the rack in the middle of the table and wiped the sauce from his hands and face. He grabbed the pitcher of beer and filled their mugs. He set it down and calmly said, "Since Pharmco has me bottled up, I was hoping you would work with me outside, in a new area. If it pans out, perhaps we could go off on our own and start a business together...incorporate. You could be my partner."

Reagan picked up her beer mug and took a swig. She felt herself flush with unease and glanced dartingly over the crowd. His egotism was limitless. She fought to hold her temper. "Off the top that sounds farfetched," she finally managed. She felt his eyes on her. She tugged the basket of wings to her side of the table. "So what do you want from me?" She grabbed at a chicken wing, but the sight of the greasy pieces and smell of the hot sauce turned her stomach. She pushed the basket away.

"What I really want to do is experiment with recreational highs—for one thing, try to produce effective arousal to help cure sexual dysfunction. I'm also well along calibrating the stimulation necessary for nanites to cause mimicking of the pleasure and hallucinogenic effects of recreational drugs on the brain." Parnevik kept eye contact. "Pharmco turned me down because they already produce hugely profitable medications that handle sexual dysfunction. Obviously, I didn't broach the recreational drug topic. Like I said, I've reconstructed the delivery vehicle.... I need you to help me write destination programs."

Reagan felt her mouth go slack. The spurious congeniality and the insult of assuming she would consider lending her reputation to help him was too much to take. She was speechless, feeling small and frail. The fear was paralyzing. She was a mouse caught in a maze, but she reached deep and gathered a semblance of control. She stood, taking her jacket from the stool back and shouldering her purse. "I have to leave," she said, fumbling in her purse and tossing a twenty-dollar bill on the table.

Parnevik had watched her reactions, knowing he had her where he wanted her. "I think we could make a lot of money," he said facetiously as she turned her back and walked away.

***

Shaking off the residual memories, Parnevik pushed off the lab table and spun on the swivel stool. Miss Driscoll had come through with the key brain-map programs he'd required, including unencrypted navigational commands, and that was all that mattered.

Since then, he'd had complete freedom to follow his own research agenda. With minor assistance from one of Pharmco's junior programmers, he'd learned to write code to any one of the brain map's over 12,000 defined sites in the cerebral cortex.

His first sortie was experimenting with brain section 1746, the pleasure palace located in the brain's parietal lobe. Progress towards his goals had been steady and secret, but it bothered him he would always have to forgo peer recognition. *It was her fault. If she'd joined him....* He idly swiveled on the lab stool. He'd have to find ways to fix the recognition problem, but now Reagan Driscoll was a clear threat to his master plan. She had the power to expose him. It was time to take care of that and do it prior to ridding himself of gridlock and corporate restrictions. The endless FDA submissions and testing had him hamstrung, keeping him from creative expression. He felt locked in a box of his own contrivance, but fortunately, he had thought far ahead.

He smiled and swung back around to continue proofing the sheets of schematics spread on the lab table. Tape analysis of the old woman's death at the nursing home had led to adjustments in the strength of the nanite's electrical charge and recalibration of the target location in the brain. He shook his head; it had taken a while, but he was confident he'd perfected a benevolent pathogen of sexual arousal. Next stop, live testing in the singles bars, and then *Amor* should be ready for its début in front of a commercial audience.

 Three

Pharmco Corp

"AND MISS DRISCOLL, she's privy, isn't she?" Jim Doggett paced in front of the CEO's desk, shirtsleeves rolled up, suit coat draped over a chair.

An inventory of nanites developed under Pharmco's top-secret DOD contract had revealed missing drones, altered bulimic nanites derived from the company's first commercial nano-project and presently undergoing the rigors of FDA testing.

"Reagan? She's key to the whole research group, but she doesn't work with nanite development. She produces encrypted software that guides them to targets in the body. She's totally loyal and indispensable. I don't think she could be involved."

"We have to look at everyone with access." Doggett halted in front of the desk. "She has access." Jim Doggett had been head of Pharmco security for sixteen years and sat on the Board of Directors.

"You won't find anything, but I understand. It's your call—I assume you'll look at Parnevik's department first. He's been responsible for all the engineering, and he controls the inventory." Dr. Safford leaned back in his desk chair, casting Doggett a concerned stare. "Jim, make this quick. If you have to go outside for additional resources, do it. I'm counting on you. Every lab room and storage unit has card security. Video cameras cover every square inch of the labs. It would seem you have all you need."

"The systems have been up for two years. That's a lot of tape, but I'll get on it. My first take is to hire a DOD-approved outside contractor to do the screening, and perhaps ask Reagan if she can design software to make the job easier."

"Fine. We're scheduled to announce submission of Memory 247 to FDA testing at the end of next week. We've got to make this go away. I'd be forced to report an incident like this to the DOD. They could shut us down, and we'd be out of business."

 Four

Chicago, Illinois

"WE'RE GETTING CLOSE." Mallory raised her hands in the air, her long, caramel-blond hair dangling, curls in matted disarray. Dirty jeans hung on her slender hips, and a filthy plaid shirt was half tucked-in. She saw her reflection in the freshly Windexed, glass office separator, and images of her sister briefly caused her to smile. Though much had changed from college days, they both still wore their hair the same way, albeit Reagan's was shorter now.

The new offices weren't exactly plush, but the old, heavy wooden molding and thick double doors left by the predecessor accounting firm gleamed with new life, lending the office spaces an air of stodgy competence.

"Yeah, all we need is furniture, rugs, a coffeepot, places to nap, some portraits of the famous, and a conference table to seal deals." Jane collapsed on a metal folding chair, the only item in the reception area.

Hands on hips, shaking her head, Mallory took a fond look at Jane Cobb, her partner in the new law firm of Driscoll & Cobb. She was a mess, clad in a dingy, white tee shirt and knee-worn Wranglers, sticky and stained with varnish, and her black hair hung in tangled strands.

"At least we have windows," Mallory came back, "and the view isn't bad for the sixth floor."

"You know, we deserve this, Mal. We paid the price. Working for the D.A. and learning the ins and outs was rough. Now we get a chance to put it all into practice." They laughed at the metaphor as Jane rose from the chair.

They entered one of the three private offices. The ornate wooden door and matching wainscoting solidified the desired impression of authority and reliability. Meandering to the six-by-ten-foot window, they looked up and down the brightly lit corridor of the windy city's famed Michigan Avenue.

"This is going to work," Mallory said, hands back on her hips. "And never despair again, Miss Cobb. I want you to know that last weekend I lined up furniture and knick-knacks you won't believe from an estate sale, including portraits of JFK and Winston Churchill. Thank you very much."

They laughed uncontrollably until Mallory started coughing. "Then all we need are clients." Jane patted Mallory on the back, tears rolling down her cheeks. She towered above Mallory by six inches, looking like a friendly stork consoling a stricken member of her brood.

"The D.A.'s got us at the top of the list." Mallory looked up at her partner with affection. "The pay isn't much, but we can make ends meet. Good public defenders are hard to find. We'll be as busy as we want to be. I just know it. And we'll be free to begin pursuing what we both want."

"We're going to have to live in here to make it." Jane shuffled to the small room connecting two of the offices. "We have storage space, a sink, and a toilet. We can take sponge baths. There's room for a double bunk bed. It's doable."

"I spent our last bucks at the estate sale, but I still have room on my MasterCard. We ought to be able to find some cheap chests of drawers and whatever else—hot plate, microwave. Worst case, we might have to wait tables at night."

"I can live with that."

"So let's go celebrate." Mallory was deviously grinning and waving her right hand in a rallying circle. "And by the way, I meet with Doug Pearson at Menard Prison in Joliet tomorrow—He's the convict I told you about a couple of weeks ago. If I think he's telling me the truth, I'll seek grounds to reopen his case."

"Mal, we can't do pro bono work on day one."

"Not to worry. Pearson's ex-wife has money. While I was attending parole hearings and becoming interested in his case, I ran into her and we got to talking about it. She doesn't think he's guilty. I'm pretty sure she's still in love with the guy. I told her I'd look into it if she was willing to retain us, and *if* I decided he had a chance. She said *yes*. I think we may have our first client." Mallory led the way back to the reception room and with a sly grin turned to face her partner. "Come on, Jane. It's almost Christmas. Let's hit Pedro's on Rush Street."

 **Five**

Corey Parnevik

HOW MANY TIMES had he traversed these long hallways, paneled walls heavily laden with framed portraits of Pharmco Corp's elite and the short form of their engraved vitas? *What a crock.*

Parnevik was about to begin the adventure he'd painstakingly designed over the last three years. Seven years of hard work in these labs, self-imposed introversion, staying on task and on time accomplishing company objectives, had taken its toll on Parnevik's limited patience reserves. Being constantly reined in by narrow-minded mediocrity had been excruciating torture; however, the end was in sight.

His part-time assistantship at the Georgia Tech Nanotechnology Research Center had been extended for two more years, enabling continued access to sophisticated equipment if needed. A sabbatical from his responsibilities at Pharmco would provide the opportunity to set the stage for his permanent exit without raising a red flag. He needed a block of unfettered time to recharge and begin implementation of his master plan.

Carrying a single manila folder, his mind wandered as he closed the distance to the CEO's office. No one had the slightest idea. No, that wasn't quite true. Reagan Driscoll did, and he'd rectify that before he started on sabbatical.

Approaching the visitor's waiting room, his mind switched channels, and he couldn't help but gloat. He was about to land a big fish. The Genovese Family had responded to his proposal to test *Amor* because, as he had put it to them, "it was in their best interests."

Passing through the waiting room, he neutralized his facial expression before acknowledging the CEO's secretary with a wave. He needed to appear tired and bedraggled.

"Sit down, Corey. I was just thinking it's been a while since we last had a one-on-one." Dr. Safford was a congenial leader, and he knew who was responsible for his company's success. He rose from his desk, motioning to the informal seating arrangement next to a long bookcase occupying the wall on one side of the office. "Too many impersonal conferences and meetings in-between."

They took seats in opposing leather chairs separated by a glass table.

"Dr. Safford, you know I'm not one for small talk, so if you don't mind I'll get right to the point."

"Of course, Corey."

"I'm burned out again and need a break—seven or eight days this time. Christmas is just around the corner anyway. You know how I get. I can't help it. I'm taking my prescriptions, but the long hours in the labs have sapped my attention span. I'm jittery and anxious—the same old signs."

"I trust it's not progressively worsening."

"No. It's just time to re-energize."

"I must admit you look a little pale. Have you had your quarterly medical exam?"

"I thought you'd ask." Parnevik leaned out of the chair and slid the folder across the table.

Dr. Safford scanned the two pages and returned the folder to the tabletop. Parnevik suffered from hyper-anxiety and a form of paranoia usually leading to panic attacks. "I'll add this to your file. The clinic doesn't recommend an increase in the dopamine dose, so I assume you're basically okay. I also assume you have your responsibilities on auto pilot."

"All the testing deadlines are ahead of schedule. I've labeled and containerized our nanite inventory in case the DOD wants to see our standard storage protocol. Nothing else should require my attention for a while. I should be able to take care of the few things remaining by the end of the day. Tomorrow's Saturday. I'm planning on leaving town over the weekend."

"Before you go I want you to sit in with John Doggett. As you know, we're trying to find out what happened to the missing inventory. He'll want your input. After that, you have your eight days, no more."

"Thank you, sir. I'll see to it."

"Where will you go?"

"I haven't decided. Some place isolated, different, where I won't be disturbed."

"What if we need to contact you?"

"You're welcome to try my cell phone. I may be out of service range for short periods, but I'll respond when I can."

Six

Newark, New Jersey

SATURDAY MORNING, COREY Parnevik landed at the Newark Liberty International Airport. A text message left on his cell phone last night directed him to search out Yellow Cab, number 2019.

The cab driver delivered him to a shopping center in the Newark suburbs and told him to walk to the rear of Costco's, out the back, and down the loading dock. A dark-blue Lincoln Town Car would be waiting.

The back door of the Lincoln opened as Parnevik was taking the steps alongside the loading platform. Jacketless and clad in Docksiders, a blue-striped tieless shirt, and navy blazer, he carried his favorite black leather Flison Field Satchel, his face passive, stride confident, ignoring the icy cold of the Jersey winter. He slid into the seat and offered his hand to the single occupant.

"Why the change in instructions and this elaborate transportation ruse?" Parnevik took in the lean Italian man at the other end of the seat. In his mid-fifties, well dressed in a charcoal business suit, he sat cross-legged in the plush interior.

Somewhat surprised at the unassuming manner of the young scientist and discounting his lack of respect, the Italian passenger was impressed with the well-thought-out method his guest had devised to win this hearing. "It's nice to meet you, Mister

Parnevik." Tony Gatturna turned his head—no handshake. He raised his eyebrows over a cold stare, his face hardening in a moment's pause. "To answer your question, no location is considered secure unless it has been freshly created. Government agencies hound us constantly. Wireless technologies allow them to eavesdrop from afar. Our regular phones are tapped. We've been forced to develop our own sophisticated software to protect communications through the Internet. We purchase customized, encrypted satellite phone services from the Chinese. Protocols are altered weekly to stay ahead of U.S. government hackers. It is very expensive to conduct business, Mister Parnevik. Your cab ride served to scan you for unwanted gadgets. This car is clean. We were not followed. This conversation will be private. I hope that explanation is sufficient for you…Mister Parnevik."

"I didn't mean any disrespect, Mister Gatturna. I now can appreciate your precautions." Parnevik smiled slightly. He'd selected the Genovese Family because of its reputation for attention to detail, its successful diversification into legitimate businesses, and its ability to conduct effective business without bloodshed. It had learned to adapt in a constantly changing world.

"Call me Tony." Gatturna peeled the wrapper off a cigar and tapped the end of a clipper against the glass partition. The driver turned a knob on the dashboard, and an increase in conditioned air entered the sealed-off space. "I am curious, Mister Parnevik, why did you pick us for your query, and how did you know we owned the restaurant in Atlanta?"

"I'm not interested in doing business with the Mexican drug trafficking organizations that dominate the Atlanta region. They're unreliable and their kingpins are out of country. The Jamaicans and Blacks aren't organized well enough and can't be trusted. The Genovese Family is known as the wealthiest and most secretive of the Five Families. I want sophisticated distribution worldwide and to work with an organization that isn't reliant on the production end of hard and soft drugs. I need a working relationship with deep pockets, major muscle, and the ability to act quickly. As for the restaurant, the owner, Alfred, is well known in Italian circles to be Daniel, *The Lion*. I figured it was a way to safely get your attention."

"Smart." Gatturna lit his cigar. "No one saw you leave the container on the hostess stand, and nobody but Alfred read your note requesting delivery. The sealed container arrived by special courier and the key through regular mail. Impressive. We have studied the dissertation on your work, and we took our time checking you out. What you propose is captivating. What you can deliver for our scrutiny appears to be the logical first step." Gatturna puffed out several smoke rings, watching the circulating air whisk them apart, aware of Parnevik's relaxed composure.

"I agree," Parnevik said matter-of-factly, "and I propose a live test of *Amor* in Atlanta at your convenience. Perhaps a trusted family representative can contact me through your protected e-mail system and make the arrangements."

Caught off guard by the insolent instructions, the Italian boss said, "I will discuss this with others, and you will be contacted." A scowl screwed up Gatturna's facial features. He reached into the breast pocket of his suit and handed Parnevik a card with an e-mail address, identification code, and password. "I think we're on the same wavelength for now," he stated dismissively. "Perhaps we will meet again, Mister Parnevik." Gatturna picked up a small hand mic from a side-door pocket. "Dorian, our guest is leaving us here. We'll go back to the office."

Parnevik offered his hand as the door of the Town Car popped open, but Gatturna didn't make a move.

"Go back the way you came, Mister Parnevik. Your cabbie is waiting. Have a safe trip back to Atlanta." The car sped away.

***

"What do you think, Paulie?" Gatturna said, after relating his impressions and the gist of the meeting. He'd spent the time on the return trip from Newark back to New York City in quiet thought, analyzing what he should do. One of his secure working offices occupied two back rooms of Angie's Italian Restaurant on Manhattan's Lower East Side, and the Family used a sterile conference room in the basement for serious business discussions.

"If what he proposes is for real, it could be big business." Paulie Torentino sat in his usual place, a leather couch opposite Gatturna, who reclined behind an old, heavy wooden desk that had seen better days. Paulie was the Genovese Family Capo, the *consigliore*.

"And if it's for real, we'll need a way to tie him down…but that's for later. I want the guy watched, and I want you personally at the test. Set it up. Let's see what he's got. I gave him an e-mail ID in our system. If it doesn't turn out, I want him put down permanently. We don't want outsiders knowing anything about how we do business."

***

Disembarking three hours later at Atlanta's Hartsfield International Airport, Parnevik had just enough time to ride MARTA from the airport to Buckhead, make a quick stop at his condo to alter his appearance, and present himself for his appointment with the owner of a small construction company. The man was an engineering acquaintance from his graduate-school days at Georgia Tech and impeccably honest.

It had been uncomfortable masquerading during their dealings. Parnevik would have enjoyed flaunting his career success and sharing his nanotechnology accomplishments. The ruse was unfortunate but necessary.

Parnevik had recently purchased a residence off Peachtree Battle Street in Midtown, using his very first manufactured identity, the documentation of which had cost him dearly. The construction company had just completed the refurbishments to the old Tudor house, including substantial alterations to its cellars in preparation for Parnevik's first laboratory and excavation of a hidden exit from the cellars to the front yard through the middle of a fountain and rock-falls complex.

Parnevik wanted to make sure the house was ready for final inspection. He intended to spend most of the coming Christmas holidays moving from his condo and organizing the house furnishings. Then he would disappear.

 Seven

Lake Rabun, Georgia

"WHAT ARE YOU working on now?" Mrs. Leonard asked, entering Professor VonMitton's library and wheeling in a vacuum cleaner.

The professor sat at his polished mahogany desk next to a window with a panoramic view over Lake Rabun, a smooth steel blue under wintery grey clouds. The scent of wintergreen lingered in the quiet. A banker's light reflected off his reading spectacles as he craned around at the interruption. His attention had drifted from an article in the *New England Journal of Medicine* to thinking about the Driscoll sisters and Ryan McKenzie. It was two days before Christmas and he hadn't received the expected holiday cards from any of the three.

"I don't suppose you'd consider knocking? You take such liberties. It's most distressing."

"I see you're in one of your snits," Mrs. Leonard said. "Are you going to tell me about it?"

"It's the Driscoll sisters and McKenzie. I can't seem to get them off my mind. Something's not good. I can feel it. I'm going back into town tomorrow. I'll poke around in the Medical Library. There are a few things I need to look up before Emory closes for Christmas break. I'll be back the day after Christmas, and I'll call on Reagan. She's working in Dunwoody at some pharmaceutical company. Maybe I can get clear of this."

"You don't think—?"

"Let us hope it's not that—but you know, I had a similar feeling years ago at that wonderful dinner they threw for me to say goodbye after graduation, but it dissipated. We'll see. I didn't realize how much I've missed them.... Strange."

Once a week the professor ventured out from his renovated, 1920s era country house on Lake Rabun, an hour and a half north of Atlanta, to teach a neurology class at the Emory Medical School. It kept him in touch with academia and gave him access to the university research facilities. Ever since the first incident back in 1986 with the appearance of the dry-ice personality of his schizophrenic counterpart, he'd spent a great deal of time on neurological research, trying to discover more about his peculiar gift of foresight and the periodic manifestations of his other self.

 Eight

Miami, Florida

THE NEW REGIONAL Director of the DEA twisted in his chair. He'd been given an understaffed office overseeing one of the most prolific drug regions in the country, and he was compelled to make a decision that wouldn't be appreciated by the staffer who sat in front of him on this day before Christmas. "McKenzie, we're spread pretty thin here. I have to ask you to take a field case. It's only an investigation."

"Sir, I'm a lawyer," Ryan McKenzie said flatly. "When I signed on, the DEA gave me assurances. I prepare cases for trial, working the crossword puzzle of evidence. I don't even carry a weapon."

The director took stock of McKenzie. He'd only seen him a couple of times in the three weeks since he'd arrived from D.C. The guy certainly looked the part of a field agent. He was obviously in great shape; he had a graceful way of moving and a gentle but precise demeanor. He was the Inter-service Pistol Champion five years running. "Do me this favor. I won't forget it. It's just a request from Pharmco, a pharmaceutical company in Atlanta. They're missing inventory. It should all be internal. You'd be working with their chief of security. *And*, in compiling the file on the situation we found one of your close acquaintances from

Emory is a department head there—Reagan Driscoll. You could catch up with old friends. What do you say?" The director passed McKenzie the file, leaned back in his black leather chair, and steepled his fingers.

McKenzie had empathy for the new director. He'd been given an office short three agents, and the next graduating class from Quantico was five weeks away. Replacements would be raw and require seasoning before effectively integrating into the way the region was managed. Two of the remaining six field agents in the office were taking holiday time. It was clear the request was not negotiable. McKenzie took a short moment to reflect: the Christmas holidays were coming. He had no plans. He'd have his routine back in short order, and it *would* be great to check in with Professor VonMitton and Reagan. Seven years had gone by since graduation and he hadn't visited. No one had kept in touch. He wondered how Mallory's life had unfolded in Chicago. No one had reached out, just Christmas cards. That reminded him he hadn't sent out his cards. *Where does the time go?*

"When do I leave?"

"You're booked on a 3:00 p.m. flight. My secretary has your itinerary all set up. Look, I appreciate this. Check with the Deputy Director in D.C on field protocol and get refreshed on procedures."

"Nice timing. I assume you knew I didn't have any plans for Christmas."

 Nine

Club Elan

"IT'S A FRUSTRATING drive from the airport, Mister Parnevik. Your rush hour is just as bad as New York City." The Genovese Family *consigliore* had chosen to rent a red Mustang convertible. The Atlanta weather was unusually warm, and he fancied the fast flashy car. He also wanted to control the transportation aspect of the meeting with Parnevik. As agreed, he'd picked up Parnevik in front of his upscale, high-rise residence in Midtown. It was 7:00 p.m.

Paulie Torentino could have passed for a stereotypical, middle-aged stockbroker if it weren't for his long, slicked-back, black hair and narrow, feline facial features linking him to an Italian ancestry. "What's the schedule? My plane leaves at 12:05."

Both men were dressed in three-piece suits as Parnevik had advised.

"Sorry about the drive. I would have picked you up at the airport." Corey Parnevik sat in the front seat, relaxed and in control. He'd taken an extra dopamine dose to quell the anxiety that constantly plagued him. Its pounding presence would shortly return but not before the test. He had to be smooth, deliberate, and decisive with this hoodlum. "It's Friday night and it's Christmas Eve. We're on our way to the hottest spot in the city for the single business elite. On a night like this, human nature says they should have nothing to do but go hunting."

***

Club Elan was located in the middle of Dunwoody's upscale Perimeter Mall, just outside I-285, the interstate circle around the heart of the Atlanta Metropolitan Area about ten miles from city-center.

Corey Parnevik and Paulie Torentino walked through the first set of glass doors behind two gorgeous, long-legged women, who glanced back and seductively smiled. There was a short line to get through the second set of glass doors in front of a well-dressed bouncer taking five-dollar bills and stamping wrists. The place was packed, a dazzling, high ceilinged, high-tech menagerie designed to captivate the senses and facilitate ease of movement among two tiers of dining tables and up to an elevated bar made of jade tile. The bar was shaped like a four-leaf clover. Stand-up tables filled a twelve-foot wide area six feet from the meandering edge of barstools.

The pedestal bar area was brass-railed all the way around and crowded with smiling faces, libating, talking, expressing, eyes wandering. Empty glasses hung three feet deep from a network of fancy wire-mesh racks hovering over raised liquor-bottle displays set on light-enhanced glass shelving.

The bar's color scheme was green, white, and chrome. High-topped bar seats, constructed of formed Plexiglas and polished chrome tubing, lined the bar top. Several stepped aisles accessed the bar area from a double row of circular tables around the perimeter. The 20s to 50s crowd was well dressed, fresh from work, in twos, threes and fours, hooking up with friends and looking for action.

Parnevik led Paulie up the steps to the bar, where they blended into the stream of bodies moving around the two-deep stack of standing patrons. "Nice, huh?" Parnevik said over his shoulder.

"I seen one place like this in Jersey. It was a gold mine while it lasted. Fickle yuppies move to the next in spot without reason. We never got involved with this business."

Parnevik spotted the bartender he was looking for, waved to get his attention. The tall blond man in his mid-20s wore a long-sleeved white shirt with a paisley tie and dark-green belted slacks. All the bartenders were similarly dressed, clean-cut young men whose primary job was to keep the women coming back—the flowers attracting the bees.

The bartender motioned, pointing to the bar in front of him. Parnevik couldn't see through the gathered horde, so he carefully excused himself through the milling mass and led Paulie to two seats marked "Reserved".

"You got some pull?" Paulie slid onto the hi-tech barstool.

"It's just money in advance. I set it up yesterday. The band's getting organized on the other side. It won't start for about an hour. I want to get this business over with before more noise and alcohol consumption significantly alters the mood of the clientele. You saw the bouncers—the guys in buttoned suits positioned around with their hands in front of them?—it can get macho in here after the crowd gets juiced up and starts dancing."

Paulie craned around, slid off the stool, and took a moment to scrutinize the place over the layered humanity packed around the snaking bar. Nearly all the tables, two steps down from the bar traffic lane, were full, and bouncers were strategically placed along the outside railings. He retook his seat and found Parnevik engaged in conversation with an attractive woman in her early 40s, short black hair hanging straight, dressed in a tight black suit with the blazer open and her unbuttoned white blouse flaunting just enough cleavage to mandate inspection.

"This is my friend, Ned," Parnevik said. "I'm sorry. I haven't asked your name."

"Patricia—Pat Delorian."

Paulie nodded, trying on a smile and adjusting his stool.

"Nice to meet you, Pat. My name's Peter Hampton," Parnevik said and then turned to Paulie as the bartender set down two gin and tonics. "We were just talking about this place and why we like it. We were at the point of discussing the noise level. You have to change the normal pitch of your voice. It's irritating and makes you feel unnatural. Scoot your seat over a little." Parnevik got up and slid his chair back about two feet to make room for Paulie, and Pat angled a little toward them.

The woman appeared to be alone. Not uncommon, but most of the ladies arrived in pairs or threes for moral support. Singles were usually meeting up with someone. If you were unattended for long at Club Elan, the trollers lined up.

"Pat, are you having something to eat or just winding down?" Parnevik asked.

"Waiting for one of my co-workers. I wrongly thought Christmas Eve would be more subdued here. I wanted to have a private conversation with him about some issues—I'm his boss. Would you mind saving my seat for a few minutes? I'm going outside to see if I can get him on his cell and turn him around to some other place."

"No problem." Parnevik stood and moved so she could get clear, at the same time shedding his suit coat and draping it over the stool back.

Paulie adjusted his stool. "Nice babe. A little old for you."

Parnevik ignored the comment. "This is perfect." He reached around the stool into his suit-coat pocket and pulled out a bottle of aspirin.

"You got a headache already?" Paulie leaned in closer. The ambient noise was distracting.

"No. This bottle of aspirin is product. Even the label looks like Johnson and Johnson. But it's just rock candy. That's all a chemical analysis would reveal." Corey screwed off the cap and tapped out one tiny pink capsule. "Completely benign, nothing to draw any attention."

"That's it?"

"Yup." Parnevik slid Pat's mixed drink close to the edge of the bar top, took a quick glance around, and dropped in the tablet.

Parnevik had adjusted the intensity of the nanite's electrical charge based on his analysis over a year ago of the old woman's room video at the Brightview Nursing Home. He had also made minor modifications to the nanite target in the brain, sending it to several sites in proximity of number 2114. Another test at a Georgia Tech fraternity party several months ago had convinced him *Amor* was ready.

Paulie watched the tiny pink pill sink to the bottom of the glass. "Won't she see it?"

"It only takes about sixty seconds for the candy coating to melt away. What's left is a nanite one tenth the size of a pinhead covered in a shell that only dissolves in human stomach acid."

"Pretty slick, but what if she doesn't drink the whole drink?"

"When the sugar coating is gone, the nanite is less dense than water and rises to the top, invisible."

"How many in a bottle?"

"Five hundred. At twenty dollars a pop, that's ten thousand dollars in retail street value. Think how easy it will be to distribute."

"Here she comes." Paulie reached for his gin and tonic.

Parnevik rotated around on the barstool. "Did you find him?"

"He's going to meet me here. There's a quiet café in the mall down by Sachs. We'll go there—anybody try and take my seat?"

"No, but the bartender almost snatched your drink. I saved it."

"Thanks." She eased onto the stool and wrapped her hand around the glass. "He's only about thirty minutes away. Well, here's to Christmas." She raised her glass.

Parnevik clinked his gin and tonic tumbler against her rocks glass.

Paulie listened to their small talk, keeping a close eye on the woman for any change in tone or mannerisms, skepticism written across his face.

Five minutes later, without seeming aware of arranging her skirt repeatedly, she started on her blouse, reaching inside to adjust—shake her bra straps. Then her left hand was on Parnevik's knee and she ran it up and down his thigh. The conversation had turned to sex.

"Pat, you better get a grip. People are looking." Parnevik pushed her hand away.

Writhing on the barstool now, Pat swung around and began to openly grope two guys in sport coats jammed next to her, who were trying to carry on a conversation.

"Hey, lady, what's your thing here?" one of the guys said, moving out of reach.

"Take me to the restroom," Pat said to him, sliding off her barstool, pressing her spread legs against his side.

The guy looked bewildered. "I don't think so. Somebody get this nut away from me."

Pat pulled on the guy's belt. A sheen of moisture glistened on her forehead and her cheeks were red splotched.

Parnevik had left the bar area as soon as Pat turned away from him. He came back with one of the bouncers. By the time the bouncer had a grip on Pat, she was weeping and hysterical.

Another bouncer arrived, and the two of them escorted the thrashing woman through the gaping crowd and off the pedestal bar. Parnevik and Paulie watched them disappear through the double doors leading to the Club Elan offices.

Ten minutes later, two police officers came through the establishment and headed for the office. Parnevik and Paulie sat transfixed as the policemen dragged the handcuffed and clearly confused and agitated woman out to a waiting paddy wagon.

"That didn't go so well." Paulie's brow was furrowed. "Looks like you got more work to do, Sonny. I've seen enough for now." He looked at his watch.

"Minor adjustments. It appears women are more sensitive to the stimulus. It works just fine on men, and she was unprepared. In a voluntary situation, the effects would be expected and the user goes with it." Parnevik saw impatience written across Paulie's face. "This presents a unique opportunity, however."

"Whadaya mean?"

"The police will take her to a hospital for blood tests to determine if she's under the influence of drugs. They won't find anything. The nanite is constructed with sugars. The body breaks them down into common metabolic compounds. I assume you have access to the workings of the Atlanta Police Department. I suggest you get hold of a copy of the tests and records generated by this arrest. It will tell you that your future users and distributors will be impervious to possession charges. Your distributors will be selling candy."

"What do you think will happen to the woman?"

"By the time she gets to the police station, the arousal will have worn off and the nanite dissolved away. She won't like what she remembers, but she won't have a clue. The only conclusion would be that somebody slipped her a Mickey, or else she had some kind of episode and should undergo a full psychiatric examination. Even if they charged her with disturbing the peace, she'd get off. She probably doesn't have a criminal record and is an upstanding person. My bet is they'll let her go."

"Well, nothing more to be done here. I'm gonna take off."

"I want you to take this back with you." Corey handed Paulie a labeled aspirin bottle containing three small pink capsules. "You should conduct your own tests. You need to know that if you attempt chemical analysis, the nanite will self-destruct. But feel free to try if you must. I mean no disrespect, Mister Torentino, but surely you must realize this product will completely change the face of the drug business."

Paulie nodded. "You want a ride?"

"I'll stay here for a while and soak up any aftermath. Then I'll get a cab."

"We'll be in touch." Paulie rotated out of his stool.

"Mister Torentino, one other thing. You should see to it that the video cameras in this place have a problem with tonight's coverage. It's like a casino in here. We wouldn't want anyone to know we were sitting next to Pat. I'm leaving for Europe in a few days. I'll be gone for several weeks—but I'll be checking my e-mail."

Ten

Atlanta PD

"CAPTAIN, I HAVE a DEA agent out here. He says you wanted to see him." Sgt. Jones was Capt. Trussel's secretary-assistant, like a military first sergeant.

McKenzie almost felt at home, standing tall in front of the police sergeant. The Marine Corps had left its permanent mark.

"Send him back, Jonesie."

The sergeant pressed off the intercom button. "It's the glassed-in corner office down there." Sgt. Jones gestured over the open room of desks and activity. "And a merry Christmas to you."

Geographically divided into situation cells, the huge square space was filled with projection screens and computer monitors keeping track of police actions in real time. McKenzie took a circuitous route, weaving through the hustle-bustle of animated cross-desk discussions, paper shuffling, and telephone chatter. The glass double doors were open.

"Agent McKenzie is it? How'd I get the DEA's attention so quickly?"

McKenzie shook a strong hand over the captain's desktop and took a seat in front of the metal desk strewn with files, newspapers, and McDonald's wrappers. He was a fireplug sort of man, small and compact, middle-aged, white shirt, sleeves rolled past his elbows, round face, coarse featured, full head of salt and pepper hair.

"I was on my way to Pharmco Corp out in Dunwoody— They'd requested assistance. You contacted the Miami office over an incident Christmas Eve. I was told to report here before I checked in with the company."

"I appreciate it, and I'll get right to the point—Hell of a way to spend Christmas. The incident took place at a high-profile club in the suburbs. The place was packed—Friday night before Christmas. Some middle-aged woman lost it and allegedly was sexually explicit with two men at the bar—groping them in plain view and demanding sex. Witnesses reported she seemed all of a sudden to come unglued and spaced out. Bouncers subdued her, and we sent a wagon to bring her in. The two guys she assaulted didn't want to be involved, and the club refused to issue a complaint. She was a regular—some sort of bigwig."

"How can I help you, Captain?"

"Well, I'm not sure. By the time we got her to the station, she was acting normally. We sent her to Emory University hospital for a work-up and kept her overnight. We assumed somebody must have slipped her a Mickey, but the tests came back negative—no evidence of drugs. Alcohol level was within limits. She wasn't drunk. We let her go, but before I close the file, I wanted to get the DEA's take. Anything like that in your experience?"

"It's out of my league, Captain. I'm a DEA agent, but I'm actually a lawyer. The field office was shorthanded with the holidays and all. They prevailed on me to respond to Pharmco's need for a consult. But I'll check on it and get back to you. What did the woman have to say?"

"She remembered feeling tingly and suddenly overwhelmed with desires she couldn't control. She was embarrassed to talk about it and worried the incident would follow her to her job. We agreed to report it as an unfortunate and dangerous prank on an unsuspecting patron of the club, names withheld."

"Did you post an inquiry through the law enforcement database and overseas?"

"No bites." Capt. Trussel frowned. "The incident's been bugging me." He stood and pushed his chair back against a bookcase. "We had an old lady pass away in a nursing home a couple of years ago from a stroke. Nothing unusual about that, but the home reported the death because the video record from her room the night she died showed unusual behavior. She was examining herself sexually, smiling and mumbling to her husband who was long deceased. I saw the tape. She seemed to be in panicked ecstasy, out of control, and then her face went blank, eyes open wide. It wasn't pretty. Somehow I can't get it out of my mind that the two are linked. It's just gut feel."

 Eleven

Pharmco Corp

"I THOUGHT I might find you working overtime. You mind if I join you, or are you going to continue to avoid me?" Parnevik spoke the words in his usual pursed smugness. He stood in front of Reagan Driscoll, balancing a plastic tray of food with both hands. They hadn't talked face-to-face in weeks. Strictly business. It was Sunday, the day before his scheduled departure for Europe, and his plan for her still lay unhatched.

"No, not at all," she lied. "I've been crushed with the FDA requests for information. They don't understand how my software works, so I've had to explain without allowing them access to the actual programs and encryption codes. You know what I'm talking about."

Parnevik pulled up a chair across from her and arranged his cafeteria plates in precise order on the gray metal tabletop. "It's the same with me. Their requirements are driving me crazy. I'm getting out of here for a while to unwind," he stated, carefully placing his napkin over his lap. Her body language clearly told him she was uncomfortable.

"How goes your outside research?" Reagan sensed she needed to placate him and extricate as soon as possible.

"It isn't. I got discouraged, and with the company investigating the missing nanite inventory, I decided to cease experimenting after my last test."

Parnevik sensed Reagan digesting his statement. Admitting awareness of the inventory shortfall, she might deduce he wasn't using Pharmco nanites and someone else was responsible.

"I'm sorry it didn't work out, but I'm glad it's not you. Security will eventually find out who's responsible."

She glossed over it. So, *she didn't believe him.*

"You said you quit after your last test. Did you ever do anything with the impotency-target program I gave you?"

She was quickly devouring the last of her salad, no eye contact, throwing out inane chatter, preparing to leave. But Parnevik had lured her in. "I did. It was the last test. I tried it out on a random female at Club Elan on Christmas Eve."

"You have got to be kidding! On a human being? You must be out of your mind," she said too loudly, spitting bits of food across the table. She glared at him and lowered her voice. "You used my programming?"

Parnevik leaned over his plates on arms and elbows. "So you're an accomplice," he whispered, "a co-creator whether you like it or not—but settle down. No one needs to know. Just like no one needs to know I might have been involved with the inventory loss." His face was solemn, uncreased, his black eyes cold, fixed on her like a gloating stone gargoyle.

"What did you do? What happened?" Perspiration had collected across her forehead. She collected her napkin and utensils. Her stomach had soured.

Parnevik leaned back in his chair, took up his fork, and picked at his salad. "I sent a six-point-five volt delivery to 2117." He glanced around the cafeteria to see if anyone was taking notice of the conversation. "Let us just say the patient was successfully aroused."

"Unbelievable! You didn't sit here without an objective. I won't help you."

It had always been obvious Reagan's integrity and commitment to her work were risks he couldn't afford. At one point, he'd conjured up a scenario framing her for the stolen inventory, but it wouldn't work if she altruistically came clean. "I want you to do nothing," he said, black eyes glaring. "And I guess this means we aren't going to be partners. I *so* looked forward to having a competent co-worker. I hope we understand each other?"

"We don't." She attempted to steady her gaze at him.

In her eyes, Parnevik saw a cornered rat running a maze with no exit. He stared at her until she turned away, collected her plates and remaining utensils, stacked them on her tray, and headed for the dump station.

Part II

The Mentor

 Twelve

Professor VonMitton

REAGAN STOMPED OUT of Pharmco's cafeteria, shaken and confused, but as she headed for her lab work area, she channeled to automatic pilot. She would call Emory and see if Professor VonMitton was in his office; he often spent a weekend in private research. His competent company would be therapeutic, and it would be great to see him. It had been at least a year since the last time.

Relieved to find him still working, Reagan drove to the campus, parked in the visitor's area in front of the Admin Building at Emory's Medical School, and got out of the car feeling limp inside, helpless and guilty at the same time. She'd successfully avoided any contact with Parnevik outside of Pharmco but always harbored remorse in the assistance she'd given him two years ago. Now, she felt threatened and afraid.

Reagan vowed to think it out over the holidays. She and her boyfriend, Bob Faust, were finally getting away over New Year's for a few days in Las Vegas. Before they left, she had a scheduled investigative interview at Pharmco about the inventory. Surviving unscathed was the goal. But right now, she needed to talk to someone. Her career was at stake. Legal advice might be required. *What a mess.*

She climbed the granite steps of the building in twos. Professor VonMitton had been on the verge of embarking for his Lake Rabun house and a week's retreat. The heavy oak-paneled door to his office was ajar. Reagan pushed it open and peeked around the doorframe. The high ceiling, stout Victorian chairs, matching conference table, huge wooden desk from the 1920s, the scent of wax, all blended, creating an atmosphere of quiet sanctuary. The professor rose from behind the desk, dropping his reading glasses to the chain around his neck.

"Thanks for seeing me, Professor. I hope I didn't disturb your plans."

"Not at all, my dear. Come right in and sit. It's been too long." He rose and motioned her to a comfortable leather chair at the side of the desk next to his high-backed recliner. "Believe it or not, I was just going to phone you at your apartment when you called. I hadn't heard from you, Mallory, or Ryan in such a long time."

She took the chair, fondly reminded he always wore English-cut blazers whether in his office or lecturing, never succumbing to the casual decorum of the modern university atmosphere. Prim and proper, he combed his full head of long, gray-brown hair impeccably behind his ears and down his shoulders. His eyes gleamed playfully on top of a welcoming smile.

The professor took his seat and leaned toward Reagan. "What is it that brings you here, young lady?—though I wish it were just to see an old friend."

Reagan related the two-year old story: her meeting with Corey Parnevik at Fat Cat's on a football-frenzied Saturday afternoon, learning he was experimenting outside Pharmco with *borrowed* nanites, developing the directional programs for him, the missing inventory at work, and then today's scary confrontation in the Pharmco cafeteria.

Professor VonMitton was attentive and had allowed her to go at her own speed. It took fifteen minutes before Reagan ran out of words.

"I don't know what to do," she said, frightened that much more by having gone back over her travesties. "Should I get a lawyer? If I get the police involved, I'll probably lose my job—maybe go to jail. This guy is definitely off his rocker. I can't believe I avoided confronting this situation. I always kept him at arm's length for my own benefit. It was selfish…. He even said we were co-conspirators. He could involve me in the whole thing—the missing nanites—whatever. It would be his word against mine."

"Reagan, settle yourself. Remember your training. It comes down to ethics. My advice is to let the chips fall where they may. Go exonerate yourself—up front. Tell the story to Pharmco—right to the CEO. I've known Doctor Safford for years. He's a good man. You made a mistake—several mistakes. They have the legal resources to help you. If you tell the truth, it will show through. Safford will do the right thing."

Reagan left Professor VonMitton's office resolved. He was right. She would put this behind her before she and Bobby left for Las Vegas. It was the only way she could hope to enjoy the holiday they'd planned for weeks.

***

With Reagan's departure, Professor VonMitton sat immersed in the silence of his office, surrounded by the emptiness of the building, staring out the window. The last glimmer of sunlight filtered through the tree limbs of the campus grounds below. He was suddenly disturbed, almost transfixed with anxiety, and he recognized the symptoms. It had been four years since he'd last experienced what always felt like a classic anxiety attack, the harbinger. And, on top of this, there was something profoundly dangerous about the path Reagan Driscoll was about to take. He sensed it. It could be a precursor to a possible Titus Smythe awakening.

He would require the support of Mrs. Leonard. He called his faithful housekeeper and placed her on notice. It was possible Titus Smythe would pay a holiday visit to his Lake Rabun home.

 Thirteen

Ryan McKenzie

IT WAS THE day after Christmas. McKenzie had spent Christmas in his hotel room, reviewing the Pharmco briefing papers he'd taken with him from Miami and running DEA databases to see if anything turned up to help the Atlanta PD.

Jim Dogett, the head of Pharmco Corp security, met McKenzie at the circular security hub inside the main entrance. He was in his early fifties, reasonably trim, curly black hair, dark-blue three-piece suit. He looked like any other pasty-faced executive, except for the stern stare and the hardly noticeable bulge under his left arm.

"Glad you could make it on such short notice." He offered his hand. "I guess this kind of ruins your holidays. Sorry about that."

"No, not really. I'd just be puttering around on my boat, maybe taking a little sun. I live alone. My mom passed away recently, and my dad visits Europe this time of year. I don't have brothers or sisters to bother."

As they were talking, McKenzie was aware Dogett was giving him the once-over. He probably wasn't used to business types with unruly hair, wearing quick-dry outdoor pants, charcoal herringbone blazers, and Sketcher running shoes.

"We better get started. Give your ID to Officer Peters here, and he'll take your picture. Then sign in." He pointed to an oversized logbook on the counter. "Doctor Safford is waiting on us."

The Pharmco administrative and executive offices were plush, taking up half of the top floor of the five-story building. Each of the floors was about the size of a Best Buy. A portrait gallery of the company's corporate lineage lined the fifth floor's main hall.

After appropriate greetings and a secretary taking coffee orders, the three men took seats around one end of Dr. Safford's oval conference table. A floor-to-ceiling bookcase separated it from his desk and working space.

"Agent McKenzie," Dr. Safford began, "we trust you had sufficient time to go over the briefing paper we provided?"

"I did, but I don't understand why you requested our assistance. It seems like a small internal matter."

"There are complex relationships not outlined in the briefing paper. At the present time, your level of clearance prohibits access to the information."

"I assume my regional director is aware of these security relationships, as you put it?"

"No, he is not," Dogett put in. "Suffice it to say, our request came to the DEA through contacts we have in the Department of Defense."

McKenzie sensed this was going to get dicey. Even his regional director didn't know the DOD was directing the play. "Okay, let's get on with it. How can I help you?"

"As you know," Dr. Safford smoothly transitioned, "we are a major manufacturer of FDA-approved drugs and invest massive amounts of capital in R&D. A significant part of our research efforts are in the field of nanotechnology. You have a full briefing paper—but to reiterate—we concentrate our activities on stimulating the areas of the brain that control memory, govern motion, produce sensory perceptions, and harbor the way we interact with one another—areas involved with psychotic behavior. Our objectives are to find ways to reverse or alleviate the effects of diseases like Alzheimer's, ACL, Parkinson's, MS, and a plethora of psychological conditions. We are also attempting to use nanotechnology to repair areas of the brain damaged by stroke—especially those affecting loss of hearing, sight, and motor function."

"What you don't know is that forty percent of that effort is dedicated to top-secret DOD contracts," Doggett said.

"The complex relationships you can't tell me about." McKenzie was aggravated, feeling boxed in.

"Precisely." Dr. Safford moved off his chair to the library-like wall of shelved books. He refreshed his coffee from a pot on a hotplate next to a mini-bar built into the shelving.

"McKenzie, what we need is forensic support," Dogett said.

"Mister Dogett, with all due respect, the Atlanta Police Department has all the resources you could possibly require."

"They don't have the clearance, McKenzie." Dogett's face had reddened.

"It's Agent McKenzie to you." He felt the back of his neck heating up.

"Sorry for the tone." Dogett backed off. "It's been frustrating from my end. Internally, I haven't been able to track down evidence linking anyone at Pharmco to the missing inventory. It's out of my purview to go outside with covert actions, and private services are out of the question for the same reasons as the police."

"At least you must have a list of people with access. They have to be your prime suspects."

"We do, Agent McKenzie." Dr. Safford's voice was calming as he walked around the table with his coffee. "From all our video tape reviewing and procedural checks and rechecks, it comes down to the same three people, Corey Parnevik, responsible for all nanite engineering and manufacturing, Reagan Driscoll, our Director of Computer Management, and Ernest Kelto, her assistant. These three are directly involved developing the programming responsible for nanite movement inside the body and engineering the nanites. Parnevik is on sabbatical somewhere in Europe, Kelto has just given thirty-days notice, tendering his resignation, and Miss Driscoll is leaving tomorrow for a Las Vegas holiday…. So we called in the DEA—and hence you are here—to assist on a strictly confidential basis.

McKenzie was looking forward to seeing Reagan while he was working the case here. He'd have to track her down today if he didn't want to miss her.

"We've completed all the staff interviews," Dr. Safford continued. "The transcripts are here for your holiday pleasure." He pulled a thick manila folder from the bookcase, dropped it on the table, and sat down. "It appears that all we can do is have these people investigated using your resources—pursue a course of observation—whatever you people do."

"I'll go over these and see if anything turns up."

"Time is becoming an issue, Agent McKenzie." Dr. Safford put his coffee cup down on the table. "Besides the missing bulimic nanites we've cited, last week we discovered three structural, nanite prototypes were missing—nanites Parnevik had programmed to self-duplicate. They're involved with the DOD contracts. Their squad of due-diligence investigators is scheduled ten days from now. They could shut us down."

A tinkling chime sounded from Dr. Safford's work area.

"Excuse me," he said and briskly left the table. He stepped behind his desk and reached for the intercom. "I asked not to be disturbed."

"I'm sorry, sir, but I thought you would want to attend to this. Miss Driscoll is here to see you. She says it's important. She seems a little distraught."

"Send her in. Thank you, Ali. I didn't mean to bite your head off."

Reagan Driscoll stepped into Dr. Safford's office, obviously agitated. When she saw McKenzie, she threw up her hands. "Rymac, what are *you* doing here?"

"Hey, Reagie, it's a long story," McKenzie said, automatically standing.

"We didn't know you two knew each other." Dr. Safford raised his eyebrows.

"We went to Emory at the same time," McKenzie said.

"Very well. Please take a seat, Miss Driscoll." Dr. Safford gestured at the conference table. "We were in the middle of something—"

"It's personal, sir."

"Please," Dr. Safford said, a sweep of his hand taking in the others. "Nothing leaves this room. Please."

Reagan had left the Medical School's Admin Building and walked the Emory University quadrangle several times, rehearsing her story. She had boiled it down to a simple apology and her volunteered resignation.

Her delivery had been smooth and deliberate. Straightening her back against the chair, she quickly cast a glance at each man and then looked at her hands in her lap, tears coming.

A long silent minute passed. Dr. Safford stood, face firm and resolved. "Reagan, it took a lot of guts to come clean. You may find this surprising, but my first instinct is one of thanks. This meeting is about the missing inventory. We now know who is at fault and can take appropriate action. For your part in this, I will take it up with the board. I see no reason at present to keep you from your work. You will have to make a formal written statement. Mister Dogett will see to it. Please wait outside for us to complete our business here."

The door closed. "Agent McKenzie, I think you can now see why it was important for the DEA to be involved. Your offices can conduct a routine investigation of Mister Parnevik's outside activities and see to securing any evidence at the Georgia Tech labs."

"We can't have any of this reach the media or local law enforcement," Dogett said. "DEA presence is not to be public knowledge. We want to keep it that way."

McKenzie interlocked his fingers and set his hands down on the table. "Without local police cooperation, we'll have a tough time executing a formal investigation—taking statements or getting the courts to issue search warrants or subpoenas. We can't get ahead of ourselves, gentlemen. There's no evidence linking Parnevik to the missing nanite inventory, only Reagan's story. She claims he threatened her. If it came to it, it would be her word against his. It will appear she's a conspirator unless we have conclusive evidence. I'll run our databases on Reagan, Parnevik, and Kelto as well as everyone with access to your nanite inventory. We'll see what comes up. In the meantime, I'll talk to Kelto. You say Parnevik's on sabbatical?"

Dogett stood. "He told us he was thinking of going to France."

***

McKenzie paced around in a vacant office next to Jim Dogett's while Reagan wrote out her statement. When she finally finished, he could see she was drained. He waited while she said goodbye to Dogett and took her by the elbow as she exited his office, guiding her down the long executive hallway to the elevator.

"I'm sorry you had to be here, Rymac. I sure screwed up."

"That's an understatement."

"What do you think will happen?"

"I don't know, Reagie. But I assume since you weren't fired, it depends on getting the goods on Corey Parnevik. I hate to be harsh, but if I were you, I'd hire a good lawyer.... What about Mallory?"

"She's in Chicago—has her own practice. I'll call her. It's been two years since we've seen each other. Did you ever touch base with her?"

"Nah. I'm sure she has a busy life."

"Come on, Rymac. You're a big boy now. You've both proven yourselves. Wasn't that the big bugaboo with you two when you split after graduation?"

"Yeah, I suppose so."

"So?"

"I thought about it, but time has a way of making it difficult."

 Fourteen

Parnevik: Day Before Sabbatical

IT WAS PERFECT. *It all fits so nicely,* Parnevik pondered as he watched the stone house from a bench across the street on the sidewalk bordering Piedmont Park.

Reagan's roommate was just leaving. Emma Kitsumi had evidently come home for lunch. He knew from experience Reagan seldom left the office at lunchtime, preferring to wolf down cafeteria food and return to work. She'd be trying to accomplish as much as she could before she left for Vegas with her hairdresser boyfriend.

Parnevik was confident in his disguise. He'd rented an electrician's outfit from a prop and casting shop in Midtown. He'd learned a lot in his four years with the acting academy at Georgia Tech, and the private investigation classes he'd taken at Atlanta Technical College had prepared him in the latest spook technology.

Emma's little Honda Civic melted into the traffic down Tenth Avenue as Parnevik crossed the street and walked straight up to the screened-in porch of the old stone house. No one on foot gave him a second glance. He opened the screen door and stepped up to the polished oak entrance. The lock clicked to his master key, and he entered as if he owned the place.

Struck by the silence as he closed the door, he felt oppressed and claustrophobic in the forbidden space, a thief, an interloper, uninvited amongst the private space and personal possessions of others. He stood inside the doorway for a moment, mesmerized, taking in the aroma of cooked ham lingering in the air, and then elation bloomed with the immensity of the plan festering in the bowels of his mind.

He had taken an extra dose of his neuro-medication, a dopamine blocker that passed through the blood-brain barrier to ensure staying calm. He still felt a little pressure, and tiny exploding lights stirred behind his eyes from deep inside his anterior frontal lobe.

Gradually, over a period of months, his medication had reached its efficacy limits, and he occasionally experienced emotional disturbances, causing him to see and hear things that didn't exist. Without proper balancing, his elevated production level of dopamine often produced mania and moved him closer to schizophrenic behavior.

He'd found a semblance of relief through trial and error. The cumulative condition could be neutralized through experiences of horrific fear and physical exhaustion. Adrenaline neutralized the excess of the neurotransmitter, soothing the racking build-up inside his head. He was far overdue for a revised prescription.

Moving from room to room with unnecessary stealth, odd curiosity overwhelmed him, and a sense of perverse righteousness came forth. Everything was so orderly, so perfect.

He slipped into Emma's bedroom and quietly opened her bureau drawers, compelled to caress her undergarments and inhale the lingering scent of the lemon drawer-freshener. Transfixed, he suddenly felt a loathing. She had rejected him. He wanted to hurt her. He slammed the drawer shut, the sharp sound returning his focus. He didn't understand why his mind wandered away from his control.

Fantasies often overwhelmed his attention, sometimes for several minutes at a time. A reccurring and distracting picture would form in his mind...of a knight bringing greater good to mankind, a savior for the addictions of the weak, accompanied by a feeling of virtuousness.

He felt his lips slack apart, a numbing of the facial skin, and raced to Emma's bathroom to peer into the mirror. He was involuntarily grinning, face drooping, and his eyes were vacant and dilated from the dim light in the apartment. Was this the image of insanity?

He splashed water on his face and toweled off. The cool liquid was a magic elixir, bringing him back together again. He folded and replaced the towel; slipped on hospital-grade, Latex operating gloves; and went directly to Reagan's bathroom. She had always been a health nut, trying to get him on a regimen of vitamins and minerals. Her bottles lined a shelf next to the sink. He reached into a pouch on his tool belt, brought out a bottle of the brand of Vitamin C she favored, shook out the dozen capsules he'd prepared, and switched out pills from Reagan's bottle.

The third-generation "B" nanites were programmed to release an electrical stimulus to sites 764-778 in the pre-frontal cortex three times as great as the ones he planned to eventually market through the Genovese Mafia Family. Uncontrollable *Bliss* was not only unpleasant, but fatal. She would survive long enough to realize who was in control.

His last stop was an exquisitely carved redwood box containing Reagan's private jewelry and mementos. He placed a tiny, glass inventory vial next to a diamond ring in an arcane setting.

Exiting the back door of the house, he released the latch on the one-way gate controlling vehicle entrance and walked to the sidewalk. He crossed Tenth Avenue and headed down a shallow bank and over the grass soccer field to his Jaguar in Piedmont

Park's parking lot. The next stop was Hartsfield International on his way to New Jersey to meet with the Genovese Family. If all went well, he would then be off to Quebec City and the next step in his plan.

 Fifteen

Mallory Driscoll

7:30 IN THE morning found Mallory arriving at the Driscoll & Cobb law offices. Her level of anxiety had been on the rise since her sister's call last night. A fitful night left her with growing trepidation, and she'd hurriedly dressed and headed for downtown Chicago, hoping to sort out her feelings on the drive.

Ryan McKenzie showing up in Atlanta on DEA business was the least expected of events, and he'd been in contact with her sister in her time of need. She'd received his cell number from Reagan.

Mallory stopped her pacing a few minutes after entering the office reception area and flipped her cell phone open. "Reagan called last night and filled me in. She said you were assigned to the Pharmco investigation...so that's why I'm calling. She wanted my advice."

McKenzie was surprised Mallory had taken the time to track him down at his Dunwoody hotel. "It's always nice to hear from you early in the morning," he said, flatly.

"I'm sorry, Ryan. How have you been?"

"I guess we can get into that later." She was obviously agitated. It sounded like the years hadn't changed her much.

"I was sort of astonished when she said you were there."

"Is that a good thing?"

"Stop it. From your end, what's this all about?"

"I really don't know yet. It appears to be a simple matter of missing research samples from their inventory, but the company won't tell me the whole story. They say I don't have the clearance. My regional director sent me here on sketchy rationale. Orders came from outside the DEA—are you going to represent Reagan?"

"I told her I'd come down and determine the intentions of the company, so I guess I am. They would have to file charges with the local police if there's going to be criminal prosecution. They could file suit in the County Superior Court for breach of contract—any number of avenues."

"They didn't fire or suspend her, and that seems unorthodox. She admitted sharing proprietary software with Corey Parnevik, the prime suspect. They haven't even reprimanded her. I don't think they want the local police involved because of the publicity. Maybe you can get something out of them. It's not my business. Pharmco's got me acting like their private police department. I'm supposed to find Parnevik and evidence linking him to the missing nanite inventory. I'm just a consultant with DEA resources."

"Well, maybe we'll run into each other. I've made reservations to come down on New Year's Day. Do you think you'll still be involved?"

"Actually, Mal, I'd rather be somewhere else. The DOD top-secret contract with Pharmco is about ready to blow up in their face. I don't know how long I can remain effective. I'll be playing it by ear."

 Sixteen

Parnevik: Next Day

THE E-MAIL INVITATION from Paulie Torentino had been short and succinct. A plane ticket would be waiting at the Atlanta airport. Corey Parnevik had been summoned to a meeting at a restaurant on Manhattan's Lower East Side. The Genovese Family had agreed in principle to his terms. It appeared they were anxious—or perhaps Italians didn't believe in the sanctity of New Year's Eve.

Parnevik took a taxi from LaGuardia International, grateful the driver wasn't in the mood for small talk. He removed a water bottle from his backpack and took an extra dose of medication. Displaying any signs of claustrophobic behavior or anxiety would be unacceptable. He needed to stay calm and in control, wits sharp.

Angie's Italian Restaurant was nondescript, a hole-in-the-wall on a side street ten blocks from downtown Manhattan. A sign tacked to the crosshatched half of the dark, wooden doors read, "Closed Until Tuesday the 2nd."

The doors opened before Parnevik had a chance to knock, and a short, stout man with slick, black hair, dressed in a sharkskin suit, waved him inside. No words were spoken as the man expertly frisked Parnevik and then trailed him through the dimly lit kitchen into a back office.

The space was much larger than it had looked approaching the marked door from the kitchen. Stale smoke mixed with the scent of oregano and tomato sauce attacked his nostrils. Three men in white shirts, sleeves rolled to the elbows and collars open, were seated at a hefty wooden table in the middle of the room, enjoying a spaghetti dinner, red wine, loaves of Italian bread.

"Sit, Mister Parnevik." Tony Gatturna motioned from the head of the table and gave Parnevik's escort the thumbs-up.

At the other end of the table, Parnevik recognized Paulie Torrentino from the Christmas Eve test and took the indicated seat set with plates, glassware, and utensils.

"You know Paulie," Gatturna said, waving his fork at Parnevik. "This is Joe Joe, my cousin," he pointed the fork at the heavyset stoic man across from Parnevik. "He works for Paulie—help yourself. First, we eat and drink. Then we have questions. Nobody wants to miss the Cotton Bowl at four."

***

Gatturna dismissed Joe Joe after directing him to clear the table and take wine and a plate to the man serving as lookout at the front of the restaurant.

"Mister Parnevik, your presentation was impressive. The PDF document was unique. Our people tried to take it apart as you recommended. The encryption was outside that offered by Adobe. It disappeared without a trace, but we took notes as you suggested—the bottom line is if you want our money, you do what we say."

"I don't require funding, Mister Gatturna. I will pay cash up front for the lab equipment, supplies, and documents I requested.

You have the resources to make the purchases and arrange delivery at the designated locations in an untraceable fashion."

"We want to be able to protect your production process," Paulie said. "It's like insurance."

"Mister Torrentino, the labs will be small and compact, taking up less than 400 square feet and set up in obscure locations in secret, creating no suspicion. No one is to know the locations. Any observation you would propose could cause suspicion and compromise the facilities."

"How do we know you can keep your end of the bargain?" Gatturna lit a cigar and stood to stretch.

Paulie took Gatturna's lead. "I need to take a piss," he said and left the office.

"Preparing a distribution network takes time and muscle," Gatturna said, bringing two ashtrays to the table, taking his chair and resting his feet on an empty seat.

"That's your investment. I make mine. You make yours." Parnevik reached into the inside pocket of his blazer, dragged out a Lucky Strike, lit up, and moved an ashtray to within reach. It was going well.

"This production end may be a deal breaker. Controlling production is sound business."

"It's not going to happen, Mister Gatturna. And I need to warn you up front. If we do business, do not tamper in any way with the product. Safeguards will be chemically embedded to make an incursion quite expensive."

Gatturna's composure remained nonplussed. "For now, we let it ride.... Your proposal says nothing about delivery."

"I purposely left it out until we reached this point. Three well-known manufacturing companies located in Pakistan, South Korea, and Vietnam will produce product from my ingredient specifications. As orders are received, I will air freight the necessary nanite delivery systems I produce in the labs. You order product from the manufacturers, specify delivery instructions, and remit fifty percent down and the balance upon receipt. All legal."

"We need to talk about the split."

"Not negotiable, Mister Gatturna. Ten percent is our bargain, based on a retail price of twenty dollars per tablet. You have a lock on costs. The manufacturing facilities produce drugs for major corporations all over the world. Your business with them will be small potatoes at first and the costs will reflect that reality, but with volume, the costs go way down. You send my ten percent to the Lichtenstein account I've given you. Receipt is acknowledged by the shipping documents you'll receive from the manufacturer and freight carrier."

Paulie came through the office door. "Boss, your wife called. She wants you home for the early family dinner."

"Okay, Paulie. We're getting close here. Sit down."

Paulie lumbered into the seat next to Parnevik, an intimidation factor.

"Okay, what's the minimum order? I say we get our feet wet if the lay out ain't too much and Paulie agrees."

"A minimum shipment is a case of twenty-four bottles to a single designated address. Five hundred pink tablets in each bottle, labeled *Sweetness*, looking like aspirin and tasting like candy. At a pegged initial street value of twenty dollars a pill, each bottle is worth ten thousand dollars to a vendor—two hundred and forty-thousand per case. Upon receipt of my ten percent, I place the order with the contract manufacturer of my choice. You will receive instruction from the manufacturer to wire the first half of their payment and cost of delivery. The airfreight carrier confirms shipment to you direct as in normal business practices—tracking numbers via your account on their website. Upon taking delivery, you pay the remaining balance to the manufacturer."

"So what's the cost of this initial order?" Gatturna looked at Paulie and took a long drag on his cigar, blowing smoke rings.

Parnevik kept a straight face, but he was enjoying the dialog, pages of his plan unfolding. "The prototype run for one case is expensive—it comes to five hundred dollars per bottle. It goes down to fifty dollars at a hundred cases. I'll send you a rundown on costs versus volume. The initial order costs you twenty-four thousand up front to me—my ten percent of retail value—and two payments of six thousand each to the manufacturer plus airfreight.

"So, we're out thirty-eight grand plus freight. Paulie?"

"It's your call, boss. We know where he lives."

"What if we need to meet?" Gatturna said.

"We don't. My proposal specifically states we never see each other again unless I instigate it."

Gatturna rose, adjusted his suspenders, and nodded at Paulie. "I say we go. We use our network here with tight control—do a test. See if they like it. See if business will cross over." The boss turned to Parnevik. "It's done, Mister Parnevik. But we don't go until you pay for the equipment and supplies you asked us to gather on your behalf. You come across with the money and everything will be delivered within three days." Gatturna put out his cigar in the ashtray, glancing at Paulie, smiling, a twinkle in his eyes.

Parnevik quickly figured the Genovese would be sitting twenty thousand dollars ahead with the markup on the equipment, supplies, and special documentation requested against the total outlay of the initial transaction.

"Paulie will take care of it. Now, I have to go home to my wife, the Cotton Bowl, and a big family gathering."

***

Parnevik left the restaurant and boarded the Air Canada 4:30 p.m. LaGuardia flight directly to Quebec City. Through their secure e-mail system, the Genovese Family had transmitted his requirements to the owner of a print shop. The documentation for his three new identities would be waiting for him in a lockbox at Jean-Lesage International Airport. Tony Gatturna had given him the key and contact information for the creator in case he had questions.

The identity documents had been very expensive. The elderly Italian craftsman, a Mr. Giovanni, had masterfully fulfilled his assignment from the Genovese. From his stock, he chose American, French, and Canadian IDs, exactly as Parnevik had ordered. The documents were impeccable, complete with fabricated backgrounds that would withstand strenuous scrutiny.

Parnevik had commissioned a local cartographer on his own. The aged gentleman was waiting with his tools in the lounge of the Chateau Bonne Entente Hotel, five minutes from the airport and three blocks from Old Quebec City. Parnevik had taken a room and discretely negotiated permission from the front desk to briefly occupy a private conference room in the hotel. The technician imbedded the photographs Parnevik had taken of himself in three disguises into the driver license and passport documents while Parnevik connected his laptop to the hotel's Wi-Fi. He opened separate bank accounts online at Barclay's bank branches in the countries of domicile, wire transferred initial deposits from his Lichtenstein account, applied for check cards, and transferred $85,000 to the Genovese's designated account.

He spent New Year's Eve at the famous five-star hotel-spa and booked a morning flight back to Atlanta under his new Canadian name.

The next morning, prior to departure, he paid another visit to Mr. Giovanni's print shop. He needed a blank passport for a local

Atlanta ID he was creating himself. And he made Giovanni an offer he was unable to turn down, giving Parnevik unfettered access to future services outside of Genovese reach.

 Seventeen

Professor VonMitton

THE CHRISTMAS AND New Year's holidays are typically a calm and peaceful time of year for visitors and residents spending time on Lake Rabun, a reservoir built in the 1930s by the Corps of Engineers. It was nestled in the North Georgia Mountains, over the decades providing convenient escapes for old-money Atlanta families. Like most years, many of the homeowners and their guests were here celebrating New Year's Eve around cozy fireplaces. There was frost most mornings and the air was typically clear and crisp.

It was mid-afternoon when Professor VonMitton returned from his research at Emory University, and he'd been at his library desk for the last two hours, fidgeting and uncommunicative.

"I spoke with Reagan Driscoll," the professor finally offered.

"You *said* you were going to talk to her. What's bothering you?" Mrs. Leonard sat with him, knitting in a rocker next to the library fireplace. "You've been like a caged cat since you got back. I recognize the signs. Tell me before I have to drag my bones out in the cold for more wood. It's New Year's Day and you're acting like a spoiled child."

Professor VonMitton turned away from the reading material spread across his huge Victorian desk, rose, and faced the window looking out over the lake. "Don't be snippy. I'll get the wood. You make us a toddy—it's the *gift*. It's bothering me. Now go, and we'll have a talk."

***

"It *is* a bit nippy outside," Professor VonMitton said, shutting the side door to the deck. He mechanically stacked the wood and built a fire in the main living area's huge central fireplace, his mind jumbling over the dreams and flashes he'd been experiencing over the last several months. Rubbing his hands together, he looked around for the steaming cup of powerful buttered rum Mrs. Leonard was so adept at concocting.

"It's right here." Mrs. Leonard tapped her knitting needle on the weighty wooden coffee table between leather loveseats. "Sit down and tell me what's troubling you."

"Ah, thank you." He let out a breath and sank into the soft folds of the sofa. He sighed once and leaned over the table to cradle the mug resting on a cheerful Christmas-colored napkin. Carefully slurping the hot brew, he relaxed in the loveseat's comfortable embrace. "It's the curse pushing through again. I'm sorry, Mrs. Leonard. I know you hate dealing with it."

"What is it this time? It's been at least four years."

"It's Reagan Driscoll. Dreams in bits and pieces for months now. I met with her yesterday. She revealed severe ethical and legal problems at work and asked for my advice. The pressure's been relentless. I'm afraid you'll have to deal with him again. I have no option but to back away. He's coming, and now I can understand why."

"His quarters are untouched, just as he left them. I'll dust and vacuum."

 Eighteen

Atlanta PD

CAPT. TRUSSEL ARRIVED at headquarters before the morning shift-change to check the overnight log, wanting to be assured everything was running smoothly so he could enjoy the day's football games with his friends. Four of them traditionally spent New Year's afternoon at his house, glued to his sixty-inch high definition TV, betting and gorging on pizza and beer.

As he passed his office, he heard the international communications phone ring. The call was brief. He placed the phone back in its console slot on his desk, a scowl etched across his face. His buddies would be pissed, but maybe he'd only miss the first game. He pushed the intercom. "Whose got the desk?" he croaked.

"I got it, Captain."

Trussel recognized Sgt. Flannigan's rough Irish tongue. "You won the lottery again. You pulled the same duty last year, didn't you?"

"Aye, sir, but at least it's been quiet. Why are ye here, sir?"

"I'm expecting faxes from the Las Vegas Police and I want to check their system postings from last night. It appears one of our residents on vacation jumped out a thirty-two-story building. They want permission for an autopsy. It's a Miss Reagan Driscoll—

works at Pharmco in Dunwoody. Find out contact information on next of kin for me and get back ASAP. I'll handle it."

 Nineteen

Mallory Driscoll

"WHEN DID YOU get in, Mal?" Emma Kisumi stood in the doorway. It was all she could think to say, at the same time trying to hold back her tears. Mallory entered the porch, shaking off her umbrella. She flopped on the hanging swing, looking off across the street at the green, treed expanse of Piedmont Park, not wanting to face her sister's roommate.

Emma had shared the beautiful, white stone house with Reagan ever since they both started careers at Pharmco Corp. It was late morning on a dismal rainy day, the kind that dampens and suffocates the spirit.

"I came here straight from the airport," she said, voice cracking, "and I want to thank you for taking me in like this. Anyway, the cops called me yesterday, on New Year's Day of all ungodly things. They wanted permission for an autopsy…. Em, her body is due in tomorrow. I had to organize the funeral from Chicago. I feel helpless and pissed off."

"Mal, I'm so sorry. I still can't believe it. She was like my sister." Emma yanked a handkerchief from a pants pocket and sat next to Mallory on the swing, blowing profusely. "I don't want to talk about it anymore."

Mallory was dressed in jeans, lightweight hiking boots, and a charcoal parka. Her hair was bunned and wrapped inside a black knit cap. "Em, I'm sorry, but I need to know if there's anything you can tell me. Was she feeling okay? Depressed? Work going well? Bobby?"

"She was good except she felt guilty for helping Corey Parnevik a couple of years ago with his outside research."

"I remember him. Never liked him. Shifty."

"He talked her into decrypting the software she'd developed so he could experiment at Tech's nano-lab."

"She mentioned something about that when I talked to her last week. It was two years ago?"

"Yeah. She tried to put it out of her mind, but I knew it bothered her. She had always avoided him, and then the other day he frightened her—sat at her table in the cafeteria, told her to keep quiet, that they were co-conspirators."

"So she went to Vegas upset and frightened?"

"No, not really. She went to Professor VonMitton for advice. He convinced her to tell the story to Pharmco's CEO. They didn't fire her—oh, and guess who was in the CEO's office when she went in? Ryan McKenzie."

"When I talked to Reagan before she left for Vegas, she said he'd been sent in to help in the missing inventory investigation. He's acting as a DEA consultant. Guess I'd better give him a call and let him know about the funeral. It's the day after tomorrow, three o'clock, at the Baptist Cemetery—are you still seeing Parnevik?"

"Are you kidding? That's been over for a long time."

"I need to talk to him as soon as possible."

"Nobody knows where he is. He's supposedly taking time off. He goes on sabbaticals to sky dive somewhere. I don't ask.

Pharmco lets him do pretty much what he wants—what are you thinking?"

"I'm thinking he may be involved—Emma, anything unusual happen lately?"

Emma dried her eyes and blew her nose. "Mal, I don't want to seem silly, but you know how meticulous we both are…"

"What?"

"I think someone was in the apartment just before Reagan left for Vegas. My underwear was disturbed, and the drawer was hard to open, like it had been shut too hard. It made me look around, and I think someone was in my bathroom. The guest towel was crumpled, and we never use it."

 Twenty

Ernest Kelto

"WHY ALL THE secrecy, Corey? Nobody at work knows anything." Ernest Kelto was talking to Parnevik from a pay phone inside Atlanta's Perimeter Mall. Parnevik had e-mailed him to make the call at 1:00 p.m. from that specific phone booth.

As Julian Trebar, Parnevik had arrived in Atlanta from Quebec City late last evening. He'd spent this morning as Trebar at the Buckhead branch of the Bank of America, organizing a trust relationship.

This afternoon he would pick up equipment and supplies held at the main UPS warehouse near the Emory University campus in the suburb of Decatur. The Genovese had proven true to their word. He'd received email confirmation of the UPS delivery, and his Lichtenstein account held a fresh $24,000 deposit from an obscure credit union in the Cayman Islands. The first order was committed. Parnevik had produced a sufficient quantity of the *Amor* nanites at the Georgia Tech labs to satisfy thousands of times the first order.

On his way to Bank America, he'd mailed off the raw product to a Pakistani manufacturing facility to produce and hold inventory and execute delivery orders according to his instructions. His focus now was setting-up several laboratories in preparation for mass production of nanites and design of new products. He was anxious to leave for France and a well-deserved break.

"I need your further assistance," Parnevik said. He had paid for Kelto's reluctant cooperation in the past.

"What do you want? I may not be able to help you. Did you know they offered me Reagan Driscoll's job? But I've been thinking of resigning."

Kelto had worked on several projects with Parnevik under Reagan's supervision, tweaking the targeting programs of robotic nanites used to stimulate areas in the brain controlling memory. These refinements would eventually lead to FDA approval of animal testing, the first step in paving the way for use on human patients with Alzheimer's and other diseases or injuries affecting memory loss.

Parnevik didn't like the mealy-mouthed computer scientist. He was an arrogant ladder climber, but Parnevik had always gone out of his way to cultivate the young man's inflated ego. There was something satisfying, even amusing, about observing the reactions.

Over time, he'd learned a great deal about nanite target programming and had commissioned Kelto in the past on his own time to proof his outside work. Now, he required his expertise one last time to review the master program he'd completed to enable development and testing of his envisioned line of designer drugs.

"How nice for you, Ernest. You should take the job," Parnevik said, a shudder of disbelief causing him to shake his head, thinking what would become of Pharmco's creativity. With Reagan Driscoll gone, the mediocre computer geek could only follow directions, not formulate them. The company would lose its competitive advantage. "I've written a general targeting program I'd like you to review for errors, if it wouldn't be too much trouble. I will pay for the consult."

"Why don't you wait until you return...? I understand you're going on one of your sabbaticals. We can talk about it then."

"Ernest, I may not be coming back to Pharmco. I'm thinking about going on my own. Perhaps you might be interested in joining me—at a later time, of course—after I'm established?"

"Corey, you can't be thinking of using the brain map. It's proprietary property. Pharmco would never sit still."

"Functional areas of the brain are universal knowledge. Applying a three-dimensional grid and assigning codes to plotted locations is elementary geometry. They wouldn't have a case."

"This is a little much for me right now, but let me think about it."

Kelto's tone of voice had changed; his avarice was palpable and Parnevik could almost feel the workings of his little mind, all cooped up in the privacy of the phone booth. "It's a straight fee. Nobody will know. Cash in a brown bag."

"What are you offering—and where are you anyway?"

Parnevik had him. The flashy little fellow was already dreaming of the Porsche he was always talking about so he could seriously attract the female gender.

"I'm in France," he lied. "My sister's family is here. She was killed in an automobile accident several years back."

"I didn't know—"

"What about a Porsche?"

"You've got to be kidding." Kelto's heart started to pound.

"I could make that happen if you could stretch a little and secure several of the government test nanites I need for research."

"Nah, no way. I couldn't afford a Porsche on my income anyway. It would look suspicious. Besides, there's already a missing-inventory investigation going on."

"What if I could fix that?"

"Come on."

"People die and leave wills, sometimes with unusual covenants. And I'll return the nanites to you within twenty-four hours. Trust me. Just listen."

***

Two hours later, Kelto was engaged with the manager at the Bank of America in Buckhead. Following Parnevik's instructions, he requested the envelope left in the manager's care for him by Mr. Julian Trebar, a Canadian customer of the bank.

The bank manger handed him the envelope after he initialed a receipt form and directed him to the security and privacy of the bank's safety deposit vault. Kelto opened the envelope; there was a key and a one-page letter with an attachment—a draft of Parnevik's target program. He was directed to proof it, draft any notes or suggestions, and use the key to retrieve the contents of a safety deposit box, then return to the bank within twenty-four hours and place a vial, of the nanites Parnevik had requested, in the safety deposit box.

Kelto opened the box. A nine-by-twelve inch, unmarked manila envelope was inside. It contained a copy of trust documents created by the last will and testament of Mrs. Gracie Willcot, a deceased British citizen. The papers included a letter of direction by the executor of the estate, Mr. Julian Trebar, to the trust department of the Buckhead Bank of America to make a cash payment of the money it had received from the estate to Mr. Ernest Kelto. The letter explained the heartfelt appreciation to Mr. Kelto for graciously assisting an out-of-sorts elderly lady in safely navigating a busy London street many years ago. Kelto sat in the quiet vault thinking, *250,000 dollars….*

He'd long ago learned the encryption codes Reagan had formulated to protect her target programs. He'd been carefully working on his own time in the Pharmco labs using the test nanites Parnevik had developed under the DOD contract, experimenting on motor-skill targets from the brain map. He'd had considerable success enhancing strength, stamina, and sensory responses in lab animals. He wasn't about to entertain a liaison with Parnevik. He had his own agenda on outside research. He could care less what Parnevik was up to. Anyway, the guy was a psycho. He never looked you straight in the eye, seemed to be constantly wired, high-strung, aloof. All he could remember of their professional interactions were curt commands…. But it was a lot of money. All he had to do was get several *Fuerte* nanites out of Pharmco. Not a problem; he'd been doing it for months. Perhaps the Porsche didn't have to wait any longer.

 Twenty-one

Julian Trebar

HALF AN HOUR after terminating the call with Kelto, Julian Trebar preened in front of a full-length mirror in the anteroom of his residence. He saw a lean, handsome Canadian in his early fifties, well-tailored in a charcoal suit, conservative striped tie, dark-gray wavy hair, blue contacts, and metal-framed glasses. He was proud of the disguise and didn't mind the confinement of the business garb. The pliable plastic facemask produced a marked change: thicker nose, squarer chin, and high cheekbones gave his face an Indian look.

Kelto had surprised him, divulging he'd already devised a method of safely transporting nanites through Pharmco's security procedures. It proved what he'd long ago suspected: his cohort was experimenting on his own. Inevitably he'd get caught. He just didn't have the smarts to lay out a thorough plan. But Kelto's activity might help cover his own carefully planned deceptions. Planning was everything.

Parnevik left his Peachtree Battle residence and rented a double-door panel van from National's midtown location. He presented his identification at the UPS Warehouse near Emory University, loaded a score of boxes and crates into the van, and circuitously drove through downtown Atlanta. As soon as he turned up

Peachtree Street toward Buckhead, he realized a black, four-door sedan was following him. It had to be the Genovese. He knew it wasn't the Italian way to trust an outsider, no matter what kind of agreement had been struck. It was their nature, and he was prepared. It was time to remind them of their covenants.

He pulled into a gas station at Sixteenth Street, parked the van, and walked to the public phone booth near the sidewalk.

"You are following the van that picked up my materials. You will desist. Complete anonymity was a condition of our relationship."

"Mister Parnevik, please tell me how you got this private number."

"I asked for it. I assume Mister Gatturna didn't inform you."

"We are only interested in protecting our investment." Arrogance pervaded Paulie Torentino's tone.

"The Mexicans may, after all, be better suited to keeping a bargain. You are forcing me to consider the competition. Is that what you want?"

"We have a bargain, Parnevik. You have our money. You just concentrate on delivery. One word from me and you're a dead man."

"Threats I can live without. I want confirmation from Gatturna via our e-mail setup within the next hour. No more tails. You leave me alone. That's our bargain. I'll be waiting."

Parnevik hung up and talked the gas station manager into leaving the van parked for a short while. He removed his briefcase containing his laptop and accessories from the van, locked up, and walked down Peachtree Street. Within several blocks, half a dozen restaurants and coffeehouses offered complimentary Wi-Fi.

Beginning his second latte at Starbuck's, the e-mail arrived.

I apologize for the misunderstanding. I am told unkind words were spoken.... We will not hinder you further and will respect your wishes, although we continue to be troubled without adequate control of the relationship. We will see how this trust plays out for now. Doing solid business will further cement that trust.

A smile spread across Parnevik's face as he snapped the laptop cover closed and packed it away. He would continue with his plan: driving to his house on Peachtree Battle after his housekeeper left for the day and under the cover of darkness.

***

Dense bushes, contoured to the height of the wrought-iron fence, hid the residence from view on all four sides. The corner lot had been perfect. Constructed in 1864, the Greek Revival mansion was built like a fortress. The giant, white Doric columns along three sides of the house defined sprawling porticos and supported elaborate cornices holding second-story balconies. A wide band of intricately carved wood framed enormous entrance doors, and the windows were set in six-pane glazing.

A small, local family-owned company of artisans had expertly executed the exterior renovations. The expansion and conversion of the deep wine cellar had been separately sub-contracted to two Quaker craftsmen brought in from Pennsylvania by his local contractor friend.

Thanks to the funds from his mother's estate, the house had become Parnevik's pride and joy. The remodeled cellar contained the working spaces necessary to carry on his nanite research. A three-hundred square foot, level-three clean room contained the micro fabrication facility and occupied the core of the room. The remaining nine-hundred square feet housed his communications equipment, computers, and two circular, microelectronic workstations. One contained a Scanning Transmission Electron Microscope (STEM) with resolution capabilities down to 1.5 angstroms—sufficient to display patterns with feature sizes as small as 20 nanometers. The other station supported specialized Atomic Force, Confocal Raman, and Laser Scanning Microscopes, together capable of displaying particles as small as atoms.

***

It was time for installation of the stainless steel tables and animal cages and organizing the small tools and devices. Parnevik drove the van down the residential streets that made circular routes off Peachtree Battle, ensuring no one was prowling about or following him. He remotely opened the heavy wrought- iron gate to access the grounds. Forty meters away, the double lanterns guarding the massive, wooden front doors were casting diffused light through the foggy night air, insufficient to embrace the circular drive. Pitch darkness consumed the grounds.

He extinguished the van's headlights, crept along the gravel driveway, and pulled to the far right side of the circle next to a large fountain he had personally designed. He turned off the engine, stepped out, and quietly opened the van's side-panel doors, aware of his steps grating over the gravel and the gushing of the fountain. The air was heavy with the scent of evergreen, and the misty fog shut out the starlight. White vapor billowed with each breath as he looked over the grounds and decided one lap around the mansion would be prudent. It always paid to be thorough.

The temperature must have gone below freezing, he thought as he crunched over the sprouting winter rye he'd added to the lawn. Craning over the depths of the property, he reviewed the hidden exits from his escape tunnels, adrenaline seeping into his circulatory system, narrowing his focus, spiking his senses.

Quiet pervaded. Rounding the other side of the building, he sloshed through wet grass as he approached the driveway. The buried water pipes from the street were warding off the frost. Fifty feet away, the van and fountain were shrouded in mist, and he could hear water trickling.

The fountain was a masterpiece, a result of Parnevik's creative engineering, a miniature of the white Greek Revival mansion, water falling down its columns into a four-foot wide moat surrounded by luscious plants chosen to bloom with the seasons. The back of the fountain structure was flat and skirted by shrubs. A short stone walkway led over the moat to its middle, and a framed bronzed plate the size of a door held an engraved statement dedicating the fountain and the house to his mother.

The square plate responded to a sequence of hits from Parnevik's remote control, sliding open against the inside left wall of the miniature building. Stairs led to the laboratory thirty feet below.

***

Three hours later, Parnevik had completed his work and collected and returned the cartons, crates, and packing materials to the van. He surveyed the grounds as he removed his rubber gloves. Nothing stirred. It was getting colder, and frost was visibly accumulating over the shrubbery and foliage and across the surface of the lawn. He double-checked the area around the fountain for telltale debris, footprints, anything that might indicate his presence on this night.

He hastily pulled a bottle of medication from a jacket pocket and choked down two capsules. The soothing effects of adrenaline neutralizing excess dopamine were wearing off and would soon be replaced with crippling paranoia, rendering him jittery, impatient, and confused. He thanked the gods for medicine.

Taking a last look around, he let out a sigh. Secrets never remained in perpetuity. Eventually, they gave up their coveted cache. But he felt secure for now, insulated. Years of planning, designing layers of illusion, had provided him with a diverse menu of backups. He was in control. All that remained was to drop the second set of supplies and equipment at the backup lab location across town in southeast Atlanta's warehouse district. And then, he was off to France.

 Twenty-two

Oakland Cemetery

IT WAS A small gathering at Atlanta's historic cemetery a mile east of downtown. Mallory invited a few of Reagan's close friends and Pharmco co-workers. Their parents had both passed away, and they'd never established close relationships with their one aunt. Mallory dismissed the idea of a wake. Reagan wouldn't have approved.

It was a chilly, late-afternoon January day in bright sunlight. Frost was still melting off the tree branches and evaporating, bathing the air in fresh-smelling moisture. With the Atlanta skyline as a backdrop and the sun blazing behind the Peachtree Plaza Hotel, Pharmco's CEO, Dr. Safford, delivered a short but powerful affirmation of Reagan's character and work ethic. Mallory closed with a prayer.

Ryan McKenzie and Mallory stood together next to Emma Kisumi and Professor VonMitton, watching the casket lowered to the bottom of the grave. They stood motionless for several minutes as one by one the mourners passed by the grave, paying their last respects.

"I don't recognize that guy, the one on the right next to Safford," Mallory whispered to Emma.

"That's Ernest Kelto, Reagan's assistant. He recently gave his notice, but Safford offered him Reagan's job. He's not the right caliber."

Mallory turned to Professor VonMitton. "Thank you for coming, Professor. She loved you like a father, and I do too. I'm so sorry after all these years that this is what brings us together."

McKenzie and Emma pulled away from them and followed the last of the gathering down the long tree-lined sidewalk that sliced through gravestones and ornate mausoleums separated by rusting picketed ironworks.

"Do not bother yourself with such thoughts, Mallory. My heart has always remained filled with the likes of you both, seen or unseen. How are you getting along with your ex-boyfriend?"

"We haven't talked since that night we said goodbye to you at Phaedra's Grill."

"That's preposterous! Perhaps this time something may manifest."

"Oh, Professor, dream on. We'd better leave. I'm staying with Emma for the time being, but Ryan's giving me a ride. At least we'll finally have some time to talk. Are you spending the night?"

"No. I've been here consulting with peers and researching for a week—but do give me a moment before you go off." They were standing alone now. Professor VonMitton's voice had hardened. "I have an important matter to discuss with the two of you. I need you to favor me with your presence at my Lake Rabun country house on Wednesday. It regards Reagan. I can say no more or Mrs. Leonard will have my skin. Shall we say four-ish? You will be spending the night."

 Twenty-three

Take a Run

"WHAT WERE YOU and the Professor talking about?" McKenzie had driven the rental car out the back way from the cemetery and down Highland Avenue.

"He wants us to come up to his place day after tomorrow to discuss something important about Reagan. He wouldn't elaborate. I said we'd be there."

"That's strange. Any clue as to what could be on his mind?"

"None, but I could tell he was concerned—almost worried. Can you get away?"

"Yeah, no problem.... Do you want to go straight back to Emma's?"

"No...yes—I don't know. My stomach is upside-down, and I feel like crying some more, but I'd rather get even. You know what I mean?"

"Pent-up anger. Let it go. What do you want to do?"

"Find Parnevik. Find out what happened.... I told you what Emma said. He threatened Reagan. She thinks he broke into their house the day before Reagan left for Vegas—messed with her things and used the bathroom."

"Look, how about I pull into Piedmont Park? It's a little cold, but I think a run would do you good—clear your mind. Then we could go somewhere and talk like we used to. I've got my stuff in the back. I can change in the car and wait for you while you suit up at Emma's. Maybe we can figure a way to work together, beginning with the visit to Lake Rabun."

***

There was still an hour of daylight; the sun was bright and the air still. The spot-ice had melted off the park roadways. People would soon be returning home from their workdays. The winding internal roads and pathways in the park would shortly fill with joggers, walkers, and leashed animals.

McKenzie warmed up next to the car, stretching and watching across Tenth Street for Mallory to bounce out the front door of Emma's house. What could he say to her? It was awkward, but she must be feeling the same way. Neither had made contact since graduation until she called him at his hotel. Since then, there hadn't been a moment together not buried in the remorse and sadness surrounding Reagan's tragic death.

Mallory shot out the front door, dressed in matching Georgia Tech, green-and-white long-sleeved shirt and running shorts. She ran across Tenth Street and took off along the sidewalk skirting the park boundary. Ryan crossed a soccer field to intercept her.

Five minutes later, running side by side, they were completely comfortable in the icy air. McKenzie wore an old, short-sleeve Peachtree Road Race shirt with bandanas wrapped around his neck and forehead. Even though the temperature was scarcely above freezing, without much wind, body heat produced a comfortable equilibrium.

They did five loops along the park's main road with a minimum of small talk, enjoying the mellowing effects of the endorphins. A half-mile from McKenzie's car, he caught her smiling.

"Last one to the car buys the grub," she shouted and got the jump on him.

McKenzie was six or eight feet behind, matching her pace. *Maybe this wouldn't be so bad after all*, he thought and gave it the gas. "And the beer," he taunted, catching and passing her, laughing as if the last seven years had never taken place.

***

"I don't know any more about the missing inventory at Pharmco than I did when I arrived." McKenzie crunched on a chicken wing. They had cleaned up at Emma's place and walked the six blocks down to The Prince of Wales Restaurant just outside Piedmont Park's west gate. "I've spent endless hours reviewing tapes with their security personnel. So far, nothing of substance. We need evidence."

"Can't you get the local police involved?"

"Pharmco won't file a report. They're afraid of bad publicity and drawing the attention of the DOD—and they don't want anything jeopardizing their FDA nanite testing applications." McKenzie looked over at her sitting on the other side of the small high-top table. Her face was full of sauce, munching on a wing. He topped off their drafts from a half-full pitcher and waved the empty in the air at their server. "Almost like old times." He pulled a double sheet of paper towels off the roll in the middle of the table and handed it to her. She was holding both ends of the gooey wing, gnawing voraciously.

She tossed the wing in the basket for waste and wiped her face and hands. "You said Reagan gave a statement implicating Parnevik."

"She did."

"Well, we can start there. It's a sworn statement. That's evidence."

"Of what?"

"That Parnevik stole the nanites. The DEA could file on its own. Screw the local police. That's what you're there for. Right?"

"I'm a consultant. I'm only supposed to advise—and the DEA's on a DOD tight leash—information is to stay strictly internal."

"Well, you can advise them to file, asserting grand theft and identifying Parnevik as the suspect vis-a-vis Reagan's statement. Then we can work with Atlanta PD and go after this guy." She dabbed a celery sprig in blue cheese dressing and abruptly cast her gaze to McKenzie. "You know, all of a sudden Reagan's death seems too convenient. Maybe Parnevik is a killer."

"I'll see what my director wants to do. Like I said, though, it's not my call—but you know, I think I better go over Emma's place with a forensics kit just in case. Maybe we'll get lucky if someone was really in the house the night before Reagan left."

Mallory took a long pull from her beer mug. McKenzie noticed her face had changed texture, hardened. The old pit-bull juices he remembered so well.

"Maybe you could take a look at Reagan's luggage and personal effects?"

"I can do that."

"It's all at Bobby Faust's house. I should go talk to him anyway and pick it up—see what his take is. The cops haven't even talked to him. Evidently, Reagan's death isn't under investigation."

Another pitcher of beer arrived, and they dug deeper into the basket of wings.

"I guess this *does* mean we're working together," Mallory said after demolishing two legs in a row.

"I don't know, Mal. They could pull me off this at any time. I told you, my office doesn't know exactly where our orders are coming from…. I'll do what I can while I can."

"So, how's your job been working out?"

"It's good. They're pushing me to get field experience. I'm at the top of my pay grade. They think I'm promotion material."

"How's your mom?"

"The cancer took her last summer. Dad's spending the winter in Madiera. He's remarrying. I don't talk to him—we never got along." McKenzie lifted his mug.

"I'm sorry about your Mom. I liked her.... Reagan said you had a boat."

"Yeah. I'm living the dream—self-sufficient, anchored off Diner Key—you know, next to Coconut Grove. She's a fifty-two footer and ready to go."

"I remember you always wanted to live aboard." She dropped eye contact and grabbed another wing, dunking it into the blue cheese dressing.

McKenzie noticed her facial features seemed to soften as if she were daydreaming.

"What about you?"

"My partner and I just opened our own office. We're gun-slinging lawyers now. We both cut our teeth defending people without the financial resources to hire a decent defense.

"What has happened is we found so many uncaring public defenders just working the numbers with helpless defendants that we decided to start researching cases of the convicted and incarcerated, looking for possibilities of innocence. When we found one, we contacted relatives to see if there was a strong conviction of innocence and enough determination and financial resources to do something about it. If we believed them, we would take them on as clients and go about trying to uncover evidence to reopen cases."

Her impassioned tone impressed McKenzie. He felt a little envious. She was making a difference—dedicated to helping the underdog. He liked that. She was waiting for him to say something. "I think that's admirable, Mal. I'm proud of you. Sounds like you're very busy…. You ever hook up with anyone? I mean—"

"No time, Rymac." Mallory popped off the chair, wiped her face and hands again, and groped through her purse.

"I've got it." McKenzie placed his MasterCard on the rim of his beer mug. "It's a legitimate expense."

"Thanks. Are you going back to Pharmco?"

"You read my mind. First thing in the morning, I have a review with the powers that be. I'll find out everything I can about what Reagan was working on and try to get a copy of her statement. That may be sufficient to convince law enforcement to classify Parnevik as a person of interest in Reagan's death if the DEA goes along."

"I'll get a deposition from Bobby Faust and pick up Reagan's stuff."

"I'll meet you at Emma's as soon as I'm done at Pharmco— do the forensics on the apartment and check Reagan's luggage. If I can get a copy of Reagan's statement on behalf of family, it may be time for you to talk with the local police whether Pharmco likes it or not. I can send the house forensics and Reagan's personal effects to the DEA labs."

Mallory's face brightened; her eyes sparkled.

"Then, we're off to see the professor."

 Twenty-four

Pharmco Corp

AGENT McKENZIE DIDN'T sleep well—hard hotel bed, unpleasant dreams, feelings of emptiness. His stomach knotted as he crossed through the atrium of Pharmco's attractive, first-floor lobby. His assignment was specific: help Pharmco recover the missing inventory and find any evidence of criminal involvement. The death of Mallory's sister was spurring him to do more. And, of course, there was Mallory…. He was getting entangled.

He didn't know any more about the missing nanites than he had ten days ago when he first arrived. DEA forensic experts combed every square inch of the Pharmco building. He'd gone over months of surveillance tapes, sensitive area videos, personal computers, telephone records, and communications saved on Pharmco's servers. Personnel interviews hadn't turned up anything of substance. If Corey Parnevik, Ernest Kelto, or anyone else with access had pilfered the inventory, he or she was adept at defeating a multilayered security system.

Over the ten days they'd worked together, McKenzie had developed respect for Jim Dogett. He was sincere, a knowledgeable security professional, and he had been tireless and consistently optimistic that they'd find the culprit. But optimism had all but faded away at every staff level in the face of the DOD inevitably sweeping in and discovering breaches in Pharmco's contracts.

McKenzie walked down the sterile, third-floor hallway, the faint odor of disinfectant reminding him of a hospital. He almost expected to see nurses and rolling carts of instruments coming in and out of the rooms. Dr. Safford and Jim Dogget were waiting in Safford's office, sitting at his conference table, a repeat of his first visit.

The usual greetings were exchanged along with offers of coffee and something to eat. McKenzie opted to fix a cup of coffee from the set up built into Safford's bookcase. He stirred in a slug of creamer and took a seat, the hard-backed chair immediately offending the small of his back.

"Doctor Safford, I have nothing new to tell you. Mister Dogget and I have come to the end of it here. We haven't found a single clue. Have you heard from Parnevik? He's the only one I haven't interviewed."

"All we know is he went to Europe," Safford said. "He doesn't answer his cell phone. When he takes these short leaves, he doesn't want any contact. It's a medical thing. He has to have quiet and stimulating activity to rejuvenate. You've seen his file."

Parnevik's file had been detailed. He'd been vetted to the nth degree and the DOD had required a top-secret military clearance. The only anomaly appeared to be the instability of his mental condition, controlled through drugs that managed the level of neurotransmitters. The records did not include a DNA analysis, but fingerprints had been taken.

"Look, Doctor Safford, you refuse to file a complaint based on Reagan Driscoll's statement prior to her leaving for Las Vegas. Without that statement, we have no evidence to justify tracking him down for questioning. The DEA can't act in a vacuum."

"It's internal. You know we don't want publicity. That's why you're here—at the government's request, I might add."

"I get the picture. But you need to wake up. Reagan's sister, Mallory, is an attorney. You met her at the funeral. She's an old friend. There may be a more sordid picture unfolding around Reagan's accidental death, and if that's the case, I'm sure Mallory will convince the locals to open a complete investigation—she knows Reagan gave a statement before she left for Las Vegas. If she finds sufficient cause, she'll subpoena the statement along with your precious government contract and anything else she wants to look at."

"I had no idea this was happening," Safford said. "That could be catastrophic for the company." He darted a glance at Jim Dogget and pushed a file folder across the conference table toward McKenzie. "But there's a more important purpose for this meeting." Dr. Safford crossed his arms. "Ernest Kelto, Miss Driscoll's assistant, tendered his resignation yesterday. Coincidentally, additional inventory went missing, but this time it was part of the experimental nanite group under one of the DOD contracts."

McKenzie didn't open the file. "Don't you think it's about time you told me exactly what's going on here?"

"Agent McKenzie, you don't have clearance. We're bound by government covenants. Suffice it to say, the nanites are capable of self-duplicating, and in the wrong hands are dangerous beyond belief. The loss of self-duplicating nanites effectively breaches our contract with the DOD. Under the secrecy terms, they could conceivably close down our business. We've notified them of the loss and are waiting to hear what they intend to do."

"As far as we're concerned here," McKenzie said, "without full disclosure and cooperation, I can't do anything more for you.

All I can do is brief my supervisor as soon as I leave here and see where it goes from there."

***

"Look, McKenzie, I know less about this than you do."

"Sir, it's a stalemate here. I need broader authority to operate if you expect me to make any progress—Pharmco needs to cooperate. Parnevik threatened Reagan Driscoll just before her *accidental* death. I think we may have enough to go to the local police. I'll know more later in the morning when Mallory Driscoll and I go through Reagan's house and the luggage from her trip."

"I'll go back up the chain and get back to you. In the meantime, stay away from the local police—just stay out of it until I get clarification."

 Twenty-five

Mallory Driscoll

BACK IN HER college days, Mallory hadn't spent much time with Bobby Faust. She recalled he'd started dating Reagan the semester before she and Reagan graduated from Emory. He wouldn't have been someone she'd have chosen for her sister, but then again her sister was her opposite in so many ways: gentle, understanding, patient. The only clear personality trait they shared was the Driscoll backbone. Mallory had always been curious why, after some seven years, the relationship never went anywhere. But she knew the answer. Reagan had been married to her work.

Even though Mallory was still full of beer and wings she'd ingested with McKenzie at The Prince of Wales, she'd invited Bobby for a beer and nachos at his favorite sports bar hangout, asking him to bring Reagan's luggage. The place was full of patrons waiting for the 8:00 p.m. football game. The rowdies had arrived in force. The smell of frying grease floated in the air, and the floor was already littered with peanut shells, a bar trademark.

Bobby came through the doors five minutes after Mallory had taken a seat. He looked dejected ambling toward her table next to the bar. He tried on a smile as he pulled himself onto a beat-up stool.

"Hi. Your car was open, so I put her bag and purse in the backseat and locked it." Bobby turned his baseball hat around backwards and gazed over the patrons at the bar.

"Thanks for coming, Bobby. I figured Ernie's would be a good spot. I see your haunt hasn't changed much."

"Look, I know you want me to tell you what happened, but I gave the police everything I know. I really don't want to go over it again."

"Bobby, I know you're hurting. I hurt too. But I'm hoping you can remember more detail than you gave the police. Do you remember Ryan McKenzie?"

"Sure. I saw him at the funeral. You and he were a thing back at Emory when I met Reagan. A couple of times we had beers together."

"He's a DEA agent now and assigned to help Pharmco with an internal investigation. We're working together, and we think Parnevik may have had something to do with Reagan's death."

"I don't see how."

"I don't have time right now to get into it—"

A young, heavily made-up blond girl, chewing gum around a pierced tongue and outfitted in a low-cut white blouse, leaned an edge of her service tray on the table and off-loaded a pitcher of Bud, two frozen mugs, and a huge plate of cheese-covered nachos. "You need anything else?" she asked, repositioning her gum and adjusting a dangling earring.

"We're fine. Thanks," Mallory said.

The server nodded and moved to the next table.

"Some things never change." Mallory raised her eyebrows. "How 'bout them nachos? I took a chance they were still your preference."

"Mal, it was terrible," Bobby blurted.

It surprised her. Something unspoken must have changed his attitude, or maybe it was just being around someone else who cared.

"She spaced out, got wide-eyed and had a silly grin on her face. It happened so fast."

"Bobby, start from the beginning." Mallory poured the beer.

"Okay, okay. I'll try. It was our first morning. We'd cooked a breakfast together in the suite. She was still suffering the guilt trip over helping Parnevik, but she was coming around. We were starting to laugh like we used to. After we did the dishes, I was reading a book and she had the bathroom first.

"She took her time. When she came out, her hair was wrapped up in a towel and she apologized for taking so long and said something about deciding it was time to put Parnevik aside and get real."

Mallory kept eye contact and took a sip of beer. So did Bobby. She wasn't sure he was going to continue. He looked tentative.

"I asked if she wanted a glass of the Sauvignon Blanc we had at breakfast." Bobby hesitated and looked away. Mallory took another swig from her mug.

Bobby's face went slack as he brought his eyes back to Mallory. "When she looked at me—and I remember exactly—she said, 'that would be perrrrrfect.' But she said it in a strange tone of voice, like an actress overplaying a part. Well, I got up and, on the way to the kitchen to pour two glasses of wine, I pushed the Play button on the CD player. When I came back in the living room, she was standing in the corner, caressing the branches of a potted palm and babbling incoherently, something about beauty…. Mal, she was wide-eyed. I put the glasses down and tried talking to her. She ignored me like I wasn't there, or she wasn't listening. If I didn't know better, I'd say she was on LSD—not that we ever—"

"I know, Bobby, I know. You're doing fine."

They exchanged glances and Bobby's face softened. "The police don't know that part."

"I understand."

"She started wandering around the room, touching things and jibber-jabbering away and thanking God. Then she started flapping her arms in the air and skipping through the suite, grinning and shouting she could fly. Mal, before I had a chance to do something, she'd slid the balcony doors open. I'll never forget the instant terror. I scrambled after her and almost had her, but she sailed over the railing, giggling. All I could do was watch her trying to fly, and then she shrieked. I had to look away."

 Twenty-six

Ryan McKenzie: Next Day

BY 10:30 IN the morning, he'd finished scouring Emma's house for potential evidence. The effort produced a used towel from the guest bathroom, a slew of fingerprints he'd processed and packaged, and a glass vial in Reagan's jewelry box embedded with a Pharmco logo. It looked empty.

McKenzie smelled the brewing aroma of fresh Viennese coffee as he packed up his forensics kit and entered the kitchen. Mallory's Bobby Faust interview was rewinding in her recording device on a countertop. He and Mallory had gone over it when McKenzie first arrived. It hadn't added substantially to the body of knowledge, but Bobby's description of Reagan's behavior brought sheer terror into the morning mood.

"You know, it's strange there weren't prints on the vial." McKenzie sat next to Mallory at the kitchen table as she nursed a cup of coffee. "Whoever it was wiped off any prints, or they wore gloves. Reagan wouldn't have a reason to do that."

"Even without a copy of Reagan's statement, maybe we have enough," Mallory said.

"It's supposition, but maybe. The vial must have been planted. I'm going to send her suitcase along with the towel and vial to the lab in D.C. for thorough forensics. I'm assuming there won't

2

be evidence of drugs—that should help. They'll come back quickly. Maybe we'll get lucky and they'll find something in her personal effects."

***

It was 12:10 p.m. when they departed out the back door of Emma's stone house and jumped into McKenzie's Ford Taurus. Mallory drove while McKenzie used his cell phone to arrange a meeting with Capt. Trussel at the Atlanta PD. He also alerted the DEA forensics lab, making sure their people knew the vial might contain nano-objects. On the way to the police station, they stopped at a UPS Store, and McKenzie overnighted the items.

"It's too bad you couldn't get a copy of Reagan's statement," Mallory said, breaking the ice. McKenzie hadn't said a word since taking over the driving at the UPS Store. "But Faust's interview, the vial, and you witnessing Reagan's Pharmco admission should be enough to get the cops to open an investigation. They aren't going to like it when you tell them you sent potential evidence to D.C.... What's bothering you? I can still read the signs."

McKenzie kept his eyes on the road. No matter what time of day, the traffic on Peachtree Street was always heavy going into the city core. "I called my office again while I was in the UPS Store. I was feeling guilty about going with you to the Atlanta Police. My boss directed me not to make contact. He told me to stand down and return to Miami. He declined to explain—and I should report finding the vial to Pharmco."

"And?"

"This whole thing has me pissed off. I didn't tell you before because it didn't seem relevant, but I met with Atlanta PD when I first arrived. Their captain has suspicions there may be connections between two bizarre incidents currently under investigation that have to do with aberrant behavior." McKenzie took a quick look at Mallory. Her face was stony.... "I requested a leave of absence. He didn't say yes."

"So, you think—"

"I'll let the captain tell you firsthand. Then you can draw your own conclusions."

"What are you going to do now?"

"The boss is supposed to call and let me know. That means he has to go upstairs to wherever this thing was initiated. What am I going to do? Right now I'm going to introduce you to Captain Trussel of the Atlanta Police Department."

"You're going to lose your job if you're not careful."

"Back at the UPS Store I decided that finding out what happened to Reagan is more important than my job. If it goes down that way, so be it. Besides, the job has been getting too confining. I am losing my creativity, working in the background setting up drug cases for trial lawyers." McKenzie slapped the steering wheel. "So let's get the thing rolling, just like lawyers do. Screw Pharmco and their contract."

"Rymac, what will you do if you lose your job?"

"I don't know. I'll figure something out."

"You don't have any money."

"Since I was a child, every year Mom and Dad put the gift limit into a trust in my name. It's made me self-sufficient. I don't need a job."

"You could work with me in Chicago."

"It's too cold there, and you'd be a distraction."

"Is that such a bad thing?"

"Let's not go there right now."

 Twenty-seven

Atlanta PD

Capt. Trussel had them escorted to a soundproof interview room. He tossed a file folder on the table and sat down. It took twenty minutes for Mallory and McKenzie to bring him up to the point where McKenzie summarized the essence of Reagan's Pharmco statement.

"Nothing incriminating turned up in the autopsy," Trussel said. "No trace of drugs. The cause of death was severe trauma from the fall, and the local Las Vegas police ruled the death a suicide based on the boyfriend's statement."

"Reagan was happy," Mallory said. The three of them were sitting on hard, metal folding chairs around a heavy, wooden table bolted to the floor. "She'd just come clean at Pharmco about helping Parnevik—guilt, yes, but no reason for despondency—she wasn't fired. She certainly wouldn't commit suicide. I know my sister well."

"Can I see a copy of the autopsy?" McKenzie asked.

Capt. Trussel reached across the table, pulled out a single sheet of paper from the folder, and passed it to him.

He scanned the document. "This is generic, basic. Since no trace of drugs was found, they didn't take tissue samples."

"It stays a suicide for now," Capt. Trussel said. "But if we did open an investigation into her death, the first stop would be her house, and now you two have fouled the scene."

"Hold it, Captain. We didn't foul anything. I followed strict DEA procedures."

"That's just ducky. I suppose the DEA authorized this evidence gathering. I don't think so. They would have followed protocol and contacted me."

"Captain, I would have coordinated with you but the DEA directed me to keep clear. Some higher ups in the Department of Defense are telling the DEA what to do but not why. It has to be the government contract that Pharmco refuses to reveal. They wouldn't tell me what Reagan was working on either, and like I said, they wouldn't release her statement."

"Maybe Miss Driscoll is responsible for the missing inventory." Furrows formed across Capt. Trussel's forehead.

"Forget it, Captain," Mallory burst out. "You didn't know her. She was totally loyal—"

"So your sister wiped the vial clean."

"She wouldn't have any reason to," Mallory said as if talking to a child. "But maybe somebody else did."

"Who?" Capt. Trussel glared at her.

"Reagan's roommate thinks someone was in the apartment the day before Reagan left for Vegas. A guest towel had been used. Agent McKenzie sent it off with her luggage and the vial to the DEA trace lab."

McKenzie scooted out of his metal chair and started to pace. "Hopefully the visitor left epidermal evidence and we'll get DNA. Maybe they'll find something in her luggage. And the vial could be important to Pharmco."

"I want the DEA report and everything you sent returned," Capt. Trussel snapped at McKenzie, iron-faced.

"I don't see any reason why they wouldn't comply if you formally make a request, but you're on your own. I've taken a leave of absence. I'm going to help Miss *Mallory* Driscoll find out what happened to her sister, and the first thing we're going to do is find Parnevik. It would help if you could track his finances, credit cards, cell phone—"

"Unless I have a copy of her sworn statement and it says what you say it says, he's not a person of interest. There's no suspicion of a crime. Until I get something tangible pointing to him, I can't open an investigation."

"You remember Christmas when we first met?" McKenzie said. "You were bugged about possible commonality of the scene made by the lady at Club Elan and the death of a nursing home patron. Well, I was present at Reagan's Pharmco interview. She said Parnevik told her about a test he'd conducted on Christmas Eve—at Club Elan."

Capt. Trussel pushed his chair back against the wall and abruptly left the room, the security door clicking in place. The quiet was stifling. Mallory and McKenzie looked at each other. Mallory shrugged. "What's happening?"

"I don't know."

Capt. Trussel came through the door, pushing buttons on a cell phone. "Sorry. I forgot this." He took his seat at the table. "Bear with me a minute." He pressed the phone to his ear. "Lieutenant, we need to reopen the Brightview case from two years ago. I want to know everything that happened to that old lady the day she died. They have comprehensive, twenty-four hour video coverage—and the Christmas Eve groping caper. Find out who the woman was talking to before she freaked out. See if Club Elan has security tapes—talk to the staff. Keep me informed." Trussel slid the phone onto the tabletop and frowned. "I'll post the behavioral symptoms and our two scenarios into the system on the off chance we get potential matches—and it'll serve to alert all law enforcement agencies."

"Will you go after Parnevik now?" Mallory was losing patience.

"If what McKenzie says is verified by your sister's statement, I'll open an investigation. We'll show up at Pharmco with a search warrant and keep it quiet if they cooperate." Capt. Trussel glanced at his watch. "Judge Harrison should be back from lunch—if that pans out, we can start at Parnevik's residence as well as talk to Kelto, the other guy with possible involvement."

"We'd like to be there," McKenzie said.

"You said you're on leave—and you," Capt. Trussel pointed at Mallory, "stay out of the way. You're a lawyer, not an investigator."

"I beg your pardon. I'm a certified Illinois P.I. about to file in Georgia and I have the right to provide attorney services to the Driscoll family—which is me."

Capt. Trussel shook his head. "And I suppose McKenzie here is your assistant?"

"Of course!" Mallory stared at the captain, face flaring.

"Okay, okay, you win, but *after* we go over the place," Capt. Trussel said, matching her gaze. "Clear?"

"Clear."

"On another matter." Capt. Trussel opened the file folder on the table. "Do you know a Professor VonMitton?"

"He's an old friend of ours," McKenzie said.

"He e-mailed me the day after New Year's, introducing himself. Said he'd had a conversation with Reagan Driscoll that might be of interest prior to her leaving for Las Vegas. Who is he, some relative?"

"He's just a good friend," Mallory said. "He kind of mentored us all through college."

"Well, that's not all that's strange about this. He volunteered the help of an acquaintance, a Dickerson Phelps. I had Phelps checked out. Over a twenty-two year period, he has a record of critical assistance in half a dozen police cases, four in the States and two in Europe. He's some kind of psychic. Pops up out of nowhere when a case interests him. Nobody's been able to discover anything about him. No address, no social security number. It's as if he doesn't exist—except for a simple website citing his *modus operandi* and a contact form. The sight is hack-proof. I brought the dossier in case you're interested." Capt. Trussel tapped the open folder. "I'll leave it on the back burner for now."

***

It was after six before they left the Atlanta PD and headed to Emma's house to drop off Mallory. It had been a long day. They'd hung around Capt. Trussel's office as officers sent to Pharmco successfully secured a copy of Reagan Driscoll's statement. The officers said the Pharmco head of security told them they had no idea where Parnevik had gone other than to Europe—possibly France—he'd done some bungee jumping there before. Dogett and Dr. Safford hadn't hid their displeasure at Mallory and Agent McKenzie's obvious responsibility for bringing in a local police investigation.

Lt. Sullivan, the officer assigned to re-open the Brightview and Club Elan cases, reported that the Club Elan tapes of the evening in question had been damaged, but interviews with one of the bar staff produced a description of two men conversing with the stricken lady just before the incident. The bartender remembered because one of the men had slipped him a twenty to reserve two seats at the bar. Sketches of the men were being analyzed.

"You want something to eat?" McKenzie asked halfway to Emma's.

"You mean you're inviting me to dinner?" Mallory cast a quick look at him, eyes wide.

"You have to eat. I'm being considerate."

"You want to have dinner with me. Is that correct?"

"Sure."

That is so insipid, she thought. "Fine, there's a Wendy's a block up on the right. I'll get takeout. I need to turn in early anyway."

"Okay, I think I'll head over to Emile's Bistro for his special of the night, like we used to do. It's a shame you're so tired."

"Stop." She was staring down Peachtree Street. "Perhaps some other time." *That didn't sound right.*

"I guess we'll have to see," McKenzie said, searching ahead for Wendy's.

"By the way, why didn't you tell the captain about the structural nanites that were mssing?"

"I didn't think it relevant, and it would be violating Pharmco's confidentiality when they divulged the information to me as a DEA agent. I need to find out more about why the loss is so important."

"Georgia Tech has a Microelectronics Research Center. It's a federally funded nanotechnology lab. I'm sure someone there could help you."

"Good idea. I'll check it out in the morning."

The familiar muffled chime of Mallory's cell phone sounded from her purse in the backseat. "Hold it." Mallory reached back for it. "Hello.... Oh, hi, Professor.... I guess we could do that. Do you want us to bring anything...? Okay, see you around six."

"What now?"

"Boy, that was strange." Mallory looked perplexed. "He sounded different. He changed the time to six. If I didn't know better, I'd say it wasn't him. He almost sounded too British—maybe Scottish. Weird."

 Twenty-eight

Lake Rabun, Georgia

MALLORY AND MCKENZIE had never visited VonMitton's Lake Rabun country house. Normally, it would have been a pleasant two-hour drive, but it had taken an extra half-hour wandering the winding road carved above the lake's eastern shore before the professor's directions paid dividends. Address numbers for individual homes were absent, and massive first-growth trees and steep terrain down from the roadway hid many of the structures.

They finally located the professor's mailbox amongst a dozen or so posted in a group and inched along the roadway, continuing to look for the house VonMitton had described. A hundred meters along, the gabled roof was barely visible through the trees. Nestled on a rock outcrop, built in the late 1920s by Atlanta's socially prominent Chandler family, the three-story stone house was constructed to survive for a millennium.

An ungated driveway, bordered by a line of dense bushes, led down in switchbacks to a flat parking area of cobbled rocks in front of the grand old home. Three stone steps led up to a simple screen door and a screened porch circling the first floor. Heavy, polished wooden doors with two brass knockers greeted would-be guests.

"Quite a place." McKenzie turned off the Taurus' engine.

"The lake is beautiful." Mallory cast her gaze out over the blue-green water shimmering in the late afternoon sunlight. She reached around in the back seat for two bottles of K.J. Chardonnay, the professor's favorite.

"This is the oldest lake built by the Corps of Engineers," McKenzie said as he opened the car door, "and it's partially spring-fed. It was the playground of the Atlanta wealthy in the '30s and '40s. Most of the original homes were passed down within families, but some have been sold to the *nouveau riche*. This side of the lake still has that old-money feel."

McKenzie was about to tap the knocker a third time when the door squeaked open, revealing a short, squat, elderly woman with a beaming face framed in short, gray hair. Little wire glasses fit snuggly on her perky nose. She looked like a Quaker, clothed in a dark-red flannel dress flaring at the ankles, and a matching vest over a long-sleeved, lace-fringed blouse buttoned tight to her throat.

Warm air billowed from the doorway, permeated with the unmistakable odors of a brewing country stew.

"Hello." She gave a short curtsy. "I'm Mrs. Leonard, Professor VonMitton's housekeeper, but he calls me his caretaker." She smiled meekly. "Please come in. I've heard so much about you two." She opened the doors all the way. "It's getting cold. We're to gather in the living room by the fireplace having toddies"

"Nice to meet you, Mrs. Leonard," they said in unison.

"We've brought the professor's favorite wine." Mallory handed off the bagged bottles. Massive timbered walls and beamed ceilings greeted them, darkened by time and the fumes from a five-foot-high, twelve-foot long stone fireplace surrounded by a semicircle of brown leather sofas, footstools, and wooden end tables. An oval, glass coffee table was the centerpiece.

Mrs. Leonard shut the doors behind them and skittered across the planked flooring onto a wide, patterned runner leading to the fireplace. "Come ahead. Don't be shy." She motioned to the couches. "I shall return in a few moments with toddies. Do sit. The professor desires that you read the scrapbook I've laid out."

The sun had set, and the crackling fire shed light throughout the vaulted great room along with the gaslights of two intricately carved chandeliers. One hovered over a library at one end of the room and the other over a dining area. A heavy, wooden country table was set for four but was clearly expandable to accommodate much larger numbers.

Mallory and McKenzie settled into a soft loveseat, the scrapbook spread out on the glass table.

"She's quite a character." Mallory tucked her purse at her feet.

"What a place." McKenzie waved at the native-Indian wall hangings and coats of arms displays at each side of the fireplace. "The Chandler Family had the bucks. This place is irreplaceable. Local craft-workers and tradesmen built it. Today, nothing remains of those talents."

"How do you know so much?"

"A buddy at Emory. His family owned one of these old houses just down the road. We used to go there and party."

Mallory's nose turned up. "Let's do the assignment." She repositioned herself in front of the scrapbook. "We want a good grade in this class."

For McKenzie, it seemed the years had suddenly dissolved away and college days were just yesterday. She was still the driver personality, directing the action like a traffic cop. But it was good to see her smiling again. He scooted next to her.

The oversized book, bound in expensive tan leather, was open to the first page, entitled, "Titus Smythe," handwritten in large, sweeping calligraphy.

Mallory held each page open for what she considered an adequate period, leafing through the book to get a feel for it. Clipped newspaper articles and a half-dozen pictures labeled with dates were spread over the twenty-page volume. The pictures were of the professor from 1986 through 2012, dressed like a southern gentleman of a bygone era and looking ageless, but his name was Dickerson Phelps.

Tucked between the last pages was a single sheet of fancy paper made out in the professor's clear hand, dated yesterday, and addressed to them. It took several minutes to read the chronology.

"Whoa! This is unbelievable," Mallory blurted. "A double life."

"Who would have guessed?"

"And Mrs. Leonard is supposed to fill in the gaps, he says."

McKenzie leaned back into the folds of the loveseat.

Mallory followed the move with her eyes. His face reflected the glowing fire, and for a fleeting moment, she was strangely moved. "So we're going to have dinner with the professor's alter ego," she said.

Mrs. Leonard strutted into view in front of the fireplace, carrying a tray of ceramic mugs and two stainless steel pitchers. "We will all probably need this." She set the tray on the table. "During winter in this house, we either drink my buttered rum toddies or hot Courvoisier XO with Kahlua and cream. Pick your poison. I hope I gave you enough time to peruse the book." With a kindly smile, she poured a steaming stream from one of the pitchers. "That's my rum toddy. Have at it." She took the mug and curled up in a leather chair on the opposite side of the table.

"The rum toddy? McKenzie stood, raising his eyebrows at Mallory.

"Perfect."

McKenzie poured two mugs and settled back next to Mallory.

Two sips later, Mrs. Leonard began. "Before Titus Smythe arrives—I presume you figured out he calls himself Dickerson Phelps—I'm going to give you a little background."

Mallory and McKenzie were all ears. The great, open room was silent except for the crackling fire.

"The professor's parents died in a car accident in Evanston, Illinois, where they both taught at Northwestern University. He was just a teenager. His mother's younger sister was my mother. I was only eighteen at the time, but I was a practicing nanny and I moved to Chicago and took him in like a brother. I never married. Anyway, to make the story short, we pulled up stakes when he was accepted to Oxford and moved to London. He received his medical degree, and, after internship and residency in Manchester, he talked me into moving to Atlanta, where he accepted a position as Associate Professor at the Emory Medical School. Emory had agreed to allow him to pursue a law degree at the same time, something he'd always wanted to do—and to work on a neurology specialty. That was in 1970. You know most of the rest. We've been in Atlanta ever since." Mrs. Leonard brought her mug to her lips and took a short sip.

"From the professor's note, you know he discovered his schizophrenic condition quite abruptly in 1983. He refers to it as his curse. I prefer to call it a gift. I was with him when it happened. It was a windy day, and we were having a cocktail before dinner on the front porch of the little house we were renting in Decatur—close to campus. He was daydreaming and listening to the wind chimes we both enjoy. Suddenly, he began talking to me in a derisive tone. His face had lost its usual softness, and he stood, looking at his clothes and the surroundings. He was clearly out of sorts. I still recall the whole bizarre conversation. He introduced himself as Titus Smythe as if he'd just met me. He said he lived in Edinburgh and claimed to have PhDs in chemical engineering and microbiology, and was a professor himself at Edinburgh University in Scotland. You can imagine how the conversation shocked me, especially when I came to find out he thought it was 1982. Well, as he was explaining his circumstances, he abruptly calmed down and the diatribe drifted to nothing. His eyes rolled over and he sat back down. And then he asked what time it was, but it was the professor talking."

Mrs. Leonard took another swig. She seemed to be waiting for questions.

Mallory finally said, "So, from the scrapbook it appears this Titus—or he's called Phelps later on—sees the past?"

"Not exactly. Over the years, Smythe has only surfaced when some tragic event in the present affected the professor's sensitivities. What makes it even more confounding is since his early twenties, the professor has demonstrated an overly keen sense of prognostic premonition. The way he puts it, he has inklings of trouble—and he always knows when there's going to be a "Titus" event. Then Smythe just shows up and takes charge. And, it gets even more bizarre. Smythe has the gift of discernment. He can see bits and pieces of someone's past. In the case I'm going to tell you about, it's an animal.

"The first time he literally took over was a police case outside Seattle in 1985—you saw the article in the scrapbook. A cougar mauled and killed a little girl a hundred yards from a public campsite on the side of Mt. McKinley. It was all over the news, a particularly brutal and bloody scene, and the professor was deeply affected. The little girl had been a second cousin. It was Titus's first appearance since the time on the porch two years before.

"I told you the professor always senses the coming of a Titus event. In the Seattle case—before this first Titus transformation actually manifested—he was able in advance to take the initiative and phone the sheriff of the town with jurisdiction. He introduced the persona of Mister Dickerson Phelps—an identity the professor created out of the blue—a licensed private investigator—a person of exceptional tracking ability who wanted to volunteer his assistance. The sheriff welcomed any help he could get. He hadn't had any luck tracking down the animal, and local residents, tourists, campers, and hikers were so afraid that they shunned the whole county."

It was time for another pull on Mrs. Leonard's toddy. "Well, Titus—Phelps—led the authorities and a search party on a ten-mile chase after the cougar. He could actually see the cat and its surroundings as it roamed the mountainous landscape. They cornered and shot it.

After that first time, the professor never had a problem with any investigative agency accepting assistance from Dickerson Phelps. He's helped solve several kidnappings and serial killer cases since then—even twice going to Europe."

"You say he's showing up here?" Mallory said. "I mean the professor—whatever."

"Yes, and I dare say you will find him abrasive and abusive. He is an arrogant man with a merciless tongue, not the Professor VonMitton you know. So, do be prepared." She raised her mug and grimaced. "He thinks he's in his late forties and a dashing dresser. His makeup is impeccable. I've looked after him all these years, dressing him like a valet and coordinating his activities."

"How does this ability of knowing the past show itself?" McKenzie appeared miffed.

"All we know is that he is able to pick up on intense emotion-al feelings of a person he's led to pursue—or, as we've seen, an animal. He has a limited window of time depending on the person's emotive state. There was even an interview and article written about his abilities after he assisted in a police case in Philadelphia in 1986. The newspaperman somehow got Titus to talk with him. It was published with little fanfair, but Titus never again allowed an interview."

"Can we see the article?" Mallory said.

"I'll see if I can find a copy, or at least the source."

"The newspaper coverage is sketchy," Mallory said. "He's never credited for his contributions."

"Police departments probably wouldn't go out on a limb to connect case results with psychic ability," McKenzie said. "It wouldn't be politically prudent to skew the image of good local police work with a hint of the paranormal."

"That's exactly what's happened," Mrs. Leonard said. "But he *did* develop an unspoken reputation with law enforcement, and it led to scientists and the government wanting to study him and law enforcement agencies trying to track him down to request assistance. The professor found it necessary to create a shield around his persona. Contact with Dickerson Phelps, Georgia private investigator, is through a website and form—he secretly contracted—with state-of-the-art encryption technology. He created a background for Phelps that included a documented amnesia incident. The professor just handles inquiries—politely turning down requests on various grounds."

"How can he afford to support this ruse?" Mallory asked.

"I don't know the details, but there's some kind of a tax-exempt foundation that accepts gifts. It gives Phelps credibility and a source of funding."

"Dear me," Mrs. Leonard sighed, "I didn't mean to go on. Perhaps we'd better top off." She stood, refreshed her toddy, and picked up the pitcher, pouring refills into the two outstretched mugs.

"This is quite a lot to swallow," Mallory said. "Would you mind if I spoke with Ryan privately for a few minutes?"

"Of course not, my dear. I'll see to the dinner and check on Mister Smythe."

"Well, what do you think?" Mallory rose from the loveseat and stretched her legs.

"From the professor's note, he says Titus is coming out to help us find who killed Reagan. Evidently, he believes there's been foul play. And, as he says, it's been on his radar for some time. He said he'd been uneasy over Reagan since our good-bye dinner seven years ago."

"Here she comes," Mallory whispered, "and I'll take a guess at who that is with her."

 Twenty-nine

DARPA

THE DEFENSE ADVANCED Research Projects Agency was charged with supplying technological options to the Department of Defense. Its mission was to prevent technological surprises, like Sputnik, and foster the development of unique technologies for use against potential enemies.

Focusing on near-term needs and requirements had driven the research efforts of the Army, Navy, Marine Corps, and Air Force at the expense of major change. The DOD needed an autonomous action arm, free from bureaucratic impediments and standard operating procedures, whose *only* charter was radical innovation.

With management levels limited to two, DARPA's 240 eclectic, world-class technical staff enjoyed the free and rapid flow of information and ideas and the luxury of instant decision-making. The agency had clearance to require cooperation from any DOD resource without question. It reported to senior Department of Defense management and worked directly with universities, foundations, and private industry. Product development was handed off to the military services or contracted with the commercial sector.

"Christine, what's the situation at Pharmco?" David Blanton, MD, Director of the Defense Sciences Office (DSO), one of five DARPA agencies, sat in his laboratory-like office with Christine Johnson, his senior team leader.

"They notified me yesterday that three of their replicating nanite prototypes were missing—and one of the generics was recovered by the DEA agent we sent in. It was contained in a Pharmco vial that came to us direct from the DEA forensics lab here in D.C. We sent it to Penn State's Nanofabrication Facility. It was a single generic nanite in a vacuum, one of the original missing drones created by Parnevik—without brain-map programming or an electrical stimulus payload. So, this technology is loose in the marketplace."

Blanton crossed his arms, scowling, as Christine Johnson continued.

"According to McKenzie, the DEA agent from Miami, following Reagan Driscoll's death, only two people remain who had access at Pharmco, Parnevik, the genius design engineer, and Ernest Kelto, a programmer also working on our *Fuerte Project*."

Run by small, purpose-built teams, DSO focused on projects with a two to four-year fruition period. It was authorized to make contractual investments in the most promising technologies across the broad spectrum of science and engineering research, with the intent of developing radically new military capabilities. The fact that failure was not viewed by the DSO or DARPA as negative, and that funds were virtually unlimited, served to empower DSO personnel to make investments in highly speculative ventures without fear of job retribution.

Dr. David Blanton was a neurologist with an MBA from MIT's Sloan School of Management. Over his nine-year tenure as head of DSO, the activities of the field teams had taken the shape of covert venture capitalism. "If the media gets wind of this project, we'll be in deep shit. We either cut bait—expunge all evidence of contact with Pharmco—or call in military intelligence to secure Pharmco's ongoing day-to-day operations and clean up outside leakage, including taking Parnevik and Kelto into custody. They could both be bad apples. Then we see if the project can be salvaged and put Pharmco back together again."

"Kelto's a computer geek operating in the blind," Johnson said. "Parnevik is the key lead in the contract. Without his robotic engineering expertise, the project is dead for at least a year until someone else with the skills, aptitude, and clearances can be recruited and brought into the fold."

"What's so unique here?"

"He's the only researcher in the world to have created a scale mock-up of a delivery nanite, complete with computer hardware and motion apparatus—and then successfully program it to replicate its structures in miniature using a controlled supply of raw materials. He built the nanites with sugar molecules. He produced inventories of generic, delivery nanites only lacking brain-map software downloads and charged batteries. The *Fuerte* Project was close to producing prototypes for testing in monkeys—the last step."

"So we find him," Blanton said, squirming on a stool across a lab table from Johnson. "He's on some kind of vacation in Europe—but it's the terrorist potential that worries me. Parnevik has already shown he can construct test products on his own. According to the copy of Reagan Driscoll's statement, he's been working at Georgia Tech's nano-labs for at least three years, experimenting on animals. And then a couple of weeks ago they think he tested one of his creations on some poor woman at a bar. Conceivably, he could program generic nanites with electrical overdoses and direct them anywhere in the brain. And if he has the replicating prototypes—"

"It's the perfect weapon," Johnson said. "Introduced selectively into the food chain, millions of people could be killed. It would be impossible to trace. Potential buyers will be numerous."

"Christine, our exposure at Pharmco is minimal. Only the CEO and the Director of Security know about the contract. Right? Any employees working on the project were doing so with FDA drug testing as the cover. The project is too important to sever ties. I'm thinking we need to clean it up and fast. I say we go in—but what about the DEA agent, McKenzie? I was told he's taken leave and is helping Reagan Driscoll's sister investigate her sister's death. They're the ones who got the Atlanta police involved."

"The release of Reagan Driscoll's statement to the Atlanta PD opened a homicide investigation. Right now the police aren't a problem," Johnson said, "but they could become one unless we intervene and close off information to the media. I think the prudent thing to do with McKenzie and the Driscoll sister is to invoke the national security umbrella on their personal probing before they realize exactly what's at stake and let the cat out of the bag. Maybe we could offer them cooperation. The other option is sanction."

"I agree. You confront the Driscoll sister and McKenzie—they'll have to go along when you explain the alternatives. And I think it's time to call in the military, especially since the project has been undertaken for their benefit. Army Military Intelligence can do the job. I'll brief them. They should be eager to provide the investigative resources. If we play our cards right, we won't have to get the FBI involved, but if we can't contain this situation, we'll be forced to call them in and the project will be out the window. Homeland Security could face a national security nightmare. Everyone loses."

 Thirty

Titus Smythe

MALLORY AND MCKENZIE sat next to the huge stone fireplace, cocooned in the comfortable, dark-leather sofa. A tall man followed Mrs. Leonard, distinguished looking; a stiff, hardened expression was pasted on his face. Dressed formally in a black suit—circa the 1920s—tieless, a white mock shirt embroidered at the neck with a line of yellow butterflies down the front, he wore black suspenders, securing trousers against his corseted midsection. Long, thick black hair hung straight and spread over his shoulders. He could have been late forties or perhaps fifty, but the image of a tyrant was unmistakable. It was hard to believe this man was a personification of Professor VonMitton.

"May I present his majesty, Mister Titus Smythe." Mrs. Leonard waved her hand, bowing like a servant, indicating a matching leather loveseat on the opposite side of the table from Mallory and McKenzie.

"Professor, is that really you?" Mallory gaped, eyes wide, questioning, holding in the desire to laugh.

"I do not entertain flippancy, young lady. You'd do best to mind your manners. I am pleased as always to be rid of the old man. I see not everyone here is so pleased." He glared at Mrs. Leonard.

"Stop it, Titus. I detest it when you demean me. These kind people came a long way at your bidding. See to your own manners."

"I didn't mean any disrespect, Mister Smythe," Mallory said, her face flushed and contrite. "I just didn't expect—"

"Call me Titus."

Mallory brightened. "Titus…this is Ryan—"

"I know perfectly well who he is. It is time to get down to the business at hand…. May I?" he asked Mrs. Leonard, nodding toward the pitchers on the table.

Mrs. Leonard adroitly scurried to the tray and stooped to pour a cup of her toddy creation. "I assume you prefer the Courvoisier?"

"Of course, and you may retire while I get acquainted with these two young people. I'm sure you have matters to attend to in the kitchen. I am looking forward to a decent meal for a change."

"You know I'm not going anywhere, Titus, and you will refrain from debasing me in front of our guests. Keep to our bargain." She handed Smythe the steaming mug. "I look after him," she said over her shoulder. "He needs ministering from time to time."

"That's enough. If you must, you must, but do sit quietly."

"Mister Smythe, this, ah, situation is unusual to say the least." McKenzie was adjusting.

"It's Titus, Agent McKenzie, just Titus—"

"It would be nice if you would explain what it is you want from us." McKenzie tried not to look for the professor.

"I see my caretaker and quasi-jailer has shown you the record of my endeavors." Smythe stabbed a finger at the tan scrapbook. "So kind of you to display my resume, Mrs. Leonard. It is a travesty that we find ourselves unable to explain publically the mechanics employed to assist in those malicious cases. But then, of course, who would believe the truth?" Smythe leaned up to the table and plucked the professor's exposed note from the back of the scrapbook. "The elements of our society are plagued with narrow-mindedness and fear anything that eludes their understanding."

Resting back in the couch and crossing his legs, Smythe read the professor's note, grinding his teeth as he went along, and then sighing as he tossed the page back on the table. "So now you know. I am indeed aware of most events that have transpired. Because of his caring for you two and Reagan, the professor released me to assist. As you now know from his explanation and the cursory reports of my endeavors, I can experience random past activities and feelings of those on which I concentrate. Intense emotion heightens the perception. Most of the time, the effectiveness is limited to one or two days, but in Reagan's case I was able to go back far enough to experience her death. It was frightening for me. I have never died before. It was most certainly contrived. There was nothing natural in how she jumped from that balcony. She was outside the real world. Something put her there, and we are going to find out what. Moreover, as we speak, I am being flooded with flashes of your activities and subsequent reactions in recent days, but do not take offense. I am unable to read your thoughts. What is the current status of police involvement?"

"They obtained a search warrant, and Pharmco delivered a copy of Reagan's statement yesterday afternoon," McKenzie said. "She gave it before going off to Las Vegas. No one has seen or heard from Parnevik since he left on sabbatical before New Year's. The police are going to search Parnevik's Atlanta house tomorrow. Captain Trussel told us we could go in and take a look after 2:00 p.m."

"I will accompany you. I need to see and feel this person's surroundings, find pictures of him, and secure any personal items he used frequently. This is important to enhance the degree to which I will be able to keep up with his recent past."

"Tell him about Club Elan and the Brightview—"

"I am aware," Smythe said, cutting Mallory off. "It appears this Parnevik has been experimenting on people for at least two years."

"But we really don't know why," Mallory said.

"The police have opened those cases," Smythe stated. "We will find out soon enough, and I am confident Parnevik's house will release some of his secrets."

A buzzer sounded in the background as McKenzie was placing another log in the hearth, and Mrs. Leonard rose from the couch.

"Ah, even the air holds the fragrance of your kitchen prowess, Mrs. Leonard. Venison stew, I dare say. You do me justice after all."

"That is my call to duty," Mrs. Leonard announced, shrugging. "Dinner will be served in five minutes."

"I'll give you a hand." Mallory stood and collected the tray from the table. "A refill, gentlemen?"

"No thank you," Smythe said. McKenzie shook his head.

"How can you let him treat you that way?" Mallory spoke low as they walked together past the pre-set dinner table.

"I tolerate his abuse. I'm afraid I may be equally responsible. I do goad him. I have to maintain a position of semi-equality. He can be very dangerous. Without his medications, he can become truly psychopathic. He recognizes no social boundaries, and his temper is uncontrollable. I allow him to believe he is independent. He thwarts me, pretending to take the medications I give him twice a day. I let him dispose of the tablets in various fashions he's crafted and force compliance through his habitual dietary intake. Fortunately, I am immune to his gift, as are many others. Sometimes he can only perceive vague flashbacks, and most of the time he is responding to intense emotions from the person of interest."

"So you're with him 24/7?"

"That is correct, young lady, and it is stressful indeed."

"What if he sneaks away or you have a problem with him?"

"Safeguards are in place." She pushed open the double doors to the kitchen. "If I have serious resistance with him, I press this button." She fingered a handsome jeweled pendant from a heavy-linked sterling chain around her neck. "The professor developed a contract with a hired agency to respond appropriately should I summon it."

"It is a beautiful adornment," Mallory said as they entered the kitchen. "And what a kitchen. It's huge."

"This is the old Chandler summer house. Chefs and servants prepared grand meals for up to a hundred people and served them on the massive veranda built out over the lake at the south side of the house."

Mallory took in the high ceiling and lines of hanging pots and pans, stainless steel worktables, wooden cutting blocks, and antiquated gas stoves.

"It's all original, just like it was after the Great Depression."

"Amazing.... I'm curious, Mrs. Leonard. Why does Mister Smythe seem to loathe the Professor?"

"He despises him for his memories. Titus has to live with them. He has few of his own after some time in the early '80s. For the sake of preserving his individuality and self-worth, he prefers not to discuss the professor, but I'm glad you asked. You'd best not mention him again or you may lose Titus's cooperation."

"It's hard for me to understand how you cope."

"It's not so difficult. I'm the doting parental figure to them both. A valued and irreplaceable servant-associate to Mister Smythe, and a housekeeper-companion to Professor VonMitton."

"Are you in—"

"No, my dear. Strictly a mother-sibling relationship," she said, shuffling off to the stove and dropping the massive oven door. Several pans on the stove were steaming, their lids merrily clinking. "And do share what I've told you with your beau."

"He's not my boyfriend."

"You sure could have fooled me." Mrs. Leonard reached for the hot pads on a nearby metal counter. "I saw the glint in your eyes."

***

"Moments without her presence are to be cherished," Smythe said when he was sure the two women had passed through the kitchen doors. "But in truth she is inimitable. We are somewhat of a team.... Now, since the autopsy was generic and incomplete, I believe the body should be exhumed and the brain examined. Emory should run the blood and urine samples again, just in case. I will need the guest towel from Reagan's house. It may help prod my senses. I may be able to tell if it was Parnevik even without forensics."

"I'll talk to Mal. She can get that going through the Chief of Police. He's starting to cooperate. The DEA's sending its lab results to the Atlanta PD and returning Reagan's personal items and the towel and vial I found in the apartment."

"Good. We have a beginning. And what did you find out at Georgia Tech?"

McKenzie leaned forward from his comfortable sitting position. "How did you know I went there? That was this morning."

"I have no time to waste indulging your petty fears of privacy. You discussed it with Miss Driscoll yesterday. It was within my range."

"You'll have to give me some time to get used to your gift, Mister Smythe."

"Titus."

McKenzie stood and picked up a brass-handled broom from its fireplace rack, brushed the accumulated ash back across the hearth, and added two more logs to the fire

"Agent McKenzie, I need to know why Pharmco is so upset."

"The structural nanites that recently went missing are replicators. Supposedly, given the raw materials—elements and compounds—these nanites can duplicate their structures—be programmed to build things—anything, a car, a bridge, a factory. It hasn't been done yet. It's theoretical. Their contract with the DOD is at risk."

"Yes, I see…. Reagan's past is somewhat more open to me because of VonMitton's long relationship and caring for her—and you two as well. She worked with her assistant, Kelto, on programming to control the replication process. Theory suggests there is a risk of replicating nanites running amok, unable to stop replicating. Parnevik's job was to engineer nanite prototypes and nano-computer hardware. Reagan Driscoll programmed the hardware for the nanites to move inside the body to specific locations in the brain and deliver electrical stimuli. Pharmco has three nanite delivery systems up to the FDA for testing approval in animals."

"Dinner is served, gentlemen," Mrs. Leonard said as she and Mallory came through the kitchen doors, both carrying the large pot of venison stew and placing it on a wooden stand next to the dinner table. The two men approached like obedient cattle coming to the trough, Smythe in the lead.

After everyone was seated, Smythe said, "So we meet at 2:00 p.m. at Mister Parnevik's house. Agent McKenzie, you will see to it there are no problems."

"The professor introduced you to Atlanta PD," McKenzie said. "Dickerson Phelps is expected."

Smythe reached in his pocket and pulled out a cell phone. "This is a satellite-powered, personal communications system. Its frequency setting is reserved, and voice communications are automatically encrypted. It's been designed to thwart tracking technology. I have one, Mrs. Leonard has one, and you two will share this one. It works like any other. There is only one number. The number seven is a speed dial that rings to each of us at the same time." Symthe handed the phone to McKenzie. "Use it only in an emergency. We don't want to test its communication bands against modern hacking unless compelled to do so."

"You'll need Parnevik's address," Mallory said, writing it down on the back of one of her business cards and handing it to Smythe. "How will you get there?"

"We drive, of course," Mrs. Leonard said, looking piqued. "I should say *he* drives, and like a maniac. His Porsche is in the garage beneath the house, next to the boats."

"It's a candy-apple, twin turbo S-type," Smythe said.

Mrs. Leonard's mouth curled, and she looked away. "Whatever," she said. "Titus will show you after we finish dinner."

Part III

The Thickening

 Thirty-one

Ernest Kelto

HE STEPPED OFF the court, sweaty, legs feeling like overdone spaghetti. Several years had slipped by since he'd played racquet-ball. He leaned over his equipment bag propped up against the wall between courts, prodded around inside, and clutched his water bottle. He took a big swig and surveyed the layout of the university fitness club. Except for some decorative painting and the conversion of the basketball court into exercise space for classes and a spin-room, it hadn't changed all that much. He'd been brought up in Charlotte and attended here at the Charlotte branch of the University of North Carolina.

Kelto was participating on the daily challenge court. The old geezer he'd been playing seemed to be well known to the others watching from benches behind the full glass back wall, waiting their turns to play the winner. They called him Doc, and he crushed Kelto 15-4 with his accurate serves and pinch shots.

Kelto returned the water bottle to his bag and pulled out a fresh one. Doc had just come out of the court to wait for the next person in the challenge line to warm up.

"Good game," Kelto said. "Doc, isn't it?" He handed him the water bottle. "Be my guest."

"Thanks. I think everyone calls me that so they don't have to remember my name. You used to play here, didn't you?"

"Yeah, about five years ago when I was a student. Pretty rusty now."

The slamming sounds of the compressed racquetball shots ceased, and the player inside the court tapped on the glass near the entry doorway, letting Doc know he was ready.

"Got to go." Doc recapped the bottle and handed it back to Kelto. "They all want a piece of this old ass."

"Go get em, Doc." Kelto tossed the bottle back into his equipment bag and took a chair with the rest of the challengers. The two players shook hands, and the challenger, a cocky air-conditioning technician ranked number two at the club, entered the service box.

A sense of well-being crept over Kelto, and the gym noises melted away as his thoughts wandered. Before leaving Atlanta for the drive to his parent's house in Charlotte, he'd received confirmation by express mail that his Porsche was scheduled for delivery within the month. Everything was perfect. If today turned out well, he was on his way to a marketable product. It may not be as strongly affecting or as long lasting as the levels Pharmco wanted to achieve under its government contract, but it didn't have to be. All it had to be was something of significant interest to Pharmco's competition.

He'd removed Pharmco inventory from the premises, utilizing the heavy, plastic, vacuum-sealed vials Parnevik had developed to elude the security machinery. The nanites he'd withheld from the Parnevik delivery were hidden in the insulation of the freezer door to his condominium refrigerator. *So the game goes*, he thought. Parnevik was experimenting outside Pharmco for his personal benefit. It didn't matter what he was up to. Two could play the game.

A body heavily slammed against the glass back wall, startling Kelto back to the present. He needed to pay careful attention. He was confident with the brain map location from working with the *Fuerte* Project. It was the calibration of the electrical charge that was in question.

The game was going quickly. The young technician was just too fast and powerful for Doc. It was 9-1 within five minutes. Then something unusual happened, and the dozen or so people watching the game were suddenly silent. The old man was all of a sudden everywhere. His speed off the line was explosive, and he power-pinched every shot that came even a foot off the back wall. At five serving nine, Doc drove the ball with such force it burst on the front wall. He turned to face the glass back wall, face flushed, waiting for someone to toss in another ball.

Doc served out the game with accurate drive serves that cracked against the sidewall just over the short line. The young challenger couldn't return a single one.

Exiting the court first, the loser stripped off his glove and jammed it and his racquet into his equipment bag, grabbed it by the shoulder straps, and headed straight for the locker room, too embarrassed to make eye contact or say a word.

Doc came off the court. His face was pasty, and he appeared confused. He reached a hand back to steady himself on the edge of the open court door.

"You okay, Doc?" someone said.

A blank look came over his face, his eyes went wide, and blood started dripping from his nose. His legs crumpled, and he slid in a heap against the glass court door.

 Thirty-two

Parnevik's Residence

As SCHEDULED, TITUS Smythe pulled up to the mansion on Peachtree Battle in the heart of old Atlanta at exactly 2:00 p.m. Mallory and McKenzie had just arrived in McKenzie's Taurus.

McKenzie walked over to the driver side of the candy-apple red Porsche. Mallory went to the other side of the racecar, greeted Mrs. Leonard, and assisted her exit. No squad cars were present, but the Atlanta PD evidently hadn't finished combing the grounds; the yard was cordoned off with yellow tape.

"I understand you had no difficulty with the police captain," Smythe said to McKenzie as he exited the sleek Carerra. "He's more cooperative since securing Reagan's statement. If there is time, we will go directly from here for a little visit with the dear captain. The first exposure is always the most difficult. I need to go over the evidence returned from the DEA. So tell me what you know about Parnevik." He turned away from McKenzie and started up the fifty feet of flagstone walkway leading from the graveled circular drive to the front door of the residence.

"I can only give you hearsay from talking to Emma Kisumi, Reagan's roommate." McKenzie followed at Smythe's back. "She had on and off contact with him for a couple of years, but he was too weird for her." McKenzie hesitated. His attorney instincts told him hearsay might not be helpful.

"Do continue." Smythe stopped at the massive wooden doors. "I need to have a feel for him before we inspect the house."

"Well, on the positive side, his intelligence is off the charts. He's a loner and aloof, high-strung, impatient, self-absorbed. He schemes and plots. Emma said he was a phony and incapable of nurturing a relationship."

"Wait up," Mallory yelled. She was negotiating the stone walk, arm-in-arm with Mrs. Leonard.

Smythe and McKenzie turned around.

"I gave her a week off," Smythe said, "but she insisted on coming." He slapped his hands against his thighs. "But, never mind—According to the statement taken by the police, Miss Kisumi hasn't seen Parnevik since before Christmas, and he didn't tell her where he was going."

"Correct. I assume you know all this because of your ability to see the past."

"Yes. The last five days or so of yours and Mallory's activities are relatively clear, although hers are clearer than yours. Perhaps because she is Reagan's twin sister."

Waiting for Mallory and Mrs. Leonard to catch up, McKenzie noticed Smythe was outfitted exactly as he'd been at dinner the night before. The stiff afternoon breeze flapped the oversized lapels of his '40s suit coat and played with the brownish curls hanging from under his Stetson.

"Okay, let's go," Mallory said approaching the doorway. "The key is on top of the portico. We are advised by Captain Trussel not to touch anything."

"I am familiar with police procedures, young lady. Who do you think you are dealing with here?" Smythe reached into a breast pocket and pulled out a pair of latex hospital gloves.

"Watch your tongue, Titus," Mrs. Leonard said. "Do as you are told with as much courtesy as you can muster. And cease playing the leader of the pack. You will wait for me to accompany you as always. No deviation."

"The police found nothing of interest in the house," McKenzie said.

"I am aware of that, Agent McKenzie. All the more reason for me to experience the interior. I need a recent photograph of Parnevik. You two will examine the house and find me a picture and any clothing that may have been used recently."

*****

The interior was like a museum, with furniture and antiques formally displayed; the fragrance of fresh lemon wax filled the air. Parnevik had duplicated classic Greek Revival décor, dominated by plain white plaster walls, intricately carved moldings, and ionic columns. Moldings around doors and windows were fluted, and the corners contained square blocks carved in bold relief.

In the middle of the round entrance foyer, a crystal chandelier hung twenty feet from the ceiling's circular apex. It supported four ornately etched brass arms terminating in ball-shaped oil lamps. A dramatic marbled staircase wound along the circle's perimeter to the second level.

"This is something else," Mallory said, mostly to herself, admiring the sweeping grace of the brass-railed stairs.

Smythe had quickly gone on into the next room and was busy darting around, examining everything in a flurry. Mrs. Leonard followed him closely, watching his every move as he clamored around the furniture, hovering over objects and randomly running his hands close to walls. He appeared to choose carefully among the numerous, artistically arranged antiques on which to focus his attention, almost caressing their surfaces.

The living room of the house was open. Double, parlor-pocket doorways led off to the reception foyer, lounge, and dining areas. Polished amber wood floors outlined the edges of a plush Persian rug. In contrived groups, carved mahogany tables rested on clawed legs, covered with books and periodicals. Matching chairs with oxidized bronze armrests gave the impression of library-like research stations.

Mallory entered the living room and gestured at the semi-circular hearth of a massive, obsidian fireplace. "Look at that."

A huge *pier* mirror set in an ornately carved Egyptian frame hung from heavy chain above the cavernous opening, canted slightly to reflect the entire room to those entering. The fireplace lacked a mantel, instead offset by Doric pilasters topped with bronze-carved capitals.

McKenzie came into the mirror's view and stood, self-consciously staring at their images, admiring the effect the reflection had on the contents of the room. "These furnishings are priceless."

"I didn't realize you were into antiques," Mallory said.

"After my mom passed, I collected a little when I did the boat over. Pirate stuff, not exquisite like this." He took his eyes off their images in the mirror and pointed. "Now that's a table." Opposite the fireplace, McKenzie was peering into the dining room dominated by a dark wood table raised on saber legs with brass toecaps.

"I'm going upstairs to look for pictures and clothes," Mallory said.

"Have at it." McKenzie watched her athletic form move gracefully through the doors into the reception foyer. She grabbed the brass railing and started taking the stair steps two at a time. Then she glanced back, caught him looking at her, and smiled. McKenzie felt naked. His face flushed. College was starting all over again.

He pulled his attention back to the living room. There was coldness about the room. The perfect layout eliminated any feel of hominess. The chairs and divans didn't seem to invite use and the antique lamps and pottery didn't entice scrutiny.

"See here! Come pay attention!" Titus Smythe's demanding voice echoed from out of sight in the next room.

"You are not to touch anything," Mrs. Leonard bayed. "Behave yourself."

The old lady's fearless, McKenzie mused as Mallory came up behind him.

"I got some pictures." She flashed two framed photographs at him as she went by and headed off to respond to Smythe.

They found him in a small antechamber leading to the kitchen. He was studying a bronze figurine embedded in a circle at eye level in a six-by-eight-foot interior wall of unadorned plaster. Below it was a claw-legged table displaying a multi-colored vase. "This piece is *Nike*, the Greek goddess of victory. Beautiful." He moved closer to examine it. "Yes, we do have something here."

"What is it?" Mallory and McKenzie were peering over his shoulder.

Smythe reached out a hand.

"Not to touch, Titus." Mrs. Leonard took him by the other arm.

"Leave me be, you insufferable appendage…. The statement Parnevik's housekeeper gave Atlanta PD claimed she hadn't seen him since Christmas Eve, but I assure you he has been here recently, though just briefly."

Smythe took a quick look at Mrs. Leonard, at the same time placing his hand around the Nike figurine. "I believe this should do it." He turned the statue body clockwise, and the plaster wall rose with an electrical whine and disappeared above the molding along the ceiling. "I'm beginning to get fleeting pictures of Mister Parnevik."

"Captain Trussel didn't say anything about this," McKenzie said, noticing Smythe's look of arrogant triumph. At that moment, he realized Titus was going to be trouble.

Wooden stairs led down into darkness. Mrs. Leonard dropped her hold on Smythe's arm, and he carefully moved the table to the side.

"What are you picking up?" McKenzie stepped in behind Smythe as he took the stairs, Mallory close behind.

"I'm quite sure the captain didn't discover it," Smythe said, ignoring McKenzie and turning back to face them. "Did you find what I asked for?"

Mallory had a foul-weather jacket slung over her shoulder and was holding two framed pictures from the master bedroom. "All his suits and shirts were encased in plastic fresh from the cleaners. I didn't find any dirty clothes. The bathroom had the usual personal items. It seemed very organized, but no comb, brush or items that might have prints or DNA. I assume the police dusted the house. They're processing whatever they found. If we're going to visit Captain Trussel, we'll find out."

"Let me see the pictures—where did you find the coat?"

Mallory passed the frames around McKenzie. "In the foyer closet."

Smythe examined the pictures. One was of a man in college graduation garb accepting a diploma. "This is of no use. It was taken from at least twenty feet away." He looked at the other one.

"That's Parnevik with his mother," Mallory said. "Emma told me she passed away while he was working on his doctorate."

"This is not Parnevik," Smythe said, handing the pictures back to Mallory. "The man I'm glimpsing doesn't look anything like this—Give me the coat."

Mallory tossed him the garment.

"Watch your manners, Titus." Mrs. Leonard glared at him from the top of the staircase.

Smythe cast a scowl of acknowledgement in her direction. "It's well used." He went over the lining and sleeves with his hands. "Yes, this is his, but he's drastically changed his appearance since the picture."

"How can you tell he was here?" McKenzie asked. "I thought your gift was only good for a couple of days."

"Sometimes my perceptions can go back further. It's all a matter of emotional intensity. The combination of the house, the pictures, and the coat have given me a clearer and deeper sense of this man. He was here about five days ago and charged with anxiety and fear, the kind one gets when playing hide-and-seek. But I can tell you that now he is in France and has taken a cottage, feeling proud of himself. More will come. Let us see what lies below."

"He's converted the wine cellar into a laboratory," Mallory said after taking in the space. "I think I've seen similar machines and microscopes at Pharmco. Reagan gave me the tour a couple of years ago."

"Come, Mrs. Leonard and the two of you. I've seen enough." Smythe stood at the opposite end of the room from the stairs leading up into the house. He was fingering one of the bottles in the built-in wooden wall of labeled wines. "Shall we go out the back way?" The wooden rack swung through the wall on three sets of heavy hinges, revealing another set of stairs.

After examining the doorway they'd come through at the back of the fountain in the front yard, Smythe said, "Very nice work, first class. The man has a flair for the macabre, and he's a perfectionist."

"This must be how he comes and goes without the house-keeper knowing." Mallory checked out the front of the fountain. "We'll sic Captain Trussel on this. Maybe he can figure out what Parnevik was going to do down there."

"The big microscope still had the manufacturer's plastic protector over the eyepiece," McKenzie said, holding Mrs. Leonard's arm. She had taken the whole experience in as if nothing surprised her.

"The police won't find anything," Smythe snapped. "It's a lab. He never used it. It's all newly installed. He wore surgical gloves and went up into the main house once to pack. Look." Smythe walked away from the fountain, pointing at the nearby driveway.

They met at the edge of the graveled circle. Smythe bent down on one knee. "Dual tire tracks. A large van. Perhaps four or five days ago. I can't see it clearly, but I'm positive he secretly brought in the equipment."

"Maybe we should bug the place," McKenzie said.

"He's too smart for that," Smythe scoffed. "I would bet he has his own bugs. He's a *perfectionist*. He'll know we've broken into his private sanctum. I don't think he'll return here."

 **Thirty-three**

France

FOUR DAYS passed while Parnevik established a residence and daily routine in an older, sedate section of Biarritz, the charming and magnificent French playground destination. Located on the Atlantic coast on the southwestern tip of France, eighteen kilometers from the Spanish border, Biarritz was a Mecca of restored eighteenth-century architecture that glistened with money. Nestled in the French Basque province of *Labourd*, the luxurious seaside town boasted two elegant casinos and some of the best beaches in Europe, attracting rich tourists worldwide and supporting a permanent surfing culture addicted to the powerful waves and mild climate.

Parnevik leased a two-story, Mediterranean-styled bungalow near the top of a rocky cliffside for the remainder of the year. His veranda faced the Bay of Biscay, overlooking a small marina and the pleasure-boat activities in the harbor. He had a view of the spectacular cliffs and lookouts lying to the west of the glitzy main beach and the steeples of St. Martin's Church off to the east. The famous Barriere and Bellevue Casinos were a hundred meters away on the beach directly below.

Arthur Dubois appeared to be just another young French jet-setter. He typically dressed in expensive casual clothes or color-coordinated biking tights and racing shirts. He roamed the city and environs on his 350 cc Ducati motorcycle, freely spending Euros and innocuously interacting with the locals.

***

This morning he'd changed identities and taken the high-speed French railway from Biarritz to Lyon, France's second largest city some 300 km northeast. The winter day was bright and the air crisp.

He sat outside, alone, under an umbrella-shaded table, at *Le Chia*, an intimate rustic café near the edge of Lyon's business district. He was warm, clothed in a dark gray, Italian-cut business suit and herringbone topcoat, and was looking forward to his meal.

He'd frequented the café many times over the years. It offered seclusion at this time of day and had Wi-Fi. His addiction to Beaujolais red wine accompanying a traditional French brunch had always been consistently satiated through the establishment's fine cuisine and wine list.

Sweet aromas from a nearby bakery hovered in the air, adding authenticity to a truly local dining experience. Today he ordered *saucisson de Lyon* (sausage), *andouillette, coq au vin, esox* (pike), *gras double* (tripe cooked with onions), and *salade lyonnaise* (lettuce with bacon croutons and a poached egg).

On the morrow, Mr. Julian Trebar from Canada was meeting with *Monsieur* Maurice Goulet, the Managing Director of the renowned Cha Wan Tea Company, at their headquarters' store. It would be Parnevik's pleasure to spend the night at the famed Villa Florentine, which offered sublime panoramic views of Lyon, and indulge in a fine Parisian seafood dinner at its five-star restaurant.

As he was finishing the last of his brunch, pressure and severe pain suddenly struck the base of his neck at the top of the spinal cord, the beginning of the medulla oblongata. He fumbled at the buttons of his topcoat and probed in the side pocket of his tailored suit coat for the plastic vial he always kept close. The pain brought seeping paranoia, and heat waves encircled him like creeping lava. He gulped down two tablets, swallowing them dry, and clenched his fists to wait. He'd neglected to take the medication before boarding the train. It didn't happen often but when it did, he had to defocus, lock out stimuli from his surroundings, and hope he could suffer in place long enough for the meds to take effect. If he was unsuccessful, uncontrollable rage could overcome him, as had occurred once in the past when he'd gone on a rampage, running from imaginary dangers. The fiasco had terminated in overnight incarceration.

His body was reliant on neutralizing the production of the neurotransmitter, dopamine, which his brain produced in excess. His medication included adrenaline, which helped balance his body chemistry, and produced a short period of relaxed euphoria, like an addict's fix.

"*Monsieur* Trebar," the waiter said softly, "are you all right?"

"Yes, yes, Francis," Parnevik said, grimacing. "The coffee or fruit I had on the train must have been bad." He could feel perspiration dripping through his sideburns, and his silk shirt was sticking to his ribcage. But the attack was subsiding, and his mind was clearing. In a few minutes, he would be himself again.

"May I get you another glass of wine?"

"That would be nice. Thank you, Francis."

A short time later, as the waiter cleared the table, Parnevik scooted to the opposite side, opened the message-managing and video software on his laptop, and re-read the e-mail from Paulie Torentino. His business had hit a snag.

***

The train ride from Biarritz to Lyon had allowed him time to access Pharmco's website. It was strictly curiosity. His stomach had turned at the announcement of Ernest Kelto's resignation and the naming of a replacement. His immediate reaction was that the stupid nerd was going on his own, and he would inevitably get caught. That could end up revealing the link between them and make it impossible for him to return to the United States. He'd taken careful measures at every step along the way to leave no trace of involvement with the missing nanite inventory. Reagan Driscoll had been his only breach until Kelto. He'd remedied the Driscoll situation. Now it was obvious he should have cleaned up his connection to Kelto before leaving the country.

Parnevik slid the chair back, irritated, just as Francis was approaching with the bill. He thanked the young man, handed him his Royal Bank MasterCard, and took his attention back to the laptop.

"We have to talk," Parnevik tapped out on the keyboard, immediately clicking the Send button.

It was after seven in the morning in New Jersey. If Paulie Torrentino was still asleep, he would be awakened by the family's monitoring system, but Paulie was one of those rare hypersensitive people that required less than five hours of sleep per night.

"You interrupt a perfectly good breakfast, Mister Parnevik, but I'm glad we are finally hearing from you. We have problems." Paulie's image showed him relaxing in a recliner. The room looked like a home library.

An Internet video chat line was part of the encrypted system on the Genovese's private server. Parnevik's access had been downloaded as part of his business arrangement.

"I am only responding because it's early in our relationship. As far as your problems are concerned, they're your own, so spare me."

"You don't need to take that tone with me, Parnevik. Just hear me out." Paulie squirmed in his seat and reached for a cup of coffee. "I see you're in a private place."

"An outdoor café. No one's around." Parnevik hoisted his wineglass and tried to look casual.

"First the good news. The street distributors love the product. We decided to let it out in your hometown. Once they got comfortable with the ease of marketing and positive feedback from users, word spread. One of the distributors was brought in by the police on suspicion of trafficking. He was released the next morning. The cops caught him with candy drops, just like you said. We're expanding distribution there and plan to launch in the twenty largest metro areas. You need to convince us you can deliver product. We have placed a large order in the usual way. Check your bank account. We need immediate delivery at the set destination."

"No problem. The Pakistani manufacturer has sufficient ingredients on hand to produce about 100,000 bottles. What else?"

"Mister Gatturna is concerned that you won't be able to keep up with demand, and we want samples of the other products you outlined in your original proposal."

"You have no reason to question me—"

"We think we do. Our sources at Atlanta PD tell us they searched your residence, and you are a person of interest involving the death of a Pharmco co-worker. You and another guy at Pharmco are also suspects in the theft of valuable test products. And, our contacts tell us an accidental death in Charlotte yesterday may be related to a similar incident at some nursing home in Atlanta—and to the little test we enjoyed together on Christmas Eve.... Mister Parnevik, they found your lab in the basement of your house. There's an APB out on you. How are you going to produce product as a fugitive?"

Parnevik hadn't thought the local police would become involved so quickly. Pharmco would have done everything in its power to keep its research out of public scrutiny. And he was positive he'd left no trace at Reagan's apartment. Over the years, he'd been meticulous with his Georgia Tech activities, including sterilization after recently manufacturing the first large batch of raw *Amor* nanites.

"Mister Torrentino, I have a backup production lab. As far as *Amor* is concerned, I will be able to supply you endless product very quickly. The *Bliss* product will be ready for testing in the near future."

"I'll tell Mister Gatturna what you said. Unlike your pink candy that gets people horny, he believes the big business is replacing hard-core drugs. He wants you to reproduce the heroin and cocaine highs. Your proposal indicates the *Bliss* drug is designed to do the job."

"That is correct. I will ponder on this and let you know what I believe is workable." As he was talking to Paulie—on a hunch—he'd brought up the Charlotte newspapers and scanned yesterday's reports of the old racquetball player's unusual behavior and sudden death. Kelto was brought up in Charlotte. It had to be him trying to go out on his own, using stolen *Fuerte* nanites from the government contract. Pharmco's inventory had not undergone Parnevik's latest alterations, optimizing voltage and duration at Georgia Tech using lab rats. Kelto was stupid. He had no idea what would happen to a human being. "Mister Torrentino, I have a favor to ask."

 Thirty-four

Atlanta PD

"Finally it's starting to move." McKenzie glanced into the back seat, taking a quick peek at Mallory sitting next to Smythe. Mrs. Leonard was dutifully quiet on the passenger side. They were all on edge. The traffic had piled up, and what should be a short trip downtown to police headquarters was testing their patience.

"Bloody hell, this is." Smythe wrestled a new sitting position in the back seat. It was his fourth outburst.

Mallory saw McKenzie grimace through the rearview mirror. Smythe had become increasingly irritated and impatient, leaving Mallory on edge not knowing what to expect from him next.

News over the radio had reported traffic snarled on Peachtree Street, Atlanta's main drag, due to an accident near the Langford Children's Hospital, a mile and a half from downtown. Cars had clogged the side-street alternatives, so they'd elected to stay on Peachtree and had been virtually stuck for the last thirty minutes.

At the first signs of aberrant behavior, Mrs. Leonard had cajoled Smythe into taking a dose of Ritalin, the standard fix-it. Back at the country house, she'd shared with Mallory and McKenzie that without it, and timed ingestions of medications worked out over the years, Smythe was capable of rampaging out of control. It had happened twice. The last time was in Rhode Island in 1993.

He'd nearly beaten a stubborn, rural deputy sheriff to death while assisting in tracking down a serial killer. As his medications wore thin, he became exceedingly strong physically, belligerent, self-absorbed, and lost social perspective.

The car inched along behind the traffic pileup, finally spilling into the streets of the central city. Smythe had ceased his scathing verbal abuse of the situation and became steely quiet. The Ritalin had done its work.

A security guard recognized McKenzie and passed the Ford Taurus rental car through the crash gate into the employee underground parking.

Mallory let out a breath. "Well, we made it."

"Are you up to this, Titus?" Mrs. Leonard hissed.

"I am. You needn't fret."

"Captain Trussel said to meet him in his conference room on the third floor." McKenzie slid the car into a visitor parking space next to a patrol sedan.

"I would prefer to enter his presence first, if you don't mind." Smythe exited the back seat. "And leading the way is my modus operandi." He strode toward the mauve-painted block structure housing the elevator bank.

Mallory assisted Mrs. Leonard, and McKenzie brought up the rear.

The elevator only stopped at the third floor, opening into a security station manned by two uniformed police officers. McKenzie pushed ahead, identified the group, and surrendered his Glock to the holding locker.

"Any other weapons?" The locker guard passed a receipt to McKenzie and glanced down the line, scowling at Smythe with his outdated black trench coat and top hat.

"He doesn't carry a weapon, Sergeant. We're all clean. Just like in the movies," Mrs. Leonard said with a straight face.

They passed through the scanning equipment one at a time, Titus Smythe in the lead, and the officer at the terminus directed them to the glassed-in conference room at one corner of the open bullpen of activity. They walked along the edge of the room, subjected to dozens of quick takes and some staring faces. Capt. Trussel, in full uniform, stood at the open conference-room door.

"My name is Dickerson Phelps, Captain. I trust my introduction of a few days ago has served to satisfy any professional curiosity." Smythe had become southern genteel, complete with a South Carolina drawl. He held out his hand.

"Mister Phelps, you are here at Agent McKenzie's request. Here in Atlanta we've had little experience with psychics, and we're not interested in lessons at present. Can we get started, ladies and gentlemen?"

Mrs. Leonard nudged Smythe in the middle of the back before he could respond to the captain's rebuff.

McKenzie reintroduced Mallory and then Mrs. Leonard as Dickerson Phelps' assistant. The captain did not appear to be in good humor as he motioned for them to take seats at the conference table and stood at the head.

"Now, I've granted you an accommodation by allowing you into Parnevik's residence. Technically that was a breach of procedure. I did it at Mallory's request as legal representative of the Driscoll family inquiring into her sister's death. I want it clearly understood that the free flow of information will cease the moment a formal investigation is opened.... As of right now, I can only tell you that no evidence has as yet been found linking Reagan Driscoll's death to foul play—"

"Captain, what did your officers find in Parnevik's laboratory?" Smythe rose, pulled his chair away from the table, re-seated and crossed his legs, a smug look on his face.

Smythe spent the next five minutes badgering Capt. Trussel as he explained how to enter the secret cellar through the house and at the outside fountain, and pointing out the presence of suspicious vehicle tracks in the gravel driveway.

Capt. Trussel suffered through the harangue without response, then abruptly left the room and scuttled to an officer's desk near the middle of the bullpen. Ten seconds later, the officer picked up his coat and hurriedly left the room.

The captain returned, and Mallory immediately started in. "I would say we were cooperating in your investigation in a positive way. I suggest our further cooperation might be beneficial. I want the Emory autopsy results of my sister's exhumation. And Mister Phelps needs to examine the items from her apartment that came back from the DEA."

"All right. I'll have an officer escort him to the evidence room." Capt. Trussel used the phone on the table to summon another officer. "We'll talk while Phelps here does what he does."

"I'll be going with him," Mrs. Leonard said, rising from her seat and shouldering her rather large purse. "He sometimes asks for my advice."

"Very well."

While Smythe and Mrs. Leonard were absent, Mallory and McKenzie looked over the autopsy report. The captain had arranged for Emory University's top neurologist to sit in with the Fulton County Medical Examiner during the procedure.

Capt. Trussel fidgeted for a few silent minutes as the two scrutinized the document.

"The bottom line is there are abnormalities in the brain," Mallory said. "We'll wait for Mister Phelps to return. He has considerable experience—as you no doubt have determined—with forensics and autopsies. And he's proven of value to many police investigations."

"We checked him out. He appears credible, but the department doesn't have any experience with psycho-babble. It's not scientific, but I'll try and keep an open mind."

"In the meantime, have you been able to track Parnevik?" Mallory asked sharply.

McKenzie recognized the signs. She could be impatient. *Curious how personality traits hung on through the years.* His eyes strayed to her as she glared at Capt. Trussel. She still had the fire. Fleeting memories spun flashbacks.

"We know he flew from Atlanta to LaGuardia on December thirty-first and from there to Quebec City. We lose him there, but pick him back up January second leaving Atlanta for Paris via New York. His credit card usage says he's been living high on the hog since his mother passed away nine years ago. She left him considerable investment assets. We only found one bank account, the Bank of America, Peachtree Battle branch. He closed it out on December thirtieth and wire transferred $13.7 million to the Hypo Investment Bank. It's a private bank offering portfolio management and investment advice located in the Principality of Liechtenstein. They won't release information. He hasn't used a credit card since the Chateau Bonne Entente hotel in Quebec City and the Paris flight."

The telephone on the table jingled. "Excuse me," he said, frowning. "Trussel.... Okay. Thanks." He put the phone back in its cradle. "They're on their way back."

***

Once they were seated, Capt. Trussel casually glanced at Dickerson Phelps. "Any secrets mysteriously reveal themselves?" he asked, unable to sustain a businesslike tone.

Smythe stood, hands clasped behind his back, leaning against the doorway, almost sneering. "In fact, my dear Captain, I am becoming more sensitive to Mister Parnevik as a result of the examination. You will be pleased to know Parnevik used the hand towel. He wiped his hands on it, and you should find a DNA match to the epidermal scales from the collar of the winter coat taken from his residence. Mrs. Leonard, if you would."

Mrs. Leonard pulled the jacket from her oversized purse and laid it on the table.

"Look, Mister Phelps—"

"Please have your lab confirm my supposition."

Capt. Trussel nodded.

"I noticed the tag on the Pharmco vial Agent McKenzie discovered among Miss Driscoll's effects had a different date than the other items. It was returned by the DEA separately. Any reason?" Smythe shifted position against the doorway.

"It didn't come back with the rest because some DOD higher-ups held it for a couple of days. No explanation was given."

"So, now more government is involved. How interesting."

"Anything else, Mister Phelps?" Mallory asked.

"Just one more item. The vitamin bottle. Has it been analyzed?"

"There were no fingerprints on it in the DEA's report other than Reagan's," Capt. Trussel responded. "Nothing suspicious with the contents."

"Captain, you must trust me. I suggest you send the contents to a responsible outside lab. Tell them to look for any evidence of tampering with the capsules. I believe Parnevik implanted experimental nanites that caused Reagan's strange behavior."

"I'll take it under advisement." Capt. Trussel dropped his attention to the pile of folders on the table.

"We have to find something solid tying Parnevik to my sister's death," Mallory said. "If he was in the house, that's a start. For now I say let's get back to the autopsy."

Capt. Trussel opened the file and read. "'Sections through the pre-frontal cortex displayed abnormal amounts of blood and cell desecration.'"

"That area of the brain controls emotion," Smythe volunteered as if addressing a student.

"Could that have caused death?" McKenzie asked. "Did she have some kind of aneurism?"

"Let me see the file," Smythe said.

Capt. Trussel slid it across the table toward an empty chair. Smythe sat down and flipped through the pages. "There was swelling and inflammation…capillaries were collapsed, and cells had burst…. It wasn't possible to determine if it was caused by the fall."

"So we have nothing." Mallory sighed.

"Captain Trussel," Smythe said. "I advise you to look for anything similar in the Brightview case—cell damage to areas of the brain, collapsed capillaries, blood pooling. We're looking for a pattern. This Parnevik was testing his product. My intuition tells me two years ago he went to that nursing home."

"I presume this is one of your visions?" Irritation was etched across Capt. Trussel's face. His patience was growing thin.

"It is an educated posit, Captain. My special abilities do not normally allow me to see back that far in the past."

"We're on the Brightview situation," Capt. Trussel went on smoothly. "The woman's daughter has given permission to exhume the body, and officers are checking into anything unusual occurring prior to and after her death. It will take a few days."

McKenzie noticed Mallory's lips were tightly pinched. "It's got to be Parnevik. Reagan was the only person who knew what he'd been up to. It's in her statement."

"Hold it," Capt. Trussel chimed in. "All this is theorizing and supposition. There's no proof of a homicide. If the washcloth and the coat produce a DNA match—and we can get an actual sample of his DNA and it matches—we could have him on suspicion of breaking and entering. That's all. You see where I'm going with this?"

"No," McKenzie said.

"Somebody else has got to find the bastard. He's presently out of my jurisdiction in Europe somewhere. Right now, I have a situation that's starting to look like some kind of serial killer is out there using drugs to experiment on live people. Remember a couple of days ago? We put out a law-enforcement system request to be notified of deaths with unusual medical circumstances. Yesterday we got a hit. Some senior citizen playing racquetball collapsed and died at a local club in Charlotte, North Carolina after a crowd witnessed him crushing one of the best players in town, like he was some kind of young phenom. What can you tell me, Mister DEA man? You're the drug expert. Pharmco's a major drug company. You've been investigating over there."

"I'm off the case. All I can tell you is Pharmco was experimenting with nanites as a delivery system for stimulating the brain, some of them have gone missing, and Pharmco had been working under a top-secret government contract that required state-of-the-art security procedures on all day-to-day activities at their research facility in Dunwoody. We haven't been allowed to see the contract."

"Well, Mister DEA Agent, it might interest you to know that Ernest Kelto was mentioned as being present when the old guy died in Charlotte. He works for Pharmco. Correct?"

"The pattern thickens indeed," Smythe said softly. He'd been pensively sitting.

"We're getting a copy of his autopsy." Capt. Trussel glanced at Mallory. "And we'll be asking for the brain scan and microscopic sectioning, same as your sister and the Brightview woman. I think we already have enough to get a search warrant. We'll pay a visit to Mister Kelto's abode. He may also be in the testing business. In the meantime, McKenzie, as long as I have you here, I have another problem. A new drug has shown up on the street—Italian drug distributors are selling candy to their clients, one at a time, from bottles labeled "Sweets." They're pink tablets that supposedly produce heightened sexual desire, like some exotic jungle aphrodisiac. The street is calling it *Amor*, and when we brought these bootleggers in for questioning, they claim its efficacy is derived from the placebo effect. Half of them can't even pronounce the word. They don't know how it works. Customers are flocking to street corners from all walks of life where twenty-dollar pills are being sold in the open. We can't do a thing about it. Our labs can't find anything to analyze. Sound familiar?"

 Thirty-five

New York City

"I DON'T CARE what he said, Paulie, I want that backup lab found and staked out, and I want Parnevik under our protection, permanently. The Atlanta market is crying for more, and we're about to go national. Reliance on one individual operating independently is unacceptable. Tell me you can take care of this, Paulie." Tony Gatturna was pacing the basement office of Angie's Italian Restaurant like a mad rooster.

Paulie Torrentino sat on a leather couch along a sidewall, smoking a cigar. "No problem, boss. I hated having to talk to the arrogant asshole. It's the right move. We can hide him and his equipment in the Bronx or offshore someplace. We can convince him to share the manufacturing techniques. In the meantime, we can set up our own lab and check it out. I'll start working on finding the science types among our young people."

"Okay, but remember, Parnevik warned us not to tamper with the product." Gatturna had stopped moving around and slapped his hand against the top of his desk. "I think we take a shot—and find out what IDs were prepared by our used-to-be friend in Quebec City. Get his credit card numbers and track down his bank accounts. We tap some favors and shut him down wherever he is. No access to money—he'll have to come to us eventually—but we don't wait. We start looking for him now—Before we give the go-ahead on this increased commitment, we have him in-house.... And Paulie, after you get the ID info, take care of that loose end. Got me?"

***

By the end of the day, Paulie Torrentino had traced the rental van used to move the equipment the Family had delivered over a week ago to an Atlanta storage facility as per Parnevik's instructions. The storage facility video provided the lead, and the GPS system installed in the van by the rental company produced a timed travel record of its usage by one Julian Trebar, a Canadian citizen.

The Family's contact at the Atlanta PD tracked the van to a three-hour stop at an abandoned fire station on the southeast side of the city core. The contact confirmed the presence of unopened crates and boxes of laboratory equipment stacked in the fire station. Paulie ordered a 24/7 watch on the property.

A short visit by a Family member to the Giovanni household in Quebec City revealed Giovanni had moved to Asuncion, Paraguay, leaving his nephew to live in the house and run the printing business.

 Thirty-six

France

ACCORDING TO THE *Feng Shui* principles of Chinese geomancy, Lyon, France, where the La Saône River flows into the Le Rhône at the foot of the *golden hills*, was considered the perfect site for cultivating creative energies. In 1991, it became the location for Cha Wuan's first exotic tea store, expanded in 2000 to include its headquarters.

Since then, the family-run business had captured some twenty percent of the French tea market, opening eleven stores in France and stores in London, Brussels, Berlin, Barcelona, and Rome.

Cha Wuan's French country store occupied the street-level floor of a rustic, three-story corner building on the periphery of Lyon's fashionable residential area. Parnevik arrived just after the store opened for the day. He wanted to browse the aisles and get a feel for the business. Then he would walk the four blocks and partake in the delight of another delectable repast at Le Chia before returning to Cha Waun for his meeting.

The feel of the place was homey and upscale. The plaster of the thick walls had a wave-like texture. Tastefully positioned antiques and hanging plants lent an outdoor air to the interior, and thirty-odd tea blends and their varietals from around the world occupied displays cases along with hand-scripted explanations.

With the flavor of the extra glass of Beaujolais he'd enjoyed after his meal still tantalizing his taste buds, Parnevik strolled the four blocks back to the Chu Wuan store, relaxed and confident entering the ground floor.

Monsieur Goulet descended from the floor above, along an ornate, wooden spiral staircase, arms open in an embracing gesture.

Parnevik moved to greet him at the bottom of the staircase. "*Monsieur* Goulet, it is good to finally meet you in person."

"The pleasure is mine, Mister Trebar. I have eagerly awaited our meeting, and please call me Maurice." Mr. Goulet smiled, revealing perfectly aligned white teeth. He was a small man, properly dressed as a French gentleman, mid-fifties, thin hair steeply receding, deeply etched crow's feet, and smart black bifocals.

"Then you must call me Julian."

"So it shall be. Please, follow me upstairs. Hot tea is waiting, and we will not be disturbed. I have many questions."

At the top of the stairs, they entered a circular parlor through a wide portico, a sitting area filled with furniture from the French countryside. Two large gilded mirrors hung on the flesh-colored plaster walls at opposite ends of the room, reflecting the exquisite tapestries adorning the circle.

"This is quite unexpected." Parnevik stopped to admire the unique room and its feeling of intimacy.

"You have hit the nail on the head, Julian—I think that's an American expression. Do forgive me…. All our stores and offices reflect the unexpected—French architecture from simple country all the way to the extravagance of Louis the Fourteenth. It is part of our branding."

Monsieur Goulet guided Parnevik toward an adjoining room. "Come. You will enjoy my office." He laid a soft hand on

Parnevik's shoulder and motioned through a two-foot thick archway.

This room was also round, with rough-hewn plaster walls. Two opposing, floor-to-ceiling bookcases were full of volumes; large mahogany armoires set off a giant window overlooking the quaint Lyon street below; and the center was dominated by a rectangle work table of polished mahogany supported by two massive tree-trunk sections. Four, wheat-back chairs occupied one side and a leather recliner on the other, the latter obviously *Monsieur* Goulet's command post.

A large, wireless LED screen was set in a rotator frame positioned front-center on the table, and piles of folders and papers were stacked, awaiting attention. A rollout tray containing a computer keyboard and accessories occupied a position under the center of the table. A two-level, wrought iron chandelier, hanging from heavy wooden crossbeams at the center of the twelve-foot-high ceiling, accentuated the circular space and French Country style.

"I've examined your proposal." *Monsieur* Goulet guided Parnivek to two stiff-looking divans on either side of a glass coffee table in front of the window overlooking the street. A tea service tray was within convenient reach. "And some of our most particular customers have taste-tested your blend in the store downstairs—Do help yourself." Goulet waved an arm at the tea service as they took seats.

"I must say we are in awe of the results. I even tried the tea myself with most unusual effects. From all accounts, it appears the name of the blend is justified. Word has spread, and literally all of our customers have signed up to purchase the product as soon as the store has it available, and the list grows daily with new customers coming to the store."

"I'm happy you are pleased, *Monsieur* Goulet. The blend is indeed unique."

"No doubt you will share your recipe?"

"That was not part of my proposal, sir. The blend will remain proprietary. I am only interested in providing the product through exclusive distributorships, with royalties as outlined. Your firm will package and promote the product as you see fit, so long as your orders meet the minimum volumes. I favor the lacey, amethyst-colored tea bags used to package one of your blends I saw downstairs, but that is up to you."

"I am curious how you came to experiment with tea blends? *Flower of Love* appears to be a simple white tea—I would say from China—and no different from some of our own blends. It was impossible for our chemists to determine which teas, as there are so many. But I digress."

"Let us just say I spent a lot of time in China with their shamans and leave it at that."

"The safety of the product is of concern."

Parnevik was growing uncomfortable. The man was proving to be a weaseling little bureaucrat devoid of vision. "*Monsieur* Goulet, you are free to add any quality control procedures you require to our agreement." Parnevik rose. "I think we are finished here. You have twenty-four hours to e-mail me a first draft of the agreement. I will be returning to Paris directly and will review it with my barrister. If it is satisfactory, he will draft a final, and we can be in business within weeks. The product has been produced in sufficient inventory and can be shipped in a matter of days."

Parnevik's face was drooping. His verbal delivery had taken on a hurried tone. His eyelids fluttered.

"Is something wrong, Mister Trebar? Your face has paled. Can I get you something—perhaps some water?"

"Please excuse me a moment," Parnevik said, mentally fighting the blanket of fear inching over his consciousness and sapping his willpower. "A restroom, *Monsieur*? It's the red wine I favor from this region of France. Perhaps too much at brunch."

"Please, I will show you." *Monsieur* Goulet stood and took Parnevik's arm. "This way."

***

Five minutes later, Parnevik left the privacy of the hallway restroom and returned through the parlor to *Monsieur* Goulet's office. He'd taken a fast-acting prescription drug that he carried for emergencies. It acted like adrenalin, entering the circulatory system and neutralizing the dopamine buildup. He felt the chill across his forehead as the last of the perspiration was evaporating.

"Ah, my friend, you look much better." *Monsieur* Goulet rose from his desk and joined Parnevik in the middle of the room.

"Forgive me. I'm afraid I overindulged earlier in one of your fine cafés."

"No apology is necessary. Shall we continue?" *Monsieur* Goulet waved his hand back to the divans.

"I believe our business is complete for now. As we say in Canada, the ball is in your court." Parnevik attempted a smile as he took steps toward the office archway. "I will await your communication, and I bid you good day, sir."

Parnevik breathed a sigh of relief as he left the store behind. He headed down the brick sidewalk toward the rail station. Perhaps he had been a little too abrupt. Hopefully, the Frenchman hadn't taken offense and would attribute the bad manners to his problem with the wine…. He would have to curb his appetite for Beaujolais.

His spirits soared as he walked the winding streets, focusing on the prospects of becoming a legitimate businessperson. Diversification would insulate him should the venture with the Genovese family turn sour.

The high-speed *discotheque* train would have him back in his small Paris flat before nightfall, and he could complete preparations for his foray to the *Gorge de Verdon* in the Alps of southeastern France. Assuming all went well—and he saw no reason it should not—he would return to the States refreshed to finish work on *Bliss* for the Genovese family and continue seeking new directions for his business.

 Thirty-seven

Atlanta PD

IT WAS A cold but sunny winter day. After sharing a morning run through Piedmont Park and cleaning up at Emma Kisuma's house, Mallory and McKenzie decided to walk the three blocks to McDonalds on Ponce de Leon Avenue to avoid the packed drive-through with people in a hurry and bound for work.

"Did you double-check with Captain Trussel?" Mallory put her hash browns down and picked up an Egg McMuffin.

"Of course. Relax." He chuckled. "You still order the same thing you did back in school."

"What of it?"

"Some things never change. Finish your coffee. We meet Smythe and Mrs. Leonard at Kelto's at nine. Atlanta PD will be there, and Captain Trussel said he'd call my cell to let us know when we could go in."

"I'm anxious to do something. I don't like sitting around, and I don't like trailing after the Atlanta PD." She gave McKenzie a look that sent his thoughts darting into the past. When she made up her mind to go in a certain direction, she'd all of a sudden bolt. No stopping her. It was not one of her more attractive personality traits. Over and over he'd felt rejected during their grad-school relationship; she'd make unilateral decisions without consulting him, and he was left facing confrontation or acquiescence, neither of which were pleasant. She'd never learned to collaborate.

"Smythe says Parnevik went to France." She slipped out of the booth with her coffee and pushed through the exit doors, McKenzie on her heals. "His ability to perceive Parnevik's past seems to be increasing since he went through his residence."

"I wonder if he's thinking about trying to track him down?" McKenzie said.

"Don't know."

They walked side by side down the sidewalk back to Emma's.

***

Kelto's one-story rental house was a block off Highland Avenue, on Greenwood Street, a couple of miles east of Piedmont Park. Two police cars double-parked on the street, and an officer was posted at the front door. Smythe's red Porsche was across the road, two doors down.

McKenzie pulled his rental car in behind the sports car and turned off the ignition. "I'll wait here and keep an eye out. You check in with Smythe and see if Mrs. Leonard needs anything. I'm sure spending the night in close quarters in a hotel room with him must have been frustrating. I wonder what they did for dinner last night."

"She told me they always take room service. I wouldn't worry about her. She's pretty tough, and she's been coping for years." Mallory opened the car door. "And don't tell me what to do."

"You're so sensitive. Lighten up—Hold it. Captain Trussel just came out of the house. He waved us in and went back inside. Let's go."

Smythe had observed the captain, and he and Mrs. Leonard exited the Porsche. All four crossed the street, Smythe in the lead.

The officer at the door said, "Good morning," nodding acknowledgment as they filed inside.

The interior of the house was a wreck. Furniture, electronics, kitchen wares, all smashed and cast about. McKenzie recognized pieces of a sophisticated microscope similar to one he'd seen when he visited the Georgia Tech nano-labs.

Everything appeared to have been pounded and crushed with a sledgehammer. Kelto's desktop computer and accessories were in crumpled heaps. Two officers wearing latex gloves were sifting through the rubble, taking pictures, tagging and bagging items.

The group found Capt. Trussel sitting at the kitchen table, talking on his cell phone.

"This isn't what we expected," McKenzie said.

Capt. Trussel flipped his phone shut and stood. "Not exactly a routine search."

"I'll look around, Captain." Smythe left the kitchen with Mrs. Leonard in tow.

"Don't touch anything," Capt. Trussel barked. "Does that guy ever change clothes?"

"He's unusual that way." Mallory raised her eyebrows.

"I just spoke with Lieutenant Sullivan. You remember—he's got the lead opening up the Brightview and Club Elan investigations. Now we've added this homicide. He wants to brief me. I have to get back. You're free to join me. Did you see the body?"

"What body?" Mallory asked.

"In the bedroom."

Ernest Kelto lay on a double bed as if he were sleeping. He appeared snug under a plaid comforter with his head resting on a white pillow supported by his right arm. His expression was natural, but the blood dripping from a raspberry-sized hole in his forehead and pooling around his head was not.

***

Mallory and McKenzie tailed Smythe back downtown to drop off his Porsche in the Peachtree Plaza parking garage. The police station was six blocks from the hotel, and Smythe didn't want to take a chance of vandalism parking the car on the street. The four musketeers walked to the station.

Capt. Trussel and Lt. Sullivan were waiting for them in the main conference room, hunkered down on large thermos cups of coffee, going through the contents of a file.

"Not a good way to start the day," Trussel acknowledged as the foursome entered the room. "Make yourselves at home. You passed the break room on your way. Feel free."

Lt. Sullivan rose from his chair and shook hands all around. The tall, heavyset, blond-haired lieutenant was stern-faced. Mallory thought he looked like he'd just received a reaming.

"We don't have much time to mince words here," Capt. Trussel said. "We both have a lot to do. Since we now have a homicide that appears to be a professional hit, our cooperation with you takes a hundred and eighty degree turn. From now on, all ongoing investigations are confidential until resolved. Any information on this case or anything related, you'll have to get from public sources as it's released by the department. Today is a courtesy. Lieutenant Sullivan will sum up what we have."

"I'll do this sitting down." Sullivan moved a stack of files and papers from the middle of the table to within reach. "The Brightview death is first. Two years ago, an autopsy of the woman verified stroke as the cause of death—"

"I'd like to see the report, Lieutenant," Smythe said.

"Certainly." Sullivan slid a file down the table where Smythe had perched. "According to the Brightview administrator, a Dr. Massey, a representative of the Association for the Humane Treatment of the Disabled, requested a copy of the standard video tape of the deceased's room taken the night of her demise. The guy's name was Stanton, as it appeared on the business card he presented to the administrator. Later in the day, this Stanton picked the tape up from Bob Morley, a technician at Brightview. Their video record of Stanton is not conclusive. Stanton avoided a head-on with the cameras. From what we could see, he doesn't look like Parnevik, but he's the same build and height."

"The injuries to the brain are consistent with those of Reagan Driscoll," Smythe announced. "The cells collapsed, causing bleeding, *but* in a different part of the pre-frontal cortex, an area associated with sexual arousal and desire, if I remember correctly."

"Duly noted." Capt. Trussel glared at Smythe, aka Phelps.

"The agency says it didn't send anyone to Brightview," Lt. Sullivan continued, "and there's no Stanton in the organization."

"We need to see the tapes, Captain." Smythe sat stoic, unrelenting.

Mallory flipped a glance at Mrs. Leonard, who looked perturbed. From the look on Capt. Trussel's face, if Smythe didn't change his tactics, this police captain was about to close down the meeting.

"Lieutenant, run the tapes for these people down the hall," Capt. Trussel monotoned, lips pursed. "Also the one with Stanton. I'm taking a short break."

***

Comfortably seated back in the conference room, Smythe said, "The tape clearly reveals the woman was overcome by powerful stimulation. Her frail condition couldn't sustain the shock at that level of activity."

"Thank you, Mister Phelps. Could we move on?"

"Indulge me one further observation, my dear Captain."

Mallory glanced at McKenzie and nodded; it was apparent Smythe had little respect for the Atlanta Police Department.

The captain didn't say anything, but his eyebrows rose and he slid his chair a few inches back from the table.

"I am sure if your forensics people compare Mister Stanton's eyes from the tape with those of photographs from Parnevik's house, you will find a match. The Brightview video is of sufficient definition. Presumably, the equipment is available in your forensic labs." Smythe leaned back and folded his hands across the front of his open black suit coat, white silk shirt tight against his neck, eyes darting to Mrs. Leonard and quickly resetting on Capt. Trussel.

Mallory was surprised the captain had been able to tap into additional reserves of patience. Smythe's attitude exuded palpable disdain.

"Sullivan." The captain stared at the lieutenant.

"I'll look into it, Captain." Lt. Sullivan pushed away from the conference table, pulled his cell phone off his belt, and left the room.

A long minute passed in silence as the group observed Lt. Sullivan pacing outside the glass doors and then reentering.

"The lab's on it." Lt. Sullivan retook his seat. "We should know something shortly."

"Not to change the subject," Mallory said, looking straight at the captain, "but what is your preliminary take on the Kelto homicide? It appears that Parnevik may be eliminating the competition."

"No reason to jump to that conclusion. There's no evidence pointing to him. In fact, the house appears to have been sterilized of evidence pointing to anyone, but we'll know later when the forensics are processed—we did find several vials similar to the one McKenzie found in your sister's house."

"I didn't detect Parnevik's presence in the house," Smythe stated in a smug tone.

Ignoring the comment, McKenzie asked, "How could the nanites be smuggled out of Pharmco? The company has the latest security system."

"The same way Parnevik got his out," Smythe said. "The vials are made of sulfur-silicate glass and would not register with the scanning equipment, and obviously nanites are too small to show up."

"We followed up on that when we got the vial back from the DEA," Lt. Sullivan said. "We took it to Pharmco, and they concurred. They relied on the video surveillance cameras. Supposedly, only three people had access to the inventory. Parnevik, Kelto and Reagan Driscoll."

"Who's left?" Smythe asked.

"Anything else, Mister Phelps?" The captain was near his limit.

"Yes, several matters." Smythe paused seemingly for effect. "The results from Georgia Tech's Microelectronics Research Center," he asked calmly, holding his eyes steady on the captain at the other end of the conference table.

Capt. Trussel let his head droop and he gritted his teeth. "The vial from Reagan Driscoll's house came back empty. The government could have tampered with it. We have no idea. A vitamin-C bottle from her luggage contained time-release tablets that had been tampered with—several were injected somehow with a miniscule amount of liquid. When a technician tried to analyze a sample, the liquid crystallized. It turned out to be sugar."

"That is unfortunate," Smythe said without rancor. "Mister Parnevik proves his genius again. It appears he makes his products with built-in fail-safes—any luck with the epithelial cells from the jacket at his residence when compared with any cells found on the guest towel?"

"A DNA match. Now if we can get a sample from him, we might be able to arrest him for breaking and entering." Capt. Trussel was scrunched down in his seat. "This is a circle jerk," he belted out. "Excuse the language," he said, taking stock of Mallory and Mrs. Leonard. "I have three deaths that seem to be related—foul play suspected—but we can't find murder weapons. The only suspects are either dead or missing. And now I have a professional hit to deal with."

"Captain, I understand your position," Smythe said, almost sincerely, "but do hear me out."

Capt. Trussel nodded, a faraway look in eyes.

"Kelto met with Parnevik to deliver the self-replicating nanites he'd stolen from Pharmco. And he experimented on his own. The Charlotte racquetball player was his doing alone."

"And what proof do you have?"

"The dirty clothing in Kelto's house. I always get my clearest perceptions with pictures and used clothing."

"Sort of like a dog, Mister Phelps?" Capt. Trussel was full up. "I'm sure your *perceptions* would stand up in any court of law."

"I beg your pardon, sir—"

Mrs. Leonard interrupted. "Mister Phelps, we'll talk about this in private—later."

Smythe leaned back in his seat, a blank expression on his face.

"Lieutenant Sullivan, I apologize for getting off task here," Mallory said. "Please continue."

Sullivan received a nod from Capt. Trussel. "We went back and interviewed the woman from Club Elan. She identified Parnevik from the picture you confiscated from his residence. She said she was sitting at the bar and briefly talked with him and some fancy Italian dresser sitting next to him. She said Parnevik called him Ned. She remembered going outside the bar to call a cohort, returning, and starting up a conversation with two other guys. She said she was overwhelmed with sexual desire like never before. It was scary and she was embarrassed to talk about it.

"According to the officers who collected her from Club Elan, by the time she arrived at the station she'd regained her composure and was humiliated. No charges were brought, and she was released a couple of hours later."

"I suppose you already knew all that, Mister Phelps?" Capt. Trussel asked, a supercilious expression on his face.

"I am unaware of the event. It was too far back in the past for me to pick up detail."

Mallory had been positive the meeting would end badly. But something kept Smythe from rising to the bait. She scanned the faces in the room and said, "Lieutenant, if you please."

"One more observation concerning the woman at Club Elan," Capt. Trussel volunteered. "Her statement describing her experience is similar to reports of the effects of the new candy aphrodisiac that's shown up on the street. It's called *Amor*. It's not too much of a leap to assume it's Parnevik's enterprise, but we still don't have any evidence. We can only hypothesize he's hooked up with distributors and producing the product in bulk."

"How could he mass produce?" Mallory asked. "His lab was compromised."

"He must have backups," McKenzie put in. "If Mister Phelps is correct, he used Kelto to steal replicating nanites for him. It shouldn't be difficult for him to produce quantity from almost anywhere. The equipment is available, and he has the money."

"Reagan always said he was an insidious planner," Mallory said. "Whatever went down got Kelto killed."

"Maybe he's operating in the city right under our noses." McKenzie's face lit up. "The trip to France could be a ruse."

"Anything more on Parnevik's finances, credit card usage, or movements?" Mallory asked.

"Nothing since we talked last," Lt. Sullivan said." We don't know where he went from Paris. He just disappeared."

"Hold it a second," Capt. Trussel said. "Did we get a make on this Ned guy at Club Elan? The lady said he was Italian. Parnevik wouldn't be meeting with some minor lieutenant. And did we do blood work on the woman?"

"No, we didn't put it together then." Lt. Sullivan flipped his pencil down on the table. "The lady wasn't charged with anything. The breathalyzer was within limits. No justification to take blood—the tapes at Club Elan were conveniently damaged, but I'll get a professional artist to work up a sketch with the bartender on the Ned character. We'll put it out and see what we get."

"Now would be good," Capt. Trussel said through tightened lips.

***

"Before I get to it, Captain," Lt. Sullivan said, coming through the conference room door, "somebody from the DOD just called Jonesie. You and I have been directed to the Fulton County Courthouse tomorrow at 4:00 p.m."

"That's great." The captain looked worn out.... "What's next—what have you got?"

"The eyes matched," Lt. Sullivan announced. "It was Parnevik at Brightview. We have to make an assumption here that Parnevik probably slipped something in the lady's drink at Club Elan."

"So it must have been a live test," Mallory burst in.

"The sketch artist is on her way to meet with the bartender." Lt. Sullivan had perked up.

"Maybe there *is* a link to the new drug on the street," Capt. Trussel said. "We'll brief the DEA. It's their bailiwick and a dead end for us. All we can do is put out the APB for Parnevik on suspicion of breaking and entering and as a person of interest in two suspicious deaths."

"I still think Parnevik may be in Atlanta," McKenzie said. "He has to be supplying the product from someplace."

"I'll talk with Emma," Mallory said. "Maybe she can remember something."

"Who's Emma?" Capt. Trussel asked.

"My sister's roommate. I've been staying with her."

"He is definitely not here." Smythe leaned his elbows on the table, hands steepled, moving back and forth. "I've perceived fleeting glimpses of his activities. He was in France yesterday. I've seen him riding a motorcycle on a narrow cobblestoned street curving down to a beach with two big casinos. I believe it to be Biarritz. He's calling himself by different names. He's been to Lyon and Paris and has an interest in Chinese teas, skydiving, and something called wing suit flying. He's very busy."

***

Two blocks from Atlanta PD Headquarters, Sergeant Jones was sitting in a phone booth inside a Starbucks on Peachtree Street.

"Paulie, Atlanta PD has a sketch of you with Parnevik at Club Elan on Christmas Eve. They're putting it together as we speak. I don't know if it will be enough to get a match. There's nothing I can do except keep you informed."

"Okay. Thanks. Anything else?"

"What about the fire station?"

"Stay with it. Parnevik has to come back. We've given him another big order. We want him bad."

"No problem. Oh, and the Kelto job passed forensics. No trace. Atlanta PD's turning what little they have on *Amor* over to the DEA. All they can do is the APB on Parnevik. But there's bad news. Some Deputy Director of the DOD has set up a meeting with Capt. Trussel and some state bigwigs tomorrow afternoon. Don't know the agenda. I'll let you know what goes down."

 Thirty-eight

Paris, France

As the cosmopolitan Canadian businessman, Julian Trebar, Parnevik spent the majority of the next day in Paris proper, consulting with his attorney, and shopping for odds and ends in preparation for his trip to the French Alps. The draft distributorship agreement from Cha Whan only required minor language modifications, and several faxes back and forth produced an agreement executed by the parties.

Cha Whan committed to the first order, a purchase of 50,000 ounces of the *Flower of Love* tea blend. The company would design ultra-gourmet packaging, and the first batch was to be hand-packed into light purple bags of filigreed Manila hemp, a box of twelve priced at the equivalent of fifty-five dollars US. In thirty days time, after light advertising, the product's introduction would take place simultaneously in all fourteen of their stores.

***

Parnevik left his attorney's office close to 4:00 p.m., one last stop remaining for the day. He was so pleased with himself he hardly remembered riding the crowded elevator to the ground floor, swishing through the revolving doors, and spilling out onto the sidewalk. He blended into the stream of Paris humanity, buoyed with elation and high expectations. For him, it had been something of a new experience. The concept of a legal business with controlled manufacturing and product quality, and astronomical profits without the need for permanent facilities or employees, was an entrepreneur's dream.

He turned right at the first corner, headed toward the nearby *Right Bank* section of Paris, his mind drifting over the details of his plan. He was confident he could deliver the tea on time, as well as produce the *Amor* order for the Genovese. His bank account reflected the Family's recent $100,000 payment. It would only take a few days to set up the backup lab in Atlanta. It was a pity the Peachtree Battle house was sacrificed after all the time and money spent on renovations. He loved that old place.

Replicating the nanites for the tea blend would be the easy part. The Chinese white teas he'd imported were waiting in forty-pound, vacuum-sealed containers at the UPS central processing facility on the south side of Atlanta. He'd decided to add approximately 500,000 *Amor* nanites to the 50,000 ounce order; mix the blend by hand; package it into non-descript air-sealed bags; and airfreight the lot directly to Cha Whan headquarters in Lyon.

It didn't matter that more than one nanite would end up in each tea bag when they were custom packaged. The nanites were programmed to recognize when more than one had entered the bloodstream of the human body at the same time. Only the first to enter the circulatory system would survive; a recognition sub-program triggered decomposition of the others.

Parnevik's final meeting was six blocks from his lawyer's office. It was a gloomy, cloud-covered winter day, the air thick with moisture. Outfitted in an Italian-cut sharkskin suit, black velour trench coat, and conservative top hat, he continued to revel in a sense of well-being at his new business prospects. He opened a black umbrella to keep the moisture from clouding his spectacles and allowed his mind to switch channels: Mount Blanc in the southeastern French Alps on the border with Italy would be beautiful, snowy white, and glistening. The precipitous glacial-side of the mountain would offer his coming project the ultimate rush for mind and body.

He crossed into Paris's *Right Bank* and onto *Avenue de I 'Opera*, heading for the 43-story, Crédit Lyonnais building. People streamed en masse from the multitude of office buildings lining the streets, marking the beginning of the day's business exodus.

The North Korean Consulate was located on the seventh floor. Parnevik was delivering a plain manila twelve-by-nine inch envelope to the senior attaché. A menacing armed guard greeted him at the glass entrance doors. He passed a handheld scanner over Parnevik's body and escorted him to a stiff-faced receptionist, who took his picture, asked him to sign in, and relieved him of the envelope addressed to Mr. Kim Choe—all very cold and efficient.

His errands complete, he returned to his flat to finish packing for the trip to Chamonix and Gap-Tallard. Gap-Tallard was a village located at the foot of the Haute French Alps, a two-hour bus ride from Grenoble. He was looking forward to seeing the faces of instructors he'd spent so much time training with over the last six years, as well as planting a few rumors. Gap-Tallard was one of the small number of locations where he could rent a motorized glider to recon his ground plan in the southeastern Alps.

The next morning, Arthur Dubois set off to pay a visit to the alpine town of Chamonix, home of the 1924 Winter Olympics. He took the high-speed train to Grenoble and the short spur ride to the town of 10,000 nestled in the glacial valley beneath Mont Blanc. Europe's highest peak rose astride the gushing Arve River, which flowed sixty-three miles to the Swiss city of Geneva. He'd chosen sophisticated Chamonix because it attracted world-class skiers, hikers, and mountaineers, summer and winter, all intent on traversing parts of the famous Haute Route or skiing among the seventy-six runs originating in or near the town. Away from the slopes, the bars and restaurants were lively year round. This would be his refuge. He'd recuperate here, blending in with the town's old *Savoir-faire* character and après-ski environment. Planning was everything.

Arthur Dubois had booked accommodations at the Hotel Alpina, an establishment of grand standing, replete with a large lounge with a great multi-chimneyed fireplace, a billiards room, mini nightclub, health center, and a commercial art gallery with exhibition halls.

He entered his third-floor suite, unpacked, and refreshed his appearance. He threw the velvet curtains to the sides of the balcony windows and admired the snow-covered slopes of Mont Blanc, bathed in the mysterious shadows cast from the sun's last fading light. The balcony overlooked the hustle-bustle of central Chamonix.

Now, it was time for something he'd been looking forward to: a feast at the *Panoramique Le 4810*, the famous French restaurant occupying the top floor of the hotel and overlooking the glitter of Chamonix.

***

Early the next morning, Parnevik left his travel bags in the suite. He would be gone for the day. He headed for the train station and bought a ticket back to Grenoble; from there he would take the slow bus ride to Gap-Tallard.

As he settled into his seat on the train, he was vaguely excited with the prospect of showing up unexpectedly and what the reactions might be from people he assumed would remember him. After all, he'd spent a fortune there over the years, gaining advanced certifications in base jumping, skydiving, wing suit flying, and glider piloting.

 Thirty-nine

Emma Kisumi

AFTER THE LONG meeting at the Atlanta PD, the musketeers split up: Smythe and Mrs. Leonard returned to the Plaza with plans to drive back to the Lake Rabun house in the morning. Mallory turned down McKenzie's offer of dinner in hopes of catching Emma before she went to bed.

The lack of progress and the decree to stay out of the police investigation made Mallory anxious to see if Emma could shed some light on what Parnevik was doing in France. But it was too late. Emma was fast asleep when she arrived, so she wrote a note asking for some time in the morning to talk about Parnevik.

Mallory rose early and went shopping, leaving Emma to enjoy sleeping late on a Saturday. As she climbed the stone-slab steps to the front walkway carrying bags of groceries, Emma opened the front door, dressed in her robe and bedroom slippers.

Mallory pushed open the screen door to the porch. "Hey, Emma, how about we walk over to the *Prince of Wales*? My treat."

"I don't go to that place anymore," Emma said halfheartedly, hugging herself from the chilly air. "The last time I was there was with Reagan."

"Okay. Where's a good spot?"

"Let's just stay here. I'll make some tea. Talking about Corey is not my favorite thing, but I guess you know that."

"I'll put this stuff away," Mallory said, stepping through the doorway. "Let's set up on the porch. It's a little chilly, but the sun is heating things up nicely."

"Okay. I'll get some clothes on and warm some croissants. We'll have the Chamomile you like."

***

They set the porch table with a pink tablecloth, silverware, Japanese teacups, jams, cheeses, and condiments. Emma poured the steaming green brew and brought out hot croissants. She seemed reserved and tentative, but she looked cute in white slacks and a loose, strawberry-colored long-sleeve sweater.

"You know, you're like her in so many ways and yet so different." Emma set the tea pitcher down and reached for a croissant. "You're both lightning rods. Reagan would absorb her world. You seem to sizzle in it." She looked at Mallory across the table with wide eyes. "Having you here—living in Reagan's room—has been hard for me. I keep thinking you're her. Even from the back you look the same."

Mallory smiled. "I know it's tough. I miss her too. She was so good…. Are you okay?" She cast an empathetic glance at Emma.

"Yeah." Emma shrugged.

"Look, I haven't had time to bring you up to date. Do you mind?"

"No, go ahead."

"Atlanta PD matched epidermal cells from clothes in Parnevik's house to the guest towel in your bathroom. Emma, the vitamins she took to Las Vegas were altered. There's no proof, no hard evidence, but we think Parnevik must have done more than plant a Pharmco vial in her bedroom. The police are investigating three separate incidents of aberrant behavior that seem to be related, two causing death and the other embarrassment to the lady involved. Parnevik was present at all three.

"There's no physical proof, but we all think he's been testing nanite products outside the company for at least two years.... Reagan gave a statement shortly before her trip to Vegas, saying that Corey had told her he was experimenting and he wanted her to share in the wealth."

"God, this whole thing is horrible. What are you going to do?"

"Well, the Atlanta PD shut us out of the investigation because it's now associated with a real homicide. You probably don't know yet but Ernest Kelto was killed in his condo yesterday. They think he stole important nanites from Pharmco and may have been working with Parnevik."

"Oh, my God! Kelto? I can't believe that. He was a little wormy guy. Kept to himself. Seemed to lack self-confidence. He couldn't have been twenty-five years old. He was a loner like Corey but not a creative genius."

Mallory rose from her chair and refilled their teacups. The late morning sun had raised the temperature comfortably into the high sixties. "It's actually getting hot out here. You may want to ditch that sweater." Mallory took off her jacket and slung it over the back of her chair.

A few minutes later, Emma returned, dressed in shorts and last year's Peachtree Road Race tee shirt. She appeared to have shed most of her remorse.

"You're looking better now," Mallory said. "Your eyes are brighter."

Emma grimaced. "Mal, I appreciate you sharing," she said, taking a croissant to her plate. "So now, you want me to tell you what I know about Corey?"

"If you wouldn't mind."

"Yeah, it's okay…. Well, I think I'm over trying to see him in any positive light. I've always felt bad about that relationship. I never could get away from thinking it was my failure."

"I never knew Parnevik, but all I've heard is bad press."

"I'm sure it's well deserved—I don't mind telling you about it if it helps. Maybe I need to."

"Okay." Mallory said, observing dejection spread across Emma's face.

"Well, he was stiff, aloof, and unaffectionate. We never even kissed." Emma was frowning at the memories.

"I tried to get him to talk about intimacy, but he'd just clam up and walk away. I don't think his mother gave him any affection—you know she was a successful model and died of pancreatic cancer when Corey was working on his doctorate. She left him a huge trust fund. He's been independent ever since, setting his own rules, doing whatever he wanted…. He had medical problems. Unless he stayed on his medication, he became belligerent and aggressive—a "Captain America" attitude. I finally gave up. For a while, I thought attention and kindness would melt him, that there was something inside that was soft and good. I was wrong. He was recalcitrant and manipulative." Emma cast her eyes toward the street and the green spaces of the park beyond, embarrassed by the tears.

Mallory took advantage of her pause to change the subject. "Where do you think he might be? He hasn't been heard from since he left for Paris. The police haven't been able to track him."

"He always went away on trips. He called them sabbaticals. Texas, Chattanooga, Tennessee, France. I don't know how he got the time off. I guess he was Pharmco's superstar. He never told me much except that he was into a sport where you put on a flying suit and make jumps. He craved the rush it gave him. He was obsessive and his talk about it was like an addiction.

"Do you know of any property he owns besides the house on Peachtree Battle?"

"No, but sometimes we went for car rides, looking at houses. He liked the variety in the old neighborhoods close to the city center, and he seemed attracted to Gothic churches and public buildings built before World War II. He would spout off about their architecture…. There was one building we always seemed to visit on these treks. It was an old, abandoned red-brick fire station on the southeast side of the city, near the baseball park. He fantasized about buying and restoring it into a museum. He talked about searching for used fire-fighting equipment and fire engines and refurbishing them—about traveling around to find original tooling and furnishings used by Georgia's first firefighters."

"That might be worth checking out. I'll get my laptop and Google the location and look at the property-ownership records." Mallory slid her porch chair away from the table.

"Mal, what's going on?"

Mallory hesitated and then plopped back in her seat. "I'm sorry I get so one-pointed," she said.

"That's how you are. I understand."

Mallory tucked her long curls behind her ears. Her face hardened like a resolute prosecutor. "Ryan and I believe Parnevik is producing drugs for the illicit market. He's using Pharmco's nanite delivery systems to stimulate areas of the brain. A new substance that looks and tastes like candy has shown up on the streets of Atlanta. It's being called *Amor*. We think he's back in town and has a manufacturing lab someplace locally. Emma, we're going to find Parnevik without the help of the police—you aren't going to believe the rest of this. You know Professor VonMitton at Emory…."

 Forty

Gap-Tallard, France

THE ARDUOUS TRIP, backtracking from Chamonix to Grenoble and on to Gap-Tallard, was critical. The stage needed to be carefully orchestrated for his plan to succeed on the glacial slopes of Mt Blanc.

A heavy pneumatic arm clanged and screeched, sealing the hangar's old wooden doors, shutting out the cold air and swirling snow. Parnevik stomped his boots on the mat, stuffed his ski mask and gloves in his parka pockets, and slid his Diesel sunglasses up to rest on his forehead.

The Flying Store appeared virtually unchanged since his first visit six years ago: the freestanding chalet, constructed in oak post-and-beam style, occupied the interior half of the converted airplane hangar. Several gliders and other jump aircraft belonging to the store operated out of the other half.

Inside, all the wooden beams and cross members were exposed, and a huge stone fireplace, surrounded by comfortable well-worn couches, lent the interior warmth and a homey feeling despite the ceiling height. Like library stacks, stout wooden shelves and display cases filled with the specialty equipment and supplies required by hikers, skiers, skydivers, base jumpers, and wing suit flyers lined the floor space. The only change since his last visit a year ago was the addition of a coffee bar.

The Gap, as Gap-Tallard was usually called, was a major support-training center for a variety of skydiving, wing-flying, and glider sports. The store also operated a multitude of tours using gliders, light planes, and helicopters. Glider and training camps were ongoing throughout the year.

Parnevik wandered the aisles, checking on the presence of new gadgets for wing suit flyers. Two years ago, he'd completed The Flying Store's advanced training program. The course took seven days of one-on-one sessions with Eva Guedue, the head instructor of The Flying Store's various training camps; it concentrated on acrobatics, terrain analysis, and the planning process for unique jumps.

"Ah, *Monsieur* Parnevik. You surprise us." Ars Vaanu, the owner of the store, waved from the central checkout counter.

Parnevik waved back. He'd known Ars since the beginning of his skydiving training days at the store. To date, Parnevik had completed every instructor's license the store offered, and he'd accumulated 157 wing suit jumps worldwide. He was recognized as one of the best flyers on the planet.

"We did not expect you," Ars said as Parnevik approached the counter.

"I just got the urge."

"I know what you mean."

Ars was smiling, but his face reflected something else. Parnevik hadn't made contact since completing the Wings-flyer Advanced Instructor's Course, and he was quite sure Ars must have heard of his exploits in the Wichita Mountains of Texas. He'd been ridiculed all over social media by flying peers worldwide. Rumors had circulated concerning his obsession with more and more dangerous jumps. Word was, he was unable to find other flyers willing to accompany him on his exploits and run the camera, no matter what he offered. He'd taken to strapping two GoPro cameras to his wing suit and covering his own events, later posting the videos on YouTube and Vimeo.

"Are you in for the competition?"

"I thought that was this summer in Stupins."

"The Russians talked the International Federation into moving it to next month and calling it the World Wing Suit Championship. The freelance event ought to be to your liking."

"I don't think so. Too much to do." Parnevik sensed an element of disdain in Ars's tone of voice. He had considered him a friend. Now, it seemed probable his only interest had been the money spent over the years.

Parnevik had returned to his old training ground because he thought he would feel comfortable. His intention was to stay overnight at the Tallard Inn and mingle with some of the flyers and jumpers and let out the broad elements of the jump he had planned.

Suddenly he felt cornered standing in front of Ars. Creeping paranoia reared its ugly head. His medication was losing its efficacy.

"Well, how can I help you? Maybe a new wing suit?"

"No. I'm satisfied with the Raptor I bought in Texas. It's a one piece, but I need a good set of Gortex thermal underwear and a set of the new break-down skis."

"Sure, let me show you what we have."

"Great. Just give me a minute. Restroom's in the same place?"

"Same same."

As Parnevik crossed to the other side of the store, he questioned his negative perception of Ars. But the guy's face had lit up when he knew he was going to make a significant sale, so he was pegged properly.

Parnevik ended up trading almost fifteen hundred Euros for equipment. In the process, he ran into Eva Guedue returning from her busy training day. He asked her to have a coffee with him at the fireplace after he finished with his purchases.

"So, what have you been up to?" Eva asked as Parnevik approached with two cups of coffee. The senior instructor at The Flying Store, she was a tall athletic woman in her mid-thirties; round face; short, straggly blonde hair; pink cheeks reflecting vibrant health; a classic Norwegian outdoors woman dedicated to the sports related to body flying. Parnevik saw her as his only competition. She held the wing suit world record for time and distance.

She was arrogant. He truly despised her, perhaps more than any person he'd ever met. He'd been forced to take one-on-one instruction from her for seven straight days. Constant coarse commands and harping on more than one occasion had almost driven him to slapping her across the face. He wondered if she had realized how close he had come to losing it.

As Parnevik had prepared the coffees, he'd been struck with an outrageous idea and he had to restrain from snickering. Maybe running into her was fate.

"I remember you like lots of sugar with French roast coffee." Parnevik handed her a steaming Styrofoam cup.

"Nice of you to recall," she said, seeming genuinely surprised. "I don't recollect you being this gregarious." She sipped at the coffee.

"I'm not a bad guy once you get to know me—but what have I been up to? Well, let's see. How do I put this?"

"You're all over the posting walls on Facebook," Eva said, rancor in her voice. "The Texas bad boy, off pushing the limits—ignoring the rules."

Parnevik hated superficial small talk and facetious sparring in particular. He'd never invested time conversing with this egotistical woman, even though they'd spent those training days in close proximity. It had been all business. "I don't keep up with social networking. It bores me. Innuendo and hearsay are bad company. People's reputations are painted and shaped by idiots looking through the rose-colored glasses of their fears and shortcomings."

"Don't go off on me now. I just try to keep current. I heard you came close to my record."

"That's why I'm here. I intend on breaking it."

"Oh, and where will this momentous event occur?"

"I haven't chosen the exact location," he lied. "I'm thinking somewhere down the Chaminoix Valley along the Haute Trail or down the Vallee Blanche Run."

"You need height to break the record. Nobody does the glaciers. It's too dangerous. The downdrafts are fickle and treacherous."

"I think the east side has potential. I'll be shooting for the day after tomorrow," he added, almost forgetting that important piece of information. He wanted the event fixed in time. *The bitch will certainly spread the word.*

"Suicide." She cast a glance at the coffee and carefully slurped from the cup. "The updrafts are there, but the swirls are unpredictable, and the east side dives into a steep valley of cracked ice and deep crevasses. If you get blown over the side, you'll never get out."

"Never say never. The descent angle is there to get the record."

"I can see that, but you'd have to jump from—oh no, you're not thinking what I think you're thinking?"

"I don't know. What are you thinking?"

"You can't be serious—you can't go alone."

"You know me," he scoffed, looking into her face. She was hooked. Everyone in the world would know what he planned within the day. "The eagle soars alone."

"It's your funeral, but if you're set on this, remember your training. Don't skip any steps."

"I won't. I'll do some base jumping and hang gliding first to analyze the winds. You taught me how to plan. But first I want to reconnoiter the valley in one of the motorized gliders. Can you set me up for a full day's rental tomorrow?"

"Let's take a look at the book." Eva stood. "I'm pretty sure one is available out of the Aerodrome at the Tallard airfield." She looked a little weary, bending at the hips to stretch her back. It was the end of a difficult day of instruction.

She'd completed three advanced hang gliding sessions, extremely demanding on her physical stamina, and one acrobatic-group skydiving lesson that had been stressful from a safety standpoint. The individuals in the group were qualified experts, but because there had been four of them the chance for error was compounded, and management of the jump parameters in the air had been all that more complex.

"You have a copy of your license?" she asked in an uncharacteristically gravel-like tone, sighing and moving toward the store counter.

"Of course." Parnevik followed her, grateful the small talk was over. He typically experienced creeping anxiety the longer any personal exchange went on, no matter who was on the other end.

The paperwork complete, Parnevik bid Eva Guedue a pleasant evening. He would check back with Ars in the morning to see if his little *Fuerte* tablet had enhanced the pleasure of Eva's evening.

He'd accomplished his objective, saying just enough. Cyberspace would be placed on alert, and criticisms, judgments, embellishments of past escapades, and wild projections would fill the social blogs. Now he wouldn't have to schmooze the flyer regulars tonight at the local hangouts, and he could get a good night's sleep, one he would sorely need if the ordeal he'd planned was to succeed.

Parnevik guided the heavy hangar doors to The Flying Store from clanging shut too loudly and noticed two men in dark-gray, mohair long-coats get out of a local cab in front of the converted hangar complex. He put on his ski mask and hunched into the icy wind and down the wooden walkway to the street. As they passed, he noticed their shiny street shoes and close-cut hairlines. They cursed the cold in Midwestern English, their attention concentrated on bracing against the wind and holding their city hats in place.

An icy chill climbed up Parnevik's spine, and it wasn't from the cold.

 Forty-one

Mallory Driscoll

AFTER GOING OVER Professor VonMitton's unusual story, Mallory left Emma agitated and heartbroken. She was still dealing with Reagan's death, Corey Parnevik's deceit, and now Ernest Kelto's murder.

Mallory made up her mind to take action. She borrowed Emma's Honda. Halfway to her destination, she pulled to the side of the road to answer her cell phone. "This is Mallory."

"Mallory, it's me, Mrs. Leonard. I just have a minute. We're about ready to leave for the country house. Titus is warming up the car. Dear, I don't want you to be upset with me, but I thought it necessary to keep you informed. He's deeply affected by the police rejecting his help and barring him from participation. I've only seen Titus in that state of mind once."

"He'll come around, Mrs. Leonard. Ryan and I will be here for you."

"You don't understand. The last time he escaped my administration, there were confrontations with law officers investigating a serial-killing case he was working on with them in Portland, Oregon. I had to fly in and bail him out of the situation and only barely managed to regain control of him through deceptive medicinal methods. I'm afraid he might do something again."

"I understand. I'll talk to Ryan and see if we can come up with ideas to help."

Mallory approached the old, red-brick fire station. A "No Trespassing" sign out front announced the boarded-up building was subject to a short-term lease granted by the City of Atlanta, pending application for status in the National Registry of Historical Buildings, to Mr. Julian Trebar.

She surveyed the area. The building was in the middle of a warehousing district, down a dead-end side street off Highway 41, a major north-south route cutting across the city of Atlanta.

She parked the car in front and grappled with the cell phone in her purse, second thoughts pulling at her. She should call Ryan and let him know where she was. Mallory hesitated, consumed with the desire to do something on her own. She opened the car door. *It's a dead end anyway.* She'd take a quick look and be back in time to meet McKenzie for their early dinner.

A large, red and white Keep Out sign covered the top half of the door. Mallory peeked over her shoulder several times as she approached the entrance. No one was about. A dozen or so cars were parked at the backs of the warehouses lining the street.

At the entrance, she pulled at the sign. The plastic sheet came loose of its tacks and trundled to the ground. Her heart jumped, but she recovered. Taking another look around, she tried the door. It was locked, but the glass next to the doorknob had been shattered, leaving an open space. She reached in and unlocked the door.

Fumbling in her purse for a flashlight, she clicked it on and backed against the old plaster walls of the entrance foyer, abruptly wondering what was she doing here. She let out a breath and entered, feeling a surge of adrenaline.

The place smelled musty, like moisture-soaked drywall, air stagnant from lack of circulation. All of a sudden, this didn't seem like such a good idea.

She looked at her watch and peeked outside. Same scene. She'd give it five minutes, no more.

***

"Look, Jonesie, I'm tellin' you, before we could confirm what's inside—like you told us—this broad drives right up front, takes down the Keep Out sign—like she's some kind of official—and goes inside."

"How long ago?"

"As long as it took me to call."

"All right. We got no choice. Can you get her out of there without causing a ruckus? No violence."

"I think so. There's nobody around. Whadaya want us to do wit her?"

"The apartment on Fifth. That's the clean one, right?"

"Yeah. You want us to use the masks and put her out nice?"

"Right. Don't mess this up! When you've got her under, find out who she is and call me, and we'll decide if we need the apartment. I'll talk to Paulie."

***

Mallory was stunned to find a plethora of unopened boxes and crates containing medical research equipment littering the fire station's open engine bay. Parnevik wouldn't have left delivery to a service. He must have been here himself. There might be forensic evidence. This was a break, and now she was anxious to get out of the building, tack the sign back up, and contact McKenzie.

***

The two men quickly exited the old Toyota sedan parked behind one of the side-street warehouses. Dressed in business suits, they popped the trunk. Geno, the leader, grabbed a small tote bag. They officiously hustled around the corner and up to the fire station entrance, looking back several times. No activity.

"Now what?" the follower said.

"We get her to come to us." Geno opened the tote bag. "Here." He parceled out two black ski masks. "Put it on. You grab her when she comes to the door and hold her mouth so she don't scream. I'll do the rest."

Geno slipped on a ski mask and glanced inside the building through the hole in the front-door glass. "Lady, we know you're in there. This is the police. This building is posted and under surveillance. Please come outside."

Startled, Mallory's throat went dry. She hadn't counted on being discovered. But maybe it wouldn't be a problem. She'd just explain she was a lawyer checking on—checking on what? She'd torn the sign off a boarded-up building. The captain would have to get her out of this one. "Be right there, officer." She walked toward the front door. She couldn't see anyone. They must be taking precautions, positioning themselves behind the brick wall. "I'm a lawyer…the equipment in here belongs to one of my clients."

"Just come out with your hands up. We'll talk about it."

The voice definitely came from the doorway. "Okay. No problem. I'm unarmed." As she opened the door and walked through, someone came from the side, wrapped strong arms around her chest, and muzzled a hand over her mouth. A man in a ski mask and a dark-blue suit stood in front of her, quickly bringing a towel over her nose and the assailant's hand. Her vision faded and she went limp.

"What now?" The follower was holding the woman upright.

"Inside. Quick…. Prop her against the wall." Geno pulled his cell phone from an inside pocket.

"Jonesie, it's Geno—"

"For shit sake, I know who you are. What's happening?"

"We caught the broad in the fire station. She said she was a lawyer. We put her out."

"Where are you now?"

"In the station. Nobody saw nothin'. Whadaya want us to do with her?"

"How long do you think she'll be out?"

"Say forty minutes."

"All right. Stay there. Check her ID, and don't muss her up. I'll wait."

"He wants to know who she is," Geno barked at his assistant. "Give me her purse, and go look and tell me what's inside the station."

"Jonesie, her name is Mallory Driscoll—"

"Shit! I know the woman. You hold tight. I gotta make another call. I'll get right back to you—"

"You wanted to know what's here."

The Family had only one objective: to find out where Parnevik was and get to him before the authorities did. The Family wanted nothing to do with collateral damage.

"Jonesie, all we want is Parnevik," Paulie said. "We can't afford to make waves. Do you understand me?"

"Yes, Paulie. But maybe she knows something."

"She doesn't. Trust me."

Nobody knows anything except Parnevik. Now the cops will find out about his lab. We have to get to him first. Leave the Driscoll woman there—Jonesie?"

"Yeah, Paulie, I'm here."

"Geno and what's-his-name kept covered, right?"

"Right."

"She'll have a headache—no worse for wear. Tell those two to get out of there and disappear."

Paulie cut off the call and immediately punched Tony Gatturna's speed dial. Their trap for Parnevik had blown up.

***

Mallory slowly opened her eyes. They burned and she could smell a kind of cleaning-fluid odor. She was slouched on the tile floor of the foyer, leaning against the cold plaster wall. Pushing with her feet and worming her way up the wall, her head began pounding. She stood straight-backed, stretched her tingling arms and legs, and looked around. She was nauseous but seemed intact. All she could remember was how stupid the man in the suit looked with the colored ski mask. She checked her watch. Forty-five minutes had passed. They had obviously anesthetized her. Being proactive wasn't such a good idea after all. She pulled out her cellphone.

"Are you still at the fire station?" McKenzie had allowed her to go at her own pace as he absorbed her story.

"Yes, and thank you for not reading me the riot act."

"You want me to come get you?"

He sounded concerned. She couldn't remember him ever demonstrating that trait. *He was usually blasé, but that was a long yesterday ago.* "No, I'm okay. I'll drive."

"You should probably get checked out at Emory."

"I said I'm okay—"

"Don't be stubborn. It's for your—

"I'm going to get a shower and some sleep. Give me a couple of hours. Come pick me up at Emma's."

"Okay, but look, there's been another curve ball. The DEA Regional Director in Miami called in scrambler mode while I was waiting for you. Some DOD official wants to meet with us at four o'clock tomorrow afternoon at the downtown Atlanta Public Library. I think we should go."

"We'll talk about it."

"And, I've been recalled for debriefing in Miami—They didn't care that I was on leave. The DOD is taking over the whole thing. I don't know any more, but I'm supposed to make an 8:10 flight tomorrow night."

Part IV

Chaos

 Forty-two

The Government

"THIS IS LIKE a damn James Bond movie." Capt. Trussel spat his words out. Lt. Sullivan at his side, he was striding down the marbled central hallway of the Fulton County Courthouse in downtown Atlanta. "I guess we got ourselves into the big leagues. The cops overseas will track down Parnevik. We'll get our shot when they return him to proper jurisdiction."

"It sure happened fast," Lt. Sullivan said, their shoes clacking in cadence down the empty corridor. "What do you think this is all about?"

"It's about drugs, Lieutenant."

"Why in the courthouse?"

"Neutral ground, I guess—will you look at that?"

As they'd turned the corner toward the Carter Conference Room, state troopers were standing at ease in front of every doorway and posted in the middle of the hall at both ends, effectively cordoning off the floor. The guard in the middle of the passage facing them approached, asked their business, checked IDs, and became their escort, directing them through the wooden double doors of a conference room and showing them to high-backed chairs on one side of a barren table.

Five men were positioned twenty feet away at an elevated speaker's stand, two on either side of a tall, grizzled, white-haired man dressed in a dark-blue suit, standing at a central podium. Each of the men had a microphone. The small conference room served as judge's chambers, utilized daily to hash out sticky issues with wily prosecutors and defense attorneys.

Captain. Trussel whispered under his breathe, "It looks like we're going to give testimony, for crap sake."

The man at the podium tapped the mic, and it echoed. "Good morning, gentlemen. I am Major General John Taggart, Commander of US Army Intelligence from Security Command Headquarters at Fort Belvoir, Virginia. This meeting has been called to ensure all parties are on the same sheet of music. By way of introduction, the governor's representative," he nodded to the man at the far right of the podium, "Bob Griensley. Next to him, the mayor of Atlanta, David Boyd. The head of the Atlanta regional FBI on my far left," he waved a hand. "And you recognize your chief of police next to him. Each of these gentlemen have been vetted and briefed. This meeting is to advise you," Taggart peered down from the podium at the two police officers, "as the field officers in charge of—for lack of better terminology—the Parnevik investigations—that as of 1400 today, under the umbrella of national security, Army Military Intelligence will be taking over all investigations pertaining to missing product inventory at the Pharmco Corporation. This includes apprehension of Mister Corey Parnevik and investigation of his possible responsibility in suspicious deaths over the last two years.

"A five-member committee has been formed to oversee these investigations, representing the DOD, the Department of Homeland Security, DEA, the FDA, and Army Military Intelligence. Miss Christine Johnson, a Senior DOD Team Leader has been assigned as liaison for the committee and should be arriving in

Atlanta about now. This officer will direct the day-to-day commander in the field, Colonel John Blackburn of military intelligence—the uniformed officer standing in the back of the room. Until further notice, he is hereby posted to Atlanta PD. He and his staff will dress in civilian clothes and receive unbridled cooperation and access to its resources. All evidence gathered to date will be turned over, and media inquiries having to do with these investigations will be referred to Colonel Blackburn. All facets of these investigations are confidential and top secret. To ensure efficacy, the military intelligence staff will implement security measures and procedures.

"For the information of everyone in this room, Pharmco Corporation is being placed under the temporary control of the Department of Homeland Security. Its day-to-day corporate operations will be administered by Homeland Security personnel. This action has been initiated due to recent compromises of Pharmco's research contract with the DOD, involving secret, high-technology products and research vital to the interests of the United States." General Taggart paused, his steely eyes fleetingly crisscrossing the room.

"We have been briefed by DEA officials regarding the recent boom in distribution of a candy product on the streets of Atlanta, producing effects similar to narcotic drugs. That unit will continue with renewed vigor to investigate this situation, reporting directly to the DOD Oversight Committee Liaison Officer. DEA's mission is to determine if Parnevik is involved and establish legal grounds for attacking this nefarious industry.

"During these investigations, a major objective of Military Intelligence will be to locate and detain Corey Parnevik.

"The ongoing police investigation in Charlotte, NC, regarding the racquetball player's death is being brought under the same national security umbrella and will continue under the direct supervision of Colonel Blackburn operating from the Atlanta PD headquarters.... I believe that about covers it. Are there any questions?"

"Sir," Capt. Trussel stood, "what do you want us to do?"

"Anything and everything Colonel Blackburn asks of you—and that begins with the interviews we requested."

"None of the three responded to our calls. We didn't—"

"Never mind, we'll find them." The general nodded to the colonel and the other four figures, who had remained seated and mute. The four rose from their seats around the podium, and along with the colonel, filed out of the room behind the general. Capt. Trussel and Lt. Sullivan were left simmering alone in the chamber.

"I guess we've been dismissed," Lt. Sullivan said, his eyebrows raised, hands on the hard wooden armrests.

"Let's get out of here." The captain shoved his chair back, feeling like a lackey.

 Forty-three

Atlanta Public Library

MCKENZIE ENTERED THE main library on Peachtree Street fifteen minutes early to get the lay of the land. He rode the escalator to each of the six floors and walked through the aisles and study areas looking for anything appearing out of place.

At 4:00 p.m. on a weekday, the building was sparsely populated. The magazine and newspaper reading area held a dozen or so raggedly dressed patrons, dingy from street living, quietly reading and snoozing. A few business people and two dozen or so students were researching the reference stacks scattered throughout the six floors.

McKenzie hadn't detected any suspicious glances. The conference rooms were on the fourth floor, all glassed-in cubicles arranged along aisles around the central escalator, some larger than others. Several were occupied, and McKenzie could see what was going on but couldn't hear what people were saying.

He hung over the waist-high wall framing the escalator bank, observing activity down several floors. A shapely woman of medium height, dressed in a gray business suit, brown hair bunned up, was rising on the escalator from the second to the third floor. He watched her as she turned to take it up another floor. She changed hands carrying her briefcase and patted her hair. It had to be their DOD lady.

McKenzie backed away, headed for one of several open study tables scattered between the two aisles of conference rooms, and picked up a magazine.

The woman stepped off the escalator and briskly started down the aisle for the row of conference rooms on the east side of the floor. She seemed to know exactly where she was going.

McKenzie was keeping one eye on her over the top of the magazine when she turned abruptly in his direction. "Hello, Agent McKenzie. You're early," she said, the corners of her mouth curling. "Any time you're ready." She faced front and continued down the aisle.

"I see you too," a voice he recognized whispered from the access aisle skirting the conference rooms on the other side of the floor.

McKenzie blushed. He stood as Mallory came into view, a book in hand, looking vibrant in a plaid skirt and white, long-sleeved blouse buttoned high to her neck. Her caramel-colored hair was braided in a thick ponytail and dangled down her back.

"Shall we go, Agent McKenzie?"

"I didn't see you come up," McKenzie said, eyebrows raised. He'd left her in the lobby while he looked around.

"I watched you casing the place. I think you were in Boy Scout mode." Mallory glanced at her watch. "We better go. Four-fifteen is down here." She pointed.

"I know where it is." McKenzie tossed his magazine on the table and led the way.

"I'm pleased you accepted our invitation." The attractive woman in her mid-thirties motioned them to seats at a sterile metal table. As they sat, she activated a recorder lying on the table next to her briefcase. "My name is Christine Johnson," she said. Her face brightened and filled with a genuine smile. "And I don't want you to feel self-conscious. Please relax and let me acquaint you with what you've gotten yourselves involved in."

For nearly fifteen minutes, Christine Johnson delivered an articulate briefing, outlining the DOD's top-secret contract with Pharmco and its relevance to the military.

She was the field officer in charge, appointed by a DOD oversight committee. *Operation Soldier* was designed with specific support responsibilities given to Military Intelligence, Homeland Security, and the DEA, all of which reported directly to her. "Actually, my real job is as a Senior Team Leader in a top-secret branch of the Defense Advanced Research Projects Agency."

DARPA had a unique role within the DOD. It was established in 1958 after the Sputnik launch to prevent technological surprise and to create hi-tech surprises for America's enemies. It supplied the entire department with options outside the box.

"The branch I work for is called the Defense Sciences Office, or DSO. Its mission is to facilitate the development of the most promising technologies within the public and private sectors that could lead to radically new military capabilities. The branches of the military necessarily focus on near-term needs and requirements at the expense of major change. DARPA imagines what capabilities military commanders might want in the future and offers potential options. Its operations are free from bureaucratic impediments. It hires at its own discretion. Its funding is unlimited, and it makes things happen. Its only charter is radical innovation, emphasizing high-risk investments. It seeks to orchestrate the quickest movement from fundamental technological advances to prototyping. Development and production remain the responsibility of the military…. I didn't mean to be so boring," she said, allowing a smile.

"And here I thought the military was always playing catch-up," McKenzie said. "So, why are we here?"

"If you agree, I've been authorized to enter a cooperative agreement with the three of you—Dickerson Phelps did not respond to our attempts to communicate."

"We haven't heard from him since yesterday," Mallory said. "He's very stubborn and independent. We'll try to locate him and get back to you."

"That would be helpful. I need to get to him before Military Intelligence. Their officers are meeting with the heads of Georgia State Government and the Atlanta PD as we speak. The search for Parnevik and all investigations are now in their hands, and I don't want any one of the three of you to run afoul of their activities. This is a national security matter. Now, back to the agreement." Ms. Johnson popped open her briefcase and spread out a manila file folder. "The agreement is set up to give you immunity from detainment and questioning by U.S. and state authorities. It clearly defines your activities as in the interests of national security and authorized by the DOD. Please review the document," she said, handing out two stapled packets. She dove back into her briefcase and laid three cell phones and three sets of DOD ID cards on the table. "The phones are specially encrypted and only work between programmed numbers. Each of you has been assigned a number, and the phones contain authorized contact numbers. This is how we'll communicate."

Mallory looked at McKenzie. "We can review all of this later, Ryan," she said. "What is it you want from us, Miss Johnson? I don't see how we can be of value. You have all the resources you need. I'm just interested in seeing that Parnevik gets what's coming to him. It's obvious he killed my sister."

"I'll be frank with you, Miss Driscoll. We don't want any of you to go public. This agreement puts a stop to that. Any breach will be treated as an act of treason. We get you, so to speak, off the street. It is also an accommodation on your behalf. I can guarantee you that a failure to execute will be followed by Military Intelligence taking you into custody and delivering you to a place of their choosing for the duration of their investigations. You don't want that. The agreement allows you to remain free, so long as you cooperate with investigators as requested, report your movements and proposed activities to me in advance, and take no steps to compromise or expose this operation.... You can carry on with your lives."

"Well, that's just splendid, Miss Johnson," McKenzie said, squirming in his seat. "Like Mallory said, we'll review this and get back to you."

"Agent McKenzie, you needn't take a hard line with me. I'm trying to help you."

Under the table, Mallory nudged McKenzie's leg with her foot. "We'll put the effort in on this," she said evenly, but she was seething inside, pictures of her sister suddenly flashing to the surface of her mind: playing with her as a child, school, friends. She forced a smile. They needed to buy time. "What you say sounds reasonable, but give us some time to talk it over."

"I can only give you twenty-four hours. After that, it's in the hands of Military Intelligence." Christine Johnson stood and placed the files and IDs back in her briefcase. "You can call me on the phone—speed dial number one. Twenty-four-seven. For now, I leave it to you to explain this to Mister Phelps and give him his phone. All of you must sign."

***

They followed Christine Johnson out of the conference room as far as the first floor. Mallory led them to a vacant table in the center study section of the library. They watched out the huge front window as the DSO team leader navigated the outside stairs to the sidewalk. "She threatened to take away our rights of free speech," Mallory said.

"She's actually intimating incarceration—So, what's with kicking me under the table? The woman has no intention of allowing us any involvement. She's trying to bottle us up. Can't you see that?"

Mallory couldn't remember seeing McKenzie this irritated. "I did it to buy time," she said. "I thought you were going to piss her off. Not a good idea...but I do have a suggestion. What if we each write our stories and put them in trust for delivery to the media if anything happens to us? We have to have some leverage."

"I thought she was kind of nice at first," McKenzie said, grimacing.

"Sure you did. You were gawking."

"I was being facetious."

Mallory looked away. Her face was lined and her lips went tight. She'd been sucked in and was surprised at her reactions. She let out a breath she was unaware of holding, gritted her teeth, and glanced back over at McKenzie. He was smiling, the gentle smile she knew so well. "Look, it's a good idea. We need to draft this up," she said calmly. "We can set up a trust—no, that won't work. The Feds can get at anything with a national security mandate. Maybe someone not related to us could hold the documents and be responsive to a reporting scenario. If we don't report in, they get delivered to the media."

"They can get to the media as well," McKenzie replied.

"I don't know. You figure it out. I'm gonna get hold of Mrs. Leonard and try to find the professor—or Titus Smythe—whoever. They need to know what's going on."

"Smythe won't have any of it," McKenzie said.

"I'll see what I can do. You come up with some options. I'll call you after I talk to them, and you and I can get together at Emma's and figure out how to deal with this mess."

"Yes, ma'am. I'll get right on it."

 Forty-four

Mrs. Leonard

MALLORY RODE THE library escalator down to the third-floor reference section where she exchanged a five-dollar bill for quarters. On the way to the ground floor, she scanned the aisles and study spaces as they came into view. It was unsettling to be so suspicious. She headed for one of the pay phones next to the library elevator bank.

It required ten minutes of patient explanation to bring Mrs. Leonard to a semblance of resignation with the realities and dangers posed by the government actions. "Mrs. Leonard, I'm using a public phone at the library where we met the DSO lady. Don't call me or Ryan on our cell phones. I don't think they've had time to bug your phone there, but I want you to purchase three cell phones from the closest Walmart—right now. The kind you buy minutes for as you need them. Use false names and addresses when you sign up. I'll call you later today for the numbers from another payphone. We'll be doing the same thing. That should work until we can come up with a better method of communicating. Can you do that?"

"Yes, I'll be on my way as soon as we're done here—but Titus has given us the special phones—"

"We only use them in emergencies. Okay?"

"I suppose."

"Good. Ryan and I will be figuring out how we'll handle the proposed agreement—and we could use Smythe's input. They were miffed when he didn't heed their summons and want him to sign off."

"Oh, I don't know, Mallory. He's not one to cater to anyone's bidding. And he's become even more despondent since deciding not to respond. He's worse than when we spoke yesterday."

"Mrs. Leonard, if he doesn't cooperate with this Christine Johnson, she'll send Military Intelligence to come get him. This is national security. They can do whatever they want."

"Oh dear, this is alarming. I don't know what he'll say. He hates being cooped up, and he hates being around politicians and government officials. He spent most of last night pacing around the house, mumbling. He seems to know somebody is going to try to apprehend him and put an end to his investigation. He's become obsessed now and quite unmanageable. He's aware Parnevik has gone to France, but he's unable to see his activities clearly without getting physically closer. I haven't been able to get him to eat or drink anything since we got back, so I couldn't use the usual sedative to facilitate the professor's return... And anyway, I think he's caught on to my tricks."

"This sounds bad. Are you okay?"

"Yes, yes, but it's the professor I'm worried about. These forays are taking away his life. I've lost control for the moment, and I don't have the faintest idea what's going on in Titus's twisted mind. He's stopped talking to me. He just gives orders."

"Is he nearby?"

"He just paced into the kitchen."

"Let me speak to him, and I'll talk to you later when you get the new phones."

"Titus, it's Mallory Driscoll. Will you speak with her?"

Smythe reached for the out-stretched phone. "Of course, my dear woman. Now, please leave the room."

"Hello, Mallory. Let me talk without interruption for a moment. I am aware of your dilemma. I have been able to tune in to most of what has transpired with you and Agent McKenzie. though clarity is significantly impaired due to my focus on our principal—something I can't control."

"You know about the agreement and the DSO and Military Intelligence?"

"In summary, yes."

"We could use your help to figure out how to get around all this. I want Parnevik—"

"I know, I know, but I am confident you will find a way by yourselves. Please listen now. For the time being, I believe you and Agent McKenzie should confine your activities to Atlanta. I will need you there and free to communicate. That should be your focus. Concentrate your considerable IQs on that problem."

"What are you going to do?"

"If I tell you, you will be forced to lie to Miss Johnson. It is best if you don't know. I will be in touch with Mrs. Leonard before the government can locate her phones, and she can explain what you've devised for communications. Be aware that Internet email has been compromised, so it's of no use unless you have an expensive encrypted system. And, should you pay your respects to our Mrs. Leonard, make sure she is outside the house. I would think within a few days at most everything will be bugged—including the spaces *you* live in, your vehicles, even your clothing—not to mention surveillance will be assigned. So do take great care."

"You're telling me you know what you're going to do?"

"Of course, my dear. I just need a little more time to sort out what I'm able to see. Unfortunately, what I've perceived is almost two days old. I have to get physically closer to Parnevik to have any chance of setting a trap for him. It's what we do with him that has me in a quandary. Being brought to classical justice appears out of the question."

"What do you have so far?"

"Bascially a mixed bag of fleeting images of him in France. We know Atlanta PD traced him to Paris on January 2nd. He's been very busy traveling from Paris to Biarritz and Lyon, and he's planning to visit a village in the French Alps where he's received training over the years. He's organizing some kind of attention-getting event. I can sense his excitement and can feel when he gets scattered and uptight. He is taking his medication and managing to remain somewhat calm, but his emotions are strong and I can read those clearly. I'll know more shortly."

 Forty-five

Emma's House

"IT'S ABOUT TIME." Mallory let McKenzie in through the back porch. "Why the back door?" She glanced at her watch showing 8:00 p.m.

"I picked up a tail, and I'm pretty sure my cell phone is tapped. I can hear a slight echo, so I didn't call you. I think I lost them, but I parked half a mile away—up Highland near the secondary school—and walked down to that rib place on Monroe." He handed her a white paper sack. "You remember how good the ribs are? I saved you some.... I took a roundabout route. Sorry I'm late."

"Okay. I get it. Come on in. I just got off the phone with Mrs. Leonard." She took the sack, led the way into the kitchen, and motioned to the table. "I bought several cell phones from Walmart, the ones with pre-paid minute cards and no contract. I had Mrs. Leonard do the same. So for the time being, our communications should be secure."

"Until Homeland Security figures it out, but it's a good stopgap. I'd say it'll take them a couple of days to trace recent phone sales. They'll correlate calls made to and received from locations they deem of interest, and then they'll start recording conversations."

"Sit." Mallory waved at the table. She scurried to the refrigerator, placed the sack of ribs inside, then went to the stove and poured out steaming cups of chamomile tea from a red ceramic pot. Embedded in a bay window, the small kitchen table overlooked a tree-enclosed backyard and it was set for dessert. A red and white checked tablecloth held two plates, forks, and matching napkins. Flickering flame from a huge lavender candle graced the middle of the table. The wrought-iron frame around the candle cast Rorschach inkblot shadows on the kitchen ceiling and walls.

"Smells good." McKenzie scooted onto the bench-side of the table. "What's cookin'?"

Mallory set the teacups on the table. "I don't suppose you'd be interested in apple turnovers?"

"Perfect. Aren't you going to have the ribs?"

"Already ate," she said. "Caesar salad." She removed a frying pan off the stove, moved to the table, and flipped two turnovers onto plates. She dumped the pan in the sink and returned with the teapot and coasters. "Good." She cast her white apron over a chair. "Now, let's take a few minutes and relax—just be—as if nothing was going on." McKenzie stared into her face and smiled that half smile she knew so well.

"Just being is what I like."

***

"So we sign the agreement if the changes are incorporated," McKenzie said after explaining what he'd proposed. "It should buy us some time to come up with a plan."

"It might work. We'll give it a try. It's obvious they'll put surveillance on us and everyone we know, even with the agreement. They'll bug us just like Smythe said. But if we only use their cell phones to communicate with them, we could maintain some freedom and work on coming up with a method to keep our personal communications private."

"That won't work, Mal. The phones they gave us will be GPS enabled. They'll know where we are no matter what we do."

Mallory's face went to stone, and then she said, "Okay, so they know where we are—but let me bring you up to speed with Smythe. I called Mrs. Leonard from the library after you left and told her to go to a Walmart and buy three phones and I'd call her for the numbers from a pay phone. Well, when I got to her, she told me Smythe had vanished. He examined the phones she bought, wrote the numbers down, took the Porsche and plenty of cash, and drove off without explanation. She said he took enough medication for a year, has multiple passports and IDs, and is armed with a legal Taser gun made of composite that's immune to airport scanners. He's loose, and she's frightened and doesn't know what to do. She and the professor evidently tried hard to avoid this scenario."

McKenzie sighed and pushed away from the table, collecting plates and utensils. "More tea?" he said as he cleared.

"Please." Mallory was gazing at the candle.

McKenzie poured the refills, placed the teapot back on its hot pad, and sat back down. "Well, there's nothing we can do about it now…. He said he'd get back to us through Mrs. Leonard, and he knows her cell phone numbers. So, we wait for him to tell us what's happening with Parnevik. I guess we're his Atlanta contingent…. I think we need to focus on things within our control."

"Any bright ideas for securing our story?" She cast her gaze away from the candle. "That's the only way we'll get the changes we want in the agreement." The lines across her forehead played like waves in the fickle candlelight. Before McKenzie could respond, she said, "You know if they try to put a national security lid on the media, it would never work a hundred percent. It's bound to start leaking out—hold it. I have an idea. I think I know someone who can help us. Remember Eddie Chou from law school? I used to hang out with him. Nobody else made friends with him because he was quiet and aloof. He was the only Asian in the program."

"Yeah, you guys visited your animal friends at the zoo and aquarium. He was a nice guy."

"Well, you didn't like that sort of thing." She frowned and looked away.

"So what about him?"

"We've kept in touch. He's a big-time corporate lawyer in Shanghai. The Chinese aren't influenced by the needs of U.S. national security, and they have their own communication satellite systems. I'll bet he knows people who are adept at evading foreign intelligence eavesdropping, and media that would welcome our story if it came to that. He could set the whole thing up legally—a trust with a Chinese bank—delivery instructions. Whadaya think?"

"I like it. Give me his contact info, and when I'm back in Miami tomorrow I'll contact him using the DEA network and see if he'll help."

"Good one. I'll talk with Christine Johnson—tell her we checked with Phelp's housekeeper and she didn't know where he'd gone. It'll look like we're cooperating. I'll lay on her what we're willing to sign and what we're not."

 Forty-six

Angie's Italian Restaurant

"THE PAKI DELIVERIES are due to hit the warehouse—"

"It's not enough, Paulie. We can't go any further with this until we control the product." Tony Gatturna paced up and down an aisle of the gloomily lit restaurant. The smell of pizza and wine still hung in the air. Angie's would open in another hour. The preparatory staff was anxious to clear the plates and reset the tables. They'd kept their distance from the afternoon's heated discussions as family members indulged in the afternoon meal.

"We have to stockpile it so we can guarantee product deliveries." Gatturna took a drag off his cigar and lashed out at an HP printer resting on one of the dinner tables. It clattered to the floor and shattered.

Paulie Torentino scowled and bent down to pick up the pieces.

"You say Giovanni's disappeared, so no more IDs out of Quebec City?" Gatturna mashed his cigar into an ashtray.

Four days earlier, the Family had reviewed the situation: the introduction of *Amor* was an overwhelming success in all of the ten U.S. metro test cities. The Family had organized over one hundred distributors. Newly designed display carts were ready to go. Local street vendors had been selected, licensed, and were waiting. Business in the open was a new modus operandi. The regional chiefs were restless in anticipation of the go-ahead.

Paulie disposed of the biggest printer pieces in a large trash can and faced Gatturna standing next to the group of tables that had served the family gathering.

"Paulie, the little bastard can't just disappear—with all our contacts in France, and you haven't been able to find him." Gatturna flipped his wrist Italian-style in front of Pauli's face. "Find Giovanni and you find Parnevik. Don't you think? Or are you thinking?" He stripped the wrapper from a fresh cigar and kicked a splintered paper tray lying on the floor. "Tell me again— no, give me the e-mail."

Paulie rifled through the files and papers on one of the tables and handed over a copy of yesterday's e-mail from Parnevik.

"At least he knows his house and the fire station have been compromised." Gatturna was reading every word. "He's wanted for breaking and entering—all they need is his DNA and he's in it for murder, and he says he's not concerned." Gatturna wadded up the email. "So, he's skiing in Chamonix. How nice. He's coming back to Atlanta. He says we're not supposed to be concerned. He'll be in touch. That's just great." Gatturna kicked a table chair into the aisle. "Paulie, I want this guy in chains," Gatturna shouted. "You hear me, Paulie? Get on the horn with Jonesie and come up with something. I'll inform Parnevik our sources tell us Military Intelligence has taken over anything to do with him, and he'd better watch his ass. And, Paulie, if he's skiing in Chamonix, get our people there and find him."

 Forty-seven

Titus Smythe

"WHERE ARE YOU, and how did you get this number?" Mallory's heart was jumping. To her dismay, she'd developed a liking for the mysterious and crafty Titus Smythe.

"You gave your cell phone numbers to Mrs. Leonard. I can't risk calling on those phone again. Have you come up with an alternative?"

"We've worked that out—you've left everyone in the lurch. We're worried about you."

When her phone purred, Mallory had been sitting at the kitchen table in Emma's house, poring over the directions she'd received from Eddie Chou in Shanghai. Specially configured handheld units were on their way by overnight DHSL, and she had the numbers assigned to the phones. She covered the phone and shouted for McKenzie, who was on the enclosed back porch enjoying an Indian summer morning with coffee and the latest *USA Today*.

"Do not fret, dear lady, and please, plead my case to Mrs. Leonard. With the door shut at Atlanta PD and Military Intelligence taking covert charge, I was forced to go on my own. She would have been too feeble and narrow-minded to be of assistance to me here, and it might be dangerous. I've had to cover ground quickly. Please apologize for my deceptions. I have prepared myself to hide away for extended periods, ever since my last sojourn turned sour and I discovered how the Professor gained advantage over me."

"I'll tell her," Mallory said, filing away Smythe's comment about the Professor. "Ryan's here. I'm conferencing him in."

"Very well."

"I'm on," Mckenzie said.

"Greetings, Agent McKenzie. I'm calling from a pay phone. Allow me to continue. As I suspected, as soon as I landed in Paris, Parnevik's trail became clearer. I could see much of his last several days. I discovered he'd been to Biarritz, on the southwest coast. He sublet an apartment overlooking the beach and casinos under another alias, and he's taken a flat in Paris under the name of Julian Trebar."

"Where are you now?" Mallory asked.

"I'm speaking to you from the city of Lyon. He met here with the manager of a boutique tea company. The gentleman was kind enough to share that they're testing a tea blend Parnevik has developed. I think we know what that might mean. At any rate, I may be able to catch up with him in real time. He left Paris yesterday for the French Alps. He's planning some kind of event where he uses a suit made for soaring. He's obsessed with breaking a distance record—but I'm having a problem now. As I get physically closer to him in real time, my ability to focus on his past becomes distorted. I'm not sure just how close I really am, but from other experiences my perceptions usually shut down completely at around fifteen hours."

"Aren't you concerned about running into Military Intelligence?" Mckenzie asked. "Certainly they must be in France by now, and they'd love to get their hands on you."

"They know Parnevik's in France, Agent McKenzie. They're not looking for me," Smythe snapped. "He used his own name on the flight from Atlanta to Paris back on January 2nd. I'm sure they're trying to trace his movements, but the trail is cold for them. French cooperation won't help with him changing identities, much as I have learned to do."

"What's your next move?" Mallory asked.

"Yesterday he went to the village of Gap-Tallard, near the base of the French Alps, where he'd spent considerable time over the years in various flying disciplines. He's preparing for his soaring event. I'm walking to the train as we're speaking. Lyon to Grenoble is about an hour and then another two hours to Gap-Tallard via bus."

"Be careful," Mallory said.

"I'm always careful, young lady."

"Okay, no need to get snippy. Take down these numbers. Friends in Shanghai have provided us with secure phones."

Smythe wrote the numbers on a notepad and said, "Smart move. You'll have to let me know how to pull that off when I return. I'll be in touch tomorrow." He hung up.

 Forty-eight

French Alps

THE TWENTY-MINUTE two-stage journey, the world's highest vertical ascent, traversed the *Les Pelerins Glacier* and rose up the north face of *Aiguilles du Midi* amid majestic views of the Swiss, French, and Italian Alps.

An elevator shaft carved into the rock of the central peak rose forty-two meters to the Summit Terrace, the high point of a complex ski station perched on top of Mt. Aiguilles du Midi's craggy mountain spire. The terrace faced Mt. Blanc, the highest mountain in the Alps, towering another 1000 meters above. Two-hundred feet below, the terrace overlooked the flat *col*, a ledge functioning as the departure area for the famed Vallee Blanche Ski Run, perhaps the most famous run in the world and the longest in Europe at twenty-two kilometers with a vertical drop of over ninety-two hundred feet.

As Parnevik got aboard the cramped tram, his sense of well-being seemed to compress. Stale air exuded from bustling bodies. Smiling faces spewed out expletives, words in different languages, a sensory cacophony. It was January 12th, and the heavy tourist season was well underway.

He dropped his shoulder-strapped duffle at his feet and grasped the perpendicular support rail with both hands. As the atmospheric pressure dropped, his head throbbed unmercifully. The pain was excruciating and paranoia began. He was barely holding on, resisting the screaming release he craved.

Clanging into place, the cable car secured against its spring-loaded terminus and snapped into stabilizers. The doors slid open and the day's first boisterous stream of humanity from Chamonix resorts burst into the icy cold mountain air, leaving Parnevik alone, clinging to the car's support railings and awash in perspiration.

The chaotic chatter drifted away, and a rush of fresh air washed over him. He gathered himself, shivering, his determination revived. He shouldered his duffle and traipsed out of the cable car.

Purchasing a welcome latte and morning croissant from the cafeteria, he selected a seat isolated from the dozens of skiers enjoying a last warm beverage. He sipped the hot brew and regained composure, studying the station brochure for changes since his last visit over two years ago.

A peculiar clover fragrance caught his attention as a giggling blonde-haired woman passed by his table, reminding him of a Parisian candle store. Then his mind wandered, recalling the advanced, off-*piste route* he'd taken from the Vallee Blanche Run in perfect powder, narrowly avoiding a huge crevasse that overnight had ripped along one side of an *arête* along the route and was shrouded in heavy mist. The situation forced him to ski the length of the ragged edge to gain the juncture of two intersecting glaciers to continue the run. He'd never forget the strength and depth of fear during those moments, strangely mixed with exuberant conquest.

In conditions of adequate snow, it was possible to traverse the entire Vallee Blanche Ski Run from the station at the top of Mt. Aiguilles Du Midi through seven connecting glaciers and end at the terminus of the Mer de Glace glacier. A steep set of wooden steps led to the small town of Montenvers and the lift to Chamonix. An alternate route from the terminus led directly to Chamonix, a short climb along the side of the glacial moraine and a two-mile trek.

Parnevik's glider recon from Gap-Tallard had confirmed conditions for a perfect ski run although his plan was far from just taking on the Vallee Blanche Run.

He finished his abbreviated breakfast as the bells rang to gather at the launch area below. En masse, the skiers disposed of their used plastic in trashcans, grabbed their gear stacked in compartments against the wall, and headed out of the cafeteria to meet with their professional guides.

Parnevik knew the routine. With their skis, harnesses, ice-axes, and crampons, they would traverse the ice cave on the east side of the central spire and then mount the short lift to the ropes leading down an exposed and very dangerous ridge to the terraced departure point for the Vallee Blanche Run.

Exiting the elevator at the Summit Terrace, Parnevik encountered a serendipitous event: the presence of an audience. The older couple he'd noticed on the tram up Aiguilles du Midi were bundled against the cold and wind, observing the skiers with binoculars two hundred feet below getting ready to start the run. They had been the only ones without skiing paraphernalia.

Parnevik meticulously laid out his clothes and equipment as if repacking for a long trek. The couple stole curious glances his way as he prepared. They smiled each time they looked over. Their curiosity was justified, but their glimpses quickly turned apprehensive as Parnevik stripped down to long underwear and slipped into his red Raptor wing suit.

The old man pulled out a cell phone and stepped behind a buttressed sidewall to get out of the wind. The woman started taking pictures. That was a good thing. Parnevik gave her a bow and stood full profile.

***

"Hans, what's your position, over?"

"North Peak, Chamonix Terrace, over."

"Pick up Fredrick in the cafeteria and proceed to Summit Terrace. A guy was observing the skiers getting off the lift and roping down the snow ridge to the *col*. His kids were going to do the run. He and his wife are alone on the terrace except for some clown the man reported was changing clothes right in front of them. Check it out. We may have a crazy."

***

Whatever the couple was thinking, it didn't matter now. Parnevik was ready. The custom-made red pack he shouldered held the gear he would need: a harness with 150 feet of rope, ice screws, pickaxe, and collapsible skis. The aerodynamic shape and the silky smoothness of the pack's construction material would not compromise his necessary flight angle.

The weather was ideal, the snow level maximum for the season. The rising morning winds were perfect for the first eight kilometers along the descent path from the top of the Summit Terrace to the *arête* where three glaciers met to form the Mer de Glace on the north slope of the Mont Blanc massif. The target flight path averaged two degrees of descent in excess of what he'd calculated would be required to break the wing suit distance record. The shame of it was, he'd never be able to officially claim the record. But witnesses—the professional guides and skier groups spread out along the Vallee Blanche Run—would verify the jump, and there would be no doubt who had accomplished the feat—if he survived the jump.

While the elderly man was out of sight, Parnevik repacked his duffle and stashed it against the inside wall of the observation deck. He would no longer need the clothing or his wallet, bulging with several currencies, credit cards, and usual items of identification.

When the old man returned to his position on the terrace, thirty feet down the railing from Parnevik, he and his wife stood frozen like stone statues, speechless. Parnevik had mounted the steel-poled structure, holding himself steady in the wind, one leg in between parallel rail poles, posing for the frightened couple as he carefully zipped in the suit's wings from wrists to ankles, wings constructed of semi-rigid carbon fiber and high-density foam.

Parnevik was reaching over the railing to zip the between-legs wing when the elevator dinged. He turned on the railing in time to see the doors slide open and two security guards amble into view.

"Hey, you, what do think you're doing?" The one in obvious charge fumbled for the *billy club* at his belt. "Get down from there."

Parnevik laughed. "Be good boys and watch history being made." He straightened up on the middle rail, knees braced against the upper. When he stepped up on the top rail and leaped out into the void, the woman let out a terrifying scream.

The stupefied guards charged to the rail. The old couple was glued to their binoculars. A giant red falcon had spread its wings and was diving straight down toward the roped trail to the run's debarkation area.

As the four watched in awe, the bird's wings became taut and its angle of descent diminished. It swooped above the crowd and shot out over the glacial slope. At over eighty miles per hour, it was soon a red dot against the white snow, and then it vanished into the distant background of hundreds of tiny, dark rock outcrops.

 # Forty-nine

The Mer de Glace

PARNEVIK PREPARED TO clear the spine juncture at the point where the *Glacier du Geant* turned thirty-five degrees west to merge with the Mer de Glace. He was ecstatic, body chemistry in equilibrium, mind riveted on the precise adjustments required to maintain a 2.5:1 descent gradient. He streaked toward the critical moment, judging he would have to come within twenty feet of the icy spine before banking and sailing out over the steeper grade of the Mer de Glace.

A torrent of crosswind suddenly slammed into his left side. The outside edges of his wing suit flapped, and he was whipped toward the raw, jagged rocks of the *Aiguilles Verte* mountainside. He struggled to flatten his body diagonally into the wind, lessen the angle, decrease the yawing toward instant death, but he had to take great care to minimize losing the angle of descent.

He was fifty feet off the ice, losing altitude and heading for the high side of the spine where it turned to barren rock—not part of the plan. His stomach pressed into his throat as he flexed every muscle to dampen the effects of the crosswind. Abruptly, the shearing abated—it must have been the spine cutting off the crosswind. He adjusted his body angle and shot out over the Mer de Glace, missing the rock-tipped protuberance by two meters.

On Mer de Glace side, a guide-led ski group was shocked into spontaneous shrieks of ovation as a big red bird swished thirty feet over their heads at eighty-five miles per hour, streaking out of sight over the eastern edge of the Mer.

The spine marked the distance for the record books. The station guards, the elderly couple, and dozens of skiers beginning the Vallee Blanche Run had witnessed his departure point. The group of skiers on the other side of the spine on the Mer de Glace would never forget his passage.

The eastern side of the Mer de Glace was posted along its entire length, and warnings were part of the orientation given to every skier and alpinist with designs on the Mer. Access to the eastern side of the glacier for skiing, hiking, or climbing the *Aiguilles du Dru* ridgeline was prohibited.

The constantly shifting glacial ice was brittle at its edges. Gravity literally crumbled it against the steep mountainside with the glacier's miniscule advances. This solid-ice side of the glacier fell off from the middle as it disintegrated against the mountainside, forming a steep valley—a massive crevasse—randomly littered with smaller chasms that could collapse without warning.

Many arrogant hotshots had lost their lives over the years, the ice claiming them without a trace. To an onlooker, a person going over the eastern side would simply disappear. The only way out was by helicopter if one was fortunate enough to have found a solid spot to wait for rescue. Even then, helicopters were reluctant to fly into the eastern glacial valley due to the whirling nature of treacherous gale winds.

Parnevik had control again and took a quick look back at the waving skiers. He heard muffled shouts as he catapulted over the eastern edge of the glacier. During yesterday's glider recon, he'd marked the best landing spot with a green smoke grenade.

Sailing down the sloped ice bank, crisscrossed with tunnel-like crevasses and huge potholes, he adjusted his body airfoil into the updraft rising from the bottom of the u-shaped valley.

Heading for the small, green spot against the steepest part of the ice bank, his speed decreased to forty then twenty-five miles per hour. He was a big, descending red bird. The thought that he might be able to actually land feet-first without deploying his emergency chute sent renewed adrenaline gushing to every cell in his body, a sensual euphoria.

His mind snapped back to reality. The updraft was decreasing and his speed increasing. The green spot was another 300 meters. His right hand curled behind his neck, and he yanked the chute stringer. The small white canopy snapped overhead. He grasped the guide toggles and expertly managed the descent, virtually floating on the failing updraft and drifting toward the green landing area. His heart stopped pounding. The excitement was over for him. He felt the grip of fear relinquish and claustrophobia seep in. He gently set down on the ice, an eagle on its nest.

He disconnected from the chute, allowing it to blow away. It slid out of view over the side of a gaping chasm thirty feet away. He unbuckled his backpack, hands shaking, suddenly shivering, aware of the damp underclothes he needed to expel. He fell to his knees and grappled in his pack for crampons and an ice pick. The awesome height of Aiguilles Verte Peak above and the tenuous, enclosed landing area caused a wave of paranoia. He unzipped a side pocket and groped for his medication and a bottle of water. He threw back two tablets, spread out on all fours, shut his eyes, and listened to the sharp cry of the wind.

A few moments went buy, his mind released from its debilitating compression. He sat up and fastened a framework of crampons to his boots to help stabilize the tenuous positions he'd be forced to endure attempting the climb up the glacial wall.

His thoughts wandered to the probable reactions to his feat. The newspapers, the Internet social networks, the gossiping among his flying adversaries, the media pundits expounding possibilities and motives—no one would have a clue. It was for the rush and control of the uncontrollable. Civilization was spiritually desolate, occupied by diverse peoples motivated solely by greed and the acquisition of power. He was supreme among them.

Calm and contained, Parnevik let out a breath and examined his surroundings. He had exciting things to do. He quickly zipped off the wing suit panels, changed out of his soaked undergarments, turned the body of the suit inside out to its beige side, and re-dressed. He removed a vial from his backpack and dripped out its contents at the edge of the crevasse, smearing the blood around. The red birdman capable of flying over thirteen kilometers in the air and living to tell about it was not to be. Or so the story would go.

Backpack shouldered, barbed gloves Velcroed tight, crampons fastened to his boot soles, a short pickaxe in his right hand, and climbing spikes dangling from a carabineer at his waist, Parnevik surveyed the three hundred meters of a deeply cut chute up the steep valley wall.

He'd planned it out. He was prepared. He was sure that back in Gap-Tallard, Eva would be envious, assuming she survived his little present. It was unfortunate he couldn't have observed firsthand. He was curious as to how long the dose had lasted, and he was anxious to get back to experimenting and refining. The North Koreans had responded favorably by e-mail, though with a flavor of arrogant reserve. Of course they would respond. *Who cares in what way?* What he'd offered would be a political and military windfall, another pawn in their diplomatic craziness.

The climb was a relatively standard ascent up the inner face of the chute, nothing he couldn't easily handle. The ice was thick and firm, and the cut extended without interruption all the way up the valley wall to the snow-covered mid-line of the glacier. He'd tested the ice by tossing large rocks from the glider and observing their impact as they bounced and pummeled down the chute. The sides had maintained integrity. Any marks left climbing out would quickly fill with moisture and freeze by late afternoon as the sun left the valley in shadow.

He reached the top, jittery but elated, carefully crawled over the edge and scanned the glacier for skiers. There could be no witnesses. He rested on the thick, crunchy snow cover near the top of the glacier edge, repacked his climbing gear, pulled on a full ski mask and goggles, mounted his collapsible short skis, expanded his portable poles, and waited for a gap in skier traffic to finish the four miles remaining down the Mer de Glace.

Winding toward the inner tongue of the glacier, the principal route of the Vallee Blanche Run, he blended in with other skiers in the last few kilometers down to the Montenvers Station at the glacier's terminus. Here, everyone would take a set of steps up to the short tram ride to Chamonix.

Parnevik broke away just short of the steps, dropped his pack, stuffed away his short skis, and detoured on foot to the left side of the glacier's terminal moraine. He followed a little-used trail up the slope and poled his way on the hard pack for ten minutes to a *buvette* (snack stall). The snowfall was at its peak for the season, making this time of year the only period this alternative route was feasible. He detoured around the snack stall, avoiding eye contact with the pretty, young attendant and her one patron. He quickly reverted to skis and pushed off down the five-minute run, tracking under the cable car from Chamonix on its way to the top of

Aiguilles du Midi, and then down to the *Planards* ski area for beginners at the edge of Chamonix.

He melted into the crowds.

 Fifty

The DOD Contract

"AGENTS HAVE BEEN dispatched. The French are cooperating. That's all you need to know." Col. John Blackburn was addressing Dr. Safford, Pharmco Corp's CEO. "Parnevik is no longer your concern—only progress on the contract."

Over the last three days, administrative and scientific specialists from the Department of Homeland Security had stepped into key positions at Pharmco, taking over corporate administration and rendering the company into lockdown. No explanations were promulgated, other than the DOD was utilizing Homeland Security to conduct a thorough audit of company operations. All research activities were suspended except for work on the DOD contract under the direction of Military Intelligence. Ninety percent of the staff received paid furloughs pending completion of the audit, and all ongoing business discussions with outside parties became the concern of Homeland Security personnel.

Only Pharmco staff with knowledge of the DOD contract, and those who had signed non-disclosure agreements, could access the Pharmco building and come and go freely; as a further security measure, each had been assigned a military intelligence security agent as an escort, attached like a leech 24/7.

"This is outrageous, Colonel. We can't make progress under the contract without Parnevik." Dr. Safford was agitated, his brow etched into furrows. Emma Kisumi, newly promoted to Head of Computer Sciences, sat next to him at the conference table in his private office. Emma's scientific surrogate was on her right. Jim Dogett, Pharmco's Head of Security, and his M.I. counterpart occupied the remaining seats.

"I am not interested in your outrage, Doctor Safford." Col. Blackburn sat straight-backed and stone-faced. "Firstly, I am interested in the status of Phase II and the capabilities on hand to move the project to completion. I am also interested in the degree of degradation to project objectives caused by Parnevik's absence. We need to define our problems. And finally, I need clarification from your point of view of the potential dangers that scientific theory points to in regards to a nanite replication process."

"Miss Kisumi...Emma." Dr. Safford offered a raised palm, "perhaps you had best tackle the response." Safford nodded at Jim Dogett, who reached in his suit-coat pocket for the remote control accessing the office recording equipment.

Ordered around for the last three days, Emma's surrogate had required explanations of every detail of her position and research involvement. The man was an insufferable, obese academic with thin, frizzy, gray hair. He was always clad in the same worn sport coat and shiny trousers and reeked from a lack of personal hygiene. The frayed collar of his white shirt, the wire-rimmed spectacles perched on his oily nose, and a mouth held in a demeaning pout put the finishing touches on a humorless personality.

Emma had overcome her fears and nervousness and was now bored, actively spending her private time investigating other career avenues. Without inputs from Parnevik, no further progress was possible; he had installed fail-safes in every nanite Pharmco had in inventory. "Sir, as you are aware, Phase I criteria were successfully completed to FDA specifications prior to Corey's—Mister Parnevik's—sabbatical. This was the lower lab-animal stage, resulting in effects lasting approximately two-hours."

"Please, Miss Kisumi, get on with it." Col. Blackburn rose from the head of the table and stiffly shuffled to the coffeemaker.

"Sir, increasing the longevity and functional diversity of the *Fuerte* Project can't go forward as long as the nanite inventory is stymied by Parnevik's programmed self-destruct. Obviously we can't enter the human testing phase without inventory."

"Can't you start from scratch? Create a new batch of inventory?"

"Colonel, allow me to add context to the unfolding picture." Emma's plump academic surrogate stood from the table as if to lecture.

"Proceed, Mister Hammerschmidt."

"Our Parnevik was an engineering genius. He created nanites programmed to travel in the blood stream and release controlled electrical stimuli at specific destinations in the brain, a brilliant scientific breakthrough in nano-technology. He developed a miniature master machine, and in the presence of sufficient raw materials—in this case, sugar molecules were the building blocks—he programmed it to duplicate itself. The next step was to work with one duplicate at a time to program it to miniaturize itself to nano size. The theory was he could then create inventory.

"The fail-safe is two stage." Hammershmidt gestured and nodded. "The first is for internal security. If more than one nanite is ingested, they sense each other's electrical signature and all but the first entering a subject will self-destruct. They dissolve into simple sugar molecules and metabolize. According to Parnevik's notes, this is to protect a subject from overdose.

"The second stage is even more creative. As you are aware, nanites are held within an accretion of sugars. This facilitates ease of handling. Nanites become active when the accretion is broken down in the presence of stomach acid. If you were to test one of the prototype nanites, it would have to be programmed to detect its route in the body and path of movement to a site in the brain. If not, it would self-destruct—dissolve."

Hammershmidt had been speaking and making eye contact in a side-to-side fashion. Now, he turned with a pregnant pause to face the conference table.

"Thank you, Mister Hammershmidt." Col. Blackburn frowned. "What is the good news?"

"Sir, there is no good news. Even if we could experiment on the prototypes, we don't have the formulas to instigate the duplication and miniaturization processes, or to calibrate the frequency and duration of the electrical stimulus. We'd have to start over from scratch with someone of Parnevik's genius."

Colonel Blackburn scowled at the plump little man. "Sit, Mister Hammerschmidt—Miss Kisumi, theoretically, is it possible to adjust the programming of nanites presently in inventory?"

Emma nodded. "Sir, the answer is no."

"Do we have sufficient inventory to try?"

"There are ninety-eight left from Phase I testing in animals. The objective of Phase II was to increase longevity of effects by adjusting the charge and altering the delivery mission to several different areas of the brain—not just motor skills but memory, sensory perception, and information processing. I worked with Parnevik drafting the new program. It was ready as far as I know before he left. We were going to use chimps and pigs exclusively. The animals had been ordered, but the master nanite he developed for Phase II is part of the missing inventory. We were looking at six months of hard work to develop a calibration we could call safe for testing on human beings."

"I would call that good news. Wouldn't you, Mister Hammerschmidt?"

"Well, I don't know—"

"Never mind—Miss Kisumi, you are obviously aware of the contract objectives and specifications?"

"Not really, sir. We worked off the project description and amendments Dr. Safford disseminated. All we knew was it was part of a contract with the military."

"Let me summarize. It is critical we work together to complete the project. The original objective was to develop and safely deliver nanite stimulus to the brain to enhance the strength, stamina, sensory perceptions, and analytical capabilities of our military soldiers. Parnevik was the only one outside of Dr. Safford with full knowledge. That has now changed."

***

Colonel Blackburn laid out a transcript of progress since the beginning of Pharmco's two-year-old contract. "So, by the time Parnevik departed, he'd met every challenge with a solution. To regulate the electrical stimulation over longer periods, he designed collectors built into the nanites that soaked up the natural electrical discharges from body metabolism, theoretically making the nanite-induced enhancements self-sustaining. What remained was the design of a multi-nanite delivery system, stimulus calibration, determination of the most effective locations in the brain, and measurements of the increased caloric demand and sleep recovery requirement necessary for the body to function without damage. You can imagine how important this could be to the military soldiers of the future. We need to know if this is still feasible."

Emma had taken it all in and slowly realized where it was leading. "Colonel, I said the programming existed. Parnevik kept everything to himself for security purposes. All I can do is go through our computer system and see if I can retrieve his work. If I can, it is possible I could come up with the theoretical alterations necessary to upgrade Phase I nanites to Phase II."

"Good. Let's get to work." Colonel Blackburn began gathering his files and papers from the table. "Dr. Safford, I want daily reports at a minimum."

"Just a minute, Colonel." Emma stood abruptly and shoved her chair back with her calves. "Without understanding duplication and miniaturization procedures, we're stalemated, and even if we did, it's considered a very dangerous area in nano science. As far as I know, only Parnevik has been successful. Without him, the possible hazards associated with nanite replication are immense and untenable."

"What are you talking about?" The Colonel's face was blank.

"There is the theoretical possibility that replicating nanites could accidentally get out of hand. Very stringent scientific controls on feedstock, the contained atmosphere, and electricity loads are required.... The theory is called *Grey Goo*. It posits that within hours of a control breach, replication could go unchecked and the process would invade the nearby environment searching for feedstock and electrical inputs—and produce grey goo—a massive mess of partially replicated product. The theory is open-ended. In other words, hypothetically, an outbreak could consume the entire biosphere."

"That's preposterous!" The Colonel shook his head and sat back in his chair.... "But this is a remote possibility...and by itself doesn't justify shutting down the project. We discovered this subject reviewing your files and took the liberty of consulting with scientists at the nanotechnology centers at Penn State and Georgia

Tech. They agree there is risk, and that is why scientists to date have not conducted tests, so consensus is absent. We move forward, Parnevik or no Parnevik."

"Reagan Driscoll was studying the phenomenon before her death," Emma said. "She'd developed the concept of a nanofactory that would preempt accidents by producing impenetrable production space and a worst-case shutdown methodology. Parnevik obviously solved all of the problems or he couldn't have produced our experimental inventories. Reagan must have had some knowledge of how he accomplished the feat. She was trying to bring the technology into the mainstream of scientific research without dependence on Parnevik." Emma sat back down, uncomfortable, looking down on the Colonel. "Sir, I hate to point out the obvious, but uncontained nanite replication could be considered another latent terrorist tool—"

The two were staring at each other, the Colonel's lips tightly pursed, Emma's eyebrows raised, forehead furrowed.

"We will need to review the late Miss Driscoll's work." The Colonel turned to Dr. Safford. "It appears we need to find a foolproof methodology for containing the replication process. I will give you the names of cooperative experts at Penn State and Georgia Tech who've been cleared to work with you. Design a testing modus operandi and a timeline for tests. Be prepared to brief me within forty-eight hours.

"Now," Col. Blackburn said, squarely facing Emma, "I don't suppose you could tell me what Parnevik is capable of. In other words, what are we missing by not having him in cooperative control?"

"Well, Colonel, as far as containment of nanite replication is concerned, we have no idea if his methods are safe. We only know he was successful. As far as what he can do on his own, in short, not only can he experiment and perfect *Fuerte* on his own, it's common knowledge his replication work is reflected in the street availability of a candy product producing sexual arousal and stamina, focusing the mind on satisfaction. Before her death, Reagan told me he was experimenting at Georgia Tech on a delivery system he referred to as *Bliss*. It produced a heavenly sense of well-being, a temporary relief from human problems. Its use removed the boundaries of conventionality and suspended the rules of ethical and moral conduct. The user experienced living his or her dreams. The experience was supposed to mimic the major effects of LSD and heroin—"

"Yes, it would appear he has been successful." Col. Blackburn glanced over the table. "That's consistent with our findings surrounding Reagan Driscoll's death, now labeled a homicide. Scientists at Penn State discovered five small, coated tablets embedded in Vitamin C pills Reagan Driscoll carried with her to Las Vegas. They tested one on a rhesus monkey and measured electrical discharges in the brain at locations associated with the highs produced by drugs such as LSD, crack cocaine, and heroin. The monkey died."

 Fifty-one

Palm Beach, California

"IT STARTED IN your territory, Alberto. What's happening, *mi amigo*? This meeting is to pool ideas. We need to take action. We are losing market share. Customers are turning to this candy. What's happened?" The big man sat heavily into the overstuffed brown leather chair. He was still commanding and vibrant, though overweight, in his late sixties, and referred to as "Papa." He was the titular head of the Rodriguez Cartel and had a business degree from San Diego State University.

The small, discreet conference room at the Ritz Carlton had been swept, and five regional kingpins sat around an oval alabaster slab, the marble reflecting a rippling sheen from a huge plate glass window with half-closed blinds facing the morning sun. Dark, cherry wood paneling covered the walls down to a three-foot-high, vertically slatted wainscot. A sedate Persian rug encircling the conference table rested on top of polished wood flooring.

The four corners of the room contained intimate seating for several people around glass coffee tables. One wall held modern accoutrements: a fifty-two-inch, high-definition TV, two computer stations, a printer/scanner/fax, and charging stations for mobile computers and communication devices. Aromas of espresso and fresh bread hovered in the room. The periodic breathing of the air conditioner was the only outside sound.

The five men were immaculately dressed in business suits, spoke perfect English, and all but one had received business degrees from American universities.

The Rodriguez Cartel was the dominant Mexican drug trafficking organization operating in the U.S., specializing in the wholesale distribution of cocaine, methamphetamine, and marijuana. Their tentacles extended into every major U.S. High Intensity Drug Trafficking Area (HIDTAs), and most criminal groups of various races and ethnicities obtained their drugs from Rodriguez distributors. Rodriguez Cartel members were part of an extended family, the perfect intermediaries, never walking the streets themselves.

The UN recently estimated the value of trafficking worldwide at over half a trillion dollars, and some eighty billion went through the Rodriguez Cartel. Columbian warlords were the principle suppliers of the cartel's raw product, and plans were underway to establish a Southeast Asia link for the acquisition and distribution of heroin.

"It's cheap—twenty dollars for a pill that looks like a miniature gumball," Alberto answered. "The DEA can't find anything in its chemical composition to support classification as an illegal substance."

Alberto didn't like being put on the spot, and he didn't like getting the blame. The problem had sprung up in his territory, the southeast U.S. "It started about a month ago. The Italians came out with this little pink pill. Now it's gumballs on carts wheeled around the business districts of Atlanta and major shopping malls. The vendors sell everything from hot dogs, burritos, and chips to candies and snacks. The Guineas have two distributors and only sell product to their guys. It comes via the regular mail in boxes of a dozen bottles, five hundred to a bottle. Payment is through accounts at a website. We tried to establish an account without success. The online registration form has to be bogus. User names and passwords must be given out in advance." Alberto scanned the faces around the table. They all looked like poker players. "The candy gets users horny for a couple of hours. They say it's better than Viagra, and it also works on women. Papa, it's taking a chunk out of the regular trade."

"It may be just a fad," the man from L.A. said.

"Yeah, like sex is going to wear out," Alberto retorted. "What are you, some kind of crazy?"

"Okay, okay." Papa raised his hand. "How big a problem do we have?"

Jose Salazar leaned forward. "The word spreads like fire everywhere it turns up." Salazar was the Chief Financial Officer for the cartel. A thin Mexican with a long nose, he looked more Lebanese than Mexican. He crossed his legs and sat back in the leather chair. "I'd estimate today's sales in Atlanta alone at around eight hundred K per week. If the growth curve is similar, in six months I'd say the Italians will have penetrated fifty HIDTAs and be generating sales of around a hundred and fifty million a month." Salazar lit a cigarette and exhaled a cloud of blue smoke. "It could double every six months."

"What's it doing to us so far?" Papa asked.

"Ten percent decrease in Atlanta," Salazar responded. "It's too soon to figure their new operations in other cities. I think we need to find a way to get in."

"What do the rest of you think?" Papa leaned back into the chair's soft folds.

"We crash the Guinea's party," Alberto said. The others nodded.

"I agree," Papa said, crossing his legs, "and we have the means. They bank in Panama just like we do, only our business is what, a thousand times more significant? Let's pull a few strings and temporarily freeze their money. A computer glitch should do the trick—or better yet, our bank examiner friend can assist. Let the Italians know we want to do business."

 Fifty-two

Agent McKenzie

MALLORY ENTERED THE Hartsville Arrival Terminal and strode past the ticketing floor, heading for the arrival exit next to the masses waiting in front of the security processing lines. Her feeling of anticipation was curious. She hadn't seen McKenzie for nearly two days and she missed him, always easygoing, never brusquely assertive, bright, and gentle. With the intensity of the last three weeks since Reagan's funeral, the seven-year gap seemed insignificant.

The US Airways 3:15 p.m. flight from Miami had arrived on time. McKenzie called Mallory the second the plane set down on the tarmac, and she timed it to catch him coming out the arrival lane.

She saw him a hundred feet away and was tempted to hide and let him go by, then sneak up from behind and tug on his backpack. Instead, she came out from behind a post right in front of him. "Hey, stranger, welcome back."

McKenzie smiled, dropped his backpack and gave her a hug, burying his face in her caramel curls.

Mallory hugged back, glad he couldn't see her face. What a surprise, she thought. She moved away, their hands sliding down each other's arms.

"Thanks for coming to meet me, Mal...sorry I sort of grabbed you—"

"It was nice. I returned the hug, didn't I?"

McKenzie picked up his pack, slung it over a shoulder, and took off ahead of her. "I only have one bag. I can meet you at your car," he said, striding toward baggage claim.

"Okay. It's at 2H-31." She stood there in the middle of the concourse, wondering what happened. *What'd I say?*

***

Mallory opened the trunk of Emma's Honda, and McKenzie tossed his sea bag inside. "We have to hustle. We're supposed to meet Emma at her place after work. She's taking a cab. I'd like to be there when she comes in. She sounded upset—not like her—what's with the bag? Why don't you get with the real world?"

"Sea bags have sentimental value."

"It's an Army thing?"

"Marine Corps." McKenzie shut the hatchback door a little harder than necessary.

They started out in silence, the madness of the rush-hour traffic on Interstate 75/85 taking up their attention. McKenzie's mind wandered as he cooled down. She had a way of ridiculing him without trying. He wondered if she was the least bit aware that being flippant just put distance between them. *Some things never change.* She'd been insensitive back in law school, always quick-witted and belittling, oblivious that the edge of her sarcasm often drew blood.

"I'm sorry I forgot you were in the Marines," she said, eyes glued on the snarled lanes ahead.

"Okay, so what gives with Emma?"

"I don't know," she said. "When I talked to her on the phone at work, she was trying to come across as upbeat and playful, inviting us to dinner. It didn't sound like her. Something must have happened at Pharmco. Since you've been gone, Military Intelligence has locked the place down and Homeland Security runs the business—how was *your* trip?"

McKenzie suddenly realized she'd recognized her lack of empathy—jumping ahead without the slightest regard for him and his circumstances. "Mal, the regional director took me off the case here, so I took a leave of absence."

"You what?"

"I decided it meant a lot to me to finish what we started." McKenzie tried to look stoic.

Mallory reached her right hand over to touch his face, but she couldn't take her eyes off the road. "So what happened?"

McKenzie read the surprise and tenderness. "The new director didn't like it one bit. He asked me just to take a vacation and think about it. I said I would. After that, everyone at the office just ignored me. Anyway, I got through to Eddie Chou on the DEA's satellite system. He still sounds the same. Good man. He set it up so I could access him at his law firm in Shanghai, using their secure server. He said he'd overnight phones and instructions."

"They came in yesterday. Yours is in my purse on the floor. Get it out, read the instructions, and activate it. I'm turning on Boulevard Drive to cut off the downtown—How's the boat?"

"High and dry. I did a little house cleaning and had it hauled out into a working yard and placed on stands for a month It needs the bottom scraped and repainted. Barnacles cling to everything and build up. They love the movement of the tides."

"Emma said you could stay at the house. The couch folds out, and you'll have the hall bathroom to yourself. No sense spending more money at a hotel."

"Great...just like old times."

***

"You guys know I broke my agreement at Pharmco by telling you about the Vitamin C," Emma said as the three of them cleared the dinner dishes from the dining room table.

"I can't imagine what horror it must have been for Reagan—that uncontrollable high." Mallory shivered in disgust and rage. "When did he have time to come up with that?"

"Two years ago, when we were friends, he was working on something similar at Georgia Tech."

"Makes sense," McKenzie said. "He was testing a logical addition to his line of drugs."

"He overdosed her," Mallory cried, hanging her head over the sink. "He's going to turn the illegal drug market upside down. There'll be total chaos." Mallory started scraping the plates and stacking them on the counter, tears rolling down her cheeks.

Emma gathered the condiments and silver, worry written across her face. She still had more to say.

"Cartel wars like we've never seen," McKenzie said. "It could be an international blood bath." He brought in the serving dishes, sealing them with plastic wrap, and adding them to the refrigerator.

"You guys, that pales in light of the containment test program ordered by Military Intelligence," Emma said. "They think if Parnevik can do it, we can do it. They've ordered secret experiments to attempt controlled replication and sequestered scientists from Georgia Tech and Penn State to assist. Reagan thought she'd figured out how to safely contain a replication process, using an electrical force field, but she convinced Dr. Safford it was too dangerous to test. She believed any misstep could produce a catastrophic event. Nobody really knows, but the tests are going ahead anyway. I'm plain scared." Emma was shaking as she brought the remaining items to the kitchen. "You guys can't tell anybody I told you."

"We won't compromise your trust." Mallory darted a look at McKenzie.

"Emma, you have my word." He followed her with the bundled up tablecloth and napkins.

"I'll wash, you dry," Mallory said to McKenzie, indicating a towel hanging next to the sink.

"Sounds fair." McKenzie threw the towel over his left arm. "At least now they have enough evidence to charge Parnevik. It'll be outside the criminal arena and into Gitmo. He'll get life at a minimum when they tie it all together."

Emma just stood immobile and forlorn, listening to the two of them calmly and logically discussing scenarios. They lacked the scientific background to understand the truly horrendous situation.

"If they can find him," Mallory came back. "But maybe not even then," she added, washing a plate and handing it to McKenzie. "I don't think Military Intelligence will ever process a case against him. They want him to finish their black project in secret. We need to talk to this Miss Christine, ASAP. If Parnevik is going to answer for what he's done, we'll have to find a way to get to him first. He's got to pay the full price."

"I'd say that's a tall order," McKenzie answered. "But at least we should be able to find out where *Miss* Johnson stands. It's still on for tomorrow morning to sign the agreement, right?"

"Nine o'clock back at the library. Smythe may be our ace in the hole. Let's hope he comes up with good info. Maybe something we can trade."

"I don't think Pharmco will ever be the same." Emma collapsed into a chair at the small breakfast table cuddled into the kitchen dormer. She looked up at the sink where Mallory and McKenzie were at a standstill doing the dishes. "I've started looking for another job while I still have credibility," she said and began to sob.

Mallory slid onto the dormer bench next to Emma, casting both arms around her neck. "Everything will turn out all right. You just stay with it. We're here for you." Mallory directed her gaze at McKenzie still standing at the sink.

***

With everything put back together in the kitchen, Mallory and McKenzie left the house for an evening walk around Piedmont Park, continuing to rehash the situation. Blurting out possibilities and tentative conclusions, they would say almost the same thing at the same time. It was a sure thing psychological testing would reveal them both as dominant analytical personalities with strong secondary driver traits, Mallory being the stronger driver and McKenzie possessing an amiable streak.

"We better find out more about the testing program," McKenzie said as the two of them climbed the steps to the porch.

"But we've got to be careful not to give Emma away. They'll ruin her career."

 Fifty-three

Titus Smythe

SMYTHE DECIDED NOT to suffer the train trip from Grenoble to Gap-Tallard. The old steam engine and ancient cars were rickety. Going up the mountain and over the pass had negative appeal. Instead, he anguished through the cramped, three-hour bus ride as he sensed Parnevik had done only the day before. He was definitely coming closer to Parnevik's real-time movements; it was like being pulled into a streaming vortex, a phenomenon he'd experienced many times when assisting police investigations in the past. Sensing ended at around fifteen hours. He'd never gotten closer than that during a pursuit.

He hired a taxi to The Flying Store. The driver explained the store was inside an aircraft hangar. It turned out to be a quaint structure built to look like a chalet, occupying half the interior of the hangar. Approaching the ornate, double wooden doors of the shop, vivid but fleeting scenes flashed across his mind, and a mental sorting-out process he didn't understand told him he was crossing Parnevik's actual path. The trail was indeed getting warmer.

Smythe introduced himself to the young clerk at the counter as one of Corey Parnevik's professors from the United States, a day late in meeting up with him and at a loss to make contact because he'd accidently surrendered his cell phone to the sewer of a slippery street in Grenoble.

"Yes, he was here the day before yesterday," the clerk said, a curious grin on his face as he took in the tall gentleman wrapped in a black, wool overcoat with straight, brown hair stringing down from his top hat. "Mister Parnevik left just before the terrible incident. You must have read about it."

"I'm sorry, young man, but I'm not from around here. I've just arrived from Grenoble."

The man was wound up and enthusiastically rushed on to relate the story. "One of our long-time instructors had some kind of seizure and died right here at the counter. It was terrible. Mister Parnevik had just finished talking with her over by the fireplace." The clerk motioned to the groupings of couches in a conversation pit surrounding the store's huge stone fireplace. "They were probably catching up on old times. Eva Guedue was her name. Over the years, she'd taught Mister Parnevik everything he knew. I was next to her when she was finishing the paperwork on Mister Parnevik's glider booking for the next day, and then suddenly she started shaking and wheeling around in circles, screaming. None of us knew what to do. My father's the owner. He tried to get her to the floor and hold her down, but she went crazy, smashing everything in sight. She collapsed just as the EMTs came. They rushed her to the hospital, but I'm pretty sure she was dead before they got her to the truck."

"I'm sorry to hear that," Smythe said. "How horrible for you. So, he has been a frequent visitor here?"

"Many times over the years. Like I said, Eva trained him."

"I hate to bother you with trivia," Smythe said, electing to move on, "but isn't experience necessary to rent a glider?"

"Most assuredly, *Monsieur*. Mr. Parnevik was fully certified."

"Did he say where he was going? Perhaps a hotel? He was to ring me and let me know, but without my phone I'm at a loss. I think he said something about Chamonix," Smythe inserted as a flurry of pictures flickered across his mental screen like movie previews: snow-covered landscapes, mountains, glaciers, packed trams, quaint village streets filled with après skiing enthusiasts, and a view of a small train station: Chamonix.

"He never mentioned a hotel, but I was here yesterday when he returned from his glider rental. It was odd. He never asked about Eva, even though it was all over the front page of the local paper—he talked to my father and announced he was going to try for the wing-flying distance record. Eva held the record for the last five years. I heard him say it would take place in the Chamonix Valley from some high point over the Vallee Blanche Ski Run."

"Did he say when?"

"It would be today. If you can get to the Internet, whatever is going on will be all over the social websites. There's already bantering from skydivers, wing suit types, and crazy base jump-ers—blogs from all over the world belittling his past bragging and dangerous escapades. Mister Parnevik was well known for pushing the limit. To tell the truth, nobody around here really liked him. He was arrogant and flaunted his money. That's just my opinion. Eva despised him."

"You've been very helpful, young man. I thank you. At least now I have a destination." Smythe glanced at his watch. "You wouldn't happen to know if there's an auto rental business close by?"

"If you're going to Chamonix, Old Ben at the petrol station outside the aerodrome rents one-way. There's enough traffic back and forth."

As Smythe was about to exit the store, he saw two men through the stained glass windows in the middle of the double doors twenty feet from entering. They were clad in city trench coats, necks scarf-wrapped, shined civilian shoes, hands in their pockets. Through the open hanger he saw a black four-door Peugeot parked next to the walkway to the store, spewing white clouds from its duals.

Smythe slid between the winter clothing displays, turning his back to the store entrance, and began browsing the wares as the two men entered and approached the service counter. He carefully wound his way out the back door of the store, navigating around assorted small aircraft and out the other end of the hangar to the street.

He took a cab to Old Ben's service station and was in luck. A half hour later, he was driving a ten-year-old Fiat down the highway, headed for Chamonix some 250 kilometers away. The roads were clear, and the weather prediction was for fair skies. He'd make it by 11:00 p.m., check into a hotel, scour the Internet social media sites for any news, and get a halfway decent night's sleep before trying to catch up with Parnevik.

 Fifty-four

Chamonix, France

ARTHUR DUBOIS HAD found a degree of assimilation in the decadence of jet set life among the discos of Chamonix. No one paid particular notice when he ventured out of the Alpina Hotel and walked the crowded streets.

Young people were letting go of their inhibitions, laughing, having fun. He was a young person too, and he'd watched the dancing and listened to the kibitzing, convincing himself he wasn't any different. But he kept to himself, reluctant to test the hypothesis in favor of maintaining anonymity.

The third disco club visited found him seated at the bar with the effects of his medication dwindling. Fear and paranoia were taking control as he anticipated retracing his spider-web travel route back to the hotel. He was forced to shake out a pill from the little plastic-capped tray ever present on his person.

As the medications took effect, the perceived chaos melted away and Chamonix again appeared to be a wonderful locale. In a place like this, he could spend time experimenting, being more outgoing, more interactive, find a girlfriend, have some fun. He vowed to return.

***

Parnevik checked out of the Alpina Hotel about 7:30 a.m. The lone young woman at the desk was cordial, amiable, and chatty. When she'd first started her shift an hour and a half earlier, a gentleman who sounded like an American had called and inquired if Arthur Dubois was still registered. She asked him if he wanted to be put through, but the caller declined, saying he would wait until a decent hour.

A tight ball contracted in Parnevik's mid-section, but he concealed the discomfort, thanked her, bid her a good morning, and headed for the respite of the hotel's sitting lounge. Placing his two bags next to a loveseat in a far corner of the room, he collapsed in the safety of its softness and tried to think. It was impossible. He'd left no telltale links to Arthur Dubois. He used the ID sparingly to establish a residence and presence in Biarritz when he'd first entered France and now here in Chamonix. That was all. As Dubois, he always paid cash for purchases. No way to trace him.

He understood the reasons Julian Trebar could have been exposed. Two days ago, he'd contacted the door attendant at his Paris apartment as a precaution in case the North Koreans came snooping around. To his dismay, the attendant informed him two Americans had shown up at the building and wanted to pay a visit. They were told Julian Trebar was out of the country. The authorities must have traced him from the rental van he used delivering equipment to his residence in Atlanta. But he'd worn gloves the whole time and been antiseptic in wiping the van clean.

Or, maybe it was the Kelto business at the Bank of America in Buckhead. The police would be certain to look through Kelto's financial affairs as part of the investigation into his death and discover the estate gift delivered by one Mr. Julian Trebar.

Glued to the loveseat, his mind raced ahead, but he couldn't fight off the queasiness burrowing into his core, narrowing his attention span. He recognized the signs. The shot of adrenaline from facing the desk clerk and absorbing the bad news was wearing off. He needed another dose of medication to avoid slipping out of control. He pawed at the zippered pocket of the smaller leather bag, fumbled out two green capsules from a twist-off bottle, and choked them down dry. He sat still, head bowed, willing his mind to concentrate on the innocuous carpet threading. Thirty seconds passed. His mind calmed and cleared. He sat straight. He knew what to do.

The lounge was deserted—too early in the morning for skiers and jetsetters to be up and around. Removing a small leather-covered notepad from his bag, he headed to the far side of the lobby and the privacy of an enclosed public telephone booth.

It was late evening in Paraguay, but Giovanni, the man from Quebec City, was still up and pleased at the opportunity of trading a night's sleep for $200,000. Parnevik had negotiated an agreement with the elderly Italian forger. Weeks earlier, one million dollars had convinced him to sever his illicit business ties with the Genovese family and retire among friends and extended family members in Paraguay's quiet capital city of Asunción. The only stipulation was keeping a separate cell phone under an assumed name available should Parnevik require his services.

Four sets of identification would be arriving via courier at the Marseilles International Airport at 3:25 p.m. Instructions were to deliver the package to the American Express office inside the terminal to be held for pick up by Arthur Dubois. Parnevik's long-term plan called for two sets of ID to be actual Argentineans, living in Buenos Aires. Parnivik would produce the names and personal chronologies at a later date. The remaining two sets were to be American: one chosen at random from Giovanni's collection and one blank.

To utilize an ID set, all Parnevik had to do was insert appropriate photographs of himself—prepared in disguise—memorize the background particulars, open bank accounts, and arrange for bank cards. But for now, his third set of IDs from Quebec City would soon be coming into play.

He exited the hotel and took a cab to the train station for the ride—Chamonix to Grenoble and on to Marseilles.

***

Walking the long marbled length of Marseilles' Saint-Charles Train Station, Parnevik ran his plan back and forth for omissions, anything not anticipated. Time was still on his side. He was ahead of his pursuers. The uncertainty was in not knowing who was pursuing and how he was being tracked.

Exiting onto the busy sidewalk, free of the reverberating noise from hundreds of voices filling the domed station and blending with the cacophonic announcements of arrivals and departures, he emerged into brilliant sunlight and the considerably warmer temperatures of this Mediterranean seaport city.

 **Fifty-five**

Chamonix

LAST NIGHT, SMYTHE checked into a little rooming house he'd been directed to by a friendly local bartender, unsure of what the next day would bring but pleased at the firmness of the bed's mattress and the quiet location off the tourist-infested main streets.

Rising early, he greeted the cold, calm day with vigor. The sun hid behind Mount Blanc as he wandered through the quiet, shadow-laden main streets lined with now-closed boutiques, clubs, and restaurants. Piles of freshly plowed snow lined the walkways. He finally stopped at a little café across the street from the city's *Commissariat de Police* and treated himself to tea and crumpets while he waited for the station to open to the public.

An occurrence he now expected, his mind had been streaming images since the moment he awoke, catching up with Parnevik as far as his gift allowed. It had left him excited and anxious at the same time. Fleeting scenes of Parnevik's jump had ended abruptly next to a sheer valley wall of ice. He saw a blotch of green and then nothing. From the sun's angle, it had to have been sometime late yesterday afternoon.

During a savored second cup of the hot green tea, more fleeting pictures conjured in his mind, vaguely at first, as if film was developing on a processing tray in front of him. He picked up the rush of fear as Parnevik had challenged the flying elements. He'd climbed a vertical ice-chute. Then he glimpsed a steep mountain landscape and glacial snow rushing by. He must have been skiing. The images faded just as the clock tower in the nearby square chimed the 8:00 a.m. hour. Smythe hastened out the door of the café, tucking his scarf tightly around his neck, adjusting his top hat and collar, and cinching the leather waist strap of his heavy overcoat.

***

"Good morning, officer." Smythe couldn't discern the rank of the porky, mustached gentleman sitting behind a long wooden service window.

"Good day to you, sir. You don't appear to be a sports enthusiast," the officer said, looking askance at the tall figure with long hair and top hat, an open long coat, revealing a Scottish blazer and corduroy pants. "How may I help you?"

"I was wondering if you might direct me to someone familiar with incidents occurring yesterday. I'm inquiring about a friend of mine who was supposed to meet me last night and didn't show up."

The officer snatched a clipboard from one corner of his desk and handed it to the stranger through the service window. "I'll need proper ID—a passport or French driver's license. Fill this out and you can examine the activity logs."

Smythe completed the form and handed the clipboard and his passport to the officer.

"Dickerson Phelps is it? PI, and all the way from Atlanta, Georgia." The officer stood and made a copy of pages from Smythe's passport. "You'll get this back when you leave the building, Mister Phelps." The officer placed the passport on top of a file he'd stuffed the copies into. "I'll pass you through. Enter the interview room first on your right." The officer evidently pushed a button hidden below the service window, and the door next to the service window buzzed open.

The room was sterile, containing a heavy, bolted-down wooden table and two straight-backed metal chairs. It was just like the movies, all gray, one wall filled by a rectangular window of one-way glass.

The officer followed Smythe inside and dropped a three-inch thick, oversized, bound volume on the table. "When you're done, knock on the door." He left the room. The door loudly clicked.

The log contained entries by time, bare-bone summaries written by responsible personnel investigating incidents, everything from processing the drunk and disorderly to fender benders. Smythe quickly found what he was looking for.

Yesterday afternoon, a Sergeant Boudoir had written up a radio call coming from a ski-group guide at the top of the Mer de Glace. His group had just begun the final turn down the Vallee Blanche Run and witnessed a wing suit flyer swoop over them and disappear over the crusted, east-side glacial wall. The flyer was suited in red and looked like a huge bird of prey. The group heard an ungodly shriek as the flyer hurled over the wall, causing them to reflexively duck and scatter, fearing it was something that would return to attack.

The entry was 4:35 yesterday afternoon. The sergeant dispatched one of their two police helicopters, mounted with powerful searchlights, to find the flyer. There wasn't a follow-up entry.

Smythe knocked on the door and stood waiting for a long minute. The slides streaming through his mind brought him down the glacier and past the steps leading to the small lift at Montenvers. Then a quick change into hiking boots, a short detour up a pathway climbing up the side of the glacial moraine, and he had a glimpse of a snack stall that flashed and faded away.

Suddenly, Parnevik was back on skis, sliding under a major gondola and gliding into the *Planards* ski area a hundred meters from the edge of Chamonix. And then nothing.

"Thank you, officer."

"Did you find what you were looking for?"

"Perhaps. Is Inspector Boudoir about? There was an incident yesterday on the Mer de Glace. My friend was planning to try for a wing suit jumping record somewhere over the classical route down the Vallee Blanche Ski Run. I'm hoping he was not involved."

"He's at his desk, probably working on the paperwork. There have been some rumors flying around about a person attempting such a jump. The inspector may be interested in talking to you. Wait in the lobby." The officer opened the heavy, metal door for Smythe, and it snapped shut behind him.

***

"Sit down, Mister Phelps." Inspector Boudoir returned Smyth's passport. He pulled a wooden chair from a cramped corner of the workspace over next to his desk. Even though the duty officer had prepared him for the man's appearance, he was surprised. "The duty officer tells me you have a missing friend that wanted to break a wing suit flying record over the Vallee Blanche."

"That is true, sir."

"I have a person, presumed deceased, that yesterday allegedly flew over the run in a red wing suit and vanished over the side of the Mer glacier. That side of the glacier turns into a steep-sided valley filled with crevasses of brittle ice that buckle into instant slides or collapse at the smallest of impacts. It's certain death for a skier, let alone some crazy wing suit flyer. Does this sound like your friend?"

"It does. His name is Corey Parnevik, and he was intending to set a distance record, but I had hoped he would wait for me to witness the event."

"That's him. He left a duffle bag and IDs at his point of departure. We have four witnesses that saw him jump off the observation terrace on top of the Aiguilles du Midi lift station—that's a 16,000-foot mountain about eighteen kilometers from here. He was spotted by skiers just turning into the final run down the Mer de Glace section of the Vallee Blanch Ski Run." Inspector Boudoir paused, his eyes canting toward Smythe. "In the process of tracking down his next of kin, we found he's wanted by several levels of your government. Can you shed any light on this situation, Mister Phelps?"

Smythe put on a mask of innocence. "He was a student of a friend of mine many years ago at Emory University. I have no knowledge of his personal life, other than he had a position at a pharmaceutical company in Atlanta. Because that friend was occupied and couldn't respond to an invitation to witness the student's attempt, he engaged me as his surrogate."

"We'll need a statement, if you wouldn't mind. We've been directed by French Foreign Affairs to turn over his belongings and what we gathered at the crash scene to your Military Intelligence in Washington."

"Of course, Inspector, but I've come a long way. Yesterday's log entry ended with the dispatch of your police helicopter. Would you mind telling me what was discovered?"

"Not at all. I was making the notes for today's entry when you came in." The inspector pulled back several sheets of his steno pad. "The helicopter found the alleged crash site because it was marked by green-stained ice, probably from a smoke grenade. He must have set the site up in advance."

Smythe remembered Parnevik had rented a glider for a day from The Flying Store in Gap-Tallard.

"We can't figure out why he chose to jump there. Like I said, it's certain death. Nobody straying to the eastern side has gotten out of there alive. It's even too dangerous for rescue personnel to land. The ice wall is constantly drying out from the winds, and the ice crumbles, breaks, and slides. There are huge crevasses and chutes that cut across the valley walls. Anyway, the rescue personnel spotted pieces of ripped reserve chute hanging down a deep crevasse. A scattering of red streaks and small puddles of red liquid appeared to be blood. The rescue team snagged what they could and soaked up some of the blood by lowering a towel from the chopper. We're sending everything to Washington after we take a look—you might be interested in a video we took into evidence from one of the skiers who witnessed Mister Parnevik's flight. Evidently, the group had stopped for a breather at the top of the Mer de Glace—it means the sea of ice—the final glacier of the run. It's posted on YouTube, and there are dozens of posts and blog entries on Facebook and Twitter from the day before yesterday, spouting rumors about Parnevik and his record attempt."

"Thank you, Inspector. I'll be sure to scour the net. Were you able to find out where he was staying or what his plans might have been?"

"Nothing here locally. No credit card usage in France. The only thing that came up was a Facebook blog entry posted by somebody at an equipment store in Gap-Tallard, again day before yesterday. The blog said Parnevik was there buying equipment and renting a motorized glider. It said he was going to try for a record from some high point over the Vallee Blanche Ski Run. The rest of the blog was scathing. It seems he was present in Gap-Tallard when one of his past instructors died from a convulsion. The next day, he rented the glider, never saying a word to anyone about the tragedy, and just disappeared without paying respects. Doesn't sound like he was a very nice guy."

Smythe stood, realizing it would be counterproductive to share what he knew with this local *gendarme*. "Well, Inspector, I'd best be on my way. Things to do, you know."

The inspector slid to a three-drawer file cabinet and pulled out a form he passed to Smythe. "I'd appreciate it if you would complete this in the interview room down the hall. It's a form for your statement of what you told me. Give it to the duty officer you met earlier. He'll process you out."

Smythe handed his statement to the duty officer after waiting in line while the officer handled inquiries from two Italian-looking men dressed like businessmen, clearly out of place in a jet-set retreat like Chamonix. He picked up on the conversation in broken French: they wanted to know about the wing suit flyer and the accident.

Smythe exited the police station and braced himself against the cold. He was certain of several things: Parnevik had gone to great lengths to orchestrate his own death. But what a bizarre and perilous gambit. The fellow was indeed irrational and more than a little unbalanced, not to mention insensitive, and he belonged somewhere locked in a straitjacket. He had the Mafia and the U.S. government on his tail. And he'd hideously killed again.

The moment Smythe inhaled the first breath of crisp cold air, he forgot the French police. The images began again, foggy and out of focus and then progressively clearing and playing like a slow slide show. He quickened his pace, unaware he was heading for the bunny slopes of the Les Planards Ski Area.

Sufficiently buffeted from the cold of the windless morning, he walked steadfastly, his concentration riveted on the imagery phenomena. Judging from the time of the ski guide's radio report of the incident, and allowing an hour and a half or so for Parnevik to have somehow climbed out of his deathbed and skied down the remainder of the glacier, those images he'd experienced two hours ago in the café were in fact about fifteen hours from real time.

Half an hour later, Smythe had trudged around the perimeter of Les Plannards at the edge of Chamonix and was trekking up a grade along a crude, snow-packed road. He had seen glimpses of Parnevik skiing back down to Chamonix on this same road after hiking from the glacial moraine terminus of the Vallee Blanche Run and passing by a cleverly located snack bar Smythe had identified on a visitor's map called the *Refuge du Requin*.

The way Smythe's mind functioned, confirming evidence was necessary to support the veracity of the ephemeral picture shows and his theoretical analysis. One of the fleeting images had shown a brief picture of the snack bar, perhaps from fifty feet away, and someone waving. Hopefully, that someone was working today and could remember the hiker with a red backpack.

The little kiosk was set against a solid wall of rock ten meters off the twisting roadway. It had taken forty minutes to trudge the distance from Chamonix, and Smythe would have chosen a different means of transport were he given another opportunity.

A young girl was alone behind the small clapboard structure, dark smoke rising from an open metal cylinder on the roof. She waved to Smythe as he approached. It was a good sign. Yesterday the person in the kiosk had waved to Parnevik in much the same way.

"Greetings, *Monsieur*," the attendant said, bundled up, giving him a cherubic smile. "I am not used to receiving customers from that direction. Come around to the stove and get warm," she added, clearly curious at the presence of the unusual figure before her.

"Thank you, my dear. Do you get much traffic here? I see no one's about."

"I just opened. The first of the skiers won't finish the Vallee Blanche Run for another hour. We do okay. The regulars and the guides know we're the only cup of hot buttered rum close by. What brings you here? It's a long uphill haul. You're lucky the weather has held and the snow is packed on the trail."

Smythe moved around to the open side of the kiosk, took off his gloves, and held his hands close to the open wood-burning stove. The attractive young woman was sitting on a high-backed stool next to the stove, wrapped in a blanket with her legs and feet propped up, sipping from a steaming cup. "That smells like tea. I'll have a cup if you don't mind, and, for that matter, a croissant. A plain one will do." Smythe slid onto a stool at the small table-like counter.

The girl unraveled and poured out the green liquid from a large kettle simmering on the stove into an oversized, colorfully decorated ceramic cup. She set him a place at the table—croissant and honey butter on a clean plate—and pulled up a second stool.

"Thank you." Smythe took a sip. "Good…. Tastes like Chinese white tea."

"You are correct. It's my personal stash. I normally don't serve it to customers, but you're special," she said, her gaze flitting over the strangely clad guest. His crusty, brown hair drooped across his shoulders, dripping as it thawed from the stove's heat. His reddish nose and cheeks contrasted against a pale sun-deprived face.

They exchanged small talk for a few minutes. The girl's name was Devonia Pardue. She was from Lancaster, England, taking the winter off from fine-art studies at the Sorbonne in Paris. It had been a slow day at the kiosk yesterday, but she remembered a solitary hiker coming up the trail in late afternoon with a red backpack. He didn't stop except to wave and change out his boots for short skis. It was a little strange, she'd said. Usually, everyone stopped to get warm, chat, and have a hot drink.

"Is he a friend of yours?" she asked.

"Of sorts," Smythe retorted. "We missed each other yesterday in town. He said he was going to ski the run and meet me for dinner. He never showed up. He said he was taking this route instead of the tram at Montenvers, so I took a chance coming up here to see if someone at the kiosk had seen him." Smythe stood away from the stool and pulled his gloves from his pockets. "It appears he followed his plan at least to here. Perhaps it was tonight we were to meet for dinner and I misunderstood. I thank you for your hospitality. I should—"

"Oh, look. Here comes Henri on the supply sled. He can give you a lift back. The wind is coming up. You don't want to hike back."

***

The ten-minute ride on the motorized supply sled passed in a flash. Smythe sat there mesmerized by a flurry of new images. He thanked Henri and asked to disembark at the head of Avenue Michel Croz, six blocks from Hotel Alpina. Now it began to make sense. In one of his fleeting images from two days ago, Arthur Dubois from Biarritz had registered there for a week. Now Smythe was beginning to get images from yesterday evening after Parnevik's triumphant ruse; he was enjoying the town and its fine cuisine.

He glanced at his watch, 3:15 p.m. It would be early morning in Atlanta, but he felt obligated to keep his promise of briefing Mallory Driscoll and Agent McKenzie. Then he'd return to his rooming house for a second good night's sleep, one he was sure he would need. By the morning, Parnevik's movements would be clearer.

 Fifty-six

Emma's House

MALLORY JUMPED AT the musical sound from the Walmart cell phone lying on her bedside table. The radio-clock LED screen displayed 7:04 a.m. She heaved off the covers and grappled for the phone. The instant she realized it was Smythe, she told him to give her the number he was calling from and she'd call him back on her new Chinese satellite phone.

The moment Smythe picked up, he started reeling off a summary of events since he'd been to Gap-Tallard two days ago and followed Parnevik to Chamonix. He was using a public phone at the local Chamonix police station: The police had labeled the investigation on the ski slope as an accident. Even though a body was not recovered, accidental death was presumed based on personal items left at the Aiguilles du Midi observation deck, skier witnesses on the glacier, and evidence collected at the alleged crash site. The file was to remain open until positive identification was confirmed via analysis of blood samples and DNA matching by authorities in the United States.

"I believe he tested one of his insidious nano drugs in Gap-Tallard on some unwitting instructor he'd known at a training place called The Flying Store," Smythe blustered on. "The local newspaper reported the woman died of a convulsion. I perceived him actually having coffee with her. The event was one of some intensity for him, and, according to the storeowner's son, she was afflicted shortly after Parnevik left the store with gear he'd purchased. Mallory, the instructor had held the distance wing-jump record. This man is a perverse animal, clearly beset with complex psychotic disorders. Feeling what he feels is a satanic experience for me. He has no respect for human life, and he's loose in a world full of powerful people and organizations that thrive on the fallout from heinous debauchery."

"How awful." Mallory grimaced and curled up in a ball on the side of the bed. "You sound...upset—"

"I am *very* upset. I respect your desire to bring Parnevik to justice, but I must say I now favor using any means to expedite his capture, whether he is processed through the legal system or not."

"You know, as I think about it, even in the pictures we found in his house, and the ones Emma shared with us, you can see madness in his eyes. What are you going to do now—any sign you're being followed?"

"My dear, I have taken additional precautions just this morning after reassessing what has transpired. You wouldn't recognize me."

"What else has *transpired* that you haven't told me?"

"I'm getting to it, my dear girl. As I was departing The Flying Store, I spotted two men about to enter. They looked out of place—city clothing, polished shoes, short haircuts."

"We warned you. These government people want Parnevik bad. From what we've found out, his scientific knowledge, random experimentation, and disappearance have created a critical national security issue."

Mallory filled Smythe in on the proposed agreement, the very real threat of a catastrophic event from Parnevik's need to replicate nanites, and the steps taken to protect her and McKenzie's

stories of events through the relationship Henry Chou had organized with a Shanghai bank. She gave him the numbers of their
encrypted Chinese satellite phones. "But we're both thinking we
can't trust the government, even with our depositions safely
located in Shanghai."

"Maybe you can hold out another carrot. Find a way to continue to lever them," Smythe said with conviction. "They don't
have the information I possess. You can tell them we know who
he's dealing with on the drug side of the equation."

"Who might that be?"

"I think you'd best not know for now." Smythe paused but
decided not to tell her about the Italian inquiries at the Chamonix
police station. "I'm the wild card you can use to regain some
freedom to move around unfettered. As far as the *Federales* are
concerned, I'm ahead of them for now and will likely stay that way
for some time."

"I wouldn't be so sure. They seem to be breathing down your
neck."

Smythe ignored the comment. "Allow me to complete my report."

"Sorry," Mallory said.

"The emotional intensity of Parnevik's experience flying
down that glacier allowed me to perceive his flight as if I were
right next to him. Quite chilling, I *must* say. Remarkably, he landed
on the steep backside of the glacier—he nearly lost it in shearing
cross winds. He changed into climbing gear and shimmied up an
ice crevasse to the top of the glacier, changed into short skis, and
wandered into the mix of skiers finishing the Vallee Blanche Run.
He made his way back to Chamonix on a little-used trail and spent
the night there at the Hotel Alpina, indulging himself at its famous
restaurant, *The Panoramique Le 4810.* A grand place, I should say. In
an earlier day, I—but never mind."

"So he's not dead. How did you know about the hotel?"

"A police friend of mine in Philadelphia was kind enough to trace Arthur Dubois's credit card usage. I checked with the hotel, and it seems that, prior to his visit to Gap-Tallard, Parnevik traveled to Chamonix as Dubois and took the room at the hotel, leaving his luggage. Hotel management said they didn't see him for more than a day and a half after that.

"He checked out of the hotel yesterday morning and booked a flight from Marseilles via New York to Atlanta. I could feel his trepidation. He's beginning to understand the scope of his predicament and the danger he'll be in when he returns to the States. Now that we've caught up to him, you have an opportunity to accomplish your objective."

"What's he up to, and what's your next move?"

"He has business responsibilities. He'll have to produce product. I sensed he was agitated as he boarded the train from Chamonix to Marseilles. He wasn't looking forward to the extra time he would have to spend on the two connector rides into Lyon where the high speed TGV goes to Marseilles. And then, the pictures and feelings faded. I was losing my proximity window."

"So what are going to do?"

"I'll be returning and will call when I've landed. Do what you can to intercept Parnevik. You should be able to track him as long as he uses the Dubois name—but I fear he will prove resilient. He must know his IDs will soon lose their usefulness. As we speak, I'm using the computer at the Chamonix police station and will fax Emma a sketch of Dubois's likeness drawn by a bellman at Hotel Alpina. And do not fret. I have another plan up my sleeve if Parnevik should elude you and the government again…and do smooth the way for me with Mrs. Leonard."

***

He was always hanging up on her before she could vent all her concerns, so directing and sure of himself. But it was strangely alluring being left in the dark, compelled to trust in the mystery and efficacy of Smythe's weird abilities.

Mallory uncurled off the side of the bed and stretched, shivering at the more lethal picture forming around Parnevik. He was becoming some kind of hideous force, a malicious demon leaving death in his wake, a practiced criminal with uncanny resources for staying in control. She padded into the kitchen, wrapped in the full-length muumuu she always wore in the morning. Quietly, she slipped into the living room where McKenzie was sprawled on the couch. "Hey, wake up," she said, gently shaking his shoulder. A groan said he'd gotten the message, and he thrashed about as he turned over, a reaction she fondly recalled.

She set up the coffeemaker to brew ten cups of the strong Arabian they both preferred and turned the kettle on for Emma's tea. She smiled as flashbacks of college and intimate times fleetingly drifted from her memory archives.

"Hey." McKenzie peeked around the wall on his way to the bathroom. "What's with so early?" He was bare-chested, had a girly pink towel wrapped around his waist, and his sandy hair was sticking up frizzed and matted.

"You look ridiculous," she snickered, clinking a spoonful of creamer into her cup of coffee. "Please leave my presence."

"No sense of compassion." He slinked out of sight down the hallway.

***

Emma had left for work early. Mallory and McKenzie, dressed in jeans and warm shirts, sat around the kitchen table devouring bagels and cream cheese, washed down with fresh coffee. Through the big bay window, the gray greeting of a cold rainy day added to the somber atmosphere.

"He wants us to smooth the path for him with Mrs. Leonard," Mallory added after finishing a detailed review of her conversation with Smythe. "And that reminds me, I should fill her in, poor thing. Smythe hasn't taken the time. She needs to know he's okay."

McKenzie nodded. "And *we* need a plan. Miss Johnson's e-mail said she thought the changes we wanted were doable."

"Still on for this morning at nine?"

"Yup."

"You know," Mallory said, "I don't think the agreement is important now. We need to cut a new deal. We have Smythe as leverage so long as Military Intelligence doesn't catch up with him and he keeps coming up with useful information. We just have to convince her that the three of us are valuable assets."

"We don't want to antagonize her—but you may be right. This is the only time we've held a decent hand. There's no question that any time it suited them they could make the two of us disappear without a trace. This may be our one and only chance to bargain."

"I think we wait to see what happens when we push the envelope. Let's find out what she knows. Maybe we'll have a partner instead of an adversary."

 Fifty-seven

Atlanta Public Library

COLD, PELTING RAIN swept down in torrents. Wind gusts billowed their umbrellas as they scrambled up the library's marble steps two at a time. The clock set high in the front apex of the building pealed off the nine o'clock hour. McKenzie jumped ahead and, against the wind, hauled open the heavy glass doors.

"Always the gentleman." Mallory frowned in acceptance and stomped across the threshold, shaking and collapsing her umbrella. "One good thing is she's still talking to us in a neutral location."

"Just remember the old adage, 'Nothing is ever what it seems.'" McKenzie slipped out of his rain jacket, shook off the moisture, and stuffed it in his shoulder bag. "I'm going to see if we can get the room changed. That way no surprises."

"Good idea. I think we ought to record her," she whispered at his side.

"Consider it done." McKenzie dug an Olympic audio recorder the size of a thumb drive out of his bag and gave her a conspiratorial look.

"Smart thinking." She grabbed it, turned it over, and placed it back in his hand. "It's nice to be in the presence of a competent agent," she said as he headed toward the information desk, then smiled when he sighed.

McKenzie changed the meeting room from number 414 to 424, a similar room on the opposite side of the floor.

***

Ms. Johnson was garbed out in Levis and a green and black plaid shirt. She quickly placed the papers and files she'd laid out on the meeting-room table into her brown briefcase and snapped it shut. She'd been waiting in room 414. "Lead on, Agent McKenzie," she said stiffly, tossing her raincoat over an arm, "but I tell you in all honesty, we did not bug the room."

"It seems we have a trust issue on both sides," Mallory put in.

They paraded single file around the circular corridor connecting the contiguous meeting rooms and entered the new room without further discourse. Mallory and McKenzie settled into two of the four chairs set around the plain, round table. Ms. Johnson remained standing, opened her briefcase on the table, pulled out a laptop, and plugged it into a sidewall socket. With practiced patience, she again placed the paperwork and folders neatly on the table and sat down. "I trust you will not mind if I record our discussion," she said calmly, reaching into her briefcase and placing a digital recorder on the table.

"That's ok," Mallory inserted flippantly, "as long as we can do the same."

McKenzie pulled the Olympus from a shirt pocket, laid it on the table, and clicked Record.

Ms. Johnson made a face and then looked away, seeming to gather herself.

Mallory tensed, hoping they hadn't provoked the woman.

"You two haven't kept the bargain we made three days ago. In spite of that, we have taken no action. You were given twenty-four hours to make your decisions."

"I beg your pardon," Mallory spat. "We didn't go public and we're here. And we sent you our responses to the agreement within the allotted time."

"All right. I don't want to get off on the wrong foot here. It's not my purpose to chastise you. You have positioned yourselves for serious trouble by inhibiting your government's efforts to quell a potentially calamitous situation."

"We're doing what you told us to do," McKenzie said straight-faced.

"And also doing what you've not been told you can do—this is getting off subject. Let's straighten out a few things. Agent McKenzie, your unauthorized use of the DEA's encrypted communication system for the purposes of organizing personal access to a foreign communications system is sufficient for serious charges. Miss Driscoll, you have collaborated to withhold vital information from this investigation, i.e. the whereabouts of Dickerson Phelps—and you've squirreled away an account of your personal investigation in a foreign country, presumably containing sensitive information involving an ongoing, top-secret government operation. You could be prosecuted."

"We never signed your agreement," Mallory said calmly. "That's what we're supposed to be talking about today."

"Clearly the agreement we proposed is not workable under the circumstances." Ms. Johnson seemed unruffled by the change in tack. "I discussed this with the DOD Oversight Committee, and we've concluded that it is, in fact, to our benefit to omit any written documents between us now that you have placed your deposition outside of our control with your friends in Shanghai. And, Miss Driscoll, you're a lawyer. You should know we don't need an agreement to bring charges. But we digress here. I don't want to get caught up with superfluous innuendo." She sternly cast her gaze at them one at a time. "I must have your cooperation, and

I *need* the information I believe you both possess, information vital to national security."

"You've got the DOD, Military Intelligence, the Department of Homeland Security, and the DEA," McKenzie stated. "Why do you need us?"

"We lost Parnevik's trail in France. Our lab people traced him from the tire tracks of a van that made deliveries to his home before he disappeared. The van was leased under the name of Julian Trebar, and credit-card tracking found Trebar had taken an apartment in Paris on January 5th—two days after Parnevik landed in Paris. Phelps called you and confirmed that. We located your Walmart phones—and he nicely pointed us to Gap-Tallard and Lyon. Agents went directly to Gap-Tallard, and from there to Chamonix, where they discovered Parnevik had a wing suit accident, was missing, and presumed dead. His death is being carried as accidental, and it hasn't made the papers yet. DNA evidence from the scene is on its way here."

Mallory and McKenzie sat through her harangue like bored students in a lecture hall as they allowed her to reiterate the witnessed wing suit flight. At the end, she said, "We haven't had any luck locating Phelps. We realize he is somehow tracking Parnevik. We need to know how, and we want to know what he knows."

"So, not only have you broken into our phones," Mallory said, "but you've bugged everything we use."

"Yes. It's our job. I can't offer any apology. And, suffice it to say, it's just a matter of time before we hack into the Chinese communications service you are now using."

McKenzie took a quick look at Mallory. Her facial expression said they were on the same page. Ms. Johnson evidently hadn't been privy to the latest Smythe reports via the new phones. They still had leverage.

"Look, you two," Ms. Johnson's tone softened, "the country needs to get this lunatic off the streets before the unsavory grab him or he places the country at risk with his experiments. The scientific consensus is he could unleash a catastrophic event. I don't want to threaten you with incarceration. But you need to know we can literally whisk you away under the guise of national security—suspend your rights as suspected terrorists. Do I make myself clear?"

No response.

"If you'll cooperate and work with me, we'll bring Parnevik to some form of justice."

"I want him dead, Miss Johnson. I want my sister exonerated. She's buried, and all her friends and relatives think she was some kind of crazy crack head. Her boyfriend even has his doubts."

"I can promise you a proper media release to cleanse your sister's reputation. And I can guarantee Parnevik will never be released into society."

"I want him dead."

"I can only assure you he will be dead to this world, but right now the important thing is to capture and contain him. Then we'll neutralize the effects of his activities. And please, realize the paramount concern is not the drugs he's unleashed into the marketplace. It's the process of production that's become the focal point. Science says that if nanite replication gets out of control, there could be a world disaster."

"What does *disaster* mean?" McKenzie pushed back in his seat.

Ms. Johnson opened a manila folder and distributed copies of an eleven-page report produced by the Defense Sciences Office (DSO), labeled in red letters "Top Secret." The report was entitled, "Controlled Nano Replications," and elucidated several hypothetical procedures with an outline of potential risks.

"The bottom line is that Parnevik is using replication to make product. To date, scientists have not attempted calibrated replication because foolproof containment hasn't been designed. Parnevik is a walking, talking, environmental time bomb. He's somehow performing the impossible without the scientific resources to handle inevitable mistakes or unforeseen events."

Ms. Johnson's demeanor had progressively changed. Her facial lines had deepened, and she held her mouth rigid. "Worst case scenario is an uncontrolled replication event could lead to conversion of the planet into a mass of grey goo. Does that get your attention? I need your ironclad verbal agreements of cooperation. And that means we share everything."

"I think we need a minute," Mallory said.

Ms. Johnson nodded and started working on her laptop.

They stood to leave the cubicle. "We'll be back," McKenzie said.

Though the meeting-room floor was virtually deserted, they assumed the DSO woman had probably found a way to eavesdrop on the whole floor. Mallory and McKenzie took the escalator down one level and began a slow stroll around the perimeter corridor, discussing the situation in hushed voices.

They didn't command the resources or authority to effectively trap Parnevik on their own, and there wasn't anything they could think of to force the government to process Parnevik through the civilian legal system. At a minimum, with national security invoked, anything to do with the black project at Pharmco would be classified and inadmissible in a court of law. Parnevik had breached his top-secret project agreement and used classified intellectual property for material gain. He had effectively defined himself as a terrorist. They concluded that if and when he was finally captured, no acknowledgement would be forthcoming. He'd be put on ice for eternity.

"She *did* volunteer the replication risk," Mallory said as they took the elevator back to the meeting-room floor.

"She wanted to scare us and show us she was cooperating at the same time, like a good little government employee. We're forced to take a leap of faith, so score one for her. She thinks she's gamed us."

"I agree," Mallory said. "But I say we don't query her about the testing going on at Pharmco. It keeps suspicion away from Emma."

"I don't know, Mal. It sounds like the military is meddling with something they don't know enough about under the pretext of making progress on the DOD government contract. I'm getting the feeling that one hand doesn't know what the other is doing. I'll bet Miss Johnson isn't aware. We should find out."

"Maybe you're right." Mallory looked McKenzie in the eyes. "I *would* like to know how high up what they're doing here goes. Let's play it by ear. See if we can find out. Maybe allude to the status of Pharmco's government project without letting on we know anything."

"What have you decided?" Ms. Johnson blurted as Mallory and McKenzie reentered the room, all evidence of cordiality absent. She was standing with her arms folded."

McKenzie looked at his watch. "Sorry we took so long. It seemed like only a few minutes, but I see it's been fifteen. Sorry."

"We've decided to cooperate," Mallory said, facing her. "But no surveillance, no gizmos, no GPS, no phone taps. And you need to realize we can't control Phelps or promise he'll buy into this. He has his own agenda."

"I can live with that as long as you share what he knows, or thinks he knows. Very shortly, our people will no doubt pick him up, and I'll deal with him."

Mallory face was turning red. "Miss Johnson, we'll have to level with Mister Phelps, and you need to keep him in the field, free to do his thing."

"What is his thing? We need to know how he was able to track Parnevik without the resources our ground teams employ."

"Well, he has this psychic gift. He can partially see, I mean perceive, Parnevik's recent past—"

"Miss Driscoll, I realize he has been credited with several documented tracking assists in crimes brought successfully to a close because of his insight, but we can't base our efforts in this critical situation on paranormal mumbo-jumbo."

"It's not mumbo-jumbo. Because of his *gift*, we know Parnevik didn't die on the Mer de Glace glacier. He staged the event, walked away, and spent the night partying in Chamonix."

"That's just hearsay to me, Miss Driscoll. There's no evidence. Our people are in Chamonix at this moment, waiting for the stubborn French police to comply with a diplomatic directive to share their final incident report and release all evidence to the CDC in Atlanta. We can tie the forensics to the Parnevik DNA we have from his residence and clothing—cooperatively provided by Mister Phelps and yourselves. Then we'll make our own evaluation. For now, the position is that Parnevik died on the glacier."

"Look, lady." Mallory grit her teeth. "Phelps thinks he's about fifteen hours away from Parnevik in real time. You've got to open yourself to valuing his input. Do I gather correctly you are unaware of the Arthur Dubois identity he's presently using?"

"We weren't privy to that information."

McKenzie threw Mallory a glance of confirmation. The two women looked like two peacocks facing off.

"Well, I suggest you get on it." Mallory said. "As Dubois, he used credit cards in Chamonix. He stayed at the—oh, what's the name?" She gave McKenzie a forlorn glance.

McKenzie's face was blank, and then suddenly he blurted, "Hotel Alpina."

"Thanks. Sorry I'm jumping on this alone," she said, locking her gaze on McKenzie.

"You're doing just fine." McKenzie nodded and stepped next to her, facing Ms. Johnson.

"He's arriving in Atlanta," she blustered on, "via New York City from Marseilles at four-thirty this afternoon."

Ms. Johnson searched Mallory's face. "Who?"

"Dubois. And maybe you could check this out. A—guess who—Julian Trebar visited the North Korean embassy in Paris on the afternoon of January 8th. Of course, I'm sure you knew that too."

The DSO agent's face flushed; the wrinkles around her mouth deepened. "I'll get on it. We should be able to verify Dubois in minutes. Please wait here while I go outside to do a little communicating."

Five minutes later, Ms. Johnson, still engrossed on her cell phone, came down the corridor and tapped on the glass wall, signaling them she was coming back inside.

She didn't skip a beat, starting in as she packed away her laptop. "I've given your information to the Military Intelligence teams in France. One is already in Chamonix as I've said. They will check out Dubois. I hope you're right about this. Another team will attempt to confirm the North Korean contact in Paris. If Dubois is aboard a flight to New York, and if we can make it in time, we'll be waiting. If we miss him, there will be dozens of Atlanta police, DEA, and Colonel Blackburn's Military Intelligence people at the airport to greet Mister Parnevik in Atlanta.... I appreciate your cooperation. Now, please sit down and take a few moments to recall any other pertinent information received from Mister

Phelps. If this pans out, it appears I will have to embrace the veracity of your friend's gift."

"We'll stand if you don't mind." Mallory glanced at McKenzie. She was perturbed at being directed here and there by this woman. It didn't seem to indicate equality in their new cooperative relationship.

McKenzie shrugged. "I don't guess you'd like to know who's buying Parnevik's *Amor*?"

"Of course we would. When the time comes, we'll need to snuff out all ends of this fiasco."

"Well, Phelps says he knows," McKenzie led in, "but he won't tell us until he returns to the States."

"And Parnevik has a business deal unfolding with a tea boutique in Lyon," Mallory said. "He posed as Julian Trebar, so it shouldn't be too difficult to ferret out."

"My, my, this gets more disturbing by the minute. And when will Mister Phelps be gracing our presence?"

"He said he'd be in touch," Mallory answered. "But I know he doesn't want any interference, so I don't think he'll be very cooperative." She hesitated. Her thoughts were pouring out without a filter, and she held back. One thing was for sure: the closer Smythe was to Parnevik, the clearer he was able to sense his activities and the nearer in real time he got. So by now, he had to be on his way to Atlanta. She decided to keep that under wraps. She and McKenzie were needed as long as they had access to current information from Smythe. No telling what would happen if that terminated.

"We need to have an understanding of liaison with him for the record," Ms. Johnson said. "Even though it will be verbal. Will you facilitate that? You have my word whichever way it goes, we'll leave him on his own if that's what he wants."

"We'll give it a try when he makes contact." McKenzie tried to look serious, but Ms. Johnson wasn't noticing, reverting back to packing up.

"Thank you," she said, abruptly making eye contact. She grabbed her raincoat off the back of her chair and moved toward the glass door.

"There's one more thing, Miss Johnson," Mallory said, still standing and blocking her way. "What is the status of the government project at Pharmco? From what you've told us and reading between the lines, the military wants successful completion of the research contract. I'm wondering if anyone has thought about making sure overzealous actions to accomplish military objectives don't take place, putting the public at risk for a colossal accident." Mallory canted her head and pursed her lips.

"I am not up to speed on that end and will check it out.... In light of our new détente, I'll get back to you if it's appropriate. It'll only take minutes to get confirmation of this Dubois flight. If it's a go, I'll be tied up organizing the airport intercessions. If it goes down at the Atlanta airport, would you two like to attend the party?"

McKenzie thought she sounded a little haughty, self-satisfied, a hint of a smirk on her face. "You may find this useful." McKenzie pawed through his layered clothing and retrieved a folded-up copy of the faxed sketch Smythe had sent earlier that morning and handed it to her. "It's Dubois."

She scanned it. "I assume you got this from Phelps.... Thanks. I'll call you as soon as I know something, so please stay available."

***

Several minutes later huddled under an umbrella, Mallory and McKenzie were clomping down the marble steps of the library and racing for McKenzie's rental car parked in the multi-story public lot next door.

"She's going to want to put a collar on Smythe," Mallory howled against the buffeting rain and wind. "And she's directed us to stand-by. She just wants to keep an eye on us."

"I concur, but actually I thought it went quite well. She seemed to accept that Smythe could be left to his own devices."

"We can't trust her, and we need to keep Smythe appraised or I'm afraid they will put an end to his *investigating* permanently. I wish we could find out if they really *can* tap into these new phones. Until we know for sure, I think our window is short for using them to convey anything important to Smythe. So, that means we call him right away. And it means we'll have to figure out how to get debugged.... We should call Eddie Chou in Shanghai and see if he can convince us the Chinese phone system is hack-proof."

 Fifty-eight

Christine Johnson

SHE SLID INTO the bank of pay phones on the way out of the library. "Colonel Blackburn, this is Christine Johnson.... Yes, I'm on my way to our meeting. I need to know when you've penetrated the Chinese satellite phones. And I want Mallory Driscoll and Agent McKenzie under total surveillance—everything you've got."

"Miss Johnson, that is already in place. We will discuss it further when you arrive."

She didn't like the patronizing tone. "Colonel, one more item. Anything yet on the Dubois identity switch, credit cards, flight itinerary?"

"We're working on it. You didn't tell me what the source was."

"A highly reliable source, Colonel, and I need the information now. I hope that's clear. His probable disposition somewhere over the Atlantic Ocean makes it a priority."

"What is this reliable source?"

"We will discuss it further when I see you." She hung up, feeling guilty having to mislead Mallory and McKenzie, and she sensed it wouldn't be the last time she'd be on the receiving end of macho reluctance from the colonel. This spy business was not within her purview.

The meeting at Atlanta PD with Colonel Blackburn was brief, the content cursory, and Christine Johnson felt a hollow spot in the pit of her stomach. The information she requested about the Dubois alias and his alleged activities was still unreported. A copy of the Chamonix police report listed Parnevik as missing and presumed dead. That wasn't a surprise, but the forensic evidence collected around the crash scene was on its way to the U.S. Army's bio-labs at Fort Belvoir in D.C. It should have gone to the CDC in Atlanta where the samples of Parnevik's DNA had been processed.

Military Intelligence wasn't fully cooperating. The colonel had an attitude problem, an army thing, a female thing, whatever. Abruptly it was clear; she'd had little real briefing from them and was being insulated from their investigation. What she knew had come from Mallory Driscoll, Agent McKenzie, and Dickerson Phelps. It was time to inform her DARPA superiors.

Ms. Johnson snuck down the hall from Colonel Blackburn's temporary office, through the Atlanta PD bullpen, and tapped on Capt. Trussel's glass door. "I need a favor, Captain."

She waited in his conference room. Ten minutes later, he rang her on the intercom with the Dubois landing information and credit card history. Perhaps the captain had a soft spot for the lady from DARPA.

Part V

R

The Chase

 Fifty-nine

Marseilles, France

A CAB DELIVERED Parnevik from the train station to Marseilles' Provence Airport, 27 km. northwest of the city. He had over two hours before Dubois's scheduled flight to Atlanta, via Lisbon and New York City. He paid the cabbie and entered the departure terminal for Iberia Airlines. Next, he went to the ticket counter and received his packet of boarding passes for the flight. He stored his large bag in a pay locker next to a string of food and beverage kiosks and processed through customs and security with his carry-on bag.

In the departure waiting lounge, it took less than half an hour to ferret out and cultivate the avarice of a passenger waiting for the flight to Lisbon. On the pretense Parnevik, as Dubois, didn't care for his assigned aisle seat, he exchanged boarding pass packets with an American man about his age and physical build traveling alone on his way back from business to Atlanta. It was incredible what money could buy.

After the exchange, heart racing, Parnevik visited the restroom across from the waiting area. Then, making sure the man he'd exchanged passes with wasn't watching, he retreated back down the concourse, smiling, jubilant, blending in with the flowing traffic of arriving passengers headed for baggage claim.

He retrieved his bag from the locked bin, returned to the main terminal area, checked the arrival board, and took a seat in the waiting area for the American Express office. The flight from Asunción via Barcelona was on time. He looked at his watch. Adding ten minutes to deplane, the messenger should be there within twenty minutes.

Parnevik's heart rate rose as the armed courier entered the American Express office with a cuffed satchel. The thought suddenly stabbed him that everything could go wrong if his man in Asuncion had not done his job. Panic gripped him and he grabbed his suitcase and over-the-shoulder carry-on. Deliberately—without undo haste—he willed himself to walk to the restroom. Cursed by the unwanted effects on his demeanor, he could not afford to draw attention. He took a stall for the disabled, pulled out a bottle of Evian water, and washed down an anti-neurotransmitter to soak up the dopamine, an Arthrotec for the pain, and a Valium to smooth it all out.

Ten minutes later, he emerged, trepidation abated. All he wanted now was to relax, climb into a first-class seat, and enjoy a comfortable trip across the Atlantic. But first, he had work to do.

With the American Express package safely tucked away in his shoulder bag, he took a shuttle the short distance from the airport to the lobby of the Hôtel Balladins. He paid cash for a day's access to the health club.

Locking himself in a private massage room, it required forty minutes to access his equipment kit, insert the picture of Professor Harold Pedersen, PhD, into his new U.S. passport, enter the appropriate passport stamps, review the dossier, and examine his new credit cards and driver's license.

Professor Phillip Pedersen, PhD, was a Pennsylvanian Quaker, son of a furniture maker, who disappeared last year without a trace while visiting his father in the little town of Sonesburg,

Germany. He'd always been a loner, without family or friends to question his comings and goings, led a Spartan life, and worked as a researcher at the Penn State Nanofabrication Facility located on the main campus at University Park, PA. The university hadn't questioned his abrupt letter of resignation based on family medical problems.

Admiring himself in the mirror, Parnevik was elated with his new disguise. He repacked his bags, exited the health club, and shuttled back to the airport. A few minutes later, lined up with his bags at the *Portugália* Airlines ticket counter, he purchased a cash ticket to Charlotte, NC, via Paris and New York City, arriving in Charlotte on Delta at 8:45 p.m. He would have plenty of time to renew himself in the luxury of first class, continue to memorize his new character, and ponder the modus operandi of his pursuers.

 Sixty

Atlanta Hartsfield International Airport

FRESH FROM THE library meeting with Ms. Johnson, Mallory and McKenzie made a quick stop at Emma's apartment to check e-mail, call Eddie Chou, and then hit the Chick-fil-A drive-through.

They pulled out of the fast-food restaurant, intending to take the meal back to Emma's and relax, but both their government satellite phones went off simultaneously, and minutes later they found themselves airport-bound, driving the congested I-75/85 corridor through downtown Atlanta and on to Hartsfield International. Ms. Johnson had informed them they'd missed Dubois in the short New York stop-over. He was due to arrive in Atlanta at 4:30 p.m. A greeting party was in preparation.

"At least the rain let up," McKenzie said as he carefully entered the stream of traffic branching off onto I-85 toward the airport exit.

"So, I guess we use the phones," McKenzie said.

"I believe what Eddie said. The Chinese launched satellites to solve the same problem. They randomly change the encryption logarithms daily. His firm relies on the system."

"Well, we should still watch what we say."

A few silent moments went by as the traffic thinned out.

"Rymac, let's listen to the tape and make sure we didn't miss anything. The airport's still twenty minutes out."

"Good idea." McKenzie fumbled in his jacket pocket, pulled out the recorder, and handed it to Mallory. She depressed the Play button. Nothing happened. She pressed Rewind, waited—Pressed Play again—nothing. Fast-forward, Play—nothing.

"What's the matter?"

Mallory scowled and stared out the window. "It's blank. She must have had a jamming gadget in that briefcase of hers. So much for our new *détente*."

***

Before parking in the short-term lot, McKenzie drove the Taurus rental up the arrival lane at the airport to get a feel for the situation.

"What's the FBI doing here?" Mallory asked as McKenzie maneuvered the car to the outside lane. Jacketed officers were milling around in front of the building. Yellow tape cordoned off a hundred-foot sector of the inner two lanes in front of the international arrival doors, and three black Suburbans with their engines running lined the curb ten feet apart. A dozen Atlanta PD officers were posted at opposite ends of the inner lanes, presumably ready to stop traffic and facilitate a quick exit.

"How would I know? I'm going around to park. Call the lady and see what's up."

Mallory punched in Ms. Johnson's speed code on the government phone. "Hey, we're here, heading for the parking lot. What's with the FBI?"

"I'll explain when you get here. Just come through the arrival doors at Air Jamaica. We're set up in the airport manager's office on the second floor above the mezzanine. Take the stairs. The guard knows to let you through." Mallory heard the dead sound of the phone shut off and looked at McKenzie.

"Well?"

"Park it near Air Jamaica. She's going to explain when we get inside."

***

The elevator was taped off, so Mallory and McKenzie climbed the stairs to the administrative offices. Christine Johnson came out one of the doors along the second-floor catwalk and hung over the rail. "We've got half an hour before he lands." She nodded at the guard to let them pass and then disappeared back behind the door.

McKenzie led the way. "That's supposed to mean follow her inside," he barked over his shoulder.

As they came through the door, Ms. Johnson said, "Please take a seat." She gestured toward a long glass table in the center of the room where three men stood. This was obviously the airport operations center. One sidewall was glass, looking out over the vehicle arrival-lanes and the three-story parking area.

Files and papers were scattered on the tabletop, surrounded at intervals by eight, futuristic chrome chairs. A roll-in cart next to the table held coffee, assorted beverages, and lunch items. The inside wall contained six contiguous workstations housing surveillance monitors covering the airport.

Ms. Johnson introduced the FBI's Atlanta Station Director and the airport's general manager.

"We know each other," Capt. Trussel gruffly inserted, nodding. The Atlanta PD chief moved to the cart, scowling as he poured himself a coffee refill and sat down at the table. Mallory felt for him, having to kowtow in his own backyard to Military Intelligence and now the FBI.

"Miss Johnson, you mind telling us what the FBI is doing here?" Mallory said. Neither she nor McKenzie had elected to sit down.

"Gentlemen." Ms. Johnson cast her gaze over the men at the table. "Could you give us a few minutes?"

They shuffled out of the room without a word.

"Things have been moving in several different directions since this morning's library meeting." Ms. Johnson smiled and motioned to the roll-in cart.

Mallory gave her the once-over. She looked particularly composed, dressed in a dark gray suit with an orange and light blue DARPA logo over the blazer's right breast pocket. She wore black and gray cross-trainers, making her appear even shorter than the five-four she estimated. Her sandy hair was efficiently barretted back above the ears. She wore little makeup, but her eyes sparkled through the lenses of an unusual green-and-black-patterned frame, producing a commanding air.

"I don't want anything, thank you." Mallory crossed her arms and cast glances around the operating space. "What's happening?"

"We were able to verify the visit by Julian Trebar to the North Korean Embassy in Paris. Don't ask me how. This is a most disturbing event. The possibility of secret scientific information falling into the hands of the unpredictable North Koreans is now a major concern. The investigation was ratcheted up. The State Department and the FBI are now fully involved. Together they represent the international diplomatic resources and investigative manpower to deal with this. I think you will be pleased to hear that Army Military Intelligence was placed on hold regarding its investigative and administrative duties. There will be no experimenting at Pharmco…. I gather you got wind of this from a friend whose name we won't need to know?"

"I really don't recall." Mallory looked at her watch. "Well, what's the plan?"

McKenzie strode to the food and beverage cart and grabbed a pre-packaged chicken salad sandwich. "Anybody want anything?" he asked, goading them both.

"Nothing." Mallory leered at him, wondering how he could be flippant at a time like this.

Ignoring Mallory's question, Ms. Johnson adjusted her blazer and headed for a bank of portable monitors organized against a section of a long glass window overlooking the catwalk and the international arrival concourse. "We can watch it from here. The three on the far left are set up for the operation. The first one is outside and will scan the docking canopy when it's rolled out for the plane—Look, the camera's panning. It's catching the plane's approach.... The middle one is inside showing the arrival bay, and the third is covering the view from the security entrance down the concourse toward the arrival gate. She pointed at the middle one. "There's a plain-clothes, FBI snatch team mixed in with the passengers waiting to board. The plane's going on to Miami. It should be an easy apprehension."

Mallory had positioned herself next to Ms. Johnson. "How do you know he's on the plane?"

McKenzie stood behind them munching on the chicken salad sandwich.

"We were able to verify he got on the plane at Marseilles from the boarding passes checked through. He was already over the Atlantic by the time our meeting ended this morning, but we got a message to the federal marshal aboard the flight to visually confirm that Dubois' seat was taken and to come back with a description."

"We gave you Smythe's sketch," Mallory reminded her.

"We had no way to get it to him. The plane didn't have the latest Internet technology. We gave him a general verbal description, Caucasian, dark short hair, mid-thirties, 180 pounds, probably dressed casual. Anyway, the marshal confirmed. He's been directed to exit the plane behind Dubois, and the FBI team will be waiting to collar him the minute he comes through the exit tunnel into the waiting area."

"What if it's not him?" McKenzie raised his eyebrows.

Ms. Johnson pointed to the monitors, paying no attention. "It's docked. Should only be a few more minutes. Here's a picture of the marshal." She handed Mallory a three-by-five photo. She snapped a handheld radio off her belt. "Team leader, everything's a go. You need to line up at the airline counter and interact with the service attendants. Look businesslike. And make sure you have people ready to block the curious once you engage." Mallory and McKenzie could clearly hear the "roger that" reply.

"So we watch," Ms. Johnson said, but her posture in front of the monitors was stiff as if she was wondering whether she'd overlooked something.

Mallory stood straight, watching everything that moved on the screens. Elation stirred. They were finally going to get the maniac. He wasn't so smart after all. She turned to take a quick look at McKenzie, who was still stuffing his face.

"Okay, they're starting to come through," Ms. Johnson said. "Dubois should be somewhere in the middle. There are two hundred and eleven passengers. Everyone was ordered to disembark so the plane can be serviced. In another hour, it will reload for Miami. There's the marshal," Ms. Johnson said.

The moment the marshal laid a hand on the shoulder of the man in front of him, the FBI agents were all over him.

"That doesn't look like the Dubois in the sketch," Mallory said.

"I agree." McKenzie had tossed the remainder of his sandwich in a wastebasket. "His physique is about the same but not his face. Maybe he changed his appearance."

"He didn't do it on the plane," Ms. Johnson snapped. "The marshal would have reported. And he didn't do it in Marseilles. His passport photo would have to match him when he checked in *and* when he went through security."

The radio cracked as they watched the monitor. The FBI team spread the suspect against the far wall of the concourse walkway and began a thorough search.

Suddenly a flight attendant filled the monitor picture as she ran past the camera toward the Federal Air Marshal, waving a sheet of paper.

"We've got him, Govy Six," Ms. Johnson's phone belched. "Hold one.... A stewardess has just brought us a fax from the plane. She got it when the airport Wi-Fi kicked in.... It's a drawing that's supposed to be him. This isn't the guy. His passport says his name is Larry Kenfield. Hold on. He's kind of shook up.... He says he's an accountant working in Atlanta.... I gave him the sketch.... He says that was the guy who gave him two hundred dollars to exchange boarding passes. He says he never saw him again and didn't look for him on the plane. What do you want to do with him?"

"Standard operating procedure. Run him through the mill as if he were a terrorist suspect. Bring him up here first." She clicked off the radio. "Shit, this is a fiasco."

She pulled her satellite phone from the case at her belt and spent the next ten minutes briefing her DSO boss, resulting in direction to take an early-morning flight to DC. A full review would take place at 10:00 a.m. She was to summarize all available information in advance and send it through DARPA's secure emailing system. The DOD Oversight Committee would meet during the night to redefine the mission.

 Sixty-one

Peachtree Plaza Hotel

Parnevik hired a one-way car rental from Charlotte and, exhausted, finally settled into a Peachtree Plaza Hotel suite around 11:30 p.m. It had been the only room available.

Setting up his laptop on a small, polished rosewood table, he felt wary, unsure he'd covered all the loose ends. He threw open the curtains to the balcony view of the city some twenty-one stories below and waited for room service to deliver nutty, Osetra caviar, Egyptian wheat crackers, and an ice-cold bottle of French Sauvignon Blanc. The thought of those favorite tastes ameliorated his uneasiness.

Gradually, he was gaining confidence in his new identity. The feeling of vulnerability would pass. It always did.... Whoever was tracking him was far behind. It certainly couldn't be the Genovese, even if they'd discovered their mutual friend in Paraguay. And it wouldn't be the Atlanta PD; they no longer had jurisdiction. The Genovese had informed him had taken over at Pharmco, and Military Intelligence was responsible for all continuing police investigations. Parnevik understood their dilemma: the DOD contract was in jeopardy, the fiasco at Pharmco had to be kept quiet, and they needed him.

The restful time spent on the Atlantic crossing hadn't generated a smidgen of new insight, but the uneventful rent-a-car drive from Charlotte to Atlanta produced a feasible conclusion: it had to be the FBI, and with their unlimited resources, he'd have to be doubly vigilant.

Room service arrived, and he seated himself back at the table. The distraction of such fine food took his attention. He hadn't realized how hungry he was.

Five minutes elapsed. Abruptly, he set his napkin down and rose to stretch. Tightness had collected in his midsection, and he started pacing, the remainder of his meal forgotten. His mind pushed a steady stream of lamentations over the unfairness of his world onto his consciousness screen. The beautiful home he could never return to. A career of respect he could in no way recover. Lost recognition of achievements gone to the credit of others. Sacrificed production capabilities at his beloved fire station. Even the soured relationship he'd attempted with Emma Kisumi.

He'd been through this process innumerable times, involuntarily perseverating over the same facts, feeling the rage. He always came to the same conclusions: He'd done it all for the sake of humanity. He had led the way by innovating—cutting the laborious testing timetable required by antiquated bureaucracies. Special stalwart individuals made sacrifices to protect and benefit the masses. He was the good shepherd. He had the knowledge—the skills and creativity—and the forethought to give birth to a utopian world…. But in order to continue, he had to maintain control. He must use his wits and wealth, *stay the course—execute the plan.*

As his anxiety dissipated, it became clear: the only way the Feds could have caught up with him was due to his presence at The Flying Store in Gap-Tallard. Taking a seat facing his laptop, he realized he was fortunate to have been successful in Chamonix;

he had remained Dubois when he stayed in town recovering from the dive. As he'd predicted, poor Eva had spread his plan to break the record to Flying Store personnel, and soon after he'd departed Gap-Tallard, the Internet had been full of comments from his detractors and jealous competition—the incessant Twitter and Facebook. *That* had placed him in Chamonix. The solitary action that kept him from discovery had been changing back to Dubois after his tremendous feat and his oh-so-clever deception at the glacier crevasse.

No matter who was after him now, and if they had somehow caught on to Arthur Dubois, the trail should have run cold at the Atlanta airparthort. The precaution of paying his way in cash since Chamonix had provided him with added insurance. Everything felt back in its proper place. He was in control. He took a deep breath, mentally completing the retrace to the present. Nothing could link him to Professor Harold Pedersen.

In the near term, Dr. Pedersen was about to be resurrected—at least for one last research project. Self-assurance on the rebound, and the last fingers of tension draining from his neck and shoulders, Parnevik connected to the hotel's Wi-Fi system, entered the appropriate codes to access his encrypted email software, and brought up his management program, thoughts drifting to the next moves on the chessboard.

Soft chiming signaled he had unread email. He sat paralyzed in front of his laptop. The email notice had elicited a fleeting shot of excitement. He quickly opened the email sent to his protected Genovese address. It was from a Chinese website server. He'd left that email address with the North Korean Embassy in Paris along with his proposal memorandum.

The email held a website link and directed him to follow it, stating that the link would disappear once followed, and the website page would delete thirty seconds after the email was opened. There was no signature.

Captivated by the esoteric nature of the contact, he clicked the link. A page opened showing Parnevik's proposition, including the demonstration date and proposed meeting location: 5:00 p.m., January 30th, at the lounge bar, Marriott Cornhusker Hotel in downtown Lincoln, Nebraska, near the University of Nebraska main campus.

Two lines of text were at the bottom: *Dear Mr. Trebar/Parnevik: Our representative, Mr. Hwang Jang, will be present at the appointed time and place.*

How had they discovered his real name? He would do well to realize that spies were everywhere.

The mystery fading, he realized his energy was waning. He needed rest. Fresh in the morning, he would attack the next elements of his plan: a working lab to produce product, and a methodology for remaining insulated from pursuit.

 Sixty-two

Elkhorn City, Kentucky

TITUS SMYTHE HELD tightly to the sturdy support pole with one hand as he stepped down and out through the bus's double doors, the other hand leading the way with his beat-up, tan duffle bag.

Elkhorn City was a little town of under two thousand souls nestled in the foothills of the Appalachian Mountains of Eastern Kentucky, merely a Greyhound bus stop along Highway 80, 150 miles west of Blacksburg, Virginia.

It had been a thirteen-hour nightmare since deplaning in Washington DC: cramped space, seedy passengers, bodily odors, screaming children, fast food stops, boredom, bags and sacks everywhere, and little sleep aside from an occasional nod-off. Bodies exited and arrived at every stop, keeping the aging bus packed like a can of sardines. Elkhorn City was stop number fifty-one.

The airbrakes hissed and the bus groaned on, leaving a gritty trail of black exhaust. Smythe looked at his watch, blessing the quiet and fresh air that enveloped him. Nine thirty-five in the morning and he was stiff, thirsty, and in desperate need of a shower and a long, uninterrupted night's sleep.

***

Smythe had arrived at Washington D.C.'s Reagan National Airport in the early evening from Marseilles via Paris. His first order of business was packaging up no longer required clothing and personal effects from his trek in the French mountains. A UPS store in the terminal facilitated sending the package to Mrs. Leonard back in Rabun, Georgia. Smythe also instituted some changes to the way he looked and dressed, no longer the Irish academic clothed in a natty tweed blazer and corduroy pants, an umbrella a constant companion.

When he exited the stall for the disabled in the airport restroom, he was a tattered-looking old man with long, curly gray-brown hair and a stringy brown beard. He was clothed in a wool, checkered work shirt, khaki bib trousers, and a black brimmed hat with foldout earmuffs—the way he presented himself the last time he visited this town as Dickerson Phelps, Private Detective, licensed in the State of Georgia. He was hoping some of the Elkhorn town folk might still recognize him.

During the time he'd spend here, he would pay cash for necessities, as he always had while working a case, and dissolve into Kentucky Appalachia.

***

The oak-log Clinchfield Railroad Station sat in the middle of town. Now renovated, the polished, ancient grey planks of its boardwalk led to a gift shop, post office, small Chamber of Commerce stall, and a hole-in-the-wall ticket counter. Three restored rail cars, an antique steam engine, and a caboose rested on a rail cutout next to the stationhouse. They would stand idle until the summer tourist season renewed the train's plodding over the sixteen-mile route up the hillsides, skirting the white water sections of the scenic Russell Fork River.

Smythe took the steps up to the stationhouse platform and walked the boardwalk to a slatted waiting bench with a view down the tracks and along the main street. He brushed the peeling green surface of the bench with a gloved hand and took a seat.

Long ago, Elkhorn City had shriveled up, as had hundreds of other small towns in the southeast affected by the movement of textile, apparel, and furniture manufacturing to cheap, overseas labor pools.

The town didn't appear to have changed much since his last visit. Mr. Franklin's general store in the center of the downtown strip was still the prominent building, and across the street he could see the neon sign poking up on top of Becky's little diner. But the old, three-story rooming house where he'd stayed for two nights had been replaced with a CITGO gas station. He'd have to stay in the Day's Inn at the edge of town if he wanted to clean up and get some sleep, unless he could get a lead on a local room from the bulletin board at Franklin's General Store. It would be a blessing not to have to avoid the motel's surveillance cameras.

He sucked in the crisp fresh air and was grateful for a few moments of silence. It had been a similar early morning in September 1986, when Smythe experienced his first foray as a private detective. He'd disembarked right here from the then-active Chesapeake & Ohio passenger train.

Smythe had been working with the Philadelphia Police Department to help capture a ruthless serial killer, who for four years had been stalking nurses in the metro area, brutally defacing them and slitting their throats. Smythe's gift was of great value to the police, but as was the case with the present search for Parnevik, he was unable to track closer than fifteen hours from real time. It stymied him, and that's when he'd stumbled across the Hagger Clan.

The clan had lived for generations in the *hollows*, locally pronounced "hollers," outside of Elkhorn City. They were proud of their subsistence life style: thriving in the natural environment, hunting, fishing, and gathering in the Jefferson National Forest; gardening, bee keeping, and raising chickens, goats and hogs. There were fifty or more clan members—depending on who was counting—and they gathered twice per month in town to trade with the locals for what they needed. The few times nature had turned her back on their production routines, the clan men went to work in the coalmines to bridge the gap.

The Hagger Clan also raised dogs—very special dogs—loosely referred to as Bluegrass Bloodhounds, the oldest and largest breed of hounds hunting entirely by scent. At the time of Smythe's last visit, Pappy Hagger, the ranking clan leader, was running the breeding kennel. Their bloodhounds brought the highest prices in Appalachia.

Smythe had heard a fable in a local Philadelphia pub, a story reading like a fairytale, about a bloodhound who could follow a trail as old as a month, even on cement. Over the years, local journalists had written several articles centered on the dog's amazing abilities. One instance reported the dog had successfully tracked criminal suspects traveling in a vehicle. In another incident, he followed a prison escapee on a twelve-mile trolley ride through the city of Paducah, Kentucky.

The Haggers had allowed Smythe to borrow Alfred. With the dog's ability, the Philadelphia Police Department ran the killer to ground in twenty-four hours. The regional population was ecstatic with the apprehension, but the Philadelphia PD put the clamps on the amazing story. Both Smythe and Alfred's assistance never made it into the public record; the police felt it would be deleterious to the image of their city's law enforcement agency to credit the capture to a person and an animal with paranormal abilities.

Smythe rose from the bench and set the straps of his worn duffle to backpack mode, just as he'd done so many years ago. It was unlikely, considering the intervening years, for Pappy to have remained at the head of the Hagger Clan; he must have been in his sixties back then. But, he'd find out soon enough. Franklin's General Store was just up the street.

It turned out the manager of Franklin's was the son of Fred Franklin, whom Smythe remembered quite fondly. Back in '86, Fred had sat patiently as Dickerson Phelps poured out the horrific story over four years of murderous tragedy that had befallen Philadelphia. He had been so very accommodating, directing him to the Haggar's breeding kennel, writing an introductory note to Papa Haggar, and offering Smythe his Ford Ranger. He'd even insisted while he was in town that Smythe take lodging in a rooming house nearby operated by his wife, Greta.

Fred Jr. was equally empathetic, absorbing Smythe's discourse of events surrounding the search for Parnevik and offering his assistance. The kennel was located in the same hollow, a glacially carved-out bowl between two ridgelines some twenty miles from town, and although Pappy was still alive and kicking, his eldest son, Raymond, had succeeded him as the Hagger Clan's leader.

Fred Jr.'s review of town news since Smythe's last visit revealed little had changed in the backwoods Kentucky town. He was kind enough to make a few calls on Smythe's behalf, and by noon Smythe found himself in the comfortable back room of a small house near the middle of town. The gentle widower who volunteered the accommodation informed Smythe he was welcome to take the evening meal with her at 6:00 p.m. sharp as long as he freshened up a bit. She also offered the use of her twenty-year-old Subaru the next day if he would top off the gas.

 Sixty-three

North Korea

TWELVE DAYS HAD elapsed since the Parnevik individual, posing as the Canadian Julian Trebar, hand delivered his memorandum to the North Korean embassy in Paris.

The file in front of Hwang Jang was two inches thick, the contents currently spread out on top of a cheap, eight-foot-long table taking up one wall of his office. The room was bare bones, claustrophobic, like a sterile operating room without the medical equipment: cement block walls, ten-foot ceilings, high square windows, off-yellow latex paint, squares of shiny gray linoleum reeking of disinfectant. He was scanning the contents of the file into his computer, page by page, making notes and moving related pages into sub-files.

He thought he had a realistic picture of this man: a demented soul, lost in the foul soup of western intrigue and capitalistic plundering. Dr. Corey Parnevik was a brilliant researcher, broken and enslaved by his own government. His sanity had been controlled by drug therapy since he was a teenager in an attempt to normalize behavior driven by genetic deficiencies—a mind permanently skewed by the effects of an imbalance in chemical neurotransmitters affecting his autonomic systems.

An Oxford-trained psychiatrist, Hwang Jang empathized with the man's evolved personality disorders: fits of obsessive-compulsive behavior, depression, the need to succeed, desire to strike out, antisocial conduct, the complete lack of conscience, disdain for moral and ethical responsibility, and incapacitating paranoia.

The memorandum delivered to the North Korean Embassy in Paris had passed to the Research Department for External Intelligence (RDEI) in Pyongyang. Its North American subsection had subsequently produced the research, and the Central Committee had immediately authorized action by the Department of Integrated Sciences, a misnomer for North Korea's secret studies of biological, chemical, and nuclear agents.

Located on a sprawling campus of buildings, surrounded by concertina wire and patrolled by military security personnel, the DIS was twenty miles outside the city limits of Pyongyang. Twelve hundred plus scientists and engineers daily processed through the gates. Medical technicians employed sophisticated scanners to examine the retinas and fingerprints of anyone entering each building, verifying identities and checking for any alterations against previous digital records.

Hwang Jang pushed his chair back from the computer workstation and rolled over to an HD monitor and the secure network computer utilized solely for communications. It was his responsibility to make recommendations.

An earlier PhD in pharmaceutical engineering at the University of Michigan had exposed him to nano environments, and yes, the premise of affecting behavior with a directed nano-agent programmed to stimulate sites in the brain was feasible. However, not a hint of this kind of research had come to his attention through the scientific journals, and searching the Internet produced old news.

The RDEI research of public records summarized Pharmco's nanite projects and the status of FDA-approved, animal testing programs using stimulant nanites to mitigate bulimic tendencies and help the brain repair synoptic pathways inhibiting memory. The potential applications were indeed mind-boggling. But how this demented researcher claimed to have solved the core problems was frightening. It wasn't the difficulty of producing engineering plans for a machine operated by software. But, to have created subroutines that directed the machine to miniaturize and replicate in a safely contained environment in the presence of calibrated raw materials, had never been accomplished. Many nano researchers were emphatic in their speculation such replication attempts could very well get out of hand and threaten the environment.

The final *coup d'état* was to have programmed the machine to replicate to a certain specified nano size. The exclusive use of sugar, a carbon-based raw material, was conclusively a mark of genius. The development of a three-dimensional body map by Pharmco was equally a unique achievement. But perhaps most exceptional, in its twisted way, were the fail-safes Parnevik claimed to have built into the structure of his creations. He programmed an auto-destruct into his products, eliminating the possibility of analysis or tampering.

As Deputy Director of DIS, Hwang Jang's responsibility was to decide what to do and how to do it. His decision was to move forward with the test Parnevik had proposed in his memorandum. The first thing he needed was approval from the Central Committee of the Korean Worker's Party. Then, he could require full cooperation from the General Intelligence Bureau. Traveling to the United States for a demonstration would require credentials, a background history, a legitimate business scenario, and extraction contingency plans. He would direct the Intelligence Bureau to form a surveillance team in the U.S. to monitor Parnevik's activities and afford Jang in-country protection. Secure communications would be essential.

He sat in his roller chair, contemplating. The situation was personally daunting. It had been seven years since Jang's last trip outside the country, receiving permission to visit his mother in Australia after she'd sustained injuries from a freak car accident in Sydney. Before that, it had been twenty years since Oxford University and twenty-five years since the University of Michigan.

He sighed. Many high-profile politicians had been briefed on the research produced and the awesome military potential of Parnevik's claims. Jang was surprised he hadn't heard from the military. That smelled like the handiwork of Party interests.

Ordered to report his recommendations directly to The Party, he bent to touch the dark monitor screen. It morphed to the log-in page for the Party's Central Committee.

 Sixty-four

Atlanta: Parnevik

A FITFUL NIGHT'S sleep found Parnevik tense and confused from the remnants of one of his standard nightmare themes: excruciating levels of frustration in not finding what he was looking for. This time it was searching for a bathroom under the duress and agony of a coming bowel movement.

He shook his head, took a few deep breaths, and made a curt call to room service. Hissing to himself, he scrambled to the bathroom for a hot shower. The shock of the heat always relaxed uptight muscles and the pounding at the back of his head.

He exited the bathroom, thankful for relief. Room service knocked as he doled out the morning's medications and finished toweling off. This was a day for planning tomorrow's events surrounding a young girl's birthday party.

His breakfast consumed, he noticed the time had crept into business hours. Before the day's scouting mission, he needed to make a nine thousand dollar cash withdrawal at Barclay's Atlanta branch, just under the limit for automatic reporting. Prior to his stateside flight from Marseilles, he'd visited a Barclay's branch and closed the Julian Trebar and Arthur Dubois relationships, subsequently opening and funding his Harold Pedersen account.

He chose to walk the short distance to the bank, and by the time he'd returned to his Peachtree Plaza hotel room a wall of apprehension had manifested. Tomorrow evening he was planning to let another person into a spoke of his planning wheel, and that meant he'd relinquish an element of control and incur additional risk.

 Sixty-five

Titus Smythe

FOLLOWING THE CHAOTIC mess at Hartsfield International, Mallory and McKenzie returned to Emma's house. They spent the evening and most of the early morning hours going through their personal effects looking for eavesdropping devices. McKenzie broke out his DEA debugger kit and checked out the house and their two vehicles. Ms. Johnson either had been good to her word or hadn't gotten around to bugging them.

Both of them were tuckered out and ready for what little sleep the remaining morning could provide, when Mallory's new satellite phone signaled from the kitchen. McKenzie plucked his out of his backpack and conferenced in.

"It's good of you to be so concerned," Smythe said after fielding Mallory's initial outbursts. "But please be assuaged, Miss Driscoll, I am perfectly fine, and yes, I do take the prescription dosages if in need."

Smythe was preparing to head out in the dark, early morning hours to visit the Hagger Kennels outside of Elkhorn City. He'd retired early after sharing a country meal with the kindly widow who'd offered him the room for the night. He'd slept soundly in the meticulously kept back bedroom. Six hours wrapped in a cozy featherbed blanket and surrounded in treasured silence had done wonders for his attitude. He'd taken time before calling Mallory to collect his bearings and sort out the glimpses of Parnevik's most recent movements and jumbled emotions.

"You are beginning to sound like Mrs. Leonard, endlessly badgering me with her motherly concerns."

"You're calling from a public phone, I hope. Where are you and—"

"Settle down, young lady—"

"Titus, listen to me." Mallory told him about Dubois not showing up on the flight from France and the possibility of an alliance with the DSO lady.

"So, the situation has tightened up," Smythe said. "But we knew that was going to happen. You must search your belongings, the apartment, and any vehicles you use, everything. Agent McKenzie should have those talents."

"We've already done it," McKenzie said. "So far everything is clean."

Mallory jumped in. "Titus, where are you? What are you planning, and where's Parnevik?"

"You needn't be concerned. All will soon be clear. As to Parnevik, he's managed another creative escape and has a new identity. I just picked up on it as I revived from a nice night's sleep. I know he came into the U.S. yesterday in the late afternoon through Charlotte with the intention of renting a car, and that brings me to the limit of my perception. If I am successful in my present endeavor, perhaps we will have a chance to trap him. I will be calling the police friend of mine in Philadelphia to try and narrow down where he's gone. It would most likely be a one-way rental. But, know this. His mental capabilities are deteriorating. His thinking is becoming convoluted—he perseverates over his decisions. The intensity of his paranoia and rage are increasing. This frustrates his need to dominate and control, a most dangerous escalation. I sense he may be intermittently taking his medications, or perhaps he has run out—another avenue of investigation you can offer to the authorities, gratis from me. However, for now, I suggest you do nothing to draw attention to yourselves. Trust me. I will call you no later than six p.m. tomorrow with a plan of action. Promise—"

"What's his name—?" Mallory pulled the phone away from her ear, exasperated. He'd hung up on her again. If he'd revealed Parnevik's new name, she and McKenzie could have started tracking him themselves. This was totally exasperating.

Talking to Smythe, Mallory had been pacing back and forth from the kitchen to the living room, mostly listening, while McKenzie was plugged into the call from the hall bathroom. "He hung up on me again," she grumbled, storming into the hallway, lips drawn tight.

"I heard," McKenzie said calmly, poking his head around the bathroom door. "Let's get some sack time. It's four in the morning."

 Sixty-six

Corey Parnevik

HE AWOKE WITH a dry tongue and a foul taste clinging to the roof of his mouth, standard for a typical night of restless dreaming: phantoms relentlessly chasing him, wanting to wound but not kill, always with long blades swinging and slashing, but they never caught him.

He washed his face with a washcloth soaked in water as hot as he could stand. Gulping down a glass of OJ with his medications, he scrambled to the phone and ordered room service; a continental breakfast would suffice.

He sat stiffly in a straight-backed chair, closed his eyes, held his throbbing head, and felt his heart rate subside as the meds hit his system. His faculties needed to be sharp to transact the morning's business.

Slowly the muscles of his neck and shoulders loosened and the throbbing faded. Anxiety eased, the dreams dissolving away into nothingness. As the process was transporting him to calm awareness, he remembered he was running out of critical medications.

Dressed in a conservative brown blazer, khaki Docksiders, an open-necked, white button-down shirt, and black and tan Sketcher shoes, he sat down at the settee along the balcony window. The early morning sun spilled city shadows over the western faces of the city-center buildings, and the gold-capped capital building gleamed like a jewel. He poured coffee and picked at the room-service tray, waiting for his laptop to boot up on the rosewood working desk.

The familiar ding and pop sounded, signaling that Skype had opened. The account had protected his anonymity on many occasions. Through an Internet connection, his subscription enabled telephone communications to any mobile or landline phone almost anywhere in the world. He'd set the program to disable caller ID and prohibit all in-coming calls.

It was time to set down the first layer of bricks in his master-piece. Doctor Edward Sarcorcee, Director of the Georgia Tech Nanotechnology Research Center, would act as the catalyst for solving his production problems. Then he'd enjoy dinner with Georgie Boy, an old engineering acquaintance. He'd call him at his workplace, and even if the despicable pea brain had plans, what he wanted to discuss with him would instantly take precedence. Everyone had his or her price, and George Randle was as avaricious as one could be.

 Sixty-seven

DOD Oversight Committee

CHRISTINE JOHNSON WAS considered a straight arrow by her co-workers. Dr. David Blanton, Director of DARPA's Defense Sciences Office (DSO) had worked closely with her for four years. She was a competent scientist with a PhD in biochemistry and was one of five DSO team leaders. Director Blanton had chosen her not only for her technical competencies, analytical abilities, and emotional stability, but also because she'd elected to utilize her Masters Degree in Law Enforcement to pursue a career, serving five years with the NYPD and climbing to the rank of homicide detective.

Blanton had met her on a case involving the death of a researcher in corporate America who was deeply associated with a DSO contract. He'd wooed her away to take responsibility for policing potential contract breaches across the gamut of the DSO's active top-secret projects. The DSO invested a great deal of taxpayer dollars in private markets to determine if promising scientific hypotheses, ideas, or inventions might have defense department applications. Its mission was to insure the DOD had constant access to "state of the art" scientific advancements.

The DOD Oversight Committee met at 10:00 a.m. sharp in the FBI's hallowed conference room inside the J. Edgar Hoover

Building. Present were: Curtis Mayborne, DOD's Director of the Defense Advanced Research Projects Agency (DARPA); Doctor David Blanton, DSO Director and Committee Chairman; Major General John Taggart, Commander of Army Military Intelligence; John Lindsay, Deputy Director of the FBI; Farris White, Deputy Administrator of the DEA; Christine Johnson, GS-17 (Rear Admiral equivalent) and DSO Special Investigator; and Dr. Amos Wrenthrow, Administrator of the Penn State Nanofabrication Facility.

The group sat around one end of a massive, polished oak conference table. Framed portraits of distinguished dignitaries lined all four walls. The room was soundproof and totally secure. U.S. Marines were posted at all four entrances.

At the termination of Christine Johnson's fifty-minute briefing, she stepped away from the podium at the head of the table and moved around a corner to occupy a leather swivel chair to the left of Curtis Mayborne. From the beginning, she'd been composed, businesslike, and direct, demonstrating professional competence.

"Thank you, Miss Johnson," Blanton said. He rose from his seat at the head of the table and shuffled in front of the podium. "As everyone in this room has had adequate opportunities to discuss the issues over most of last night and early this morning—and having come to preliminary conclusions—let us field questions or comments generated by Miss Johnson's briefing. After which, it is my intention to facilitate redirection of this chaotic situation into an operation with new objectives.

"I'll start it off," General Taggart said, pushing away from the table and crossing his legs. "I think we owe Miss Johnson an apology—military intelligence owes her an apology." He cast his gaze on Christine Johnson. "Colonel Blackburn was out of line reporting his interpretation of the Dickerson Phelps character up the line to me—and not fully cooperating with your requests. You were his direct superior. Please accept my apology and know that appropriate disciplinary measures have been taken."

"With that out of the way," Blanton cut in, "let's take aim at the big issue here." Blanton held his eyes on Christine. "Several changes have been agreed on with regards to the investigative approach and Parnevik's apprehension. Let me just jump ahead briefly and confirm that this situation has escalated into a threat to national security. Military Intelligence is not equipped—nor does it possess the finesse, geographic resources, and response capabilities—to execute the new objectives this committee will be authorizing. It is now clear that Military Intelligence should not have been charged with traipsing around the European continent running after private citizens, much less having any business dealing with a potential North Korean confrontation."

"Unfortunately, I'm afraid Colonel Blackburn was under pressure playing catch-up," General Taggart inserted.

"It's not meant as a rebuke, General.... We've decided to bring the FBI fully into the hunt for Parnevik within U.S. borders. Their organization will replace Military Intelligence operating out of the Atlanta PD Headquarters. As you aptly pointed out, Christine, they have the resources." Blanton nodded toward John Lindsay, the FBI Deputy Director seated next to General Taggart. "John, I think you have something to say here."

Lindsay raised his eyebrows, folded his hands in his lap, and focused on Christine Johnson. "Homeland Security has been fully briefed," he said, "and their resources are also available. Ed Furlow, Special Agent in Charge of our Atlanta Field Office, will report directly to you, Miss Johnson, and office space and equipment will be ready for your use upon your return to Atlanta. Ed will meet you at Hartsfield, and anything you need will be immediately procured."

"Thank you, John," Blanton said. "Can we assume Furlow is aware of this operation's national security status? And is he prepared to debrief Military Intelligence personnel posted at the Atlanta PD and sit down with Christine to hammer out the planning?"

"Yes, sir, General Taggart and myself took care of it early this morning."

"Very well then, the next major issue is Pharmco Corp. After consultations with Doctor Wrenthrow," Blanton waved a hand at the Director of the Penn State Nanofabrication Facility, "it is now thought to have been a poor decision to charge Military Intelligence with overseeing continuation of Pharmco efforts on the DOD contract. There are catastrophic risks in attempting to duplicate the nanite replication process developed by Parnevik. Doctor Wrenthrow was present during our deliberations the last 48 hours and will summarize Pharmco's contract role and the risks we have chosen to avoid. This is primarily for your edification, Christine."

"Thank you, Doctor Blanton," Wrenthrow acknowledged, docilely replacing Blanton at the podium. A somber expression written across his face, he was a diminutive man, the archetype of a researcher forever buried in the scientific milieu: classic wire-rimmed glasses, thin, disheveled light-brown hair. His nondescript, tanish sport coat and dark gray trousers were unpressed. He looked a little like Woody Allen, bug-eyed, as he removed a spiral note pad from his coat pocket. "To put this problem in context, Pharmco's DOD contract was designed to test the feasibility of creating a non-debilitating enhancement of sensory perceptions—in human beings...time controlled alterations in behavior. In short, a pill for increasing mental and physical performance—the classic ultimate soldier. Now, the pieces of the development puzzle: Reagan Driscoll, a senior department head at Pharmco, developed software and applied for patents that created a literal body-map. Corey Parnevik created nanite machines programmed to travel along body-map pathways to specific locations in the brain that controlled behaviors isolated for study. Stomach acid activated the nanites by dissolving their exterior sugar casings, which in turn triggered their programs to run, empowering flippers that maneuvered them through the blood stream to programmed destinations." The little man turned a page in his notebook and set it back on the podium. "Once in place, nanites emit a constant, small electrical charge over a set period of time. Pharmco's research—Doctor Parnevik's research—produced nanites that ran on absorbed energy from the body's metabolic electrical discharges. At the expiration of programmed time periods, nanites were programmed to break down and dissolve into their original, simple-sugar building blocks that either metabolized in the normal course of the body producing energy, or were excreted by the skin or through the urine. To date, Pharmco has successfully created nanites proven effective in substantially ameliorating bulimia and dementia in mice, and was seeking FDA approval to move to Phase II testing and refining, using a chimpanzee population.... Parnevik called the nanites developed for Pharmco's DOD contract, *Fuerte.*" Dr. Wenthrow was droning like a boring, lecture-hall professor.

Rising from his chair, Blanton interrupted. "I apologize, Amos," he said, gesturing, "but we need to get to the heart of our concern, and perhaps the present status at Pharmco is also appropriate."

"As you wish, sir." Wrenthrow pursed his lips and his eyes darted back and forth over the group. "At the present time, Pharmco has only a few of these *Fuerte* nanites left in Parnevik's test inventory. Through testing in mice, they have been calibrated to achieve different degrees of stimulus at twenty-two different locations in the brain, in effect producing super-mice. Chimpanzee experiments were next on the docket at the time of Parnevik's sabbatical. Now, the problem we have here is the considerable concern in the scientific community that these tiny machines might run amok during the replication process and literally consume the biosphere, reducing the planet to copies of themselves and a waste product referred to as 'grey goo.'" Wrenthrow looked down at his notes. "As far as is known to date—except for Dr. Parnevik—not a single replication process has ever been attempted. Software programs for miniaturizing a machine and programming it to replicate have never been developed. Furthermore, there is no consensus on how to go about containing such a replication process."

"Thank you, Amos." Blanton looked over the group to judge the patience level. "With final indulgence…for Christine's benefit, the only other person who may have had knowledge of the procedures Parnevik used to successfully accomplish a controlled replication process was Reagan Driscoll. She was allegedly killed as a result of one of Parnevik's despicable experiments. She worked with Parnevik during his development of the process and produced a conceptual paper on force field containment. It is unclear if her concepts were incorporated into Parnevik's replication procedures. Unfortunately, Parnevik kept her at arm's length and never published systematic directions internally. So far as we know, no one at Pharmco has the knowledge and skills to duplicate his procedures to produce nanite inventory.

"We also know from evidence collected at the apartment of Ernest Kelto, a deceased assistant to Reagan Driscoll—case under investigation—that Kelto smuggled out most of the *Fuerte* inventory. Authorities allege he performed a disastrous experiment on a racquetball player in Charlotte, and presumably, from a money trail still under scrutiny, was paid to deliver nanites to Parnevik. The crux of our problem, ladies and gentlemen, is replication. And the problem has two fronts. One, Parnevik is running loose making products for the drug market in ad hoc laboratory environments without any replication safeguards. Two, Pharmco was under pressure, directed by Military Intelligence, to devise a method to produce more nanite inventory in order to continue performance under the DOD contract. That has ended as of this morning. Over the next several days, Military Intelligence personnel assigned as surrogates to Pharmco staffers will be phased out and all work on the DOD contract will be halted." Blanton reached in front of the podium for a bottle of Evian and took a swallow. Setting his gaze back on John Lindsay and Christine Johnson, he continued, "Christine, you and John are saddled with tracking down Parnevik. And Christine, the DEA has re-called Agent McKenzie to full duty. You are to inform him personally." Blanton glanced over at Ferris White, the DEA Deputy Administrator. "He has been given cooperative access to DEA assets and is to report to you. His mission is to ferret out the distribution source for this *Amor* candy product infesting our major cities *and* to orchestrate a very pointed meeting in Washington between the culprits and the Attorney General at the Department of Justice."

Blanton switched his attention to Christine Johnson. "You believe that Mister Phelps has knowledge of Parnevik—through this paranormal gift he brings to bear. Is this correct?"

"Yes, sir," Christine said.

"And I—we are curious as to how it was known the Dubois person was actually Parnevik?" Blanton queried.

"Phelps gave us Julian Trebar and the North Korean contact, both of which have been confirmed. And he gave us Dubois."

Blanton nodded. "Accepting that for the moment, then if Dubois is no longer his persona, we have to assume we've lost Parnevik in Marseilles. The flight logs revealed that the person holding the KPMG consultant's boarding pass never boarded the flight and the airline filled the seat with a standby. Again, let me be perfectly clear. Parnevik's apprehension is the number one priority. He is a traitor, a murderer, and poses a threat to national security."

"And again, sir," Christine said, "so far, all we have is Phelp's gift. If you'll give me a few minutes, I'll check in with Mallory Driscoll and Agent McKenzie and make sure we have the latest information."

"Please do so. You'll have to make the call from the waiting area. This room is impervious to all outside signals. We'll adjourn for fifteen minutes."

***

As Christine Johnson returned, everyone took their seats. "Phelps contacted them about 4:00 a.m. this morning. He told them Parnevik made it back to Atlanta yesterday via Charlotte, using a different identity. He says Parnevik is extremely agitated and may have run out of his medications. I get the sense that Mallory and Agent McKenzie may be planning to catch him on their own. They want the full extent of the law brought down on Parnevik. Mallory Driscoll is adamant. She wants him to pay for her sister's death."

"Out of the question, as I'm sure you understand." Blanton cupped his chin and leaned back in his chair. "What name is he using now, and where is our Mister Phelps?"

"They claimed he hung up on them before they could ask. They said he's somewhere in Kentucky and he has some kind of surprise for them. They're supposed to meet Phelps in Charlotte tomorrow."

"Did he reveal the distribution source for these *Amor* pills?"

"No, sir." Sitting in the hot seat, it was clear to Christine that Dr. Blanton was becoming harder to deal with; he wasn't going to accept much more negative news. The redefined situation held a new kind of potential terrorist threat to the homeland. Her pre-meeting briefing papers had outlined action/reaction scenarios unique in both the national and international realms. It was clear the gloves were coming off with many of the major arms of government now invested.

Blanton appeared slightly disgruntled, and his stern façade didn't hide the hint of fear showing in his eyes. "General Taggart, you best be getting on. I want Pharmco closed up tighter than a drum. Christine, you pick up your mission assignment from my secretary. You're returning to Atlanta tonight. A DOD Gulfstream G550 will be ready by 7:00 p.m. out of Reagan National." Blanton cast a quick look at John Lindsey, the Assistant FBI Director. "Please have Special Agent Furlow up to speed and at Hartsfield to meet Christine.... Christine, you need to reel these wild cards in or find a way to control them. It's your job now. Just do it, and if you have any questions about the assignment, you can call me—I don't care what time it is."

"I will, sir—how do you want me to handle the situation if the North Koreans enter the playing field?"

"Not your concern," Blanton responded. "It's a diplomatic issue. The Secretary of State has been briefed and is working with the CIA to determine what transpired between Julian Trebar and the North Koreans. They will handle it, cooperating with Defense from then on. Besides the DOD, this Committee is charged with minute-to-minute updates directly to the Secretary of State. You just make sure we hear of anything that would help define the situation. Anything, Christine, and I'm talking about our paranormal private investigator. Should there be encounters, the FBI is your go-to resource. By the way, the favor you asked. The world's various intelligence services didn't come up with any evidence indicating the existence of Dickerson Phelps prior to 1986.

 Sixty-eight

George Randle

NINE YEARS OUT of Georgia Tech with a degree in Structural Engineering, George Randle was satisfied with his mid-level career at Lockheed Martin. He'd stagnated at the position of crew supervisor, working out of the Marietta, Georgia, facility, converting and upgrading C-130s. He simply wasn't the ladder-climbing type, and he was well aware that shy employees never seemed to get promoted.

He was comfortable and content, living alone in a three-bedroom condominium, overlooking the Chattahoochee River near the I-75/I-285 confluence, and rarely changed his daily routine: fast foods or delivery, watching TV, and secreting himself away in a marijuana-induced stupor. The lottery was also a daily addiction along with his principle hobby, spending money on nearly every Internet scheme he came across.

Never in his wildest dreams had he expected a call from Co-rey Parnevik. Taken aback at the seeming changes in Parnevik's tone of voice, Randle was left confused as Parnevik threaded together an inane litany of distorted camaraderie. He remembered Parnevik as a self-centered asshole. The moment Randle realized who was on the line, images and memories from the past flooded his mind, and the heat of forgotten anger pressured against his forehead. Parnevik had kept him from furthering the only female relationship he'd ever attempted. Emma Kisumi had been attracted to Parnevik. He never could figure out what she saw in him.

As he'd listened to Parnevik, he wondered what had happened to Emma. He recalled she'd taken a position with some company in North Atlanta. He hadn't taken the time to pursue her, writing it off in his long column of losses.

At Georgia Tech, Georgie Boy, as Parnevik always called him, had taken several math and engineering courses with Parnevik, but that was over a decade ago.

It had been late when Parnevik called, close to midnight, interrupting a good horror movie. He apologized for the late call and was generally cordial and friendly, the conversation almost totally one-sided. After hanging up, Randle was surprised he'd accepted an invitation to dinner the following evening, at Parnevik's expense. They were to meet at Linda's Café in fashionable Midtown. He said he had a lucrative business proposition to discuss. *What could Parnevik want with me?*

After the call, he sat in the quiet, allowing his thoughts to wander. At first, he felt a sense of reluctance, but that soon dissolved into curiosity and anticipation. Old friends or not, out of left field or not, it was just like playing the lottery. You had to keep playing if you wanted a chance to win anything.

 Sixty-nine

Genovese Family

TONY GATTURNA, PAULI Torentino, and three Family regional chiefs sat around a group of tables pulled together in the middle of Angie's Italian Restaurant. After the meal had been consumed and the small talk exhausted, the weekly gathering in Midtown Manhattan was strictly business. Waiters were clearing away the dirty dishes as most of the men lit cigars.

"Leave the wine and shut the doors behind you." Gatturna waved his hand at the headwaiter and tapped an ash into a glass ashtray.

"Product is ten days out from the Vietnam distribution plant," Paulie said. "That takes care of the problem for now. When it comes in, we launch Phase Two of the expansion."

"What's it been, Paulie, four days and we don't hear from Parnevik? Then today, he's kind enough to answer our day's old questions by email. All he had to do was tell us the plants had the raw materials." Gatturna was furious but he held it inside. He needed to maintain his image, and the illusion of command was paramount. His four regional chiefs looked to the Family's capabilities to support their business activities. "Paulie, I want Parnevik in the flesh—here. He works for us from now on. No more bull shit." Gatturna cast his gaze around the table. "But how 'bout you tell the boys what our contacts in France found out."

Paulie expelled a puff on his cigar. "In front of credible witnesses, he was attempting to set a record wing suit flight down a glacial ski run at the base of Mt. Blount near Chamonix, France. He went missing and the local police called it an accident. They even found the area where he went down. It was inaccessible. He was pronounced dead and the police closed the case."

"This guy is some kind of Jason Bourne," Gatturna said. "He emailed us today, so he's not dead. He wants to be declared dead so the Feds will take the heat off. Smart thinking. You got to hand it to him—none of our people could run him down."

The chiefs appeared to relax a degree. Gatturna stood up, satisfied the status quo had returned and gave Paulie an order. "As back-up, go ahead with the science kids. I'm ignoring his warning about experimenting. We need to be able to make this product ourselves."

Paulie had scoured the Family's educated youth for advice and volunteers to do the analytical work. Four from different bioscience disciplines were on-call, and facilities had been leased from a provider of research laboratories outside of Durham, a city in the technology triangle of North Carolina.

"What about the bank, Tony?" the L.A. chief asked. "Our checks are bouncing."

"Paulie, what's the status there?"

"The Panamanian banks are going through an examination. All our funds are frozen for the duration. Our banker says he doesn't know how long it's gonna take. It's a little too convenient that Rodriguez wants to meet. The Mexicans want into *Amor*, and our sources tell us it's them that put the clamps on our bank. They have great influence in Panama."

"We never should have gone into Panama in the first place," Gatturna said. "It's in the middle of the money trade between supply-side partners and distribution. They're all Latinos and Mexicans, and they give us no respect. We need to take our business elsewhere. When this passes, we move our banking. Paulie, look into it. In the meantime, run some of our cash to Cayman to meet Family payments. Does that take care of it for now?" Gatturna's gaze took in the group.

"What about the new product you've been talking about?" The Chicago Chief had been the one most interested in the prospects of alternatives to heroin and cocaine.

"It's coming, old friend." Gatturna stole a glance at Paulie. "It's called *Bliss*, and a test sample is on its way here."

***

Five minutes passed before the goodbyes, hand shaking, and shoulder slapping ended. Gatturna and Paulie returned to the table and the last of the wine and *cannolis*. "It was nice of Parnevik to say he'd call when he got back in town. Whatever the hell that means." Gatturna was building up another head of steam.

"Cool it, Boss. We'll get him when he brings the *Bliss* sample. He said he'd do it personally. I'll email him we want it ASAP."

"We'll meet with Rodriguez. Set it up. We'll agree to cut them into *Amor*. As long as we control the supply, we have them over a barrel. We don't need a war over this. And, Paulie, make it look like they're doing us a favor by helping get our money freed up from the examiners. We get our money out, and if we play our cards right, we buy time to get our house in order. The other cartels will want in eventually. We'll have to plan for that."

 Seventy

Dorie Sarcorcee

PARNEVIK LEISURELY FINISHED his breakfast and was standing in front of the bedroom's full-length mirror, scrutinizing the finishing touches to his professorial veneer: perfect blue blazer, light-blue button-down Oxford shirt, striped tie, black and grey Sketcher casuals, and khaki Docksiders. He'd dyed his hair back to its original medium brown and added a matching mustache and fashionable growth below the lower lip. With Tom Ford Metal Aviator sunglasses, he was just another associate professor off to important collegiate affairs.

Rested, balanced, confident, he exited the twenty-first-floor suite with his dark-brown, over-the-shoulder leather satchel packed full: laptop and accessories, a makeup kit, syringes, two small bottles of liquid Halothane, surgical gloves, a ski mask, and a miniature, portable X-ray unit. He took final stock of his image, passing several mirrors lining the hallway on his way to the elevator bank.

The elevator was empty on the way down to the main floor. Parnevik's rubber soles squeaked across the shiny granite squares leading to the Peachtree Plaza's reservation desk. He felt sufficiently comfortable to book an additional two days. Professor

Harold Pedersen had business to transact, and Parnevik was planning to renew old acquaintances.

That business taken care of, he crossed through the ornate lobby and rode the elevator down to the underground parking lot, all the time reviewing the fullness of the day's docket.

***

The delivery van pulled into the 7-Eleven at Twelfth and Peachtree. It was adorned on two sides and the rear with circles of hearts and colorful flower bunches making-up the company's logo.

Mobile Surprise Enterprises, Inc. specialized in creative wrapping and delivery of boutique gifts and flower arrangements for birthdays, anniversaries, awards, holidays, and other special events.

The last two days, Parnevik had followed the driver. He'd made this same stop each day to replenish his coffee and wolf down a sweet roll to hold him until lunch. Today Parnevik was in waiting.

The customer list was long, and the truck was neatly stacked with packages in many sizes wrapped in brightly colored paper patterns, strung with ribbon, and covered with fancy, stick-on paper flowers. A diverse array of live plant arrangements and corsages filled the side cooler.

Parnevik had a surprise gift he wanted hand delivered to an eight-year-old girl on her birthday, and this was the perfect opportunity to facilitate that task.

With his rental car secure across the street in the Presbyterian Church parking lot, Parnevik approached the van from the rear, watching for possible observers, and entered through the back doors. He moved cargo around to enable crouching behind the driver's seat. His right hand held a thin, finely grained sponge saturated with an odorless liquid. Halothane would provide the driver with a sound three-hour nap.

Today was Dorie Sarcorcee's eighth birthday. She excitedly negotiated the exit steps of the school bus at her usual stop two blocks from home. "Careful, honey," the bus driver cautioned. "Have a great party, Dorie, and I'll see you tomorrow." Eddie was a kind old man, always looking out after the kids, smiling and kidding around. He'd watched over hundreds during the school years before junior high.

"I will," Dorie replied, laughing. "See you tomorrow." The bus doors creaked and slapped closed. She started hop scotching down the sidewalk, changing hands with her lunch pail to maintain stability along the imaginary course. She was the only one that got off at the stop, and the streets were virtually empty on this calm winter day. All her friends and the neighborhood kids were waiting for her at home.

The Mobile Surprises van pulled up to the curb about twenty feet in front of Dorie. She read the writing on the rear doors and noticed the flowery logo. The driver came around and opened the back of the van, slid a steel ramp to the ground, and turned to face her, hands playfully resting on his hips. He was dressed in a funny pink and white uniform covered with flowers and red hearts. Even his cap had the same flowers and hearts. The silly mask he had on made Dorie laugh out loud.

"You're Dorie Sarcorcee, the birthday girl. Right?" he asked, imitating the voice of Donald Duck.

"How'd you know?" Dorie scrunched her eyes, her mouth taking on a comely pout, and she placed her hands on her hips, mimicking the funny-looking driver.

"Your dad asked me to surprise you with his present before you got to the party. Will you please follow me to accept your prize? Then you can be on your way. Everyone is waiting for you." The driver entered the back end of the van and disappeared inside.

"It's something you put on," she heard him mumble. "It will only take a minute."

"I'm coming," she giggled.

***

"You look simply gorgeous, Miss Dorie. Now don't be late for your party." The driver held her elbow as she navigated the rear ramp. She was wearing a beautiful fur coat.

"I don't remember putting it on," she said, looking up at the driver, eyes squinting in the bright sunlight. She shuffled toward the sidewalk, holding her arms out to steady herself like a tightrope walker.

The driver stood in the open rear of the van, and he had on the funny mask that grinned. "You unwrapped it yourself," he said. "It looks great. All the other kids will be jealous. Get along now, and don't forget the card from your dad. I put it inside your lunchbox." The driver stepped to the ground and held out the box. Dorie turned back a tentative step to grab the handle and noticed he had on rubber gloves.

***

The Mobile Surprise Enterprises driver began to snore, sitting on the passenger side of the delivery van. Several blocks from the 7-Eleven, Parnevik pulled the van into a residential neighborhood and parked. In the back, he peeled off the delivery uniform and again became the young professor. He parked the van back at the side of the 7-Eleven, leaving the snoring driver in the passenger seat. He would miss being present when the driver came to his senses and realized he'd been on a fifty-minute unscheduled delivery.

Parnevik exited the way he'd entered, out the back doors, focused on the next task as he crossed Peachtree Street to his rental car in the deserted church parking lot: the Barclay's Bank branch in Buckhead.

 ## Seventy-one

Mallory & McKenzie

MALLORY AND MCKENZIE slept in like a couple of college kids on weekends. Poor Emma had to put up with last night's search and destroy mission in the house looking for tracking devices, and they didn't hear her leave for work.

It was late afternoon when they finished a long run together—five times the circuit through Piedmont Park—and were cleaning up and preparing to leave for an event they'd been looking forward to. It was one of their favorite things to do back in their college days.

McKenzie was in the living room, patiently organizing a picnic basket and cooler: Irish hard cheddar, light rye crackers, port wine cheese spread, two bottles of iced-down Pinot Grigio, a loaf of sourdough bread, utensils, and plastic wine glasses. They were going to the open-air concert at Chastain Park, lie out on a blanket and pillows among the oak trees above the amphitheater, and relax like old times, taking in music from *Sting*.

A flurry of memories caught Mallory off guard as she watched McKenzie neatly packing all the items. She felt a tingling sensation creep along the back of her neck and along her shoulders. She wondered if he would want to hold her like he used to.

Mallory was about ready to follow McKenzie out the back door when her government phone vibrated from her belt case. The display showed Christine Johnson's ID. "Rymac, hold up. It's her again. You better conference in."

McKenzie was heading down the driveway, lugging the basket and cooler toward his rental car. He jerked around. "Not again. Get rid of her." He scurried to the car, opened the trunk, placed the basket inside, and grabbed his phone.

Christine Johnson was at Reagan National Airport, climbing the boarding steps of the DOD's Gulfstream G550, ready to return to Atlanta. "I didn't have time to explain earlier. I was in a very important DOD meeting in D.C., and I'm en route back. Sorry I didn't let you guys know. It all happened so fast. After the airport incident and other missteps you don't need to know about, I felt like I was losing control of my mission, and the Oversight Committee requested a review. I've been in D.C. since this morning. There have been many changes. Can we meet? I'll be on the ground at eight-o-five."

"No. We're on our way to Chastain Park," McKenzie said.

"It's important. What about eleven-thirty at the FBI's field office on International Boulevard? I'm permanently stationed there now. Military Intelligence has been removed from authority, so don't worry about the surveillance issues. That's in the past. We've got new direction and a national security mandate. I'm confident we can finally get on the same track together—and I apologize for the late hour."

McKenzie grimaced, holding the government phone away from his ear, watching Mallory's reaction in the doorway as she hung up and ran down the walkway.

"I don't like being told what to do." Mallory snapped her phone back in its case and glared at McKenzie as he slammed the trunk closed.

"Mal, if anyone knows that, it's me."

"Eleven-thirty at night. She has a lot of gall. There goes our evening."

"We won't miss the concert. Just put it out of your mind and get in the car.... It sounds to me like she wants our help now."

"No, she needs Smythe."

Mallory slid into the front seat, seemingly recovered. McKenzie stole a glance and smiled, remembering how she quickly changed channels.

The soft chime of Mallory's satellite phone issued from her shoulder bag. "It's got to be Smythe."

Another uninterrupted report from the elusive and wayward Titus Smythe revealed the Genovese Family in New Jersey as Parnevik's *Amor* distributor, and Parnevik was planning a dinner meeting with an old college friend. He hadn't picked up on Parnevik's physical location until just recently. He said his imaging had been jumbled—Parnevik hadn't been emoting or experiencing stress, a sign that he considered himself in control. This had hampered Smythe's ability to pick up on him.

"The *Amor* product is contract-manufactured into its final tablet form in Vietnam and Pakistan and delivered by order to the Genovese." Smythe's tone was even and relentless. "The tea company I told you about in Lyon also orders *Amor* from those plants. They think it's a flavor enhancer and mix it into a tea blend Parnevik has them prepare to his specifications. They manufacture the teabags and marketing containers and distribute to their fourteen European stores. I checked with the head office, and the product seems to be taking off—no wonder in that. Now, listen. If you play the cards correctly, I'm sure our government will be able to confirm those relationships and perhaps shut the supply spigot. Of course, producing and buying candy is not illegal, but if one finds the pipeline one can at least confront both ends."

"Titus," Mallory interrupted, "how do you know all this?"

"Sometimes it's from random thoughts I pick up, ones that are more intense—charged with feeling—or perseverated over—repeatedly reviewed, like this dinner with an old college friend. He's actually excited about it."

"Who is Parnevik now?" McKenzie said, leaning close to Mallory's phone. "Maybe we can track him down from here. He doesn't know what we look like, and we don't come across as Feds."

"He hadn't invested enough emotion in this new name for my faculties to discern it until now—But do give me a moment here. Agent McKenzie, I sense it is much too dangerous to pursue him randomly. He is moving very quickly. At present, his constant flurry of thoughts are confusing. He's planning ahead, and even though I only see flashes, my sense is, as I've said before, he is losing a degree of rationality. He is aggressive, unafraid of his circumstances, and uncaring about inflicting harm on others. He's obsessed with control and believes he is omniscient in any undertaking."

Mallory was losing patience. "So, where are *you*? What's your plan, and who is Parnevik now?"

"I'm visiting old haunts in Kentucky. But never mind that. We will need to meet. I want to introduce you to a new friend of mine—but for now, remember the Philadelphia police acquaintance I told you about? He put together possible connections to the U.S. originating from Marseilles around the time Dubois was pulling his little trick. The only terminal destination that made sense was Charlotte, North Carolina—it gets better. National Car Rental leased a vehicle one-way to Atlanta for cash within an hour of the flight's arrival. I feel strongly about this. I knew he rented a car. I just didn't know where. And now we know his name. Doctor Harold Pedersen."

"What are you going to do?"

"I want you and Agent McKenzie to meet me at the National Car Rental at noon tomorrow—the one at the airport. I'll be arriving in a white van with a green and black advertisement for *The Hagger Kennels*—and I don't want anything to do with this government woman you have befriended. I sense nothing but trouble, no matter how cooperative she may seem. Her agenda is not the same as ours. I'm fifteen to twenty hours behind Parnevik in real time, but I intend on remedying that situation. One final matter. It is important that you bring the winter coat we retrieved from Parnevik's residence."

"I don't know how we can get it out of the evidence locker at Atlanta PD—"

"I'll handle that," McKenzie interjected.

"Thank you, Agent McKenzie."

"Now, how is my dear caretaker, and did she receive the package of clothes I mailed from Marseilles?"

"She got it," Mallory answered. "But she's worried about you. She said you've never been away from her this long. She's afraid you aren't taking your medication and she's concerned about Professor VonMitton." She yanked the satellite phone from her ear and slapped it shut against her thigh. "He hung up."

"We have to decide what to tell Miss Johnson," McKenzie said.

"You drive. I'm going to give her the guts of what Smythe said." She pulled the government phone from her belt case and fiddled with the call screen. "Good, it has texting.… We'll be able to tell by how she reacts tonight if she's a friend or a foe."

"You're not going to tell her about going to Charlotte—"

"Of course not."

 Seventy-two

McGaw Laboratories

THE DAY HAD been physically challenging. As Parnevik made his way to his hotel suite, he longed for a shower, a fresh change of clothes, and a double Grey Goose martini. In the room, he tossed his shoulder satchel on a couch and raided the portable service bar.

Refreshed from his shower, he concocted a second ice-cold martini and sat in front of his laptop, waiting for it to power up. Sipping, he admired the smooth flavor as the heat rolled down his throat and awakened the lining of his stomach. Latent tension quickly dissipated, and he got up to retrieve last night's crackers and tin of caviar from the fridge. He checked his email: nothing. *Good.* The caviar was still excellent, but he decided to lighten up. He wanted to save his appetite for the coming meal.

It was time to take his medication and get ready for dinner. He only had one more dose of Dopamine dampener, and the other two neurotransmitter supplements he relied on to keep mental equilibrium were also running low. He'd stashed a year's supply of meds at the fire station, the Genovese having compromised that location confronting Reagan Driscoll's sister. He'd have to do something about her...just to be consistent. The thought made him laugh.

Eventually, the Feds would track any regular prescriptions he could easily obtain. He had to assume by now, along with his residence, banking, and physician relationships, anything to do with his previous life was unavailable. Besides, he needed a large supply, too large not to garner suspicion at standard retail outlets. The task lay ahead, before indulging in dinner and a plan of brilliant chicanery.

McGaw Laboratories operated a pharmaceutical warehouse in southwest Atlanta, not far from his favorite fire station. Like most of the warehouse distribution businesses in a park complex, it was located along a dead-end side street off a central feeder road.

At nine o'clock in the evening, the whole park was deserted. Parnevik hadn't used his set of master keys since purchasing them upon completion of several law enforcement classes online through DeVry University. Collecting technical gizmos in the field of eavesdropping and deception had been a hobby since he was in seventh grade.

He found a restaurant parking spot a block from the warehouse complex and walked in carrying his briefcase. He would look inconspicuous to any late homeward-bound workers, just another informally dressed management type. In case he met an inquisitive security patrol, he had the business card of a McGaw staffer he was on his way to meet.

The company hadn't changed the layout of their security cameras since he'd last visited the premises several months ago to make sure they carried a stock of the specialty drugs he used. Before coming into camera range next to the warehouse side of the building, he halted next to a telephone pole, reached into his briefcase, and pulled out a Ruger pellet handgun. One silent shot and the camera was disabled.

The warehouse cylinder lock on the side door next to the loading ramp was at least twenty years old and yielded to Parnevik's keys. The inside loading area was parallel to a forty-foot long, glass-enclosed control counter with three security windows and one access door. Drug orders were filled, packaged, and consigned to licensed delivery drivers; who drove custom-made security vans. Labeled medicines and ingredients sat organized in rows of shelves behind the counter and preparation areas.

The access door lock also yielded to Parnevik's master key set. Five minutes later, with the aid of a 130-lumen mini light, he had what he needed stuffed in his briefcase: at least a year's supply of 10 mg Valium tablets; 20 mg Dopamine gel-caps; and 25 mg Paroxetine pills, a serotonin inhibitor that reduced depression and anxiety—his go-to quick fix.

 Seventy-three

Christine Johnson

SHE PACED THE floor of her newly acquired office space in Atlanta's FBI field office, waiting for Mallory and Agent McKenzie to show up. Comfortable as government offices go, it had been Special Agent Furlow's, and he'd kindly designated it for her use; it was the only one with the necessary communications capabilities.

For the second time, she finished reviewing the police report from Chamonix, France. The bottom line was that DNA evidence from the wing-flyer's landing was on the way to the CDC in Atlanta.

Christine slipped into the comfortable desk chair, flipped off her formal flats, and curled her feet into the side of the chair, amazed at the turn of events and reluctance of the French police to respond quickly to high-level requests by the U.S. government.

She had no doubt the DNA would match with the epidermal cells left on the towel in Reagan Driscoll's apartment prior to her death in Las Vegas, and for good measure the same for the residue taken from the collar of Parnevik's winter coat brought from his Atlanta residence. The standard police work to date had accumulated sufficient evidence to charge Parnevik with breaking and entering, at least two counts of murder, bribery, grand theft, possession of stolen property, sale of elicit substances, felonious assault using dangerous drugs for the purposes of human experimentation, breach of top-secret contract covenants, and treason against the United States. But that was all academic now. Parnevik was a national security risk. He had to be captured alive without drawing public attention. From there, she could only speculate: at a minimum, he'd have to be confined, forced to cooperate with government research, and neutralize the results of his deleterious activities.

She got up from the desk and stretched her arms and legs. Too much sedentary time. She needed a good workout.

At least now she had something to work with, assuming the information from the paranormal Dickerson Phelps had veracity. It was a good sign Mallory Driscoll and McKenzie would cooperate. She'd put the wheels in motion from the G-5 flight into Atlanta. There'd be results soon enough.

Buzzing from the intercom on the office desk brought her back to the moment. Mallory Driscoll and Agent McKenzie had arrived and were under escort by the evening duty officer. Christine was sincere about establishing a working relationship with them. She had zero leads as to Parnevik's whereabouts and nothing solid to go on until the FBI got up to speed. Special Agent Furlow was anxious to get to work on it, but for most of tomorrow morning his time would be consumed debriefing military intelligence personnel working out of the Atlanta PD. Furlow was scheduled to meet with her after lunch and brainstorm how best to move forward.

***

"I have some good news." Christine offered a smile as they took seats. "I apologize. I don't even have access to a coffeepot yet. Don't know where anything is."

Mallory and McKenzie had come directly from Chastain Park. The concert was great, but it hadn't been like old times. The meeting had come like a summons and put a damper on fully letting go and enjoying the music.

"Again, I'm sorry for the late hour," Ms. Johnson said as sincerely as she could muster. "First item is I've been directed to inform Agent McKenzie that he's been reactivated by the DEA and assigned to me until our present problems are resolved."

"Hold on, Miss Johnson. I'm on administrative leave—"

"Not anymore. Your country needs you. I trust this is not going to be a problem."

"What's the deal?" McKenzie asked.

"You are to make contact with the Genovese Family, requiring a one-on-one meeting with their top decision-maker, informing that person—and only that person—he or she is to present himself or herself immediately at the offices of the Chief Justice in D.C. The meeting is covert, and you will personally organize government transportation through the offices of the Deputy Attorney General, no middlemen. You will be alone in all preliminary discussions. You will ensure that no recordings take place. You will personally escort the decision-maker to the Justice Department, using whatever guise is devised by Justice."

"These guys don't operate that way, Ms. Johnson. It's not to their benefit. There's no incentive."

"Agent McKenzie," Ms. Johnson said, her face taking on a stony texture, "you may inform the decision-maker that all members and cohorts of their family will be incarcerated should compliance not be immediate." She reached across her desk and pushed a red folder toward McKenzie. "This is now a national security matter and procedures are, shall we say, different. This is a DOD/Justice Department briefing paper assigning you your mission. It outlines procedures and actions authorized under a variety of circumstances and the short speech you are to deliver. You report directly to me."

McKenzie hooded his eyes, staring at her face.

Mallory looked on in disbelief.

Ms. Johnson moved on. "The government's objectives are clear: to capture Parnevik, dismantle his boutique drug operations, and put an end to the *Amor* blitz. From now on, Miss Driscoll is temporarily assigned to the Department of Defense and *also* works for me. No more cowboy activities. This is a national security emergency, and the two of you will conduct yourselves according-ly.... I apologize for the bluster, but the circumstances justify a harsh and surgical approach. Do you need a minute?"

"No," Mallory said evenly, having quickly adjusted. "But what fate have you assigned to Parnevik? He's killed people and my sister, and he's a proven psychopath."

"Let me back off a minute," Christine said, relieved the two people in front of her, for whom she had developed affection, had not lost it. "I'll tell you exactly why this is going down."

After a detailed review, holding nothing back, including the scientific realities, she said, "I think you can see the situation more clearly now. At least I hope so." She made quick eye contact. "An office has been prepared for you both two doors down the hall to the right. Agent McKenzie, you can review your mission file while you check out the office. I'll see you both here in this office at eight in the morning. Miss Driscoll, please remain for a few minutes."

Christine waited for the door to shut behind McKenzie. "Miss Driscoll, I'd like to call you Mallory. Would that offend you?"

"Please do. So I get to call you Christine?"

"When no one's around, if you don't mind."

"Look, Miss Johnson, according to Phelps, Parnevik has returned to the U.S. through Charlotte and has rented a car. What are you going to do about it?"

Ms. Johnson raised her eyebrows. "So you've had further contact. Excellent—but this is important info. I can't have you holding back—the situation is too critical. Do you understand?"

"Yes, I do now."

"As far as what happens to Parnevik, I am not privy at this time, but I assume if he's captured he won't be a part of society—ever."

"What's my job?"

"To team up with Mister Phelps. Though I don't understand how he does what he does, he's the only person that has been able to get close to Parnevik. I would like to learn more, but time is of the essence. Rather than using precious resources to hunt him down, you are my agent in seeking his cooperation. At present, the government has no interest in bringing charges against him. He is your responsibility now."

Mallory relaxed. It seemed there would be serious activity and she'd be included, not shunted away in the backwater.

"Did Mister Phelps say why he thinks Parnevik has returned? He's gone to a lot of trouble to convince authorities he died on the French glacier. Perhaps we *are* catching up with him—his residence is compromised. We've bugged the whole house, including his secret lab in the basement. The fire station where you found he'd stored some laboratory equipment is under twenty-four hour surveillance by Atlanta PD. He's got nowhere to go."

"Phelps says he has obligations. He has to make product to meet his commitments. The Mafia's not the only customer. There's the tea company in Lyon, France I told you about, and so far Phelps doesn't know what he's got planned for the North Koreans."

"The State Department is working out the tea company situation with the French. I can assure you their new brand will never make it to their product shelves."

"Parnevik's well prepared. I'm betting he has one or more lab backups. From all indications, he's been designing contingency plans for years—just so you know, I've agreed to meet Phelps tomorrow at noon at a rental car place in Charlotte."

"Good. It's only a two-and-a-half-hour drive." Ms. Johnson put on a smile and waved a tired hand. "You can tell me how all this transpired in the morning. You need to get some sleep tonight. But make sure you allow sufficient time in the morning to get versed on our satellite phone system and how it hooks up to the resources in place here. You'll find everything you and McKenzie might require for field work has been staged in your office down the hall. It looks like you're the point man on this operation. We'll get more fully together in the morning. Anything else?"

"Yes. Phelps says he needs the winter coat taken from Parnevik's residence. It's in the evidence locker at Atlanta PD. McKenzie was going over there around seven in the morning to request its release."

"I'll set it up," she said, wondering why the coat. She decided to wait until morning for any lingering questions. By then, the challenges in front of them might have morphed into any number of possible scenarios.

 Seventy-four

Linda's Café

PARNEVIK CONVINCED THE restaurant manager that a late meal for two in a private setting would be financially rewarding, but though cooperative, he kindly requested the extent of the dinner be limited to midnight. Parnevik would cement his full cooperation upon arrival and take care of the staff in advance.

***

George Randle hadn't been this nervous since his first day at Lockheed. He arrived at 10:15, fifteen minutes early, to get a feel for the place and slug down a stiff drink. On his own, he would never consider patronizing such an intimate café. He ate out practically every night, preferences running the gamut from a stool at a sports bar to all-you-could-eat buffets, and he loved Burger King and Taco Bell.

The restaurant was practically empty. It was, after all, a Thursday night. The manager greeted him cordially when he mentioned the Parnevik reservation and sat him at a candlelit table next to a wood-framed window with cream-colored lace curtains. Fresh flowers were set in a clear glass decanter in the middle of a fancy beige tablecloth. White cotton napkins, wine glasses, four-piece table settings, and soft ambient music nicely accentuated the cozy atmosphere.

Randle was savoring the last swallow of his Cosmopolitan martini when a hand gripped his shoulder from behind. He jerked in his chair.

"Sorry, old friend. I didn't mean to startle you." Parnevik tucked himself into the opposing seat and set his elbows on the table, a snide smile sliding across his face. "How long has it been?"

"Maybe a decade. Maybe more.... I hope you don't mind. I went ahead and had a cocktail." Randle waved the empty glass.

"Good, let's get another round." Parnevik gestured to a waiter alertly standing nearby.

Parnevik looked older. Some gray flecked his sideburns. Or maybe it was the mustache. But he still had that cocky sneer—the same inflated ego. *Funny how some things didn't change.*

Parnevik ordered the wine, a Chilean *Pinot Noir*, and both decided to take the waiter's recommendation for one of the chef's specialties: the Mediterranean shrimp scampi tossed in angel hair pasta and served with snow peas, creamed spinach, and French-cut green beans. The table bread was crisp, homemade sourdough. The meal was exquisite.

Randle relaxed as Parnevik skirted the conversation around his primary objective, concentrating on spinning a somewhat fictitious history of his last ten years: Master's Degree in engineering, PhD in bio-mechanics, Pharmco position, and working in the nanotechnology field.

Two cocktails and the red wine had loosened Randle's tongue, and with a little coaxing, he reluctantly related his work history and uneventful personal life.

Parnevik suffered though the boring renditions until a wave of paranoia crept over him. He was losing patience with inane conversation. Suddenly the signs were clear: the alcohol had neutralized his medication. It had happened before. He knew he shouldn't drink—only a glass of wine, no hard liquor. He stood and grabbed the edge of the table, responding to a sudden dizzy spell.

"Are you okay, Corey?" Randle placed his napkin aside, stood, and reached out an arm.

"A bout of vertigo," Parnevik said hoarsely, shaking his head. He had to get to the washroom immediately. In a similar situation he'd fallen, incapacitated for fifteen minutes in the middle of a banquet cocktail party until an observant waiter had understood he needed his meds from a coat pocket. "Give me a hand to the john."

Randle slung Parnevik's left arm over his shoulder and walked him to the restroom, along the way assuring the concerned manager that it was just a dizzy spell.

Parnevik's attention focused on making it to the washroom, but he was impressed at the way Randle handled the situation. He needed to lay his head sidewise on a flat surface for several minutes and then quickly reverse sides. Medical specialists had taught him the technique shortly after recovering from his first episode.

The vertigo subsided after several head turns, and Parnevik stood from the infant-changing station he'd been using, groping in a blazer pocket for his ever-present pill container. He looked over at Randle, standing several feet away, watching him like an obedient pet. "I'm good," he said. "Do me a favor and go apologize to the manager for me. I'll be right out."

Ten minutes later, they were back at the table sipping coffee. "Well, that was unfortunate, Georgie." Parnevik appeared calm and color had returned to his face. "I hope you'll forgive me. It's something I can't control."

"No problem. I'm just glad you're okay."

Parnevik was struck by Randle's sincerity. Maybe this would work out better than expected. "Well, thanks, Georgie Boy. Now to the business." Parnevik looked at his watch. Twenty minutes was plenty of time.

His pitch concluded, he reached into his satchel resting against the legs of an adjacent unused chair, removed a white, number-ten envelope, and handed it across the table.

"What's this?"

"An advance for the first stop on our schedule. You'll receive the same for the second act in the play. Cash. What do you say?"

Randle couldn't help himself. He slit the envelope open with the end of his dining knife and fingered the neat stack of hundred dollar bills. He'd never held twenty thousand dollars in his hands. "When do we practice, and how are you going to make me look like you?"

"You'll see."

"It'll have to be after work."

"Today's Wednesday. You take Friday off. If you have to, call in sick on Friday. Tomorrow after work, you come to room 1410 at the Peachtree Plaza. We'll have all evening to work out the details. For now, all you need to know is you'll be traveling to New York City Friday morning and returning in the evening. Saturday you'll be on an early morning flight to Lincoln, Nebraska, and back again that evening."

The restaurant manager escorted them to the door as a clock above the bar chimed the midnight hour. Returning to his hotel in his rented Audi, Parnevik was full of self-satisfaction. He'd picked the right guy. It was worth the money, and the relationship would be short-lived. It would work—perfect insulation against the untrustworthy Italian mafia and the crazy North Koreans.

 Seventy-five

Charlotte, North Carolina

THE HAGGER KENNEL van was conspicuously parked in front of the National Rental Car office, but there was no sign of Titus Smythe. Mallory looked at her watch: 12:04. She was on time as she pulled her one-way rental Honda in behind the van. *He's probably inside. What's with the van? And why meet here instead of Atlanta?* She turned off the engine and headed up the covered walkway toward the office, but midway she heard someone from behind call her name and turned around.

"Over here," came a voice from out in the rental car lot. No mistaking who it was. A tall man wearing a knee-length black trench coat and a black Stetson was waving his arms in the middle of the sea of cars.

Mallory waved back and jogged out to meet him.

"I trust your drive was uneventful, Miss Driscoll," Smythe said with a dour smile.

"Titus, don't you think it's time you called me Mallory? We've all been worried about you, but it's good to finally see you're okay. What am I doing here?"

"Fine, Mallory it is. Where, may I ask, is your sidekick?"

"He's been given an assignment with the Justice Department. I'm not allowed to discuss it."

"So be it. Did you bring the overcoat?"

"Yes, of course, but why are we here?"

"To meet a new friend and, hopefully, with the application of a few sweets as incentives, acquire his assistance. Please, follow me." Smythe stepped out in his characteristic loping gait with Mallory nearly skipping to keep up.

"Where is this friend of yours? Why the mystery?"

"Be patient, Miss Mallory." Smythe headed toward the Haggar van from which a baying sound grew louder as they approached. He went directly to the back of the van and opened the back doors, revealing a caged area containing a very large brown and black bloodhound with huge floppy ears.

Smythe cooed at the whining dog and nuzzled his big snout poking through a cage opening. "There, there, it's all right. Yes, I know it was a long trip." He opened the latch and fixed a leash to the big dog's harness. "Miss Mallory, this is my friend, Edwin. Edwin, this is Mallory." The pleasant grin on Smythe's face was momentary. "Please, the coat, if you would."

Mallory hesitated, tired of Smythe's commands. "No more directives, Titus. What's going on?"

"If you insist.... Please get the coat. I'll tell you the story as soon as I've walked Edwin and he's had a drink." He pointed at a small patch of grass at the side of the rent-a-car office, gave the hound some slack on the leash, and dragged behind, beseeching the dog to be a good boy.

***

"So this is Alfred's offspring, and he's supposed to track Parnevik?" Mallory grinned in disbelief, leaning against a lamppost with Parnevik's winter coat draped over her arm and Edwin nuzzling her hand. "You have got to be kidding me, Titus."

The dog whined.

"Do not be a skeptic, my dear girl. The hound is quite sensitive. See, you've hurt his feelings. Say you're sorry." Smythe patted the dog's hindquarter.

Mallory shook her head and cast her gaze at a big set of hooded brown eyes. "Sorry, Edwin—now what?" she asked, still shaking her head.

"A little demonstration perhaps, for the pessimistic. Give me the coat, please." Smythe wadded up the garment and dropped it on the cement under Edwin's ample nose. The hound aggressively sniffed and snorted, moving the coat with his forefeet this way and that, tossing it with his nose, spreading it out. Finally, with a sneeze and a short bay, Edwin headed out into the parking lot, dragging Smythe. Mallory followed.

The dog stopped, sat down, and yawned. "This is what he does," Smythe said.

"Does?"

"He's on N-47. That's the parking spot for the car Parnevik rented yesterday. It's equipped with a LoJack GPS tracking system. National puts them in all their rental cars. We can go inside, and if we're particularly pleasant, Miss Windsworth, the manager, as she was so kind to explain to me when I displayed my PI credentials, will pull the car that occupied that spot up on her computer."

***

After ten minutes of flattering small talk in front of Ms. Windsworth's desk, she turned the monitor around so the two of them could see. "It's a black, four-door Audi A-6 sedan," she said proudly, "and you can see the route the car has taken since Doctor Pedersen rented it yesterday and traveled to Atlanta. At the present time, he is wandering the city."

Once outside the building, Mallory said, "We go to Atlanta."

"Indeed. Now we have the capability of catching up with him in real time. You saw that from the log on the computer monitor.

As soon as he got into Atlanta, he headed for the place where he spent the night. I wrote down the coordinates. Use Google Earth on your laptop. Wi-Fi should work here. Then we'll know where he's staying.... We'll drop your rental at Hertz and take the van. We want to make Edwin as comfortable as possible. He is such a good boy. And, as a further demonstration, we'll let him lead us. My bet is he'll take us to Mr. Parnevik in Atlanta. You'll see."

 Seventy-six

Genovese Family

THE FAMILY'S MANHATTAN business office in the basement of Angie's Italian Restaurant needed serious renovations. The walls exuded stale cigar smoke and mildew. The leather furniture was thirty years old with multitudes of rips and burns. At a minimum, the air conditioner needed replacement.

"Everything went smooth with the Rodriguez reps," Paulie said. "They're gonna fix the bank situation in Panama—as a favor like you said—as soon as they receive the candy. I committed to 100,000 units." Paulie sat in his usual place on one of the leather couches lining one side of the office.

"Excellent. Now, if Parnevik keeps his word, in ten days we'll have a year's inventory. We pacify Rodriguez and then move the funds out of Panama to our European banks. We need to stay away from anyplace the cartels have influence."

"But we're gonna have to deal with this in a bigger way." Paulie Torrentino was charged with keeping track of the big picture and seeing to it that the Family's businesses were legal and ran smoothly. "The Asian DTO, the Jamaicans, the Black organizations, they're asking us what's going on. How they can get a piece of the action. The market's eating the stuff up. A whole new segment is coming in because there're no side effects and no dependency. It's like legal recreation for the masses, and it's out in the open. No hiding. Just walk up to the cart and buy some candy with your hot dog."

"I know, Paulie. The use of marijuana and cocaine is decreasing. Everybody in the business is feeling the squeeze. People want to make love not war." Gatturna laughed. "But you're right. We need to open up channels and talk, but first we need to protect our source. We need to get Parnevik under wraps. Maybe we keep him locked up. We make him a new deal. We let him live."

"We can do it tomorrow."

"Exactly, and he's bringing the sample. What's he calling it? Oh yeah, *Bliss*. You know, Paulie, this could work out like the candies, and then we'll have a real *problema*, as the Latinos say. It will cause revolution unless we handle it carefully.... We'll have to let everyone in," Gatturna mumbled to himself. "When's he comin' in and what's the status of the boys in North Carolina?"

"He said around lunchtime. I had to email him. He doesn't like using his cell phone. Said he'll call from a pay phone when he lands and take a cab to Angie's—the boys in Carolina are supposed to come through on Skype in about an hour."

∗∗∗

The four young men looked uneasy as the webcam window blinked into clarity on the computer screen. They were clad in assorted lab coats with bibs. White-N-100 bio masks hung from their necks. They were sitting around a card table in the middle of a drab, grey-walled laboratory filled with specialized equipment: a Scanning Transmission Electron Microscope (STEM), an Atomic Force Microscope (AFM), a Confocal Raman Microscope, a Laser Scanning Confocal Microscope, tools, and an operating room constructed to Level 10 bio-standards. "Mister Gatturna...Paulie," Fredrico, the bio-chemist head of the group opened up, "we got bad news." He cast a forlorn glance over the group. "The samples provided—we put some of it in solution to analyze its composition. It seemed a no-brainer.... Well, it turned into sugar—just a slush of simple sugars. There's nothing else we can do."

Paulie leaned over and whispered in Gatturna's ear, "Parnevik told us not to try to analyze, Boss. Remember, he said we'd be sorry."

"All this education and you guys can't figure out what it is and how to make it." Gatturna was ready to scream, but he realized the futility. They hadn't told the young men the background story other than they were dealing with a synthetic drug.

"But that's not all," Fredrico blurted. "Several seconds after the test solution turned to slush, the rest of the samples disintegrated into powder. The powder was also simple sugar. Whatever happened, we don't believe we're at fault. The test was conducted in the containment chamber. No hands touched the samples. We have no idea.... We're just sorry to disappoint you."

Gatturna clicked off the Skype program and flopped onto the leather couch next to a computer table, taking in deep breaths. A moment later, he fixed his stare up at Paulie who was standing next to the couch. "I think we gotta start over. No more bullshit. We take him down at the airport. Figure out what flight he's on coming in from Atlanta around noon. Have him met. Escort him to a vehicle, hit him with a needle, and bring him here. No more games. Get the boys in Carolina to pack up and bring the equipment up here. We can use the slaughter plant in Jersey, like we were gonna do originally. Parnevik stays with us for the duration."

 Seventy-seven

Parnevik: Georgia Tech

TO SATISFY HIS present purposes, Parnevik needed a production lab for at most a week, but he needed it quickly. When the Genovese revealed his plans for a lab at the old Atlanta fire station had been compromised, he'd immediately reacted and arranged purchases to duplicate the equipment and supplies for a future laboratory outside Albuquerque, NM, near the University of New Mexico's Nanoscience User Facility. Everything would shortly be waiting in storage.

But first things first. The scheduled meeting with Hwang Jang was three days away. Thanks to the deceased Ernest Kelto's pilfering of *Fuerte* nanites from the Pharmco coffers, he possessed a sufficient supply. A little fine-tuning and he'd be ready for the Nebraska demonstration. Prior to his Pharmco sabbatical, he'd been very close to the first chimp test under the DOD government contract. *Fuerte* was in fact an array of nanites, ingeniously packed together at the center of a ball of accreted sugar, producing a tablet that looked like a light-green breath mint. The nanites were programmed to follow the body map to twenty-seven specific sites located in the four lobes of the brain's cerebral cortex.

***

Parnevik was early for his eleven o'clock meeting with Dr. Sarcorcee, Director of the Georgia Tech Nanotechnology Research Center. Casually walking across the east side of the Georgia Tech quadrangle, he listened intently to bits of passerby conversation, enjoying the feeling of again being in the midst of academia. He took a seat on a shaded bench next to a walk-around fountain at the center of the quad and allowed his mind to drift through the procedures necessary to refine *Fuerte*. It brought back the memory of the last time he'd observed a test on a human subject.

It had been barely a month ago; the ludicrous fiasco at Club Elan on Christmas Eve: the sophisticated lady executive under the influence of *Amor* groping several young men while he and the Genovese *consigliore* looked on.... It was a pity he couldn't have remained to observe sweet Eva's demise in Gap-Tallard. Subtle modifications to the intensity of the stimulus emitted by the tiny machines at each site would eliminate the deadly convulsions. That and extending the duration of the charge would produce a successful test in Nebraska.... And the *Bliss* test sample he promised the Genovese would simply require a decrease of around fifty percent in intensity; the two-hour duration would remain unchanged. The *Bliss* utilized in his first human test had purposefully been too potent. Again, it was too bad he wasn't present to watch Reagan Driscoll—overcome in heavenly abandon—toss herself off the Las Vegas hotel balcony. The memories caused him to laugh aloud, and he craned around to see if anyone had noticed.

The few students remaining on the quad were now hurrying to class. He scooched back against the hard bench slats, picked up again on his reverie, and snickered to himself. He'd designed *Bliss* to stimulate the same areas of the brain affected by LSD. He intended to experiment on himself to reach an acceptable effect for the Genovese sample. That should be more than pleasant. If need be, he'd refine it further when he was settled in Albuquerque.

The clock tower bells at the head of the quadrangle commenced gonging the eleventh hour. He'd lost track of time. He stood abruptly, looking at his watch. *Mustn't be late.* He giggled, latched onto his briefcase, and headed toward the heart of campus and the nano research center.

 Seventy-eight

Doctor Edward Sarcorcee

ON THE TOP floor of Georgia Tech's Nanotechnology Research Center, Dr. Sarcorcee walked back and forth across the length of his glassed-in lab office. He'd searched the journals in preparation for his meeting with Professor Pedersen but found nothing published in the last two years. Even the decade prior, the professor had only been involved in a handful of mostly subjective case studies assisting in research at Penn State's nano-center. Equally disturbing was the fact that a little over a year had passed since he'd been reported missing on a trip to visit his father in Germany. The case was still open; he'd simply not shown up at his father's house.

Typically dressed in a clean, white lab coat over a white shirt and striped tie, Dr. Sarcorcee was meticulous to a fault. At fifty-five, he retained a bushy head of black hair, never a strand out of place. Generous facial features were chiseled into a head disproportionately large for his short, plump body.

Sarcorcee bunched his hands and burrowed them into his coat pockets; he was growing more irritated by the minute. His time was precious. It was a mistake agreeing to the meeting. Even though he was allegedly involved with nano-research, this academic couldn't possibly have anything of value to offer.

He sat back down at his computer. During his search, he must have missed something, anything that would shed more light on Professor Harold Pedersen. He claimed he was bringing a project proposal—an opportunity not to be passed up.

Dr. Sarcorcee was just about to put the computer to sleep when, through the corridor window blinds, he noticed a student and another man approaching his office. The man appeared to be a classic academic archetype, but rather youngish, clad in a worn, light brown corduroy blazer, tan Docksiders, open-neck patterned shirt, and penny loafers. Definitely a West Coast type, but there was something familiar about him.

Sarcorcee opened the glass doors.

"This lad was kind enough to escort me." Harold Pedersen offered his hand.

"Thank you, Brian." Sarcorcee raised a hand in the direction of the departing student. "Please come in, Professor. Take a seat." Sarcorcee led the way to two nicely upholstered opposing couches separated by a chrome-framed, glass coffee table. "Would you care for something to drink?"

"No, thank you. I've had my morning coffee and am anxious to explain the reason for imposing on your morning." Parnevik was seated, legs crossed, smiling through his beard at Sarcorcee's slackened face, eyes darting about, questioning, but not recognizing him yet.

"Please continue. I only have an hour before a meeting with the Dean of the Liberal Arts College." Dr. Sarcorcee eyed Pedersen up and down, his mouth slightly open.

Parnevik could tell he was wrestling with something he couldn't quite grasp. "Is there something wrong, Doctor Sarcorcee?"

"No, no. It's just that—have we met before?" Sarcorcee had a quizzical look on his face, and he'd come to a straightened position on the couch.

He's beginning to get it. "Most assuredly, my good doctor, but I beg your indulgence. All will be clear in the next little while." Parnevik unzipped his Filson, tin-cloth briefcase, removed a folder, and handed it across the table. "Carefully peruse the pages. It will save a great deal of time." Parnevik rose. "I'll take a five-minute stroll. I want to examine the Level 10 containment facility and adjunct laboratories to see if any significant changes have been made since my last visit."

The suddenness of the hard tone of voice and overt demand left Sarcorcee apprehensive…he'd been here before. The way the man walked was familiar. When the door closed, he opened the file.

The simple manila file contained three typed pages. Sarcorcee quickly scanned them: a chronicle of his published research papers from the most recent, going back some twelve years; a listing of equipment and supplies—most he recognized as common to nano research; the project proposal was the last page. By the time he'd finished reading, his heart was pounding, and the shirt under his lab coat was stuck to his body. He placed the page on the coffee table with the other two and slipped into the embracing folds of the cushioned couch, trying to make himself small.

Pedersen wasn't Pedersen at all. Beneath the professor façade was Corey Parnevik, a graduate student who'd assisted him during the prolific publishing period outlined in the folder. Without Parnevik's brilliance, his successful programming of rudimentary nanite machines could not have been achieved. It was him all right. *Rude, aloof, arrogant little prick without friends.*

What he was proposing was ludicrous and dangerous beyond imagination. He was going to demonstrate, step-by-step, how to program nanite machines to replicate.

To Sarcorcee's knowledge, no one had ever attempted the feat. But it would revolutionize the sciences, especially medical technology. Once manufactured and programmed, nano-machines would replicate at little cost—just the raw materials—common molecular building blocks. His mind leaped over the landscape of potential: nanites could be utilized to locate and rid the body of any unwanted cells, bacteria, viruses; disease would be a thing of the past. The applications were endless and mindboggling.

Sarcorcee sat in disbelief. Under his spiffy lab coat, the sides of his shirt were soaked. Evaporation at the back of his neck sent shivers down his spine. Why him? He hadn't heard from Parnevik since he'd received his PhD in micro-engineering and used the Georgia Tech labs from time to time on a pay-as-you-go basis. As he recalled, Parnevik had buried himself at Pharmco Corp in classified government work and wasn't allowed to talk about it. Over the years—the few times he'd run into him—his personality had coarsened and he went out of his way to taunt Sarcorcee. Everything he said was "I" oriented, complaining about the inequities in the system in grating, demeaning language. Over time the entire staff at the Georgia Tech labs had learned to give him a wide berth.

***

Parnevik came through the office door without knocking. Dr. Sarcorcee stiffened and resumed a straight-backed posture on the couch.

"I see you have digested my little proposal packet.... Ah, and you recognize me now. You look a little waxen around the edges, Edward."

"I am shocked, yes," he replied, creases appearing across his large forehead. "But I am curious at the same time. How did this technological breakthrough you are representing take place?"

Sarcorcee had rushed the words, anxious anticipation overshadowing his perplexity. And there was fear. "You don't surprise me," Parnevik said maliciously, taking a seat at the opposing couch. "Always looking out for number one, aren't you, Edward? But I'm a little nonplussed you aren't taking this opportunity to grovel in apologies for all the past breakthroughs I've given you—without collaborative credit in your journal articles. You stole expertise and took my genius as your own—and I let you. You had me over a career-barrel in those years. You held my PhD and research references hostage. But I'm not here for payback. I only want the accommodations I'm requesting in return for witnessing and logging the procedures I've designed to produce successful nanite replication. I'll even share the programming and structural specifications for the nanite machine we'll be using. What you do with the research is up to you. I have no interest in journal credits."

Parnevik paused a moment. Dr. Sarcorcee was absorbed fiddling with his necktie. His face was pasty. Blanched skin around his lips was a classic sign of fear.

"But I caution you," he continued. "If you go too far too fast, the government will come for you. What I'm going to reveal is well past what I achieved through a Department of Defense contract under Pharmco's supervision, and it's classified top secret." Parnevik leaned back in the couch to wait for Sarcorcee to come to a liberating epiphany. He was betting the chunky-headed bastard would succumb to projections of scholarly fame and commercial fortune.

"I understand…. If it makes any difference, I *do* apologize for not including you in the credits," he said with the lameness of an undergraduate freshman. "Your proposal calls for up to two weeks of lab use. You realize it must be paid for in advance."

Parnevik reached in his briefcase side pocket and handed Sarcorcee a certified check made out to him for twenty thousand dollars and identified as a personal research grant. "I trust this will be satisfactory?"

Sarcorcee scrutinized the check, gaping, his face lighting up in a bewildered smile. "Most generous and appropriate," he managed to say. "But I really can't accept." He placed the check back on the table next to the manila folder.

Parnevik sensed the man's reluctant avarice. *People never change.*

"What you want to do is too dangerous to risk university-owned facilities. You would have to be a registered user. I would have to submit standard paperwork—it just couldn't happen."

"Edward, let's get to the heart of this situation," Parnevik said, stone cold. His patience was gone. "In the Pharmco labs I've done what I've outlined dozens of times. You record the procedures and get copies of the structural diagrams and nanite directional programs. I get the time I need to refine the nanite machines I'm working on and produce some test inventory. You'll learn how to control a replication process. No one need know that the lab time is anything other than for your own research.... Make sense? I will remain as a nebulous subordinate. Someone you've invited to observe and assist. No one will notice. We'll work the hours of midnight to 5:00 a.m., and I will appear disguised as various student research assistants. All you need do is authorize the list of names I've given you and secure temporary lab IDs. The desk guard doesn't use a sign-in log. I'm sure you can figure out how to doctor the building's camera recorders as we go along, taking me out of the picture as you think necessary. I'm not looking for notoriety—in fact, just the opposite."

Dr. Sarcorcee squirmed in the couch. His mind was spinning with various scenarios. "Let me think about it—"

"No time, Edward. You put it together. The supplies you don't have in the labs I'll pick up locally. I'll see you at midnight tonight. Leave an envelope with the IDs for me at the security desk. I'll call for them as Peter Brown, the first name on the list. You be prepared to cover our tracks. Do we have a deal?"

"You're saying you actually have sample nanites you've programmed?"

He was succumbing. *Greed always trumped.* All men covet, and when an acquisition path contains no formidable obstacles, they take appalling actions to acquire their heart's desire.

Parnevik again reached into the Filson briefcase. On the table in front of them, he placed an eight-by-four-by-six-inch, olive green case of plastic construction. He snapped it open, revealing twelve padded cylinders cushioning twelve sealed vials, the Pharmco logo etched around their lips.

"I don't exactly know what to say. I'm tempted. You make a good case, but I'm troubled with the outside possibility of an accident. I'm not doubting your expertise, but nano-experts worldwide have warned of a catastrophic event if a replication attempt were to get out of control. Several have hypothesized that what would be left of the earth's surface would be nanites and waste, endless mounds of gray dust. The heat of the earth's mantle would be extinguished and the atmosphere consumed."

"Look, I've been there. This is the last time I'm asking you nicely. Are you in or not?"

"I just—I just don't know. I've got to think about it." Sarcorcee folded back in the cushy couch, arms crossed.

Parnevik thought the scene was pathetic. "You force my hand, Doctor. It's time to get ugly." He gathered the file, the check, and the green box to his side of the table and returned the items to his briefcase. He then removed another manila folder and slid it to Dr. Sarcorcee.

"What is this?" Sarcorcee asked.

"Just open it."

An x-ray photo of a human brain dated two days ago, plainly revealed a roundish lesion, a dark spot in the upper neck next to the medulla oblongata.

"Read the notation pastie on the back," Parnevik directed.

Dr. Sarcorcee flipped it over and scanned the note. His jaw dropped, blood leaving his face. "You bastard. You couldn't…. How could…?" He slammed the photo on the table. His face was beet-red. Animal survival reflexes were kicking in.

"Hold it, Doctor." Parnevik realized Sarcorcee was about to lose it. "She's fine. The implant is just under the skin. She doesn't even know it's there. Everything will be all right. We'll be done with our business together in several quick nights, and your career will suddenly take off. You'll be famous."

As Parnevik reiterated the obvious in a gilded, patronizing voice, the lines of fear stretching across the doctor's face faded. He had flashed through a milieu of feelings, finally settling on hopelessness. His daughter's life was in Parnevik's hands. One push of a remote control button and Parnevik could inflict any degree of pain he selected, even death.

Parnevik reached back into his briefcase and pushed the original file folder back in front of him. "We begin tonight at midnight. I trust we are clear?"

***

Parnevik walked out of the office, leaving a broken Dr. Sarcorcee to adjust to his fate. The big-headed oaf would rationalize his way back to stable ground, accept the situation, and invent a psychological patch to righteously support moving forward.

Parnevik had worked with the man. He would give in to his propensity to manipulate the truth and validate the unethical for personal gain.

Sidetracking out through a biochemistry lab, Parnevik avoided any undue notice by students visiting professors and advisors off the main hall. He was jubilant, but halfway down the short exit hallway, his knees weakened, and his legs felt wobbly. The corridor walls seemed to tilt. A bout of debilitating vertigo was on its way. The stress of role-playing required to crumble the greedy doctor's pathetically thin resolve had drained his control reserves.

Thankful it was between classes—leaving the hall empty—he staggered to a stainless steel drinking fountain and held tightly to an edge with one hand, fumbling with the other in his blazer pocket for the small plastic box. He flipped open a section and downed the three tablets. Holding his head to the side, parallel to the floor, his right hand against the wall, he guided himself some thirty feet down the hall and into a men's washroom. It required nearly ten minutes in a stall to perform the side-to-side head positions in his lap to neutralize the bout.

Parnevik spent the remainder of the day gathering supplies for the upcoming midnight lab session. He checked out of the Plaza as a precaution and left the car to be picked up by the rental agency. It was cash, cabs, and public transportation for this next sojourn.

Seventy-nine

The Trackers

"WHAT'S WITH THE baying all of a sudden?" Mallory asked. She was driving the Haggar Kennel van with Titus Smythe in the back, sitting on a bench next to Edwin's cage, keeping the animal company and periodically rewarding him with a doggy sweet.

"It's the exit you just passed," Smythe replied. "Take the next one and come back around. Parnevik must have made a pit stop."

They'd left Charlotte after a quick lunch and were traveling on I-20, now about twenty minutes from the I-285 convergence and forty minutes from downtown Atlanta. Edwin had been emitting a high whine every few miles, just like he did when he was first given Parnevik's winter coat back at the National rent-a-car lot.

"So he bays to change direction. Okay, I get it. The crying sound is when he's straight on the trail. It's just hard to believe."

"My exact reaction when I first met his father in 1986. Alfred took me on a bus ride across Philadelphia using the same talent. We kept in contact with the police. They followed in squad cars full of armed cops. Alfred bayed as the bus approached the stop where the fugitive had disembarked. We got off, and instead of whining and going off tracking, he sat at the bus stop and gave that yawning sound when a bus arrived he wanted to board. Incredible. On the third bus, Alfred took a spot in the aisle next to a man and whined, just like Edwin did back in the lot. I convinced the bus driver to pull over. The police screeched up and corralled a hideous serial killer of young boys."

"But, how does he do it?"

"Alfred had been a research subject off and on for years at Kentucky University's Medical Center in Lexington. Scientists believed that his family of bloodhounds possessed genes that allowed dominant individuals to tap into non-substance components of space. Researchers have known for decades that the universe is made up of particles we can detect, classify, and describe with three-dimensional physics, and other matter we can't. It is posited that disturbances from close contact between the two is discerned by the dog, a sort of fifth-dimension scenting. And evidently, the disturbances are nearly permanent, like leaving an obvious trail in the snow."

Mallory turned the van onto the exit, and Edwin ceased baying, changing to soft whining that indicated he was back on the trail. They pulled into an Exxon gas station where Edwin led Smythe into the men's washroom, made a quick walk-through, and came out sneezing. He lapped up half a quart of cold water and consumed a sweet, and once again the van was back on I-20 headed for Atlanta.

Forty minutes of differential whining and baying tones later, Mallory pulled the van into the underground parking garage at the Peachtree Plaza Hotel in downtown Atlanta. Over the course of the trip, she'd been talking periodically to Christine Johnson, bringing her the new information on Smythe's activities in France and Kentucky, and the amazing talents of the bloodhound named Edwin.

***

Once Ms. Johnson knew the name Parnevik was using, she instigated a charge card, bank account, and accommodations search. She was waiting on the results.

The FBI hooked up a direct link to the National Rental Car tracking program, which produced a two-day log of Parnevik's car movements, starting with the trip from Charlotte and an overnight in underground parking at the Peachtree Plaza Hotel. The car parked for several hours the afternoon of the next day in a church parking space on Peachtree Street. It returned to the hotel; then mid-evening, it parked at a McDonald's for two hours next to one of Southwest Atlanta's warehouse districts. Yesterday's final movements were a late night stop at Linda's Café in the heart of funky Virginia Highlands and then back to the Plaza just after midnight.

This morning he'd parked in the general parking lot at Georgia Tech University for two hours and then spent the rest of the daylight hours visiting scientific supply stores and back to the hotel.

By the time the full picture of Professor Pedersen's activities was complete, the FBI just missed him checking out of the Peachtree Plaza. At present, he was effectively off the radar with the Atlanta PD putting out an APB. The best clue Ms. Johnson had was his visit to Georgia Tech. The nano-science buildings were a good place to start. She organized a team to take the task on first thing in the morning.

***

It was 5:35 p.m. Ms. Johnson waited in the hotel lobby to meet and brief the trackers, and she was curious to finally make the acquaintance of Dickerson Phelps. She sat in the middle of an ornate, glass-enclosed atrium with an excellent field of view over the elevator banks and main entrance. She'd had a minor altercation with the hotel's general manager over access for the dog inside the hotel, but he reluctantly relented, not wanting to know the details—just that the visit would be short, uneventful and not involve other guests.

The elevator opened, and she had to stop herself from a supercilious grin. She covered her mouth with one hand. It was like a Dorothy team in the Wizard of Oz: Dickerson Phelps, the tall, thin man dressed in black with a flowing gray-brown beard and flat-topped Stetson; Mallory, exotic, long brown-blonde hair curling down her back and shoulders over a white pleated blouse, brown running shoes; the huge, brown and black bloodhound, mouth open, tongue hanging, ears flopping. Mallory saw her and waved.

"I am trusting your judgment of this lady," Smythe whispered twenty feet away.

"Be nice," Mallory hissed.

Ms. Johnson rose from an ornately carved Victorian chair with an extended hand toward the tall man holding the dog steady in its harness. "I'm Christine Johnson and I'm happy to meet you, Mister Phelps."

Smythe took her hand gently but had to firm up in response to the pressure of her grip. "Dickerson Phelps, licensed private investigator in the State of Georgia, at your service," Smythe said curtly, his head slightly bowed.

Ms. Johnson courteously greeted Mallory and motioned the odd group to chairs arranged around a small glass table. With everyone comfortable—the dog lying at Smythe's feet—she quickly itemized what she'd learned about Parnevik's last two days. "It took us until an hour ago tracking credit card use to locate Professor Pedersen registered at the Plaza. He had just checked out and notified the rental car company to pick the car up in the Plaza's underground parking lot. We don't know where he went."

 Eighty

Georgia Tech University

PARNEVIK BID FAREWELL to the lab around five thirty in the morning. The first session with Dr. Sarcorcee had gone smoothly. Albeit, Sarcorcee had been aloof and standoffish, clearly in fear for the safety of his daughter, but his eyes held a greedy gleam; his mind had made its contorted adjustments.

Parnevik allowed Sarcorcee to record the reprogramming of the stimulus intensities for the three *Fuerte* nanite packets needed for the Nebraska demonstration. Twenty remained, from the batch Ernest Kelto had stolen from Pharmco, for future recalibrations.

He'd also altered the stimulus levels on a dozen *Bliss* nanites, and then hand-prepared a blue-dyed, sugar accretion solution, creating the breath-mint tablets for the Genovese trial; the solution-accretion process was identical to that utilized on a mass scale by his contract manufacturers producing *Amor*, except *Amor* was red-dyed.

Dr. Sarcorcee had been mesmerized and amazed, busily taking notes and running the video camera. Parnevik simply altered the software programs on his computer and sent the digitally encoded changes as data bursts to nanite receivers via a common radio-frequency band.

Parnevik informed Sarcorcee he would be out of town for two days, and they agreed to meet on his return at the same time, same place. He would be true to his word, taking Sarcorcee through the machine miniaturization program and initiating and controlling a nanite replication process. He would wait until the last possible moment to reveal the structural plans for creating a standard nanite machine at full scale, along with Reagan Driscoll's body map program.

Walking off the deserted campus, the quiet and shadows casting off the campus lampposts began playing on Parnevik's mind. His meds were wearing thin and he needed sleep. But before he grabbed a convenient motel room near the campus and got some rest, he took a cab to Georgie Boy's condominium to deliver the vials of *Bliss* tablets Randle would need for tomorrow's New York City trip.

During the cab ride, he brought out a bottle of Evian and swallowed down a half dose of meds, but something was bothering him. Ever since leaving Sarcorcee's company, he'd involuntarily started checking to see if he was being followed, perhaps just a symptom of creeping paranoia from lack of medication. But the inclination to continually look out the back window of the cab stayed with him, so much so that he twice had the cab exit I-75 and pull into gas stations to see if he was being tailed.

He left the sack containing the vials inside Randle's front door and returned to the cab. During the trip back to the motel, he continued to peer out the back window and ponder what was eating at him.... He was medicated. Dr. Sarcorcee was under control. He was the only one who knew of his Professor Pedersen persona. After he no longer needed the lab, he'd release

Sarcorcee's daughter, allowing extraction of the implant. Sarcorcee could do whatever he wanted. It wouldn't matter if he reported everything, but it was more likely Sarcorcee would keep his mouth shut so he could conjure a method to rationally document his coming research of nanite breakthroughs. His future would be secure if he was careful.... And Randle wouldn't rat on him as long as things went smoothly, as they should. In any case, Parnevik would soon be long gone, and it wouldn't matter who knew what.

***

Three hours of sleep were all Parnevik could afford, but he was ready to initiate his next moves. It was 10:30 a.m. He quickly dressed and recreated the Professor Pedersen imagery, but something was still bothering him. Then, as he was about to make a flight reservation to Kansas City, one thing abruptly became apparent: Professor Harold Pedersen would only be of use one more time. He needed to disappear, and it should take place today.

He'd used the ID for four days now. The government, or whoever had been chasing him, would eventually figure out the ruse he'd pulled on the French glacier and conclude he'd gone to ground in Chamonix. Checking hotel registrations and security cameras on the day of the wing suit run would quickly lead to identification of single, mid-thirties males with his body type—and that would lead to Anthony Dubois traveling the next day to Marseilles, the nearest international airport. By running down all the passengers traveling from Marseilles to the U.S., they'd come across Pedersen, a man who had gone missing over a year ago. It wouldn't take long to pick up on his Atlanta location and Sarcorcee at Georgia Tech. Security cameras would have his picture. But at least he could count on Sarcorcee to only admit meeting Pedersen and refusing him use of the labs. No one would be suspicious of the late night sessions Sarcorcee conducted with research assistants. Parnevik was confident he'd give nothing away with his daughter still at risk and his mind focused on fame and avarice.

Having distilled what had been bothering him, he felt relieved and focused. It was shortly after noon when he checked out of the motel. He took a cab to the Federal Reserve Building a mile away, making one stop at a community bank to change a twenty-dollar bill into quarters.

By the time Parnevik entered the stone edifice of the Federal Reserve Bank, his confidence was on the upswing. He had two more sets of IDs from the courier's delivery in Marseilles; they were both Argentinean. And, he possessed a blank American passport originally ordered from Giovanni in Quebec City nearly six weeks ago.

The first Argentinean was Arturo Alverez, a businessman and consulting mechanical engineer with an advanced degree in structural engineering and fluid dynamics. Eased out of a large Argentine company at 36 years of age for drug abuse, he had successfully gone through his company's paid rehabilitation program and had been awarded a generous severance stipend. He'd been with the company for twelve years and was held in high regard as a successful and competent researcher, one known for innovation. A widower with no children, his parents and only brother deceased, he was now living alone in the suburbs of Buenos Aires in a small condominium, having nonexistent career prospects and dwindling financial resources.

The memory of the extensive research Parnevik had contracted regarding this man's life was lifting his spirits. He'd long ago planned for the eventuality of dealing with his final change of personality. But he was not yet ready to take action; there were still elements of his plan to be executed. Now, if all went well closing out his business in Atlanta, it could happen.

The second set of Argentine IDs from Giovanni were in the name of Jose Gomez, a beggar and minor thief for most of his thirty-eight years. He was an undocumented nobody living off the official radar of Argentinean society, soon to begin paying taxes for the first time in his life on interest income from a serendipitous inheritance. But Corey Parnevik was not destined to become Jose Gomez. He had other plans for Gomez.

The third identity was Parnevik's own creation, organized some six months ago around a freelance photographer named Gregory Campbell. Campbell worked out of his Atlanta home in the suburb of Marietta. Handsome, mustached, he was a black man in his mid-thirties, horn-rimmed glasses, long black hair held back in a braided ponytail. He could easily pass for a sophisticated Rastafarian.

Parnevik had run across Campbell in the lounge of the Doubletree Hotel in the trendy Buckhead section of Atlanta after a day's worth of shooting a Coca Cola TV gig. Parnevik frequented the bar because it was ten minutes away from Pharmco's headquarters, seldom crowded, and on the way to his Peachtree Battle residence in Midtown. He could relax there in the lounge's high-priced environment, knowing he'd never come across anyone he knew.

That particular afternoon, the bar had been practically empty; it wasn't a watering hole for after-work yuppies. Everyone flaunting their availability frequented the glitzy bars with upscale music and service pizzazz. Parnevik had cautiously taken a seat two stools away from Campbell, noticing he was talking to himself, apparently past his consumption limit. The minute Parnevik had gotten comfortable, and before he could object, Campbell had bought him a drink and taken the seat next to him. Two hours later, the lonely, single, generally non-gregarious individual had related his life's story. He was unhappy, unfulfilled, and at the constant mercy of the search for sufficiently lucrative work to keep ahead of his bills in a bad market.

As the time went by, Parnevik realized a golden opportunity had presented itself. He made a deal with Campbell. He would equip him with state-of-the-art equipment—sorely needed to remain competitive—and pay him two thousand dollars a month as a retainer. In return, Campbell agreed to teach Parnevik the ins and outs of planning and executing photographic and video shoots and to obtain duplicates of his driver's license and charge cards for Parnevik's use. But most importantly, Campbell agreed to disappear, when notified, to a location of his preference and to pay cash for all his needs until such a time as he was given word to return to his life. Parnevik had set up the capability to step into Campbell's shoes as needed.

Several months later, Parnevik had a local man, whose vocation was providing fake IDs for Latin American immigrants, enter Campbell's personal information and picture on the blank U.S. passport Parnevik had purchased from Giovanni.

***

The Federal Reserve Building housed an ancient bank of six, dark-wood-framed phone booths on its main floor—communications utilized fully in days long gone by. Parnevik entered the one farthest from the entrance. The antique booths had old-fashioned accordion doors, and once shut, the claustrophobic space exuded the unpleasant smell of time-accumulated odors.

Ten minutes and fourteen dollars' worth of quarters later, Parnevik hung up the phone, perplexed, a cascade of projections filling his imagination, pushing him toward overload. He felt a band of perspiration at his hairline.

He'd managed in Spanish to briefly speak with Giovanni's sister. Three days ago, after a surprise visit from two old friends from the U.S., the old man had suffered a fatal heart attack. The funeral had been yesterday.

He sat in the phone booth, claustrophobic, insecure, and exposed. He took two deep breaths. *I can do this*, he said to himself. *Yes I can*. His uncertainty was melting away. If he had to, as a last resort, he'd institute the final act of the play a little earlier than planned. For now, although he didn't like it, he would have to accept the risk of acquiring or buying one more change of identities without control over the source. But it could be done…maybe the same way he'd done it in Marseilles.

Exiting the Federal Reserve Building into the brisk winter air, his confidence was returning. First, he walked south down Peachtree and entered a Starbuck's, two blocks from his next stop at a Barclay's bank branch. He used its Wi-Fi to book a flight to Los Angles leaving in two hours.

At the bank, he withdrew a little over seventy-five hundred dollars and presented written instructions to a bank officer to close out his Pedersen banking relationship as soon as processing the debit card transaction for his round trip ticket to L.A. cleared the account.

 Eighty-one

New York City

UPON CLOSE INSPECTION, the average person wouldn't be able to tell them apart. George Randle *was* Corey Parnevik. Similar in height, weight, complexion, and hair color, even their posture and carriage were alike. Randle's hair had been cut by a professional to match. A facial mask had been constructed, and he'd been instructed in the application of the mustache and chin beard Parnevik had previously worn in the presence of Genovese Family members.

Randle felt strangely empowered, looking out through a costume at the world. A Halloween party. He could say and do anything he wanted and no one would know it was him.

Parnevik had grilled him in maintaining a clipped, self-assured demeanor, to be commanding, and to react and respond to scenarios he might encounter dealing with the Genovese. Parnevik had been nothing but comprehensive and efficient in building up Randle's confidence.

Randle wore silver, wire-framed glasses, an expensive sterling silver bracelet and was clad in the casual clothing Parnevik favored. He appeared to be a successful young entrepreneur. He even carried Parnevik's cherished Filston briefcase.

Exiting the aircraft at LaGuardia, gate G-4, he felt a sense of pride, and with each stride down the broad walkway, his bearing reflected increased self-confidence. He headed past the security area and out into the arriving-passenger greeting area where he was to call the number Parnevik had given him for Angie's Italian Restaurant, telling whoever answered he had landed and would be there shortly. It was 11:45 a.m.

Approaching the terminal concourse, he spotted two men in dark suits and black hats, the smaller one holding up a sign with Parnevik's name scribbled on it. Randle was surprised, and apprehension suddenly took hold. No one was supposed to meet him. Parnevik hadn't prepared him for this situation. He strode on straight-backed, adjusting, taking stock. He could do this.... They looked out of place, a little like hit men in a bad 1950s movie.

Well, here goes. Got to earn my keep. Randle waved as he continued to approach, keeping a neutral reaction on his face, strictly business. "I didn't expect a welcoming committee," he said without smiling.

"Mister Parnevik, please follow me," the smaller man said, turning toward the terminal exit without any gesture or word of greeting, the larger man falling in behind. "We'll be takin' you to the meeting," he said over his shoulder. His dark eyes were vacant. He crumpled up the cardboard sign and tossed it in a trashcan next to the exit doors.

A black, four-door Town Car stood waiting just outside the exit, white exhaust issuing from its duals and the trunk open. The driver was outside the vehicle, chatting away with a TSA security guard. The bigger man roughly relieved Randle of his briefcase and tossed it into the trunk. The smaller man opened the back door and Randle climbed in, fear mounting. This was not part of his rehearsals.

Randle noticed it was raining, a gloomy day in New York City. He was boxed in-between the two goons. "What's the weather supposed to be like?" Randle asked, attempting to break the ice.

The bigger man leaned over and snapped a bear hug on Randle, pinning his arms. The smaller man pulled a syringe from a pocket at the back of the front seat and jammed it home in Randle's left thigh. "It's going to continue to rain on your parade, Mister Parnevik."

***

Gradually, the fog in his mind dissipated. His throat was bone dry, and the taste on his palate was sour grapes. He heard conversation, low and far away. His eyes focused. He was alone in a square room dimly lit by a banker's light sitting on a desk full of papers, magazines, coffee mugs, and ashtrays. A fancy, wheeled office chair behind the desk was an anomaly in the middle of the clutter. The desk occupied the middle of one slate-gray wall. He was in the center of the room, tied to a heavy, metal, straight-backed chair bolted to a stained linoleum floor that used to be light brown. Pungent air left over from lengthy exposure to cigar and cigarette smoke attacked his nasal passages. A huge ceiling fan hung overhead. Two old leather couches and a beat-up wooden table covered with take-out wrappers, overloaded ashtrays, and coffee cups were opposite the desk and behind Randle. A door outlined with dirty, drawn venetian blinds occupied the middle of the third wall. A stuffed floor-to-ceiling bookcase covered the fourth.

Randle was frightened beyond any time in his memory, but he reached inside, remembering what Parnevik had told him: *No matter what happens, just keep your cool and bring the situation back to one of the scenarios. You carry all the cards, but you have to create a game to play them. You can do it.*

The door opened abruptly. Three men lumbered in. He recognized the first two from Parnevik's descriptions: the titular family don, Tony Gatturna, and the *consigliore*, Paulie Torentino. The third man was the small fellow with black eyes and stubby hands that had plunged the needle into his leg. Gatturna slid into the plush chair behind his desk and lit up a cigar. The other two sat on the couches. Randle faced the desk.

"Well, how does it feel now, Mister Parnevik?" Gatturna asked, casting smoke rings in the air. "No more of your rules, no more emails, no more travel. You work for me now."

Randle took a leap of faith and went into a prepared scenario. "I've brought you the *Bliss* sample you requested."

Gatturna eyed the couches. "Get his stuff, Barry."

The small man jumped off the couch, opened a locker next to the bookcase, and brought the briefcase to the side of Gatturna's desk.

"You don't talk to me unless I ask you something. You got it? Or do you want little Barry here to loosen your tongue and teach you some manners?"

"That won't be necessary, Mister Gatturna, but I can't in good conscience accept your offer—"

"It's not an offer, you supercilious little prick. You caused me and Paulie a lot of grief. Barry, give our new employee an initiation lesson."

In a second, the heavy-set little man with the ferret eyes was standing in front of Randle and snarling. He wound up a stubby right hand and slammed it into Randle's mid-section. Randle felt his ribs cave, the helplessness of pain, and the futile effort his body was making to take a breath.

"Now, do we have your attention and cooperation?" Gatturna continued to blow smoke rings. He'd been through this process countless times.

Randle finally was able to take in small gasps of air, but the pain was excruciating. Little Barry stood to his side like a faithful bull terrier. "I have some realities I think you need to know before we continue," Randle rasped, wincing. "A moment please."

"We don't have time for your bullshit, Parnevik." But suddenly Gatturna wasn't so sure of what his next step should be. He could lock him up until he came around to accepting his fate. Or, he could pry from him what was needed for his boys to set up a production lab and be rid of the arrogant prick.

Gatturna was glaring at Randle, evidently deciding to wait and hear what he had to say. "Well?"

"Thank you." Randle struggled to lift his head and make solid eye contact. "You need to know that I have two implanted devices within my body. One is activated by applying pressure above its location. That causes a signal to a satellite. That signal in turn initiates a short broadcast to all the *Amor* nanite machines contained in your inventory, wherever they are, to self-destruct."

Paulie stood from the couch, a concerned expression on his face. "Is that what you warned us about in the beginning?"

"No. That warning was for any attempt to experiment with *Amor* by analysis. If the tablets are penetrated in any way or brought into solution, they self-destruct and that event triggers self-destruct in nearby inventory. I assume you must have experienced this or you wouldn't be asking."

Gatturna placed his cigar in an ashtray, and his mouth was moving, a tic of contemplation. "What about the second device?"

"It's similar in function. It signals the satellite to send a detailed chronology of our relationship to the email accounts of major media editors.... And, please, don't take me lightly. The devices can't be located with today's scanning equipment. They also are nano-machines. A hundred could fit on the point of a needle, and because they are not metallic, they will go undetected.

And, please, no more muscle stuff. Our relationship can be long and profitable so long as you trust me and follow the operating parameters. To reiterate, you will not know my whereabouts—do not try and track me. That will result in changing partners. Product orders will be handled in the same established manner. If you are satisfied with the *Bliss* samples, the identical price, royalty percentage, and ordering process will be in effect. *Bliss* is now available. You contact me through email." Randle said it just like in practice, and he sensed he'd regained a semblance of control.

Gatturna made a decision. He despised having his inner circle witness an act of conciliation, but the Family was a business operating in a changing world, and he couldn't afford to be left behind. He was caught in this situation without countering capabilities. So, he'd eat a little crow.

As he'd listened to Parnevik, he realized this crafty little bastard could insulate himself from the Family's reach, but how could he keep himself out of the government's clutches? "It appears you have a winning agreement." Gatturna relit his cigar. "Barry, cut his bonds and take a seat.... We do business. Now, how can we be sure the *Bliss* product is street-ready?"

"I tested it myself," Randle said, the tightness in his chest releasing. "It's ready. I suggest you have several of your staff that are familiar with the effects of LSD try the product. In my briefcase is a green box containing twelve vials, twelve sample tablets that look and taste like breath mints. A mild dose of high quality LSD produces a similar effect to heroin. The samples are set to give that kind of trip for two hours. Unlike LSD, the trip does not linger on, leaving the participant affected for an extended period of time."

"Okay, we'll do that," Gatturna said smartly, taking a long pull on his cigar. "You want something to eat, drink?"

"No thank you, Mister Gatturna."

"Paulie, take the box and round up six volunteers—different ages and sexes. Let's see what we got."

***

Paulie organized a late afternoon meal in a small, cordoned-off banquet room at the rear of Angie's Restaurant. It had taken a couple of hours to assemble a group of close-by family members.

The six individuals participated in an opening toast to good fortune and dug into a traditional Italian feast, just as they had on many occasions at Angie's. As the meal progressed, Gatturna and Paulie observed behavior. The participants were all curious why the wonderful two-hour party had been so enjoyable: smiles and laughter; endless comments on the delicately flavored food and superb wine; the classical music had been delightful—each instrumental group clear and perfect; the lingering fragrances emanating from the fresh-cut flowers on the table were divine.

The Genovese family members were unaware they had successfully tested a product that would soon shock the world and replace hard drugs with ten times greater profit margins. And, it would all be legal. Breath mints.

***

At ten o'clock the next morning, the Genovese cadre gathered in Angie's basement office. The word had gone out last night, the minute Parnevik departed for the airport, escorted by Little Barry. The six regional chiefs were present via Skype split-screens. After Gatturna explained the background and what had transpired the previous day, the meeting turned into a feeding frenzy of projected greed. The money would be astronomical, but everyone agreed the change over process would have to be gradual, and all interested parties would have to be brought to the table. The Family would have to share the spoils. Consensus was that sharing wasn't a negative factor. The Family would literally inherit a ready-made, policed, worldwide distribution network. No overhead.

The meeting ended with Paulie taking responsibility for developing a plan to introduce *Bliss* to the world of drug cartels. They had ordered a beginning inventory from the contract manufacturer in Vietnam and made the appropriate payment to Parnevik's European bank account. They would have product within two weeks.

"Time to go home, eh, Paulie?" Gatturna said. They were the only two left in the office, and it was well past two in the morning. Though pleased and still electrified with the future prospects, Gatturna was visibly worn out: too much wine, too many cigars, and too much lingering stress from having to deal with Parnevik.

"Home it is, Boss. But we still got that same problem. The little faggot has to stay clear of the law. How we gonna make sure that happens? He goes down, everything falls apart, and we end up the baddest guys in a world full of bad guys."

The computer on Gatturna's desk softly chimed, indicating receipt of an email from the Family's system. He rose from the couch with a groan and half-collapsed into his desk chair, wondering who could possibly be sending email at two o'clock in the morning. He tapped in his password.

The email was addressed to Gatturna's encrypted email address. No other person would be able to open it. There were no signatures at the bottom of the message, no name for the sender. Gatturna read it and continued to stare at the screen, backing into his desk chair, alarm etched across his face.

Dear Mr. Gatturna:

Your attendance is required at 10:30 this morning in Room 416 of the NYC Public Library on 47th Street in Manhattan. You will be met by Special Agent Ryan McKenzie of the DEA at the fountain in front of the building. He will identify himself, conduct you to the room, and present you with important business information. The meeting is top secret. No recording devices of any kind, and there will be no record of the meeting having taken place. You are to come alone and tell no one of the meeting. Failure to attend will be interpreted as treason and immediate actions will be taken to appre-hend you, your family, and your associates. You have a total of five minutes to click on the link below, indicating your understanding and commitment to comply. This email will automatically delete six minutes after its opening.

It was supposed to be impossible for unauthorized senders to gain access to the Family's communication system. He was paying top dollar. Suddenly, Gatturna felt a blanket of palpable terror, a tide of trepidation threatening to suffocate him. His breathing turned raspy and the room seemed to grow smaller.

"What's the matter, Boss?" Paulie had waited out the minutes of silence and changes in facial expression, watching Gatturna's shoulders slump as he'd fixated on the computer screen.

Gatturna slumped into the back of his desk chair. "Water, Paulie. Just get me a glass of water," he said flatly. The concept of security was tenuous if not a complete sham; perhaps it had always been that way and he had not seen it. How could the Family adjust, let alone thrive? What could he do? What could any of them do?

 Eighty-two

Corey Parnevik

PARNEVIK LEFT THE Barclay's bank branch and took a cab to Atlanta's Hartsfield International Airport. It was 3:30 p.m., and Harold Pedersen was due to depart on the Southwest Airline's 4:35 p.m. flight to L.A. For all practical purposes, Professor Harold Pederson would cease to exist later this evening at the Los Angeles International Airport.

It had been a breeze to bribe another passenger waiting to board at the L.A. gate. Two crisp hundred-dollar bills did the trick, and they exchanged boarding pass packets. Parnevik waited until the passenger boarded and simply tossed the other man's pass in the trash on his way back to the main terminal. Pursuers should be thrown off track for at least two days before discovering Pedersen was not Pedersen. It would give Parnevik all the time he needed in Albuquerque.

The flight to Kansas City was scheduled to depart at 11:08 p.m., allowing time to negotiate what he required. He roamed the terminal food courts, looking for the perfect fit. It cost fifteen hundred dollars in cash to convince a casually dressed and unhurried man about his age, height, and build—and one who carried a passport—to purchase a roundtrip ticket in his name to Kansas City, relinquish his driver's license, and agree to reschedule his own flight for the next day. Gerald Jones could easily obtain a duplicate driver's license at his leisure, and his passport would serve as adequate identification.

Parnevik exited a taxi at the nearby Renaissance Concourse Hotel at 6:35 p.m. He rented a room to adjust his facial features and hairstyle to resemble Gerald Jones. His cash and the newly acquired driver's license should ensure anonymity for the next two days of travel. Then, back to Atlanta to finish his business with Sarcorcee and produce *Bliss* inventory for his contract manufacturers. The final act would soon follow.

***

Randle returned to Atlanta from New York City, investing his own money to upgrade to first class. His chest ached from Little Barry's gut punch, and every time he took a deep breath, piercing pain shot along his spine, causing him to bend over for relief. But, he'd pulled it off. The Genovese had agreed to every stipulation on the list Parnevik had him memorize.

A decent, relaxing meal, along with a palatable Merlot, helped make the two and a half hour flight an effective wind-down, allowing Randle to review and assess. He had one more of these human proxy trips left to perform for Parnevik.

After what had happened with the Genovese, he felt a little skittish. Some of his self-confidence had been chipped away by exposure to brutality.... It was naïve to believe all the possible contingencies would be covered inside Parnevik's unfolding gambits. He would need more assurances and a deeper understanding of what lay ahead the next day in Nebraska. And, he'd need more money. A lot more money.

***

Parnevik left the room at the Renaissance Concourse and returned to the airport at 7:45 p.m. He headed to the arrival/departure board to check flights. Georgie Boy's flight from LaGuardia was running fifteen minutes late, scheduled at 9:36 p.m. The timing was working out perfectly. He was anxious to know how it had gone with the Genovese and ensure Randle was stable and motivated for tomorrow's job in Nebraska.

Having forty-five minutes to kill, he headed to a Hudson newsstand to pick up a good book, with the intent of indulging in steak fajitas at the Chili's restaurant two shops down.

As it turned out, Randle's flight from LaGuardia was forty-five minutes late, causing Parnevik to cut the visit short.

He'd approached Georgie from the rear, walking down the exit concourse. After the initial shock of meeting Gerald Jones, Georgie related his frightening ordeal, but there was pride in his countenance. He said he was ready for Nebraska and asked about the bottled water. He also asked for a bonus. Parnevik didn't have time to bicker and agreed to wire transfer Randle's second payment and a bonus of $50,000 to his bank account first thing in the morning.

Parnevik cleared security and had to run most of the way to his departure gate. Luckily it was on the "A" concourse. He was surprised he wasn't upset with Randle's greed and obvious blackmail. Georgie Boy certainly lit up when he'd agreed to the bonus. He'd wire Randle the blood money. It was still a small price to pay for protection.

When he returned from Albuquerque, he should only need one more night at the Georgia Tech lab to complete Sarcorcee's education, make any adjustments to further perfect *Fuerte*—if the results of the Nebraska demonstration required it—and then he'd say goodbye to Atlanta and hello to the final act in the play.

Settling in his first class seat, he was actually smiling. He even bantered with the flight attendant who took his Grey Goose martini order the moment he took his seat. It was a little over a two-hour flight to Kansas City, and back in control he was prepared to enjoy every minute of it.

 Eighty-three

Emma's House

LAST EVENING, AFTER goodbyes to a disconsolate and skeptical Ms. Johnson in the lobby of the Peachtree Plaza Hotel, Mallory, McKenzie, Smythe, and Edwin re-boarded the kennel van, and with Edwin continuing to periodically whine, they headed for Emma's house.

The group had agreed to meet with Ms. Johnson outside the Plaza's entrance at 8:00 a.m. the next morning—prior to the FBI's invasion of the nano-facilities at Georgia Tech—to see if the dog could actually pick up Parnevik's trail.

As McKenzie drove down Peachtree Street, Mallory called Emma and informed her that her two additional guests were on their way. Emma loved big dogs, and though she'd many times contemplated owning one, she never acted on it; she couldn't see herself taking the responsibility for a pet and watching it grow old and pass away.

"Will Edwin be able to pick up Parnevik?" Mallory asked.

"I believe so, as long as we give him another sniff at Parnevik's coat. The trail is no colder nor more complex than situations where he's already demonstrated competence."

"It's still hard to fathom."

"He's a good boy," Smythe said, soothing the hound and massaging his hindquarter. "Don't fret, Miss Mallory, as long as he gets a good night's rest, he'll be ready."

On the way to Emma's, McKenzie stopped at a grocery store to pick up some pre-made fried chicken, potato salad, and a supply of dog food.

It was a cordial meal. Smythe was unusually candid and charming, unlike his derisive nature in the company of Mrs. Leonard. Emma appeared more relaxed now that Homeland Security administrative personnel had fully replaced Military Intelligence. Thankfully, research under Pharmco's government contract was firmly on hold. The workplace and daily routine were still restricted, but all regular business activities had resumed.

The chatty evening ended with everyone making an early exit in favor of soft beds. Emma made Edwin a cradle of old blankets on the front porch and put out a bowl of water. The pooch took to it without fuss, yawning and accepting several goodnight head-pats.

 Eighty-four

Kansas City, Missouri

PARNEVIK ARRIVED AT 12:15 a.m., Kansas City time. The quiet airplane flight left him refreshed and invigorated. Clutching his Filston, twill carry-on and bidding his first-class flight attendant a special goodbye, he was one of three people exiting the early morning flight.

Trouncing through the connector tube to the exit gate, he vividly remembered the attendant had actually gone out of her way to service his every need, more so than any of the other passengers in first class. It led him to believe he could be likeable if he tried.

He cabbed it to Kansas City's Union Station and headed for the Amtrak booth. He paid cash for a first-class cabin on the Southwest Chief to Albuquerque and strode over to the well-known Pierponts Restaurant. It was closed, as was every other shop in the station except the newsstand, so he decided to meander outside and look around.

Two blocks away, he discovered a seedy, little all-night grill and took a seat at the bar. There was only one other person in the place: a business-type at a table along a far wall, engrossed in his laptop screen, probably also waiting for a train. CNN was on the tube, going through its taped, late-night thirty-minute wrap-up of the day's events. While he watched, he ordered a Budweiser draft and a pulled-pork sandwich that turned out passably good. Finishing the meal, his mind began to wander. He felt a flood of well-being, an effervescent feeling of self-satisfaction. With only cash and a valid driver's license, he could travel anywhere in the country by train, bus, or air for that matter, with no questions asked.

With two more hours remaining before the Amtrak left for Albuquerque, his appetite and thirst satiated, he returned to a virtually abandoned Union Station. Parnevik liked it that way; he had to be very watchful in crowds. They caused his attention to scatter, resulting in a fit of paranoia. Attending major sporting events had always been out of the question.

He found a Wi-Fi table near the newsstand and instigated two wire transfers out of his numbered account in Lichtenstein. One went to the Western Union's Albuquerque branch for $9900, payable to cash and released on call to Gerald Jones; it was the cash he would need for contemplated transactions in Albuquerque. The second was for $2,250,000, payable to the Buenos Aires law firm of Marval, O'Farrell & Mairal and held in escrow for the benefit of a new client, Arturo Alvarez.

Business taken care of, he broke out the novel he'd purchased in the Atlanta airport and attempted to relax as best he could on one of the hard seats in the station waiting area. He could sleep later in his secure Amtrak cabin. He was anxious to hear how Georgie Boy was faring, but he'd have to wait to check in until the late afternoon. With Randle taking the morning flight to Nebraska, his challenges would just be getting underway in Albuquerque's early afternoon.

 Eighty-five

New York City Public Library

LAST NIGHT THE President of the New York City Library System received an unusual phone call at his home. An Assistant Attorney General with the Justice Department issued him orders to cordon off the entire third floor of the main branch in Midtown Manhattan from the next day's opening until such a time as DEA, Special Agent Ryan McKenzie released the order.

Guards from a designated private security firm were to be posted at all entrance and egress points to the third floor. Agent McKenzie and his guest were the only persons allowed access—no explanation given, except the country appreciated his patriotism. No one was to know of the activity, and compliance was considered commensurate with the highest interests of national security.

***

Agent Ryan McKenzie checked his watch. It was 10:25 a.m., and he had been waiting for fifteen minutes in the chill of the breezy morning, leaning against the base of a stone lion statue halfway up the massive granite steps to the library's main entrance.

A taxi pulled up to the curb a few minutes later, and a trim, lanky man dressed in a dark-blue business suit and wearing a '50s top hat climbed out smoking a cigar, immediately casting his gaze up the library steps.

McKenzie recognized Tony Gatturna, the titular head of the Genovese Family. He stood tall and motioned the man to follow as he turned and took the rest of the stairs up to the entrance.

He waited in a small alcove just inside the first set of double doors. Gatturna came through the doorway, startled by McKenzie's presence in the confined space.

"Get rid of the cigar." McKenzie looked Gatturna straight in the eyes. Gatturna's thin leathery face gave no sign of fear, and his long nose and smirking mouth made him look like just another gangster. "I'm Special Agent Ryan McKenzie." McKenzie displayed his badge. "Put your hands on the wall and spread your legs." McKenzie took his time patting him down. "Follow me," he said flatly. "We'll be taking the stairs to the third floor."

An armed guard at the top of the staircase stood in front of the wooden doors opening into the third floor's reference-book section. McKenzie displayed his credentials, and the guard opened the doors. Inside, it was as quiet as a tomb, the air tainted with the smell of musty old books.

The spacious floor was open, the quiet unsettling. Row upon row of ancient bookshelves separated lines of heavy, wooden study tables. The lingering scent of disinfectant rose from the granite flooring. They were completely alone.

When the double doors closed, McKenzie said, "Walk through the scanning arch. I'll be right behind you. Take a look at the screen as I pass through. This room is free of all recording devices. It's sterile."

Gatturna didn't bother to view the security monitor. "What's all this bullshit?"

McKenzie directed Gatturna to follow him, pointing behind the reference information desk to a line of offices framed in thick wooden trim that had darkened over the years.

McKenzie opened the door to the last office in the row. "Sit down. This won't take long." McKenzie gestured to a six-foot, collapsible table in the middle of the barren room with common office chairs at each end. Reluctantly, Gatturna took a chair and grunted something in Italian. McKenzie remained standing, waiting for the arrogant man to give him his attention.

"I have been empowered to inform you face to face of the following summons: You are to appear, in person and alone, tomorrow at 11:00 a.m. in Room 309 at the Department of Justice in Washington D.C. for the purpose of executing a mutually beneficial agreement with the government of the United States. Your failure to comply with this summons, or if you should reveal to anyone what has transpired today—or will transpire tomorrow—will cause your immediate apprehension as a terrorist and incarceration at facilities in Guantanamo Bay, Cuba. There will be no written or digital records of any kind today or at any time during your Washington visit. This meeting never occurred. You are free to leave."

"This is a travesty. It's a free country. I don't have to do anything you say."

"Mister Gatturna, do what you believe is best." Agent McKenzie turned and left the room, carefully closing the door, a clicking sound punctuating his exit. Tony Gatturna sat at the table, grimacing, tapping his fingers on the surface, pondering the unthinkable.

 Eighty-six

Peachtree Plaza Hotel

BRIGHT SUN AND increased humidity were harbingers of an unseasonably warm, late winter day in Atlanta. The group of three that greeted each other outside the hotel entrance was exalting the unusual intensity of the sun's warmth, only vaguely aware they were the source of rubber-necking from the dense sidewalk traffic passing them by in both directions—early workers trying to get to their places of business before 8:00 a.m. It was the tall, thin, bearded man with the flat-topped Stetson and the big brown and black bloodhound causing the attention. Agent Ryan McKenzie was due back in mid-afternoon from his meeting with the Genovese in New York City.

"Well, how does this work?" Ms. Johnson looked up at Smythe.

A short, crisp bark from Edwin startled her. The dog was actually staring at her.

"Give him another go with the coat, if you would, Miss Mallory," Smythe said.

Ms. Johnson watched the ritual of sniffs and snorts. Then abruptly, Edwin gave out a soft whine and pulled at his harness to go south down the sidewalk.

"He's ready, Miss Johnson. All we need do is let him take us where he will. But I can tell you this. After last night's sleep, this morning I sensed Parnevik spent most of the afternoon yesterday at the airport, and I believe he left Atlanta. I am sure Edwin will undoubtedly end up there. This little demonstration is for you alone. Edwin will be most useful when we are close on Parnevik's trail, where my gift, as it were, is no longer effective."

It was quite a sight. The whining and baying hound led the three of them to backtrack to the kennel van in the Peachtree Plaza parking lot.

Ten minutes later, a mile and a half down Peachtree Street, the pooch yelped.

"He wants to stop," Smythe said.

They parked in a no parking zone in front of the Atlanta Federal Reserve Building.

Ms. Johnson turned to Smythe. "What now?"

"We go see where he wants to go," Mallory cut in.

The dog led them up the stone steps to the multi-door, building entrance. Ms. Johnson badged them past the befuddled uniformed guards.

Yes, the information desk personnel remembered a man answering the description of Professor Pedersen yesterday morning around noon, asking if he could use one of the phone booths.

The next stop was the campus of Georgia Tech University. Edwin led the group to the office of Dr. Edward Sarcorcee, Director of the Georgia Tech Nanotechnology Research Center. Ms. Johnson introduced herself and the members of the group. The group stood inside Sarcorcee's glass office space, listening while Ms. Johnson grilled him.

Sarcorcee appeared stunned and hesitant when the questions were posed, admitting he'd met with Professor Pedersen yesterday afternoon, but he claimed nothing came of the meeting. The group listened to him explain why he had turned down Pedersen's request for access to the research center's equipment: there was a two month waiting list for lab space, and the professor's need was immediate; and the board would have rejected the request based on the lack of credentials required for the nano research he proposed.

Ms. Johnson directed Sarcorcee to report any future contact with Pedersen directly to the FBI Atlanta Field Office, putting him on notice that their interest was a national security matter. She also made it clear he would be called in for a more complete interview in the coming days.

As the group was returning to the kennel van, Mallory said flatly, "If I'm correct, we're at a standstill here."

"We'd best head for the airport with Edwin," Smythe said.

"And what about this gift of yours, Mister Phelps?" Ms. Johnson asked, her tone ringing with skepticism. "As I understand it, you're supposed to be able to sense Parnevik as close as fifteen hours in the past."

"That is true, Miss Johnson, though approximate. I admit my abilities are flawed and intermittent. And even when they are active, unless there are sufficiently charged emotions emanating from Parnevik, I pick up very little."

Ms. Johnson's cell phone chirped inside her purse. "Excuse me," she said, holding up short of the van, phone pressed to her ear.... "That was an FBI technician. Pedersen used a debit card to book a flight to L.A. that departed from Hartsfield last night at 11:08 p.m."

"I realize it may seem anti-climactic, but we must go to the airport," Smythe said. "I'm sensing the situation might not be so straightforward."

 Eighty-seven

Lincoln, Nebraska

GEORGE RANDLE DEPLANED on schedule in Lincoln, swiftly making his way to the terminal exit to grab a taxi. *So far so good.* No tough guys with black hair and blue suits were waiting.

It was 10:15 a.m. He had until 3:00 to do his job, meet with the pharmaceutical representative, and get seated for the match in the first round of the NCAA National Wrestling Championships. According to the plan, Randle was only interested in the match at 149 lbs. between last year's NCAA champion from Iowa State University and a freshman from Nebraska who had little hope of victory.

***

"How goes it, Georgie?"

"Nice of you to ring me," Randle said sharply, not seeing Parnevik's ID on the phone screen. He was still irritated Parnevik had cut their time short when he'd landed in Atlanta last night from his confrontation with the Genovese. He shuddered at the memory of crude Italian hospitality. There had been no time to revel in his success, but he had stated and justified his demands— and he'd felt somewhat healed this morning by the $70,000 deposit newly resting in his bank account.

"It's going as planned so far. I used the Evian uniform you gave me and did like you said. I walked right into the arena and left two cases of bottles in the main locker-room supply closet, along with the cooler icing down two bottles."

"Any trouble with the injection?"

"No, it went just like in practice…. All I have to do this afternoon is stage them. At least there are no mafia in this project."

"I'm sorry about that, George. Even the greatest of masters is imperfect. What about the rep meeting?" Parnevik was smiling. He'd been killing time at the Albuquerque train station, waiting to give Georgie Boy sufficient latitude to accomplish his morning's objectives.

What an egotistical asshole. "I didn't expect a Korean to show up as a pharmaceutical representative. He was on time in the lobby of the Marriott like you said. He introduced himself, a Mister Jang, very formal, very officious, very much to the point, not like any salesman I ever met."

"Just play along. Stick with the plan. After the match, you're done. You give him the envelope and inform him it contains the basis for further negotiations. That's all. You tell him you'll be awaiting his reply and get out of there. I'm sure he'll have lots of questions during the match, but if his probes get outside the areas we've covered together, you defer explanations to future cooperative negotiations…and don't forget to video the match. Your seats are in the front row right next to the mats. Then you come home and make a DVD of the video. I'll call you before you get aboard the flight home to see how it went and tell you where to mail the DVD. If you need to talk to me, from now on do it using a public phone at this number." Parnevik recited the number.

***

Hwang Jang, the Deputy Director of North Korea's Integrated Technology Center, a military department that studied bio, chemical, and nuclear solutions for military needs, had been directed to personally observe the demonstration.

The North Korean Intelligence Service had gone to great lengths to provide him with a business cover as a pharmaceutical representative of PyongSu, a six-year-old North Korean drug distributor headquartered in Pyongyang. He had scheduled visits to marketing executives of both the Merck and Pfizer corporations in the U.S. He was also an avid wrestling fan.

***

The University of Nebraska coliseum was located in the heart of the campus, next to the Memorial Stadium. A perfect setting for college wrestling, the Coliseum had been home to the National Duals off and on from 1993 to the present. It had hosted the Big 12 Championships the last three years in a row when Nebraska claimed overall dominance. This afternoon, it was hosting the first round of the NCAA-Division I wrestling championships.

Randle's arrangement with the Korean pharmaceutical rep was to meet at their seats ten minutes before the start of the first match in the 149-lb weight class. Parnevik's plan called for two face-to-face contacts: the strictly introductory meeting at the hotel and observing the match together.

Parnevik had picked the first round of the tournament's 149-lb weight class because the University of Nebraska's wrestling team had a glaring deficiency at that weight; an inexperienced freshman had the slot, and he was scheduled against last year's defending NCAA champion, a senior from Iowa State.

As it happened, the seating surrounding the mat for the match was packed with rambunctious students, and Randle only managed to find his seat by locating Mr. Jang in the crowd. The little Oriental man was actually beaming as he caught sight of Randle making his way along the mat's outside circumference.

"You are late, Mister Parnevik," he said, still smiling as Randle squeezed into the space where Jang had placed his briefcase to save the spot.

The North Korean was hard to miss in a Nebraska University letter jacket, wearing jeans, a Nebraska wrestling jersey, and a matching baseball cap. A pendant hung around his neck like a '60s hippy. He no longer looked officious. Randle thought he must be trying to fit in.

Their seats were at floor level in the middle of the Nebraska side of the wrestling arena. "Sorry." Randle scootched further into a more comfortable position. The crowd was noisy: students chanting slogans, whistling, and shouting challenges. He leaned over to whisper close to the rep's ear. "I had a little trouble getting into the Nebraska team locker room and convincing the head coach that he was supposed to use the sponsor's water for the match. I stayed long enough to witness the Nebraska wrestler drinking the iced-down Evian. I left two cases of unopened bottles to make it look corporate."

"Ah, so that is how the test dosage is administered," Mr. Jang said. "And what is to be anticipated? Your choice of venues was unexpected."

"We observe, Mister Jang. I don't want you to have expectations. The test demonstration should have maximum veracity with a random, unsuspecting subject. One parameter I want you to understand up front is that the duration of effects is calibrated to approximately fifteen minutes. I will be taking a video of the match, starting now." Randle pulled a Sony digital HD video camera and a small collapsible tripod from a jacket pocket. He married the two and set them up on the floorboards between his legs.

The outside of the circular wrestling mat contained a table populated by two referees and two scorers. It, along with two team benches for the contestants and their coaches, divided the circle in thirds.

The contestants entered the arena, and the spectators immediately quieted down. Each of the wrestlers wore team-colored, spandex singlets, headgear, and special shoes. The Nebraska freshman wore tight red leggings. Together with their coaches and support team, they migrated around the outside of the mat to their respective benches. The wrestlers stretched while the rest organized equipment, first-aid gear, towels, and the like.

Randle shifted his attention to the Nebraska bench. He breathed a sigh of relief, noticing a support member place the green and white cooler next to the contestant, and a case of Evian bottles was unopened and stashed under the bench. A flurry of thoughts crossed his mind. Matches were one three-minute period and two, two-minute periods, a total of seven minutes; overtime was limited to two sets of two, thirty-second periods with a minute in between. The nanites released in the digestive tract would take perhaps ten minutes to get into position and begin releasing stimulus. The plan called for the freshman wrestler to have hydrated in the locker room, which Randle had witnessed. So, he should begin to feel the effects right about now; and no matter how long the match lasted, the *Fuerte* shouldn't wear off.

Randle glued his attention to the bench. Perspiration sprouted across his brow. He wanted confirmation the wrestler had consumed at least six ounces. As if on command, the freshman contestant reached down and opened the cooler, taking out the Evian bottle and chugging a couple of swallows. The bottle was half-empty. Randle breathed a sigh. *That should do it.* He relaxed, glancing at the Korean, who seemed content, grinning, engrossed in the student mania.

Randle had told Mr. Jang to watch for an unusual level of agitation, a sign the nanite package was operative. And now, as

Randle's gaze was riveted on the Nebraska bench, there was no question the freshman was showing agitation, and not just from pre-match jitters. He was standing, jumping up and down. Then he dropped to the floor and started pumping pushups, and then jumped up again. His face was flushed, features hardened in a scowl. The coaches were attempting to calm him down without attracting attention.

Introductions of the two wrestlers took place at center circle. They sat down with their coaches for last-minute pep talks. One minute later, the referee had them in a neutral starting position and blew the whistle.

The first period of three minutes saw the freshman appearing somewhat off balance, barely managing to stave off a pin on two occasions. He was down by five points as the second period was set to begin.

The champion was in the up referee's position when the whistle blew, but in a lightning sit-out move, the freshman scrambled and stood, beckoning the champion to get to his feet. The two stalked each other, hands grabbing, feigning for advantage. Then suddenly, the freshman was at the champion's back, hoisting him in the air like a feather and smashing him to the mat. He splayed him out and broke him down flat on his stomach. The crowd was standing and dead quiet. The champion was not moving. The freshman rolled him over and pinned him. The whistle blew. The match was over. The freshman released his opponent and jumped up, screaming defiant unintelligible words. Team support personnel from the bench took control of him and half-dragged, half-carried him out of the room.

The team doctor from Iowa State knelt on the mat with two coaches, the crowd deathly quiet, observing from their seats. The head coach abruptly stood up and radioed for the standby paramedic team. Minutes later, the young man was gently placed on a gurney and rolled outside the arena to a waiting EMT ambulance. Later reports confirmed his chest had been crushed, his right arm fractured, and his broken ribs may have caused major internal-organ damage.

Randle and Hwang Jang had remained seated. Most of the students had vacated their seats and were huddling in groups, distressed by the violent event. There were no other persons within hearing range.

"Are we to assume the athlete received too many nanites?" Jang said calmly without outward expression, positive or negative, but Randle could tell the man was duly impressed; he hadn't lost his smile.

"No, the nanites detect one another. Programming permits only one *Fuerte* packet's presence in the bloodstream at a time."

"What went wrong with him? He was magnificent but had no control. A killing machine is of no use if it is unable to control its capabilities."

"The intensity of faculty stimulation was too high. Remember, this is the first test on a human being. Perfecting the dosage will require a proper laboratory setting for accurately measuring the degree of mental and physical enhancements displayed by subjects in controlled environments over a series of test trials."

"Yes, I quite concur. I believe we can offer you the security, equipment, and resources you will require, Mister Parnevik. But just one more question for now. Are there any unusual effects we should be aware of?"

"Well, for one thing, metabolism will increase tremendously. Four times the caloric intake and hydration needs will be required to sustain a man for whatever the duration of the dosage—I trust this has been a sufficiently enlightening experience for you, Mister Jang." It was time to change channels. "Further discussions must be scheduled for another time, and we should depart. People are returning to their seats. The next match will soon begin."

Randle pocketed his camera equipment and pulled out a number ten envelope, handing it to Jang as he rose from his seat. "My proposal to your government and the ground rules for further discussions are covered in this letter. Now, it is time I bid you a safe journey back to your country. I look forward to hearing from your government."

Randle left the Korean holding the envelope. Making his way through the congestion surrounding the wrestling mat, he took a quick look over his shoulder as he approached the exit. The Korean was watching him and was still wearing the same smile.

Hwang Jang waited until Parnevik left the room and whispered a few crisp words into his lapel mic. Two Caucasian men standing near the wrestling-arena entrance doors quickly exited.

Jang opened the envelope as the seats around him were rapidly filling for the next match. He skipped through it, focusing on the important elements: *a copy of the demonstration video will be delivered...$2,000,000 to be wire transferred to an account...within two week's time, twelve sets each of six newly calibrated Fuerte nanite packets will be delivered by courier...the six will be in ascending stimulant intensities and all calibrated for a two-hour duration...your scientists can perform any measurements...communicating their observations and suggestions will initiate manufacture and delivery of further test phases of Fuerte...until such a time as you are satisfied...the cost of the final product will be $20,000,000 per million doses, the minimum order...communicate via a protected server and website within your control...assign me an access code and notify me by email when communications are ready for my review...all test nanites will be programmed to auto-destruct if tampering is detected.*

Jang stood abruptly and wiggled into his Nebraska scarlet and cream jacket, stuffing the envelope in a pocket. He had taken his own video of the match with a wide-angle lens, crafted inside the pendant he wore hanging on the gold chain around his neck.

He left the arena, swiftly striding across the cement square connected to the student union building. He entered the building and located the general-use computer room. Using one of the freely accessible computers, he sat down and typed a summary of the demonstration along with recommendations into a word processing program installed on the computer. Several copier/scanners were positioned around the computer room. He scanned Parnevik's letter and converted it to jpeg images, saving the images to a small flash drive. Next, he transferred the match video from his pendant to the computer and added it to the flash drive. He used the Firefox browser to reach the Internet and sign into the Intelligence Service's encrypted email server.

A minute later, he'd uploaded all the files from the flash drive to his superiors in Pyongyang. He remained logged in, waiting. Ten minutes went by. A reply came into his Inbox. The last sentence read: *Prepare Doctor Parnevik for a long vacation. Instructions to shortly follow via satellite phone.*

Hwang Jang fed the university server with a virus that destroyed the records of the last thirty minutes of activity. He left the sports arena complex in a hurry, crossing a newly grassed soccer field and heading for a beige Mercedes parked and waiting just inside the campus entrance arches. He climbed inside as his satellite phone chirped from his coat pocket: a 747 Cargo plane owned by the People's Republic of China would be landing at Atlanta's Hartsfield International Airport in six hours. It would be transporting a load of computer peripherals to a company in Pyongyang that assembled government-approved cell phones for sale in the North Korean market. It was available for additional special cargo.

 Eighty-eight

Hartsfield International Airport

IT WAS 2:00 P.M. by the time the group arrived at the airport in the kennel van. Edwin tracked Parnevik to the United Airlines ticket counter and then to gate A-19. Ms. Johnson made a call and confirmed it was the gate used by Professor Pedersen boarding yesterday's 4:35 p.m. flight to L.A. She was beginning to believe in Edwin. The group moved over to a nearby gate devoid of an outgoing flight and clear of passengers.

"Edwin wants to go on," Smythe said, as the dog held his nose in the air, whining, tail flapping. "It appears that Mister Parnevik moved from here. He had plenty of time before the L.A. flight left."

"If he was at the Federal Reserve Building around noon," Mallory said, "he wouldn't be able to get to the airport, buy a ticket, and process through security before say two o'clock. So he had about two and a half hours to kill."

"Perhaps he indulged in a meal." Smythe gave Edwin his head.

It required twelve minutes to traverse from the "A" to "D" concourse via the terminal underground rail system and then up the escalator and down the crowded concourse. Edwin, much to the delight of passengers scurrying along on their individual journeys, whined his way to a Chili's restaurant and finally to Gate D-11. He emitted a short, muffled bay and curled up next to a seat in the last row of the gate's deserted waiting area.

"Is he done now?" Ms. Johnson asked, stooping to pet Edwin.

Smythe gave the dog a treat. "I believe so. His restlessness seems to have abated."

"So, we get lists of passengers for flights out of this gate from two o'clock on—"

"No need." Smythe cut Mallory off. "Since Chili's, I've been picking up some strong emotions from Parnevik. He's very pleased with himself. I sense his soaring spirits. It seems he spent time in a Kansas City train station."

Ms. Johnson yanked her cell phone off its belt clip. "I'm on it. If there was a flight to Kansas City yesterday out of this gate, I'm a true convert." She barked out requests and held the phone halfway to her ear as if waiting for an epiphany. She canted her head, looking Phelps over. Things were moving too quickly and the methodology was still difficult for her to accept, and it would be even more difficult to explain to her superiors. "We can't be hopping on a flight to Kansas City, even if what you say pans out—"

"Precisely, Miss Johnson. We need to wait until he settles in one place. *Then* we move with the best chance to make the most of Edwin's talents."

"Right." She moved off into the next row of waiting-area seats, holding the phone to her ear.

"We don't have a clue as to what he looks like now," Mallory lamented, "or who he's pretending to be."

A few minutes later, Ms. Johnson rejoined the others. "The FBI confirmed United Airlines' records show Pedersen had been aboard the L.A. flight. Only one flight to K.C. yesterday from this gate. It left at 11:08 last night. They'll get back to me when they have passenger lists and boarding videos for the flights."

"I'd check if there were any no-shows on the L.A. flight," Mallory said, "in case Parnevik pulled the same boarding-pass stunt he did in Marseilles with the Dubois identity."

Ms. Johnson sensed Mallory's frustration. Parnevik was eluding them at every turn, making the chances of closure in her sister's death more and more unlikely.

Mallory pressed on, "Assuming that's what happened, and Pedersen wasn't the guy that landed in L.A., then the FBI can at least figure out who it was by tracking down the no-show. They find the guy, and maybe we'll get lucky and he'll know something useful."

"It's worth looking at. I'll pass it on," Ms. Johnson said, turning away and punching a number into her phone.

"For now, ladies and gentlemen," Smythe pronounced, "I suggest we get Edwin back to Emma's kind care. He's been a good boy. He deserves a juicy meal and perhaps a bath. I'm sure Emma will be happy to lend a hand. She got along marvelously with Edwin." Smythe darted his gaze over the others.

"Okay," Mallory said. "I'll call her and tell her we're on our way. She'll probably come home early from Pharmco." She gave the dog a pat on the head, and Edwin acknowledged with a grumbled bark, yawned, and scrambled to his feet.

Ms. Johnson turned back to the group. "The Atlanta FBI office fed me some possibly relevant information. Their database screens picked up an unusual death in Nebraska. A NCAA wrestling champion was accidentally killed in a tournament by an inexperienced opponent. The local media covered the match and are reporting the story as a ferocious attack by a crazed freshman who wasn't expected to be competition for the past champion. They're spinning it as potentially drug related. The University of

Nebraska is cooperating with the local police. An autopsy has been ordered, and the freshman is under surveillance at a psychiatric hospital."

"Why is the incident relevant?" Mallory asked.

"Well, the TV footage being shown is disturbing. The freshman had been fortunate to survive the first period of the match. He was nearly pinned twice—that's how you win. Then, in the second period, he was tossing the NCAA champion around like a football. But more importantly, the FBI thinks they spotted a person sitting in the first row next to an older Oriental man, who closely resembled Corey Parnevik. Washington has recalled me to D.C. I'll see you tomorrow when I get back. Hopefully, I'll have more news. In the meantime, all we can do is wait, trusting that Mister Phelps here can tell us when and where Parnevik settles."

 Eighty-nine

Doctor Sarcorcee

THE MORNING VISIT by the FBI lady and her unusual entourage set the good doctor on edge and introduced him to potential problems he found difficult to fathom. *Interviewing with the FBI?*

If in fact, Parnevik's activities were in the realm of national security, he'd be thoroughly grilled, and they were bound to discover he'd recognized Professor Pedersen as Parnevik and that Parnevik had been one of his graduate assistants a decade ago.

He'd been in a quandary since they left, slumped in the chair behind his office desk, pondering ways to protect himself from being accused of complicity or worse. His envisioned, ground-breaking research derived from Parnevik's brilliance was fading. On the other hand, it could all blow over. Nonetheless, Parnevik was a wanted man. If the FBI captured him, which he assumed would be the outcome, they'd discover the lab visit and the after-hours pass. So, he'd be caught up in lies…. Ah, but he'd done it under extreme duress: Dorie's implant.

He squirmed in the chair. Parnevik's threats should protect him from legal prosecution. He cringed at the thought of Parnevik anesthetizing his little girl and cutting her open.

Sarcorcee sighed and rose from the chair. That was the only game he had. He would have to play dumb if the FBI called him in before Parnevik's next visit. He shrugged and headed to the break room for more coffee. He wasn't capable of giving the situation any more mental attention. More important matters lay ahead. He needed to prepare; Parnevik was due back at the lab at midnight, day after tomorrow, to teach him how to set up a controlled replication process. The magic wand.

Without Parnevik's knowledge, Sarcorcee had concealed a video camera in the ceiling over the central, computer plug-in area. It had recorded Parnevik's last session in the lab—every keystroke and screen view on his laptop as he altered the programs used to download destination, stimulus, and duration adjustments to his two nanite types. Parnevik hadn't given him copies of the programs, but the video would yield enough to allow one of his hot-shot graduate students to reconstruct them.

He had two full days to start outlining his own nanite projects. He was brimming with excitement, positive he could work out the program changes to download to test-nanites. Parnevik had promised him an adequate testing inventory of Pharmco's bulimic nanites.

As soon as his daughter was freed from the implant, Sarcorcee's vision was to secretly conduct and document history's first successfully controlled replication event. He would create a larger inventory of bulimic nanites and then reprogram destinations and set stimulus intensities and duration for testing any number of effects, first on animals and then human volunteers.

The prospects were so exciting and consuming that Sarcorcee couldn't clear his mind. There was so much to think about, to invent. He would be capable of performing medical miracles. Reversal of Alzheimer's would be his first priority. The areas of the brain affected by the disease were well documented. Constant controlled stimulation would have a hugely positive impact. That was where the money would be. In the near future, he would be known as a medical savior.

 Ninety

Agent McKenzie: Same Day

AFTER DELIVERING THE summons to the Genovese headman at the New York City Library, Agent Ryan McKenzie returned to Atlanta with the intention of taking a short break from the non-stop intensity and lack of sleep over the last few days. Moreover, he was looking forward to seeing Mallory. Strange, he had missed being close to her. He couldn't make up his mind if he was feeling over-protective or something else.

Striding briskly along the moving walkway toward baggage claim and the terminal exit, his satellite phone vibrated inside his carry-on bag.

Special Investigator, Christine Johnson, efficiently filled him in on Parnevik's movements and Smythe's last intuited location, then curtly directed him to pick up tickets at the Delta counter for a 9:30 p.m. flight to Washington D.C. He'd been assigned to provide escort services the next morning for his favorite Italian, Tony Gatturna. The family kingpin would arrive mid-morning at Washington National for an 11:00 a.m. appointment, room 309 at the U.S. Department of Justice. He'd be returning to New York later in the day.

The FBI assigned a limo to pick McKenzie up at Washington National, take him to the Hyatt Hotel in Arlington, Virginia, for the night, and do his bidding the following day.

He headed for the Delta Sky Club to clean up and grab a nap. At least the FBI had connections.

 Ninety-one

George Randle

RANDLE'S LINCOLN, NEBRASKA, to Atlanta flight landed at 8:10 p.m. He was tired but euphoric. He'd pulled off two successful performances in two days, but more importantly his bank account had swelled by $70,000.

He retrieved his car from the short-term parking area. Twenty-five minutes later, on autopilot, he'd driven north on I-75 through downtown Atlanta, out to the I-285 perimeter south and the exit to his condo on the Chattahoochee River.

The ride gave him time to think as the accumulated tension of the last two days melted away. He reveled in his good fortune and was positive he deserved it. In his view, he'd paid the price in countless ventures gone awry, none of which were his fault. It was always the deception of others, the flawed system, the unfair put downs and lack of praise. This time around, he knew one thing: he never wanted to see Corey Parnevik again. He was just plain lucky to have come out of his schemes in one piece. What was this crazy guy really involved in? He was either the most brilliant conspirator he'd ever met or certifiably insane. He didn't want to know which it was.

Maybe it wasn't just luck, he mused to himself. Just maybe he'd discovered latent abilities, sharpened his personality. Maybe he'd think more about being up front with people, especially at Lockheed. He deserved meritorious job recognition; he could run the engineering department by himself, including design. He allowed himself a smirk and shook his head, adjusting the radio volume on a Gloria Estefan song. He loved the Miami Sound Machine. Now he could indulge in some of the luxuries he'd only dreamed about: dress like a professional, join an athletic club, get in shape, even ask out the blond in accounting. No more schemes.

His mind drifted as he mechanically turned into his driveway. He pressed the remote to open the garage door, drove in, pressed the button again, and shut the car down. He turned the radio off and sat lingering in the quiet, listening to the tinkling of the motor cooling down. The next thing that popped into his mind was Las Vegas: he'd hit the town and indulge himself, have a lady on his arm, live it up. But for now, he'd eat something and hit the sack.

He retrieved his carry-on bag from the rear seat, still in semi-fascination with his prospects. A cold beer sounded great.

He unlocked the breezeway door, turned on the light, and walked into the kitchen, setting his bag down next to the refrigerator.

It was cold and stuffy inside, so he reset the air-conditioning controls to auto-heat at seventy-five degrees, opened the refrigerator, and popped the top on a Miller Lite. There were only two left. He could have sworn he had a full six-pack.

Beer in hand, he entered the living room and turned on the TV to catch the latest news, intending to flop down in his leather recliner. His eye caught a slight movement in the darkened dining room, and his heart jumped. He stood petrified, adrenaline rushing through his body. "What's going on?" he said lamely.

Two men rushed him from the shadows, halting at his side, pointing unusual-looking pistols at him.

"Pack up a suitcase, Mister Parnevik," one of them said. "We're going on a little vacation."

Randle's knees weaken. He was helpless. Multiple scenarios flooded his thoughts. *Who are these people?* "My name is George Randle. I'm not who you think I am." The two men were Caucasians. It couldn't be the North Koreans coming for him—not here in America.

"No talking," one of them said. "We don't care who you call yourself. You take a carry-on and one bag. Bring your laptop and anything you'll need pertaining to the *Fuerte* project. Where you're going you'll have everything else you require."

Five minutes later, they were traveling in a nondescript four-door sedan down I-75 back towards the airport.

"Please tell me what this is about." Randle attempted a businesslike tone. The man sitting next to him in the back seat didn't hesitate. He pulled out the ugly pistol and fired a dart into Randle's shoulder.

Part VI

The Corral

 Ninety-two

DOD Oversight Committee

FOR THE SECOND time in two weeks, the Oversight Committee meeting was taking place in the main conference room at the J. Edgar Hoover Building. But this time, the FBI's sanctified conference room was chaired by Curtis Mayborne, DOD's Director of the Defense Advanced Research Projects Agency (DARPA). The other returning participants were John Lindsay, Deputy Director of the FBI, and GS-17 Christine Johnson, Special Investigator for the Defense Sciences Office (DSO) under DARPA. The DEA and Military Intelligence roles were no longer active links in the mission framework.

After the usual pleasantries, and without the use of the podium, Curtis Mayborne began. "I was musing for a few uncomfortable moments before this meeting, so bear with me." Mayborne's face was hard, like a stone statue. "DSO's mandate is to pursue the most promising technologies within the broad spectrum of active science and engineering research communities—and fund the development of those technologies into important new military capabilities. And here we are, cleaning up the Pharmco mess and hoping—yes, hoping—to avert a disaster. Now, we have this genius nutcase—supposedly meticulously vetted—walking right through our security protocols at Pharmco like they didn't exist, and taking with him top secret technology and the ability to throw the world into chaos. I am deeply embarrassed for our naiveté in not directly supervising the Pharmco contract—and thoroughly confused by the failure to apprehend this maniac."

Christine Johnson had never witnessed the DARPA director in such an agitated state. The sheen on his face made it look like porcelain.

"It appears our efforts have morphed into a pure chase, like an elaborate international spy movie," Mayborne drove on. "If we don't get this situation under control in the next forty-eight hours, I've been told by the Secretary of Defense it has to go into the President's briefing. He'll want full accountability, and if that happens, we better be prepared to convince him we can deliver or tell him why we can't. Needless to say, our careers are on the line.... So, in my *musing,* I decided I needed to vent here.... I don't intend on telling you how to do your jobs. I'm basically a scientist, but the twists, false turns, and numerous dead ends so far have me enduring sleepless nights. I'm going to step in here and make some observations." Mayborne's facial features seemed to relax a degree as he paused, reached for the water pitcher on the table, poured a glass, and unceremoniously gulped half of it down.

"With Parnevik's track record of illusion and *elusion,* we have to assume his contact with this Dr. Sarcorcee at Georgia Tech is important. Parnevik would not approach this person with a request if there were the slightest chance he'd be turned down. And he shows up there as this Professor Pedersen. Sarcorcee hasn't admitted he's recognized him. I don't buy it. Something's going on. Christine, tell me the FBI is all over that nano research center—every bit of campus coverage 24/7 during and since Parnevik's first visit with Sarcorcee. And you *are* finding out what his real connections are to Parnevik and what he really knows, right?" Dr. Mayborne was making a super human attempt to rein in his anger.

"Sir, I assure you it's all in the hopper." She looked straight at the deputy FBI director.

John Lindsay nodded. "This morning the FBI forensics crew hit the Georgia Tech Nano Center, and copies of all campus camera coverage are being audited with University police cooperation. Sarcorcee has been summoned to appear this afternoon for a lie detector session."

"Use any methods with Sarcorcee consistent with DOD policy. We know Parnevik has to be looking for facilities to refine his nanites and produce inventory—it's the only logical reason he went to Georgia Tech. We can't allow that to happen. This is a national security priority."

"Curtis," John Lindsay spoke to Mayborne, "it's being dealt with competently. Ed Furlow in Atlanta is on it. And please be assured, Christine is doing a great job. What else is bugging you?"

The hastily called meeting ended up to be a cathartic exercise for the frustrated scientist. Mayborne needed reinforcement; he'd never faced diplomatic games at the highest levels of government, much less the prospects of being put on the witness stand by the President of the United States. He was a good man, a competent scientist, a great administrator, but he hadn't developed the stomach for the trenches.

"Okay, John. I appreciate your assurances, but let's cover the latest," Mayborne continued. "For a time, we were led to believe Parnevik was in two places at once." Mayborne cast a questioning glance at Ms. Johnson. "Just yesterday, your Mister Phelps and a tracking bloodhound he's using placed Parnevik leaving the Atlanta airport for Kansas City, but here we have an unconfirmed sighting at the wrestling match in Nebraska the same day." He tapped a red file folder on the table in front of him. "He was spotted in the TV footage of the wrestling match, sitting with an Oriental man. And then this morning, the FBI reports that comparative facial analysis proves him a look-alike. But there is no question this is Parnevik in action—using a surrogate—and he's experimenting with the DSO's *Fuerte* project and obviously pandering with the North Koreans." He tapped the file again. "Facial recognition software identified the Oriental as Hwang Jang, the Deputy Director of North Korea's Integrated Bio-Technology Center—part of its intelligence service."

"Curtis, that's how you're going to get off the hook on this," Lindsay said, noting the creases etched across Mayborne's forehead. He wasn't making the connection. "Hear me out.... I apologize for not bringing you into the loop earlier—and for your frustration. There just wasn't time, but I believe it was beneficial for us to have reviewed where we are.... I spent most of last night with the Deputy Secretary of State for East Asian and Pacific Affairs. Because of the contact Parnevik made with the North Koreans in Paris, and the reports you have in front of you, they summoned us shortly after midnight. As of now, North Korea's involvement is a state department problem and the FBI will continue its mission to apprehend Parnevik. You're out of the loop—but you need to know you've been duly commended for your leadership, Curtis. Miss Johnson is to remain temporarily relieved from her duties at the Defense Sciences Office and assigned to the FBI. She'll continue to be in charge of the overall investigation. We have to run Parnevik to ground before he makes a mistake and we end up with a calamity on our hands."

"What about the candy on the street and the mafia?" Ms. Johnson asked, thankful at the turn of events. She'd come to the meeting with great trepidation. For a while there, her boss's job as well as her own had seemed in peril.

John Lindsay glanced at his watch. "Christine, in answer to your question, Agent McKenzie is delivering the responsible party to a special meeting with the attorney general at the Justice Department in about two hours. So, that wild card is now out of our purview and directly in the hands of the Justice Department where it belongs."

Dr. Mayborne was sitting up much straighter in his chair.

"And, Curtis," Lindsay said, "rest assured the FBI, DOD, and State Department will take over any presidential briefings necessary. So, with your permission I think we can adjourn here and get back to work."

 **Ninety-three**

U.S. Department of Justice: Same Day

AGENT MCKENZIE HADN'T said a word to Gatturna since taking the front seat on the limo ride from Washington National to the Justice Department building. He'd only been here once for a DEA briefing on a case he'd helped prepare for Justice Department prosecutors. The structure was impressive and imposing, designed to represent the broad breadth of the democratic principle of justice for all.

McKenzie directed the limo driver to wait in the VIP parking in front of the building and check in with the guard detail patrolling the grounds. Maintaining a position behind Gatturna, McKenzie ordered him up the wide marble stairs, through the security search, and up the elevator. The huge wooden doors to Room 309 were bordered by carved medallions of corn, anvils, and sunflowers. McKenzie stepped in front of Gatturna and opened the massive doors. "Take a seat at the table with the file folder."

Two gray-haired men with torsos covered by sleeved black robes sat at the judge's bench, moving papers between them and whispering. This was the U.S. Court of Appeals courtroom. The base of the raised bench was paneled in walnut inlaid with wedge–shaped characters of cuneiform script. Marble squares of dark and light green floored the great room in a checked pattern. Several tapestries tastefully broke up the high walnut wainscoting. At the facial center of the judge's bench was a hand carving of a Roman axe and blade fasces. Large beams spread across the ceiling, posted along the front and back walls. Ornate, copper light fixtures designed with arrowheads and shafts hung from the ceiling, casting gentle light from yellow bulbs shaped like half-husked ears of corn. An inscription taken from Heraclitus, a Greek philosopher, was inlaid in paneled walnut above the judge's bench: *Eyes and ears are poor witnesses when the soul is barbarous.*

Rays from the late morning sun penetrated through the iron grillwork of the eastside windows, reflecting dust hanging almost frozen in the quiet. Agent McKenzie stood at the rear of the room next to the entrance doors. Tony Gatturna was the only other person in the cavernous courtroom.

Ten minutes went by without a word. Gatturna's forehead gleamed, and he dabbed at it with a handkerchief.

One man finally stood to speak, his voice booming through hidden speakers. "This meeting is held for the purpose of securing a verbal agreement between the DOJ and the entity commonly referred to as the Genovese Family. No records are made of this meeting. You, Anthony Gatturna, as the recognized family leader, are to be considered a responsible patriot so long as covenants of the agreement are not breached."

Suddenly electric window shades whined, closing off the four windows in the courtroom. The lights went out. The grating of an electric motor sounded, and a few moments later a huge screen lit up against the right-hand wall, filling with a flow chart.

"As you can see, your lines of authority and responsibility are known down to the last man and woman. The activities of these people must abide by the agreement. That is the burden of responsibility you carry away from this room. Examine the file folder on the table. There you will find a copy of the flow chart shown on the screen, an unexecuted copy of our agreement, and a factual listing of breach consequences."

At least a full minute went by in silence as the lights came back on and the window shades and slide screen disappeared into inconspicuous cylindrical containers. Gatturna opened the file and for the next fifteen minutes read over the material several times. As he read, his mind madly projected the effects and probed alternative ways to get out from under the devastating blanket of destruction: business with Parnevik was to be terminated; no more candy, no more distribution. *Amor* inventory was to be surrendered. A list of suppliers of Parnevik product was required. Methods of communication with Parnevik were to be identified—the FBI would control outputs and confiscate inputs. Family bank accounts were listed—no new accounts allowed. Six months were allocated to adjust the Family's businesses to one-hundred percent compliance and legitimacy.

Any breach of covenants meant: persons listed in the flow chart would be deemed terrorists and summarily removed without notice or public declaration to Guantanamo Bay. All associated bank accounts would be seized by the IRS.

Gatturna sat limply against the straight-backed chair, eyes glazed. A sickening knot had formed in his mid-section. This was democracy in action. Justice for all. He rose to his feet. "Who are you people?"

"You have no need to know who we are. You may keep the file folder, Mister Gatturna. No signature is required. Our business here is complete." The second man stood from the judge's bench and called out to Agent McKenzie.

McKenzie walked down the polished marble aisle to the defendant's table. He took the Genovese headman's arm and led the shaken Gatturna back up the aisle, head bowed.

"I thought that went rather well," the Attorney General said as the two men entered the conference chamber behind the courtroom to remove their robes. "Coordinate with State and devise the means and methods for dealing with those two Asian manufacturing plants. No more Parnevik business. Have McKenzie report back to Christine Johnson. He's turned out to be a resilient, reliable field agent. I think he was a lawyer researching cases in some back room at the DEA. Waste of talent."

 Ninety-four

Atlanta, Georgia

SHORTLY AFTER DELIVERING Tony Gatturna to the airport for his return trip to New York City, Agent McKenzie checked in with Christine Johnson. The timing was fortuitous. Ms. Johnson was on her way to Washington National and invited McKenzie to join her on the FBI flight back to Atlanta.

The trip gave them an opportunity to share what had transpired. Both were encouraged by the turn of events; the whole situation had simplified. The authorities had acted incisively, removing the complex legal and international complexities from the hunt for Parnevik. It was now a pure manhunt. Ms. Johnson used her satellite phone to brief Mallory and Dickerson Phelps. She caught them gathered at Emma's house and requested they all meet at the FBI offices at 6:00 p.m.

Unfortunately, it was the middle of the rush hour when the FBI plane landed, and Ms. Johnson and McKenzie suffered through a logjam on Interstate 75 to downtown Atlanta. But their spirits remained elevated, and the ride wasn't so bad in the FBI's VIP limo.

***

"Well, hello, Agent McKenzie," Mallory said as she, Smythe, and Edwin entered Ms. Johnson's glassed-in office. "Back from secret agenting I see. How'd it go?"

"Short and sweet—got a lift back from Christine."

"You look beat," Mallory said to Ms. Johnson.

"It's been a tough week—It's nice to see *you* again, Mister Phelps, and you too, Edwin." Ms. Johnson reached down and scratched the hound behind the ears.

"Young lady, we had to wait in your drab reception room for half an hour," Smythe said. "Unacceptable." Smythe was in a coarse mood; he hadn't picked up any clear imaging from Parnevik for several hours and assumed he was feeling back in control—hence, no intense emotion to be sensed.

Ms. Johnson sighed. "I'm sorry about that. Let's get to it." She clicked on a sixty-inch plasma monitor mounted on the wall at the far end of the table. "I want you to watch the video of yesterday's wrestling match in Nebraska I told you about. The FBI put together local TV station footage and tapes from the arena's surveillance cameras into a time lined event."

Everyone took seats at the conference table as Ms. Johnson slipped a DVD into the computer at her desk. The monitor flickered up the Windows Media Player screen. "There's the man posing as Parnevik coming down the interior hall, carrying a duffle bag." She grabbed a pointer off the table and moved closer to the monitor. "We traced him from his flights to Lincoln from Atlanta. He turns out to be an old acquaintance of Parnevik's from Georgia Tech. His name is George Randle. They were both in the undergraduate engineering program at the same time—he's opening the door to a supply room next to the men's locker room—FBI personnel interviewed the coaches of the contestants for their take on anything unusual. But I'm getting ahead here. There's Randle with the duffle, knocking on the locker room doors about an hour before the match. Nobody answers and he goes inside. He comes out and his duffle is obviously lighter. Turns out a guy matching Randle's description talked to the Iowa State coach about making sure the Evian sponsor's water was prominently displayed and used for the match, and he received permission to drop a case in the locker room. He also left a cooler with bottles all iced down."

She placed the video on *Pause*. "The FBI found a North Korean national registered at the Marriott the night before the match, a pharmaceutical rep for a North Korean drug distributor. Now, watch. Here's Randle sitting with this Oriental man garbed out in Nebraska colors. In reality, he's a North Korean agent.... Now, Randle gets out of his seat just before the contestant introductions and walks behind the Iowa State bench. You see? He's making sure the Evian water bottles have been brought out—and there— the coach sees him and gestures with a grimace, opens the cooler, and gives the freshman wrestler a half-full bottle of water.

"That's what we knew this morning. The FBI worked all night identifying the players and putting their movements together. There's more video of the North Korean at the Marriott, taking his seat at the match, exiting the sports arena afterwards, visiting the computer room at the student union, and using an untraceable satellite phone like ours. The technicians are putting together some of the conversation from facial recognition software. Unfortunately, last night after the match, Randle returned to Atlanta before the FBI had put the pieces together, or we'd have nabbed him. This morning they tapped his bank account and found he'd recently received a large sum of money. They'll find out where it originated. We're assuming for now he was working for Parnevik, but from there the trail went dead. Randle is currently missing in action. He doesn't answer his phones and no one has shown up at his condo.

"The freshman wrestler gave a statement to the FBI." She clicked off the monitor and took a sheet of paper from the inbox at her desk. "I'll paraphrase some of it. He said he didn't remember much except being heated up and feeling light on his feet, and then he said he felt omnipotent, and it turned into rage he couldn't control. He said the desire to win the match became overwhelming. He didn't mean to take the other wrestler down like he did. He said he was consumed with the power and didn't have time to try and control it. Now you're up to speed."

"How does this help us capture Parnevik?" Mallory had been patient during Ms. Johnson's diatribe, but aggravation had taken over. All she wanted was Parnevik.

"Mal, if we can find Randle, maybe we're a step closer," McKenzie said calmly, realizing Mallory was heating up.

"I for one am truly sorry we are remaining so far behind his movements in real time," Smythe put in. "As you are aware, my window of sensitivity to his whereabouts and what he is doing is not only limited in time, but I only pick up his highly charged emotions. I interpolate from there. For now, he must be in a state of control and remaining calm. But perhaps we have an opportunity to catch this Randle character and get a heads-up on what Parnevik is planning. Maybe then we can position ahead of him instead of lagging behind."

"Okay, I'm game," Mallory gave in. "I don't think we have anything better to do—Miss Johnson?"

"What do you have in mind, Mister Phelps?" She nodded at Mallory.

"Send the FBI to his place of residence—"

"Did it this morning."

"By chance, did they bring in some of his clothing, toiletries, bath towels?"

"I think so," Ms. Johnson said. "So we use Edwin?"

"And begin at the airport," Smythe affirmed. "He arrived last night. Get the gate number and we start from there."

"Can't you do your sensing thing on him—save us time?" Ms. Johnson asked.

"He's part of the Parnevik puzzle. I'm unable to sort him out without pictures, hearing him speak, or having a sense of his character."

They all headed for the office doors as Ms. Johnson picked up the desk phone and arranged to pick up some of Randle's dirty clothes stored in the FBI's evidence room.

"Now, you're going to witness something very special," Mallory said to McKenzie. "We're going on a tracking safari with a hound dog in the middle of a metropolitan area."

***

An hour later, and attracting the usual gaping onlookers, Edwin had taken the group from gate B-14, through the concourse and train ride, and outside the terminal to the busy cab station. Ms. Johnson called in her FBI car and asked an agent to bring Phelps's kennel van around. The group was prepared to set out and follow the bellowing dog wherever it led them.

Just before crossing a thoroughfare on the way out of the airport and onto I-85, Edwin whined and then yelped for a turn onto the road leading to the airport's commercial-cargo gates. Ten minutes later, the group was staring at Edwin as he flopped down in front of one of the main gates.

It took Ms. Johnson a few minutes to contact the airport dispatcher and receive a list of flights using that gate since yesterday night. There were four candidates: two FedEx flights to Europe, one Cargill grain flight to Pakistan, and an Air China flight to Pyongyang.

"The Air China flight took off at 10:28 p.m., she said. "That pretty much gives us our answer. I've got to call this in to FBI headquarters, and for the time being this is where it ends for us. It'll be the State Department's problem now."

The group was dejected.

"Perhaps later today or tomorrow morning I'll be able to pick up fresh information," Smythe said, stroking Edwin's hindquarter.

"In the meantime, we'd all better get some rest," Ms. Johnson said. "Mister Phelps, if you sense anything from Parnevik, please call me—any time, day or night. I'll check in with you all first thing in the morning." She quickly turned and headed for the FBI car.

 Ninety-five

Albuquerque, New Mexico

THE ALBUQUERQUE REAL estate broker Parnevik had selected several months ago had done an outstanding job communicating the attributes of properties through posted videos and pictures at his business website. The broker understood he was dealing with a Buenos Aires law firm on behalf of an Argentine client. It was as if fate had produced the perfect fit. That's what Parnevik truly believed, even without a physical inspection of the property.

It was an authentic Italian mansion, isolated, resting on top of a mesa twenty miles from Albuquerque and miles from the nearest neighbors; it was inconsequential that the house and grounds were rundown. Designed after World War II for a Chicago mobster, who demanded security along with peace and quiet, it had remained unoccupied for over twenty years.

Over the last eight months, Parnevik had invested many hours of research, and he continued on the Internet during the Amtrak ride in from Kansas City, scrutinizing images from the original plans held in the archives of Bernalillo County. His visions for the old mansion were constantly being revised and refined; the endeavor was enchanted.

He'd made arrangements with the broker to have the keys to the gate and the house left under a rock next to the entrance. He wanted to be alone in the house on this first visit, no one quacking in his ear, no distractions; and, at this time, he didn't want to meet face-to-face with the broker.

The mob boss and his acquaintances occupied the rambling Mediterranean-style house off and on until 1957; that year the mobster reportedly met his demise outside Milwaukee, Wisconsin in a suspicious car accident. Howard Hughes subsequently owned the property. After his death in the late '90s, it fell into county ownership in lieu of back taxes.

Parnevik's anticipation had built up on the over-night train ride. Debarking from the train and rushing through the station to the National Rental Car kiosk, he had a full day to accomplish objectives.

He drove out into the desert, navigated the private, quarter-mile dirt road, and stopped at the rusty gate. The view of the mansion captivated his imagination. His mind-eyed view was filled with magnificence.

After several hours traversing every nook and cranny with high-tech sonar electronics, he remained euphoric. It was run-down inside, but the opulence of the original makeover by the Chicago mobster was still present under the dust. The dry New Mexico air had largely protected the structure from significant deterioration.

He loved it. An alluring factor—icing on the cake sealing the purchase—was the information he'd secured from the company that served as the original contractor. The plans were different from those filed with the county. There were several secret passages and hidden rooms behind sliding wall panels and book-cases, one of which led to a huge wine cellar filled with cobwebs and dozens of dusty wine bottles in neatly stacked racks.

Each discovery thrilled him; he relished secrets. Finding the mechanical trick doors still functioning was a special treat. From the accumulated dust in the secret spaces, it was evident the Hughes occupants had been unaware of their existence.

***

The Buenos Aires law firm of Marval, O'Farrell & Mairal was the attorney-in-fact for Mr. Arturo Alvarez, the new owner of the soon-to-be palatial manor. To those inquiring, Mr. Alvarez was described by the law firm as a wealthy recluse, a noted hunter, collector of artifacts, and a man enamored with the southwestern part of the United States.

Two days ago, the law firm closed on the purchase from Bernalillo County on behalf of Mr. Alvarez. Cash was paid, and additional funds placed in a trust account with a local credit union to pay invoices submitted under contracts for cleanup of the property, interior and exterior repairs and renovations, revitalization of the landscaping, and installation of state-of-the-art security systems. Alvarez's real estate broker was empowered to negotiate the contracts.

***

Before he said goodbye to his home-to-be, Parnevik stashed a duplicate set of IDs for Arturo Alvarez in the secret wine cellar. He had a few stops to make in Albuquerque before returning to Atlanta on the over-night flight. The first was to open a bank account and apply for a debit card for Arturo Alvarez. Then, completion of admittance paperwork to the University of New Mexico, the state's flagship institution of higher learning; Arturo Alvarez was going to be a new student attending under a student travel visa.

The next item on the agenda was to inspect several small office spaces located in an exclusive complex of medical support practitioners and research facilities across the street from Presbyterian Hospital, the largest acute care hospital in New Mexico.

He committed Alvarez to a lease. His future research lab would be surrounded by professional activities beyond reproach.

Next to last on the list, he visited the Porsche dealership to pick up his new Panamera, waiting and paid for five weeks ago. He drove the vehicle, mindful of holding back his excitement, to a self-storage facility where he'd made arrangements, wishing he had more time. It would come.

To accomplish the last task on the list required a quiet secluded location. He entered an L.A. Fitness Center near the Presbyterian Hospital, created a membership for Arturo Alvarez, and utilized the restroom and shower.

Two nights earlier, while back in the lab with Dr. Sacorcee, Parnevik had reprogrammed six of the *Bliss* nanites to adhere to each other, work together without self-destructing, and travel to six different destinations in the brain affecting balance and cognition.

In between instructing Sarcorcee, he'd run a replication process on the packet of six nanites right under his nose and accreted the inventory together in a single, round sugar tablet the size of an aspirin.

He took possession of a stall for the disabled in the L.A. Fitness restroom and laid out equipment and supplies he'd brought from Atlanta on a baby-changing platform. He cut an inch-long incision at the midline of his right *quadriceps femoris* and inserted the plastic-coated implant. Applying an antiseptic cream, he carefully closed the wound with four self-dissolving sutures. The tablet contained millions of nanite packets, undetectable by modern scanning devices, including MRIs. A backup contrived from a paranoid mind.

 Ninety-six

Atlanta, Georgia

THE AFTERNOON CALL from Randle upon completion of the wrestling match in Nebraska had presented concerns. The freshman had thrown the NCAA champion around like a feather in the second period after nearly being pinned in the first. On the way to the hospital, the champion had succumbed to internal injuries, making adjustments to the second generation of *Fuerte* packets for the North Koreans a priority. He'd have to create several sets of test packets—scaled at different intensities—and add a full twenty-four hours of effects to the duration.

One more midnight lab session with Sarcorcee should be sufficient to complete his business commitments: work out the *Fuerte* packets, replicate test batches, air-ship them to North Korea, produce the necessary *Bliss* inventory for the Genovese, and ship it to his contract manufacturers. Then he'd get on with the last act in the play.

Prior to boarding the flight to Atlanta, he'd tried to contact Randle again to be sure nothing unusual had transpired on his return trip from Nebraska. Randle hadn't returned calls to his cell phone or messages left at his home number. It was Saturday night; he probably couldn't resist celebrating, but it left Parnevik uneasy

Twenty minutes from landing, Parnevik was still examining his present position and perseverating over every issue and detail facing him in Atlanta and beyond. The process had left him with an overall sense of jubilance.

He felt assured his crucial side trip to Albuquerque would go undiscovered: Gerald Jones had gotten him to Kansas City. His Amtrak ticket hadn't required ID, and cash left no trail as he'd moved around the Albuquerque area, ever vigilant eluding the surveillance cameras proliferating the urban landscape. Securing a one-way ticket to Atlanta had been a patented drill, again compensating a traveler for the use of his driver's license and altering his appearance.

***

The plane landed on schedule just before midnight. Parnevik took a cab from the airport to a Days Inn motel several blocks from the Georgia Tech campus, making a quick stop at a 24-hour Walmart to pick up several disposable cell phones. His mind had incessantly rambled on the cab ride, pulling scenarios apart and putting them back together again. Everything needed to be perfect.

Settling in the motel room, he realized he'd become frazzled from building nebulous projection layers, signaling the need for fresh medication, especially the anti-dopamine.

He sprawled on the bed and waited. Slowly his mind revved down, and he compartmentalized the scenes in the play to come, focusing on the present. He needed a nap, but checking on Dr. Sarcorcee came first. It was important to read the man's state of mind to detect anything that might compromise their upcoming lab session.

Reaching him at home at this late hour on one of the new cell phones, Sarcorcee actually sounded upbeat, looking forward to working through the early morning session. He related that a day after their prior lab session, he'd been visited by an FBI agent and a party of three plus a hound dog. But he'd stayed with the plan, revealing Professor Pedersen's request for lab use had been turned down. The FBI notified him he'd be called in to give a statement, and the nano center facilities had been forensically searched, camera footage from all over campus confiscated. He said he wasn't worried about it; he'd doctored the ones from the lab session. He never mentioned his daughter.

Parnevik clicked off the phone, shaking his head. Sarcorcee was pleased with himself; that could only mean he'd contrived a plan of personal gain. The man was self-centered and consumed by the malignant tag team of power and greed, a dangerous combination. He was also very naive. The FBI would get what they needed from him one way or the other. The fool had no idea he was playing hardball. With the FBI involved, eventually Sarcorcee's phone conversations would be monitored; so from here on out, using a telephone to contact him would be suicide. *What about the hound dog?* He made a mental note to find out more from Sarcorcee during the lab session and set the alarm on his watch for 2:00 a.m.

 **Ninety-seven**

Georgia Tech University

PARNEVIK USED ONE of his research passes and logged in at 2:30 a.m. as Gerald Jones, using the driver's license as ID. The log indicated he and Sarcorcee were alone in the building. Even the janitorial service had completed its work and signed out.

An hour later, seated at a small table in one of the several number ten containment rooms, Parnevik finished putting together a two-foot-square box of half-inch glass, sealed airtight with liquid silicone, then joined Sarcorcee, who was observing outside on a stool at a lab table.

Dr. Sarcorcee had patiently monitored the activity. "How did you manage to produce a nanite machine in the first place?"

Parnevik saw that the good doctor seemed to have brought his A-game. Confident, short smiles, but his eyes gleamed like a hungry rodent.

Earlier, Parnevik had given him assurances he was free to remove the device implanted in the back of Dorie Sarcorcee's neck—as simple as extracting a splinter. A Band-Aid would be sufficient to dress the wound.

"I'll answer your questions as we go along, but first I need to know more about this FBI visit."

"It was unannounced," Sarcorcee blurted. "A lady agent, a PI named Dickerson Phelps was with her…a couple of other people and an ugly hound dog. They knew Professor Pedersen had been here. I didn't deny it, but I don't know how they could have known. I told them I had to turn down your—the professor's—request for access to the labs."

Parnevik leaned against the lab's doorjamb, pensive, looking down at Sarcorcee. "A dog, you say?" He pondered a moment. It seemed like a long shot, but he'd have to look into it in the next few days—leave nothing to chance. "Did they mention my name?"

"No."

"Well, no harm. You haven't broken any laws," he said dryly. "Let's get back on track here. Sit down and I'll answer your questions."

"Aren't the necessary materials complex? I can't understand how you overcame the size versus intricacy required."

Sarcorcee was so transparent, Parnevik mused to himself as he revealed the pieces of the puzzle that had confounded researchers for decades. "The key was constructing the base machine in full size. The motor functions are simple. It's electrically powered by a rechargeable battery. The battery draws electricity from the electrical discharges produced by body metabolism. All it has to do is get from one spot to another, impale itself in the cell wall, and give off a periodic electrical stimulus."

The core brilliance was in creation of programs that directed nanite actions: movement to specific locations in the brain, collection and storage of electrical energy, release of electrical stimulation, miniaturization, replication, and self-destruction.

Dr. Sarcorcee sat mesmerized throughout the lecture. The only program he'd been unable to reconstruct from his recordings of Parnevik's previous work on his laptop was the replication program. The other programs were not that brilliant, and his graduate-student whiz kids had been able to piece them together.

Reading him like a book, Parnevik said, "So, you need to know how to construct the replication program. Then your dreams can come true. Isn't that right, Edward?"

Sarcorcee nodded like a mental patient.

Another hour went by. A full-scale prototype machine, duplicating itself to specific internal and external dimensions—Sarcorcee had been riveted to the explanations of the coding, line by line, and amazed at the simplicity of the concept.

The raw materials required were air, sugars, and electricity—nothing else—but the procedure required absolute control of those inputs in a sterile environment. Electrical impulses broke down the raw materials into molecules the program reassembled into miniature duplicates. The replication process continued until the raw materials were exhausted.

"I trust you are duly impressed?" Parnevik closed the replication software file on his laptop and switched to a folder labeled *Fuerte.*

"It truly is a marvel," Sarcorcee said flatly.

Parnevik saw his faraway look and knew the man's mind was racing with ideas.

"I assume you're setting up for a replication," Sarcorcee said.

"Yes, but first I have to make some adjustments to two nanites—like I did last time—and use the radio to download the changes. So, go do something for an hour or so. I'll come get you when I'm finished."

Sarcorcee left the room. Parnevik dug in his briefcase, connected a small shortwave radio to his laptop, and laid out a few other items on the lab table, including his green case of test nanite vials, a small, twelve-volt battery, and various wires and clips.

***

Parnevik finished forty-five minutes later. He'd removed one red and one green tablet from the vials of *Fuerte* and *Bliss* nanite packets, set the radio frequency, clipped and wired the tablets in turn to the radio output connectors, and downloaded the alterations he'd programmed from his laptop. He was ready to replicate and motioned to Sarcorcee through the glass wall, where he had been observing from an adjacent lab.

"Take a seat so you can watch the process, and don't forget to reset the camera," Parnevik said facetiously. "This will not take long." He entered the number-ten containment chamber. From a test tube, he poured out a pre-measured amount of a speckled grainy substance that looked like beach sand, making a mound at the bottom of the glass box. "This is the first nanite packet to be replicated." He used tweezers to place a red pill on top of the mound. "The replication program has been activated and placed on standby."

Parnevik reached over to a test-tube holder, removed one with forceps, peeled off the vacuum seal, and poured the distilled water over the sandy mound. Carefully placing the glass top into the silicon-beaded frame of the box, they observed the sand immediately absorb the water, dissolve the tablet, and coalesce.

The grey glob that remained quivered. "And we're ready to go. Watch closely. The air, water, and sugar are sufficient to produce the necessary construction elements for a replication of two dozen nanite packets. All that's required now is a sustained, one-ampere charge of twelve-volt current to initiate and sustain the replication program." Parnevik taped the two battery leads to opposite sides of the glass box. "The half-inch glass allows just enough current, not too much, not too little. I'm sure you can appreciate the trial-and-error time it took experimenting."

He snatched a look at Sarcorcee. His huge head was hovering over the top of the glass box as the grey blob began turning into fluffy white crystals, like snowflakes. Sarcorcee's forehead was damp. Parnevik could almost read his mind. *What a worm.*

"It will take another few minutes to consolidate into a dense circular mass. The nanite packets will be at the center, dormant and safe to handle."

"How do you separate them?" Sarcorcee asked, eyes gleaming, unable to take his gaze from the replication process.

"Patience, Doctor." Parnevik glanced at his watch. It was 5:00 a.m. He had at least an hour of work ahead. He summoned up the last of a diminishing pool of tolerance and continued. "Their programming directed them to gather. The white circular mass is leftover sugars and acts as a protective packaging case. Each nanite packet in the center of the mass finished the replication process by coating itself in layers of sugar. During the mass-manufacturing process, the crystalline masses, like the one I've prepared here, are exposed to a specifically measured solution of sugar-water, flavoring, and color pigment. The packets in the masses have been programmed to coat themselves until they reach a preset round size common to many medical tablets. The nanite packets are then left to dry out in a controlled environment and are packaged."

"Activation of individual nanites is through the human digestive system," Sarcorcee stated, impishly grinning, "dissolving the sugar coating and triggering the search for its final destination using the body map in its data base."

"You've done your homework, I see." Parnevik had assumed Sarcorcee would be able to duplicate the programs he'd accessed from his laptop to create miniaturization, give stimulus orders, and direct travel to brain map locations. The devilish little man with the huge head would have recorded every minute of the lab sessions from every conceivable angle.

It didn't matter now. It never had. Parnevik was close to his own goals. The dear doctor had enough information to either become famous or create scientific havoc. Without patience, the latter would be the expected outcome.

"One last thing before you finish here," Dr. Sarcorcee said, noting Parnevik had looked at his watch several times during the replication explanations. "Why do you program the nanites to self-destruct?"

"Purely a defensive mechanism to prevent undesired scrutiny. I keep my secrets safe." Parnevik raised his eyebrows. "If a nanite is activated in solution and the human body is not detected, it is unable to use the body map and will dissolve into its simple sugar components. Self-destruction also occurs at the end of the time a nanite has been programmed to remain active…. I've got to move on now, Edward. I have two more processes to run. One is basically a repeat. I'll be creating crystalline mass for a contract manufacturer to produce inventory of a perfected product you needn't know anything about. The second is to act as if I were the contract manufacturer and convert the crystalline mass we have created in the glass box into a dozen or so individualized, dark red pills for further testing. It's the accretion process we just went over. I'll add additional sugars, water, and flavoring and wait. You're free to watch, take notes, whatever."

***

It was 6:15 a.m. when an exasperated Parnevik finally exited the Georgia Tech nano research center for the last time, choking down a dose of meds in the hall washroom on the way out. He'd completed his work at the tail end of falling into weariness; lack of sleep was catching up with him.

The session had left him nauseated, repulsed by Sarcorcee's patronizing presence. During the hours of confinement, the despicable man had displayed every form of loathsome character trait. Forced into close bodily proximity, Parnevik had done his level best not to cringe in the presence of the man's pointed inquiries and palpable greed.

The early morning air was calm, holding heavy moisture, foreshadowing an unseasonably warm and humid day to come. He elected to walk the few short blocks back to his room at the Days Inn, all the while watching his surroundings, checking the shadows, looking for surveillance cameras, warily contemplating the mystery of how he'd been followed from France and onward from Charlotte.

Keying the door and turning on the lights, he felt contaminated from the repugnant experience of the lab session. He needed to clean up and get some rest. But first, he signed into the hotel's Wi-Fi system and entered the North Korean's website, giving notice of test samples being delivered by UPS. Then he emailed the Genovese that *Bliss* would be available to order within ten days on the same terms and conditions as *Amor*.

As he closed his laptop, he was struck by a flare of excitement, signaling the nearness of a long journey's end. He'd sleep for an hour and a half, make himself up for the coming trip, and present himself at the UPS store when it opened a few blocks down on Peachtree Street. He had two air-express packages to send off, and then the photographer, Gregory Campbell, had to catch a 10:35 a.m. flight to Miami.

 Ninety-eight

The Trackers

THE DEAD-END encountered last night at Hartsfield International Airport had left the group disconsolate. George Randle was out of reach, a presumed guest of the North Koreans. Thankfully, due to the DOD Oversight Committee's rapid response, the issue was in the hands of the State Department.

The group had agreed to meet again this morning, hoping the passing night would provide Smythe with another eight hours or so of fresh perception, possibly revealing Parnevik's location and insight into what he was planning.

At Emma's house, Mallory and McKenzie were soaking up a second cup of coffee, lounging in the breakfast nook, picking apart the morning paper, and waiting for Smythe to join them. Emma had already taken Edwin for a walk in the park, seen to his food and water, and left to spend most of Sunday at Pharmco.

"Good morning to you," Smythe said, shuffling into the kitchen, looking dapper in a freshly pressed white linen shirt, a black corduroy blazer with brown leather elbow patches, and, of all things, khaki Docksiders. The out-of-character image was completed by a pair of black and gray cross-trainers. Smythe caught their stare. "I see you approve of my attire. It's more appropriate for our work with Edwin, don't you think?"

"We put water on for your tea," Mallory said without comment. "We're anxious to find out if you know anything more."

"Very well, my dear girl. I don't know how you put up with her, Agent McKenzie." Smythe poured out a cup of hot water, squeezed into the nook while bobbing a tea bag, and reached for the open box of donuts on the table.

"Her bite is vicious first thing in the morning," McKenzie kidded. "She's much sweeter after her second cup of coffee."

Mallory's face reddened. "I'm sorry, Titus. This whole chase thing has me down. We have all the resources of the FBI and nothing's happening. Every time we get close, Parnevik dematerializes."

"I understand your frustration, Miss Mallory. I really do, and I share it with you…. Now, when I awoke, it took me a while to sort out my perceptions. They come in bundles, and I have to interpret as best I can what the pieces are saying. So, here goes—the most important first. He has further business with Georgia Tech. He was on a plane mulling over what he wanted to accomplish there, and he was—oh, how to put it—charged up. You should alert Miss Johnson immediately." Smythe looked directly at Mallory. "He's going to start a replication process."

"I'll get her on the satellite phone," McKenzie said.

"Titus, hold up on the rest of it so she can hear it firsthand." Mallory nodded at Smythe and reached for the phone in her shoulder bag hanging on the back of her chair.

****

Ms. Johnson had been at the FBI office since four in the morning, running roughshod over four FBI agents she'd assigned to research and explore potential Parnevik scenarios. "I've got Ed Furlow conferenced in," she said after Mallory revealed what she'd heard from Smythe. "When do you think he got into Atlanta?"

Mallory handed the phone to Smythe and activated the speaker. "She wants to know when he got into Atlanta."

"It was last night," Smythe responded. "I can't tell exactly, but it has to be less than fifteen hours ago or I would have picked something up. It's seven now, so that puts it sometime after 4:00 p.m. yesterday."

"That jives with what we figured out this morning," Ms. Johnson said. "Furlow and his people compared the videos of boarding passengers on the Kansas City flight two days ago with the videos of arriving passengers since then from every flight coming into the airport from Kansas City and west. We got a match screening guys of Parnevik's height, build, and age. A Joseph Carpenter, a stockbroker with Merrill Lynch, working out of the Albuquerque office, arrived last night at 11:34 p.m. They got him out of bed earlier this morning. You're not going to believe this. For a thousand dollars, he gave his driver's license and proof of insurance to a guy at the airport, but the guy didn't match Parnevik's description."

"He would have doctored himself…. It's what he does," McKenzie put in.

"So, it looks like we know who he is for now," Ms. Johnson said. "The FBI is checking the Atlanta hotels and motels as we speak. Maybe we'll get lucky."

"That's great, Christine," Mallory said, encouragement in her voice.

"Anything else, Mister Phelps?" Ms. Johnson asked.

"I only picked up flashes here and there," Smythe said haughtily. "He was traipsing around on a small mountain. I believe you call them mesas. He was very organized, going quickly from one place to another—no heavy emotions except he was pleased with himself. I don't know exactly where he went or why. He was on the move every minute, but if he's back, Edwin can track him."

"We don't want to start at the airport again," Mallory blurted. "We know where he's going."

"Georgia Tech," McKenzie said. "Maybe Edwin can cut further into Phellps's sensitivity window. Sarcorcee said the lab sessions were at night, after midnight. That could mean he might have already been there early this morning."

"I agree," Ms. Johnson shot back. "It's early. Sarcorcee will be at home. Follow me there. His house is near Piedmont Park, only a few blocks from where you're staying—910 Elm Street. And in the meantime, if the FBI comes up with a Joseph Carpenter registered in Atlanta, they'll go after him."

***

It was 8:45 a.m. Dr. Harold Sarcorcee was still fast asleep, snug in his guest bedroom's double bed. He'd returned from the lab a little after six, leaving instructions for his wife on the kitchen table not to disturb him until noon and to make an appointment for Dorie with their family physician for first thing Monday morning. He told her the school nurse had notified him that Dorie's booster shot was due.

The group arrived at Sarcorcee's doorstep unannounced, not wanting to take the chance he might bolt on them. His wife answered the door, and it took a few minutes to get her comfortable with the presence of the FBI and the strange entourage. She told them he'd been up all night working in the lab at Georgia Tech and didn't want to be disturbed. Ms. Johnson didn't push the stressed-out lady, but her insistence that it was important finally won them entry—except she didn't want the dog in the house. Smythe volunteered to stay outside with Edwin. Two FBI agents covered the back and front of the house.

Five minutes went by as Ms. Johnson, Mallory, and McKenzie sat waiting in the country-appointed living room. Dr. Sarcorcee shuffled down the open staircase at one end of the room and approached, bleary-eyed, adorned in a blue velour bathrobe tied at the waist.

"It's all right, Evelyn," his said in a husky voice directed toward the kitchen. "I know these people. Perhaps they would like coffee or tea."

"No thank you, Doctor," Mallory spoke up. "We're coffeed out."

"Very well then.... Evelyn, if you wouldn't mind, we need to be left to ourselves."

Sarcorcee beckoned with hand signals, leading them through a set of wood-paneled double doors to a den that appeared to serve as the doctor's office and library. "It will be private in here." He motioned for them to take seats in the two leather couches facing a heavy wooden table on curled, black, wrought-iron legs, an old ship hatch cover. "I presume you are here pursuing Professor Pedersen as you were several days ago. I have nothing to hide." Sarcorcee decided to play along. He couldn't tell if they were aware that Corey Parnevik was the professor.

"That is correct," Ms. Johnson said, taking over. "Was he with you in the Georgia Tech lab last night?"

"Yes."

"Why didn't you inform the FBI as I instructed three days ago?"

"He surprised me, and it was after midnight. I was working late in the lab and he just showed up."

"That doesn't cut it, Doctor. You had ample opportunity to call it in. You've impeded a national security investigation, and agents will be taking you into custody later today to take your statement. But right now, we're more interested in apprehending Professor Pedersen. How did he get access to the lab—what did he do and when did he leave?"

"Last week I arranged after-hours research passes for him to get into the labs. I don't know what he was doing. He wouldn't let me observe. He insisted on complete privacy, and he left the lab around five-thirty this morning."

"So you lied to me previously—in front of these witnesses." Ms. Johnson waved her hand toward Mallory and McKenzie, who appeared content to watch the show. "You gave him passes! Incredible. Why did you allow him access?"

"I don't want my wife to know anything about this," Sarcorcee burst out, his face contorted.

Mallory and McKenzie were glued to their seats. All of a sudden, Sarcorcee seemed on the verge of breaking down.

"If you've done nothing illegal, we'll abide by that," Ms. Johnson said.

"He threatened to harm my daughter," he blurted. "He intercepted her a week ago after she got off the school bus—on the pretext of giving her a birthday present from me. He pulled up to the curb in front of her in some sort of delivery truck and greeted her dressed in a pink and white uniform and a clown's mask, wishing her happy birthday. My daughter was on the way to her birthday party. We had it all planned. He enticed her into the truck and surgically placed an implant under the skin behind her neck, over the medulla oblongata. Dorie said she didn't remember anything about the man, except he gave her a fur coat, the present supposedly from me. I checked the implant out later after Professor Pedersen threatened me. Dorie never knew it was there. He said he could cause her great pain at will. I believed him."

"Incredible!" Mallory pushed back into the couch.

"What a bastard," McKenzie punctuated.

"We'll be checking that out, Dr. Sarcorcee," Ms. Johnson said smoothly. "And I can empathize with your situation. Now, this is important." She took a breath. "You're a noted nano researcher.

Did he give you any indication, anything at all, by his use of equipment or supplies, or by what he said, that he was going to attempt a replication procedure?"

Dr. Sarcorcee's face noticeably sagged. "All he told me was he was working on adjusting instructions to nanites he'd created outside his responsibilities where he worked. I had no idea he was an FBI fugitive."

"You'll have time later today to give your story. Expect a call from the Atlanta FBI field office, and expect a lie detector test. From this moment, you are placed on notice that this situation has been designated a national security issue. An agent will remain after we leave here. He will accompany you wherever you go. You're not to talk to anyone about anything associated with Pedersen."

The group left the house and headed back to the waiting vehicles, bearing witness as they left to the beginning of a shouting match between Sarcorcee and his wife.

Smythe and Edwin had just returned to the van from a walk down the sidewalk. "Parnevik's coat is still in the back of the van. Edwin can track him from Georgia Tech," he said as they approached.

Hearing his name, Edwin became agitated, circling out and around the limits of his leash.

"How'd you know he was—"

"I listened at the library window, Miss Mallory. I'm a Georgia PI, you know. We're definitely gaining ground on him in real time."

"Let's go then!" Ms. Johnson barked, motioning for the FBI backup car to follow.

 Ninety-nine

Gregory Campbell

SLEEPING UNEASILY FOR a brief two hours after returning from the Georgia Tech lab, Parnevik cautiously left the Days Inn at 8:30 a.m. He avoided the office and walked a block along Peachtree Street to summon a taxi. Six blocks down the road, he paid a visit to the UPS Store as it was opening for business. He disposed of his two packages and returned to the motel to prepare himself for the next phase of his master plan.

Forty-five minutes later, he left his room key in the motel room, and, again avoiding the office, walked a block down Peachtree Street, carrying his two suitcases, and hailed another taxi. Stashing the suitcases in the trunk, he slid into the back seat. He felt relaxed though a little self-conscious. Disguised as a light-skinned Rastafarian was a new experience.

It might be a little tight time-wise, but he'd make the 10:35 a.m. flight. He felt liberated—rid of the covetous little doctor with the big head as well as dependence on the Georgia Tech laboratory facilities.

He sat calmly, drawn up in the corner of the back seat, relishing the possible scenarios making headlines over the next few days and weeks. The devious doctor would most certainly find himself incarcerated, and very soon. After years of speculation by the pedantic scientific community confronting the milieu of potentially calamitous consequences, it should be enlightening to finally witness an actual nanite replication process going out of control.

He ran his hand over the top of his ponytail, testing its permanence. Smiling to himself, he pictured Sarcorcee alone in the lab, hovering over the glass containment chamber, attempting to produce a working inventory from the bulimic samples he'd left the greedy dwarf. The one instruction he'd failed to convey was setting the number of replications as part of the nanite's download instructions.

Curiously, Parnevik had grown fond of Gregory Campbell. On several occasions, Campbell had sent emails expressing his sincere gratitude for shoring up his livelihood and enabling his photographic business to weather the decline in demand from the effects of the deteriorating economy.

Prior to leaving for his business in Albuquerque, Parnevik, for the first time in their six-month business relationship, contacted Campbell and directed him to execute his end of their bargain. To his credit, Campbell never balked and was prepared as agreed.

His grandmother had a beach house outside Panama City. She was up in years and seldom visited the small house on the beautiful Gulf of Mexico. Campbell had a key and permission to visit at his leisure. All he had to do was drive his car to the beach house, refrain from using his charge cards, and stick with cash, leaving no trail. All business and personal contacts coming in by cell phone or email were to be responded to by "out of country" automated messages.

"Hey, buddy, we're here. You okay?" the cab driver said.

"Ah…yes, just daydreaming." Parnevik paid the cabby and thanked him for the quiet ride. He was still thinking about Campbell as he carried his bags into the terminal. It was an equitable arrangement and one he would keep active. Backups had become an integral facet of his life.

He halted at the lineup in front of *Aerolíneas Argentinas* and rifled through the pockets of his work vest for his passport. Gregory Campbell would shortly be on his way to Buenos Aires to shoot a TV commercial for a major Argentinean law firm.

 One Hundred

The Chase

A MILE AFTER the three-vehicle caravan made the first turn off Sarcorcee's street onto Peachtree toward Georgia Tech, Edwin began baying, pawing his feet, which meant the kennel van should make a turn. The hound whined as they passed a UPS store, causing McKenzie to U-turn and pull into the store parking lot.

Ms. Johnson checked it out alone, badging her way to the assistant manager's office. Five minutes later, she returned to the van with a description of a man who'd dropped off two packages just after the store opened. The man had said he was in a rush to get to the airport.

"That sounds like Parnevik," McKenzie said.

Mallory glanced at her watch. "We're less than an hour from him in real time."

"I sequestered the two packages." Ms. Johnson revealed them tucked under one arm as she signaled the FBI backup vehicle. Two plainclothes agents jumped out of the back seat, immediately at her side, hands on their weapons. She backed them off, telling them to speed the packages to Ed Furlow and get on the horn for another backup team to meet them at the airport ASAP. She said she'd fill Furlow in on the way.

"We obviously don't have to waste time going to Georgia Tech." Ms. Johnson climbed into the van. "I'm betting on Edwin. We may have nipped this thing in the bud."

 One Hundred One

Doctor Sarcorcee

HIS WIFE FINALLY settled down after the FBI people and the dog departed, reluctantly accepting his feeble and cursory explanations, but Sarcorcee couldn't explain away the agent left to shadow his movements.

Too agitated to go back to sleep, Sarcorcee locked himself in his library-study, slumped in his favorite reading chair, and attempted to dissect the situation and devise a feasible plan to survive the onslaught that would surely be coming his way. He'd have the evidence of blackmail in the morning when his family physician removed the implant from Dorie. But how could he protect his research plans? Parnevik had given him a dozen bulimic nanites as a starting base and wished him luck when he left the lab, christening the wish with his standard demeaning smirk.

He squirmed in the leather chair. He'd have to come clean if the FBI put him through a lie detector test. There seemed a good chance he could get away with the fact he hadn't reported the second contact with Parnevik because of the threat to Dorie's life. They'd ask about surveillance tapes. He could answer yes. The cameras were operational 24/7, but they wouldn't show any up-close detail. He'd take the chance they wouldn't ask him if he'd made his own. He'd have to admit receiving bulimic nanites from

Parnevik, but maybe he didn't have to give them all up. Even if he did, he still had the structural plans for Parnevik's generic machine and the miniaturization software program. He could design his own unique machine.... He needed to get back to the labs and take care of business, including sterilizing his computer. His assigned FBI agent wouldn't be aware of what he was up to. He'd place all the programs and files he'd accumulated encrypted in the cloud. He could still go on with his research plans after this thing blew over.

Sarcorcee pushed out of the chair, an epiphany forming. He paced the study, hands clasped behind his back. It would be logical to experiment with the nanites. The FBI didn't know about them yet and wouldn't be able to find fault with that, but he'd have to do it before they called him in.

He could create his own inventory of bulimic nanites. That would be easier than constructing a full-scale machine and going through the miniaturization process. Then he could legitimately return all the vials he'd received from Parnevik. Later, he could announce he'd created the miniaturization program. That was the key to credibility within the scientific research community. Experiments from there would be untainted by anything Parnevik might later claim—if the FBI ever caught up with him.

Satisfied his mind had spewed out most of the puzzle pieces, he compartmentalized them for later refinement. The first priority was to attempt a replication process before the FBI summons.

 One Hundred Two

Tracking Parnevik

EDWIN DIDN'T LET them down. He whined them away from the UPS store and through the turn onto I-75-85, heading for the airport.

By 10:55 a.m., the dog had navigated the party to gate D-15, about as far from the main terminal as you could get. Attendants at the gate were just changing over the signage to an Air Tran flight departing for Fort Myers later in the afternoon.

Ms. Johnson's face was tight with resolve. "You guys wait here." She pointed to the back row of empty seats in the lounge. "I'll find out where the last plane went and get a passenger list." She turned away and headed for the gate counter, returning moments later. "It went to Miami—it left at 10:35."

"We've got to nab him at the arrival gate," Mallory said, arms crossed. Neither McKenzie nor Smythe responded to the obvious as one of the gate attendants joined the group and handed Ms. Johnson a passenger-list printout.

She scanned it. "No one I recognize. I didn't think I would." She flipped the printout to McKenzie.

"You can get a copy of the boarding video," Mallory said. "Maybe we can isolate potential candidates."

Ms. Johnson yanked the satellite phone from her shoulder bag and punched in Ed Furlow's speed dial. "You know he's landed by now," she said, waiting. "It's only an hour-and-fifteen-minute flight. I'll get the FBI there. If there's any kind of delay, maybe we'll get a chance to screen the passengers as they debark. It's a long shot. The attendants said the plane was posted as coming in on time."

She turned away from the group and walked down the aisle of empty lounge seats, gesturing to the unseen party on the other end of the satellite connection.

The moment she returned, Mallory asked, "What about the Miami flight boarding video?"

"Yeah, they're on it. They should have it by the time we get back to the office—and two more items. One, Professor Pedersen going to L.A. turned out to be another Parnevik switch, and Pedersen's bank account and credit cards were closed out yesterday. Two, we've got Sarcorcee scheduled for a statement and lie detector test at six. It looks like it's going to be a long night. You're all welcome to hang out. Maybe our Mister Phelps here will pick up more on Parnevik." She smiled at the tall man sitting in a lounge seat, stroking Edwin and looking like a helpless professor.

 One Hundred Three

Georgia Tech: Day One

HE RUSHED DOWN out the doors into fresh air, informing the FBI agent he was headed for the Nano Research Center. All the way there, he took care driving, mentally rehearsing the steps in the replication procedure, the agent trailing behind in a government vehicle.

Entering the building, his insides started churning, and fear crept over him like a blanket, but he pushed through it; visions of fame and prosperity were now a viral cancer consuming his mind.

By the time he finished saving copies of his files to the cloud and checking over the clean room's operational systems, it was 3:30 p.m. The FBI agent was content to observe and not get in the way of Sarcorcee's work, interrupting him once knocking on the lab door to inform Sarcorcee of his appointment with the lie detector at 6:00 p.m.

Sarcorcee laid out his equipment on a black granite lab table just outside the glass-enclosed clean room and booted up his laptop. Two minutes later, he had the replication program up and running and the radio transmitter attached.

It had taken Parnevik only an hour and a half to complete a replication process. There was no reason Sarcorcee couldn't duplicate the effort and produce a large enough inventory of bulimic nanites to support his experiments into the foreseeable future.

He dressed in an orange, level-A, encapsulating suit with a self-contained air supply and entered the clean room, a multi-million dollar facility with filtered, vertical laminar airflow. The room's equipment supported university research in the fields of microelectronics, electronic materials, nanotechnology, MEMS (Micro-Electro-Mechanical Systems), lithography, optics, and other experimental disciplines requiring a particle-free environment.

In one corner of the room was a self-contained, eight-by-eight-by-eight foot, glass-enclosed cubicle, constructed for experiments requiring even more control of complex environmental conditions.

Sarcorcee set the air mixture in the cubicle to 75% pure oxygen and 25% water vapor and entered the cubicle carrying Parnevik's replication chamber and a plastic freezer bag of supplies. He placed the glass chamber on a small, pedestal-like steel lab table in the middle of the cubicle.

First, he removed the lid, set it on the table, and spooned out a four-ounce mound of monosaccharide sugar onto a round pewter plate fiber-glassed to the base of the chamber. He poured the contents of one vial over the mound and added six ounces of distilled water, stirring the mixture until the sugar dissolved. Then he brought in a twelve-volt battery, set it on the floor of the cubicle, calibrated the amperage, and connected the pincher leads to opposite sides of the replication chamber.

"That should do it," he said, feeling the perspiration running down his face inside the protective suit. He looked outside to make sure no one had somehow entered the locked lab. The FBI agent was in an adjacent lab reading a magazine and periodically observing through a common glass wall. The remote control to release the battery's charge was on the lab table where he'd left it.

His heart leaped when he noticed the lid still lying on the table. He removed a tube of silicone from the plastic bag and sealed the lid to the chamber. He quickly exited the cubicle and gave the inside of the clean room a last visual, then shut the cubicle glass door. He stood gazing through the glass, waiting for the sucking sound of the door to abate, indicating the seal was complete.

He exited the clean room and closed the double doors, again waiting for the sound of the air seal. Stripping off his protective clothing, he shivered as the air-conditioning hit him. Under his white lab coat, perspiration had pasted his tee shirt to his body, and droplets were rolling along his spine.

Perched on a stool in front of his laptop, all his equipment neatly arranged on the lab table, he set the radio transmission frequency just as Parnevik had done. The replication program was ready to transmit to the nanite. Now, all he had to do was press the Enter key and click the remote's *On* button.

He had about six minutes before the nanite would self-destruct, not having detected a human body in which to navigate to its programmed destination. Suddenly, the enormity of what he was about to do felt like a hundred-pound weight on his back, and he wavered. He'd gone over it dozens of times, reviewing the tapes and everything Parnevik had said and done. Did he have it right?

Sweat trickled from his hairline, down along his ears, and across his cheeks. What could he do if something *did* go wrong? Why hadn't he marked the time? He checked his watch. He had to guess.... Maybe three minutes had elapsed. He spun off the stool, ran to the near wall, and unclipped the specialized extinguisher designed to neutralize chemical reactions as well as put out fires. He verified it had a full charge and set it next to the clean-room doors. He stood back behind his table staring at it, realizing he didn't know how to operate the thing.

His mind told him everything was in order. There was nothing to fear. So, why was he frightened? His thoughts raced. He had to have the inventory—his own inventory. He could wait out the repercussions from the FBI, even totally cooperate, as long as he had inventory. The university would understand, and if it didn't, he had impeccable credentials. He could start over. It didn't matter where—to hell with tenure. Money and security wouldn't be a problem. He'd prepared meticulously.

He reached for the laptop keyboard, pressed the Enter key, clicked the remote, and scurried to a position along one glass wall of the clean room with a clear view of the containment cubicle and the replication chamber. The reaction would be immediate. He expected a whitish crystalline mass to accumulate in the center of the plate, surrounded by a perimeter of gray waste dust. Later he would use an electron microscope to separate the individual nanites—coated in their accreted sugar shells—from the crystalline mass. He had measured out the amount of raw materials for one thousand nanites.

As he watched, the crystal-like mass began to accumulate in the center of the dish. It was happening. Gray dust was forming around the mass as it grew. Within ten seconds, it was many times larger than Parnevik's process had been, but that was to be expected. Parnevik had wanted a small number of nanites.

Sarcorcee stood in awe, his breath fogging the glass as he strained to monitor the growing mass. Another ten seconds went by and it was still amassing. Then a strange thing happened. The gray dust began liquefying and covering the crystalline mass, rising and pouring thickly out over the pewter plate edges and onto the glass base of the replication chamber. That hadn't happened to Parnevik.

Riveted to the glass wall, Sarcorcee moved up and down to different views of what was taking place. To his growing horror, the gray goop seeped to one edge of the replication chamber. Steam burst forth as it made contact with the metal seams. The chamber collapsed. The glass panels fell flat onto the steel table. Now the gray goo streamed over the metal tabletop and a cloud of steam formed. The gunk dropped off the table to the floor like liquid plastic, pooling and spreading into tentacles toward the metal seams holding the floor and sides of the cubicle together.

As Sarcorcee watched the movement of the growing goop, the steel table collapsed and was quickly engulfed in gray ooze along with the battery. He heard muffled explosions of steam as the metal seams of the cubicle were disintegrating.

Now the cubicle floor was a solid mass of pulsating goop, covered over by a thick cloud of steam. Sarcorcee ran back to his table and collected his equipment, having no idea what he should do. He fled further back into the laboratory space. He stood there and watched the glass walls of the cubicle fall away and shatter to the floor; the sound was muffled, but the sight was horrific. The gray slime flowed like lava over the broken glass and across the cement floor of the clean room as if it had purpose.

Sarcorcee's heart jumping up and down as if it wanted to fill his throat and choke him to death. Millions of dollars of equipment were contained inside the clean room, lots of metal and lots of live electrical outlets. He had to do something. Call 911, but he hesitated. All his projections of the future rushed across his mind in a millisecond: his burgeoning career, his rise to fame, the money. It would never happen if he couldn't find a way to deal with this now.

He watched, mesmerized, feeling helpless, as the mass devoured the complex scientific equipment, filling the room with seething, churning gray slime that was rapidly decomposing the metal seams holding the containment walls of the clean room together.

When the explosive sound of the clean room collapsing in shattered ruin caused him to seek cover, he came to his senses. His table disintegrated as the flowing mass moved out over the cement floor of the lab in magma-like tentacles, sealant effervescing and bubbling up through the crawling nightmare like a boiling soup.

The disaster had taken less than three minutes. The process was not terminating, and Sarcorcee was in panic drive, head spinning. Visions conjured from the scientific warnings of potential consequences from uncontrolled replication were running rampant in his imagination.

He ignored the FBI agent pounding on the adjacent lab window. What was happening? Suddenly he understood. The nanites must be looking for more raw material. The process wasn't absorbing the shattered glass or the cement floor of the lab. The replication program directed breaking up the atomic structure of substances that contained the elements of carbon, oxygen, and hydrogen needed for replication of the sugar-based nanite machines. Perhaps the oxygen contained in the chemical bonds of the glass and cement didn't yield to the replication program. Or, maybe the process was getting enough oxygen from the air and water vapor and was searching for carbon. Yes, he was beginning to understand, but why hadn't it stopped? He'd placed the exact amount of raw materials prescribed in Parnevik's formula to produce exactly one thousand nanites. It was supposed to terminate when the raw materials were exhausted. Or, was it? Did he miss Parnevik placing a limit function on the reaction? Or, did Parnevik hide that from him? He was sure he'd completely absorbed the video and audio of their sessions.

Then he remembered the replication process needed a constant electrical source of two amperes or more. But that was for small-scale replications. He continued watching the moving tentacles, transfixed, tightly clutching his hands together, still frozen in fear, but his mind was working.

And then the epiphany. Whatever happened that caused the replication process to continue wasn't the issue. The thing needed raw materials and electricity—lots of electricity—and it had sucked it from the outlets embedded in the clean room's cement floor. It was spreading out looking for more. Maybe he *could* put an end to this—shut down the lab. Quarantine it. Face up to causing the damage. He still had the rest of his nanite inventory and the software.

Sarcorcee exited the clean room, ran to the control box between clean rooms, and started the pumps to create as close to a vacuum as possible. He switched off all the electrical fuses supplying the lab and set all the entrance doors to airtight seals.

The FBI agent was beside himself as Sarcorcee tried in vain to explain that an accident had occurred. He was busy on his phone as Sarcorcee continued to observe the movements of the center mass and tentacles of the process through the hallway windows. Movement was slowing. He returned to the control panel and glanced at the gauges. The vacuum in the room was 79%.

Ten minutes later, the slaggy mess was no longer bubbling and expanding. Its movement seemed limited to a wavy effect, like breathing.

A shiver ran up Sarcorcee's spine. He couldn't help projecting what might happen if the lab were breached and the process gained access to the unlimited supply of raw materials and electrical circuits waiting just outside. Some scientists believed a replication process could go rogue and within days literally devour the earth's atmosphere and surface features, leaving in its wake a layer of grey slime that would harden to slag, a dead planet. Scientists weren't even sure it would stop there. Space contains debris and invisible particles; it could jump to other planets and celestial bodies, perhaps feeding on the energy from the stars. Who could know?

 One Hundred Four

Miami, Florida: Same Day

PRIOR TO BOARDING the 1:45 p.m. flight from Miami to Buenos Aires, Parnevik made a long distance call from a pay phone to Arturo Alvarez. He was following up his last email, confirming their 9:00 a.m. meeting the next morning at the law offices of Marval, O'Farrell & Mairal in the heart of the Argentine capital.

Greetings and small talk ended quickly. "Your proposition was most interesting, if not provocative," Alvarez said smoothly in impeccable Spanish, displaying the intonations of the upper class and demonstrating his membership in society's elite. "How were you able to ascertain so much about me?"

"I employed appropriate resources, Mister Alvarez, but I respectfully request you understand my intent and not allow my actions to jeopardize our relationship. Our proposed business affiliation will be held in the strictest of confidence. The meeting tomorrow will result in full disclosure, and all your questions will be addressed." Parnevik's Spanish was near perfect; he was careful to use verbs in the formal tense, the result of four years of college language training and the efforts of his Panamanian nanny during his childhood.

"I look forward to it, Mister Campbell. Until then."

The phone conversation lifted Parnevik's spirits, leaving him confident and self-assured. Everything was in readiness.

Safely aboard the flight and in the luxury of first class, Parnevik relaxed and indulged in the finest Argentinean wines available to passengers. He would enjoy a gourmet meal and the gracious service he deserved. There would be time enough after the meal to prowl the Internet, researching the name Sarcorcee had given him in the lab early that morning.

 One Hundred Five

Georgia Tech: Late Afternoon

THE WHOLE EVENT had transpired in half an hour. Dr. Sarcorcee had no way of knowing if the process had reached stasis or was just lying dormant. He didn't want to think about what could happen if it breached the laboratory. What to do? He had to go somewhere quiet, alone, and think this out. As calmly as he could muster, he'd explained the chemical accident to the FBI agent, who called in the information to his superiors.

Almost on automatic pilot, he locked the lab, placing Off Limits signs on the entrance doors. From the control panel, he rolled down the inside shades, covering the observation windows.

Followed by the agent, he walked briskly down the hall—avoiding eye contact with passing students and fortunately not running into other staff—he retreated to his glass office, requesting the agent wait outside. He locked the doors and closed the blinds. He set the lighting low and slid into the comfortable mesh of his desk chair…. Ten seconds went by. He got up and walked to his small refrigerator for a bottle of water. "*Think*…." He sat back down in the chair and pushed into a reclined position.

He couldn't even contact Parnevik…a disastrous situation since he was the only one who could get him out of this mess.

Why hadn't he insisted on the means to communicate with him? *What about Pharmco? Someone there must know how the process works.*

Sarcorcee looked at his watch: 4:30 p.m. He plucked his cell phone from his lab coat pocket, hoping Dr. Safford hadn't gone home early for the day.

"There's been an accident in one of our clean rooms," Dr. Sarcorcee blurted after a slurred greeting.

"How can I help, Doctor?" The abruptness of Dr. Sarcorcee's tone was unexpected. He'd known Sarcorcee for years but never cultivated the man. There was something about him—something that caused Safford discomfort in his presence. His only contacts with him had been the few times he'd requested use of a lab when Pharmco's containment resources were overburdened.

"Can this be just between the two of us, Sam?"

Though immediately apprehensive at the personal liberty of using his first name, he swallowed his pride. Sarcorcee sounded very much out of sorts. "I suppose, but what could you possibly need? You have more capabilities than we do."

"Please, Dr. Safford, hear me out."

"Yes, yes. Go ahead."

"I attempted a nano replication and the containment chamber failed—"

"You did what?"

"I think it's in stasis. I was able to take away the atmosphere and access to electricity for the time being, but the process destroyed the equipment in one of our clean rooms. I don't know what to do. I have a huge mass of gray goop sitting in one of our clean-room laboratories."

"What in heaven's name led you to believe you could succeed?" Dr. Safford was at a loss; he couldn't divulge Pharmco's capabilities. They were all classified.

"It was Corey Parnevik. He instructed me—"

"Parnevik?" Panic grabbed at Dr. Safford's throat. "He's a wanted criminal," he blurted before realizing Sarcorcee couldn't know anything about that. "But never mind. My advice is to pray. I'll make a few calls to see if anyone has the expertise to assist. In the meantime, I suggest you cordon off the area and say nothing to a soul, not even Georgia Tech personnel. I'll be in touch at this number as soon as I can—and for God's sake, call the FBI."

 One Hundred Six

Atlanta FBI Office

RETURNING FROM THE airport, the kennel van and FBI trail car entered the FBI's underground parking. The group, including the ubiquitous hound dog, packed into the elevator, ascended the five floors in silence, and strode down the main hall in line behind Christine Johnson. It was almost 3:00 p.m.

Everyone was hungry, including Edwin. Riding in the trail car from the airport, Ms. Johnson had arranged with the FBI duty officer to order an assortment of Subway sandwiches and drinks.

Smythe had Edwin on a leash, bringing up the rear of the line, and he'd packed a bag with dog food and a water bowl. The hound appeared to be getting used to moving around the city, no longer skittish in unfamiliar surroundings.

Halfway down the hall, Ed Furlow, Atlanta's Special Agent in Charge, entered the corridor in front of them. "Miss Johnson, we were half an hour too late in Miami, and we screened the Miami debarkation tape with no luck. All the males that remotely resembling Parnevik's body type turned out to be either legitimate businessmen or tourists."

"That's not good news, Ed. I want to see the tape for myself."

"I'll set it up in my office. The lunch you wanted is there also. Let me know if you need anything." Furlow turned back into his office.

"He had to be on that flight," Mallory said. "Edwin would have gone to another gate."

"It *is* possible for him to err," Smythe said.

"So far he hasn't led us astray," McKenzie put in. "But if he wasn't on that flight, there's no telling where he went. He may have discovered we were tracking him—"

"Sarcorcee could have told him about us showing up at the lab with Edwin," Mallory blurted.

"We'll find out what Sarcorcee told him soon enough," Ms. Johnson said. "He's due in here at six for the lie-detector test."

***

Mallory, McKenzie, and Smythe were allowed to observe the interview with Dr. Sarcorcee as well as the administration of the lie-detector test. Escorted by his FBI agent, Sarcorcee had shown up in a distraught state, but that was understandable. After all, he was just a simple member of academia suddenly thrown into the middle of a national security manhunt. On top of it, as it turned out, he'd been blackmailed into lying to the FBI. He had to be terrified.

***

While Dr. Sarcorcee was writing out his statement of events, the group went back to Agent Furlow's office to chew over the interview session and go over the Miami tape. Strewn with Subway sacks, sandwich containers, and empty water bottles, the conference table was a mess.

Titus Smythe excused himself to take Edwin for a walk amongst the sparse greenery outside the building.

"Ed, if you could give us some alone time, I'd appreciate it," Ms. Johnson asked. Agent Furlow nodded and left the room.

"Sarcorcee's so wishy-washy, it's pathetic," Mallory snarled.

"I agree," Ms. Johnson said. "He melted too easily."

"My sense of it is he's afraid," McKenzie said. "But he passed the lie detector—I still get a lack of integrity. I wouldn't trust him to walk my dog."

"Speaking of dogs," Mallory jumped in, "he told Parnevik that Dickerson Phelps and the hound dog were with us at the lab. A little time on the Internet and even an idiot could find out Phelps' modus operandi. I don't care if he *was* blackmailed—and I don't care if he passed the lie detector. I think he's a lying scumbag."

"Maybe we haven't asked the right questions," Ms. Johnson said as Smythe returned with Edwin. "We can take another crack at him any time we want. What do *you* think about Doctor Sarcorcee, Mister Phelps?"

"I think I'm a pretty good judge of character, Miss Johnson. I don't think he has any. But I will say this. If Parnevik has done his research, he will discover how to combat my gift and befuddle Edwin's abilities."

Mallory's face contorted. "What are you saying?"

"All he has to do is be wary of intense emotion. He can counter emotions with a mantra, any mantra. It's all laid out in a Philadelphia newspaper interview I gave after working a case with their police department. As for Alfred, Edwin's father, I was questioned about his capabilities and revealed that garlic neutralizes the dog's sensitivity—Mallory, you remember when we stopped to buy dog food at the grocery store? Edwin wouldn't enter the building, and I had to take him back to the van. I didn't mention it at the time, but I assure you there was an open shelf of garlic cloves in the vegetable section."

Ed Furlow abruptly opened the office door and stuck his head inside. "Sorry for the interruption," he said to Ms. Johnson, "but you need to hear a recording of a phone call that just came in."

"What's so—"

"Trust me."

Ms. Johnson turned to face the assemblage. "I'll just be a minute." She followed Furlow out the door and into the bullpen com-center.

Wearing the set of earphones Furlow offered, she remained standing, her brow slowly furrowing and her mouth scrunching up as she listened to Dr. Sarcorcee's dilemma and plea for Pharmco's help. She played it a second time. "Ed, when did we get this?" She tossed the headset onto the desk.

"Just a few minutes ago from Dr. Sanford, Pharmco's CEO. Sarcorcee called him around 4:30. No wonder the guy was so cooperative. He was scared out of his mind—Sanford says he doesn't know what to do. He says Parnevik was Pharmco's only source of replication expertise and that we could be facing a potential catastrophic event."

"We were all afraid this might happen," Ms. Johnson said. "Get your director filled in. I'll bring DARPA up to speed. They'll canvass the scientific community for containment expertise. Then we visit Georgia Tech's chancellor. That research center needs to be quarantined tonight—without attracting media attention.... So, we go with a bomb scare and standard bomb-squad personnel and procedures—and get Sarcorcee back into interrogation and find out what the hell really happened."

 One Hundred Seven

Buenos Aires, Argentina

AEROLÍNEAS ARGENTINAS FLIGHT 403 landed in Buenos Aires at four in the morning. Parnevik had invested many hours scouring the Internet between bouts of fleeting sleep. Googling the name Dickerson Phelps had brought up a full page of entries. The third one he examined was delightfully revealing. A 1986 article in the *Philadelphia Inquirer* lauded the uncanny abilities of the Georgia PI and Alfred his bloodhound sidekick. They'd been credited with invaluable assistance to local police in tracking down a serial killer who gruesomely dispatched nine nurses over a four-year period in the Philly Metro Area.

The dog had proven his ability to track a person many days later, even across the congestion of major city streets while riding in a vehicle. The article recited Dickerson Phelps' claim of being able to tune into the thoughts and feelings of a person once he knew what they looked like and heard them speak. The so-called "gift" was said to be imperfect, its highest degree of effectiveness limited in time to some seventy-two hours in the past, but not including the most recent fifteen-hour span.

Parnevik had fidgeted away half of the thirteen-hour flight wrestling with the quandary of how to neutralize the threat. He'd almost given up halfway down the second Google search page when the entries began spawning answers. There was a similar case of assistance in Oregon, one in Chicago, another in Baton Rouge, and then there it was: another Dickerson Phelps interview shortly after the capture of the serial killer in Philadelphia. Parnevik read it over several times, thanking the Internet gods for deliverance. The Georgia PI had given his secrets away. All Parnevik had to do was massage away any building emotion with simple mantras to neutralize the clairvoyant gift. And the dog couldn't track him so long as he carried around a bunch of garlic cloves.

He sat back in his first class seat, a rising sense of wellbeing seeping into his consciousness as he looked around the cabin. First class was only half-full, and everyone was fast asleep. Then a thought flashed in his mind like an electric jolt. He'd experienced some mild stress, fear, and confusion as he'd considered the ramifications of the Dickerson Phelps conundrum. From now on, he must be ever vigilant—otherwise, they would find him.

***

By the time passengers were streaming past his seat, disembarking from the plane, Parnevik was experiencing his first test, combating creeping paranoia. Would his pursuers have discovered he'd boarded the plane in Miami for Buenos Areas?

He concentrated on remaining calm as he dissected the question, scrunched up against the window next to his seat. He watched the last of the stragglers pass by and out the exit door. The answer had to be no. The dog was back in Atlanta. He hadn't been that uptight on the flight, just purposeful, and he'd begun monitoring his emotions. They'd have to bring the hound dog to Miami...but they wouldn't. They'd never see through to Gregory Campbell even if the dog found his departure gate. The ID was impeccable. They would have to assume they'd been outsmarted again. Or maybe that he'd discovered his pursuer's weaknesses.

And for insurance, as serendipitous events would have it, the pizza he'd consumed at the Miami airport just happened to be heavily laden with garlic. He loved garlic, lots of garlic...but there was still the question of whether any of this was at all real. The authorities could be waiting for him here in the terminal. He shut his mind to it, embraced his chosen mantra, and scurried out of the first class section.

He was the last passenger to disembark, singing a Mary Poppins tune, much to the delight of the two attendants wishing him a pleasant day. *Chim chiminey. Chim chiminey. Chim chim cher-ee! A sweep is as lucky as lucky can be.*

 One Hundred Eight

Doctor Sarcorcee

LAST NIGHT, Ms. Johnson and her FBI interrogators had confronted Dr. Sarcorcee a second time as Mallory, McKenzie, and Titus Smythe observed behind two-way glass. When Sarcorcee heard the recorded phone conversation with Pharmco's CEO, his demeanor morphed into whining pleas of innocence and naiveté.

Briefed earlier that afternoon, the Chancellor of Georgia Tech University was astounded by what had transpired. There were strict rules and procedures in place for all nano-experimentation, whether conducted by staff or by outside contractors.

Dr. Sarcorcee was placed on temporary academic and research suspension, pending a university inquiry, and the FBI took him into custody on charges of impeding a federal investigation, withholding vital information in matters of national security, and lying to federal officers. He was incarcerated at the Fulton County Jail.

 One Hundred Nine

Arturo Alvarez

MIST-FILLED SUNLIGHT OCCUPIED the sultry downtown streets of early-morning Buenos Aires. It would be a scorcher after the moisture burned off.

From the thirty-fourth floor of the five-star InterContinental Hotel, Parnevik rose from a two-hour nap and watched the rosy sun ball peeking up over Buenos Aires Harbor.

He savored a typical Argentine breakfast of strong espresso, croissants covered in sweet toffee, and a grilled *tostado* filled with ham and cheese. Confident he'd attended to the details of his assumed identity, he checked out of the hotel at 8:00 a.m.

Gregory Campbell was scheduled to arrive at the law offices of Marval, O'Farrell & Mairal before it opened for business. The plush headquarters in downtown Buenos Aires took up the twenty-first through twenty-fourth floors of the *Gothic Palacio Barolo* with its high beacon tower.

Parnevik needed two hours to organize his equipment around an original Picasso painting in the luxurious vestibule. The actual shoot was to take place during the midday siesta break. Key staff members at the law firm would be participating in a carefully scripted commercial directed by professionals from the award-winning Anson-Stoner Advertising Agency.

No one at the law firm knew what Parnevik looked like—only that he was wealthy, generous, knowledgeable, and explicit. Gregory Campbell, a close friend of Mr. Parnevik, had been hired as a professional photographer, having been highly recommended by Mr. Parnevik. Campbell was scheduled to meet with Arturo Alvarez and Michael O'Farrell, one of the firm's principals, at 10:00 a.m.

Weeks ago, at Parnevik's direction, Mr. O'Farrell had drawn up an agreement, and Alvarez had reviewed it via email. The final document now awaited the signatures of Mr. Alvarez and Parnevik, through power of attorney granted to Gregory Campbell.

Alvarez was prompt and ushered into O'Farrell's spacious, glassed-in corner office by a beautiful, elegantly dressed mulatto woman. Parnevik, as Gregory Campbell, sat mesmerized on a plush couch. She was about Parnevik's age and she was stunning. All eyes followed her movements. Slender hips undulated under a short white skirt. Her armless, low-slung beaded blouse contained ample erotica as she sauntered toward the chairs and couches surrounding a glass table laden with stacks of file folders and beckoned Alvarez to take a seat.

Alvarez was a year younger than Parnevik, similarly built with comparable complexion. Attired in a business suit he could only have dreamt about sixty days ago, he appeared comfortable in the setting, over time having absorbed the serendipitous nature of the event that was to transpire this morning.

Another man was to take over the remainder of what was left of Arturo Alvarez's life. All he had to do was become someone else and inherit an estate of one million U.S. dollars. He could live as he pleased, no obligations, no strings—except to comply with every covenant of the agreement in order to receive quarterly annuity payments for life.

There were polite greetings in Spanish, and O'Farrell asked the woman to bring espresso and *empanadas*, stuffed pastries expressing social courtesy common to Argentineans.

Parnevik was so taken by the woman's gentle smile and captivating movements, he could hardly resist the impulse to follow her out of the room, engage her in conversation and learn who she was. Experiencing the attraction was entirely unexpected, leaving him confused but pleasantly calm. It also reminded him to control his emotions: *chim chim cher-ee*.

"I didn't realize you were fluent in our language, Mister Campbell," O'Farrell said in English.

"Not as fluent as our mutual friend, Corey Parnevik," Campbell responded, his eyes riveted on the woman's exit. Then, smiling, he cast a fleeting glance at Arturo Alvarez. He actually felt compassion for this man, another unaccustomed feeling.

Alvarez's formal dress was in no way a reflection of his dire circumstances. He'd been fired from his twelve-year engineering position as a result of a drug-possession conviction, sent to rehab, and given a severance check. He lived alone, no family, no relatives. After nearly a year out of prison, his financial resources were nearly exhausted, and the drug conviction had shattered his future career prospects. But he had been the perfect find, thanks to the efforts of an Argentine private detective employed by the Marval law firm.

***

Since retiring seven years ago from the Buenos Aires Police Department, Edwardo Flavantino had been a respected private investigator working exclusively for Argentine law firms.

For the last six weeks, he had been tossing and turning his way to a hot cup of tea at four each morning. He was not sleeping well. The retainer for this last assignment was exceptional, but Marval, O'Farrell & Mairal had been paying him to lie.

At first, he'd accepted it because the firm was considered impeccable, first class. But the personal history developed from his research had been edited by the law firm's staff. He was asked to sign off on it. That was ten days ago, and it still bothered him greatly.

Then, there was the strange way it had all started: a simple email from a Yahoo.com account offering him a lucrative and unusual assignment. No signature, no name, just directions to make contact with Michael O'Farrell at his law firm and then wait for the first retainer.

Flavantino had an old friend with considerable Internet and computer experience attempt to hack into the Yahoo server to no avail. His buddy told him if an email sender didn't identify himself, it was a sham, or else the owner of the account was smart enough to have opened it using false profile information from a public computer. It would be virtually impossible to find out the identity of the person.

When the first installment from the law firm arrived by cashier's check, he deposited the funds and waited a week for any backlash before making an appointment with O'Farrell.

His assignment was to locate an engineer in his late thirties, five foot ten-ish, 170-80 lbs., recently out of work, in financial straits, with no family and few if any entanglements. Work up his life story.

He'd accomplished the assignment but was immediately assigned an additional mission: to purge the personnel records where this engineer had worked, eliminating his termination event. And he was asked to facilitate, as O'Farrell had put it, the expulsion of the guy's conviction for drug possession from the Argentine legal system. This had required the use of considerable outside expertise and financial resources and had left him fearful.

Even though Flavantino was basically an honest man, he had allowed himself to become too deeply involved. The remuneration package had an overwhelming effect on him. It held the carrot of a comfortable full retirement.

***

The Argentinean element of Parnevik's master plan had its roots planted some three months earlier during his flight back to Atlanta from Quebec City. He'd used the Air Canada, in-flight Wi-Fi to conduct his research and choose the O'Farrell law firm.

One of the IDs he'd received from Giovanni was that of an imaginary Argentine citizen, Jose Gomez. Parnevik sent the law firm an introductory e-mail, wire transferred a retainer, directed the firm to utilize its resources to locate the required destitute engineer, and to fabricate a background life and documentation for a non-existent citizen by the name of Jose Gomez. Now, it was time for Jose Gomez to make his stage debut.

Marval, O'Farrell & Mairal had created two trust accounts, each operated by the law firm through limited powers of attorney granted by Parnevik. Arturo Alvarez was the beneficiary of the first trust, funded through a numbered account at a Lichtenstein bank, enabling the purchase and refurbishing in Alvarez's name of Parnevik's future home in Albuquerque.

The second trust was in favor of Jose Gomez, drawn upon by the law firm for expenses in creating the legal Gomez identity. It housed a one million dollar inheritance from the estate of a wealthy U.K. widow claiming she was Gomez's aunt.

On behalf of Jose Gomez, the O'Farrell law firm had presented an appeal up the hierarchy of the Argentine Federal Appellate Court system, finally reaching a judge who specialized in administrative matters involving agencies of the Federal Government.

A cover letter from Marval, O'Farrel & Mairal outlined the basic facts: Mr. Gomez was an indigent who had recently received an inheritance from the estate of a deceased person claiming to be his aunt. The funds and letter of direction were delivered to the law firm by the trustee, the Union Bank of Switzerland.

Gomez's deposition to the court claimed he was a homeless person, over the years scrounging out a living in the slums of several Argentine cities. He was in his late thirties, without any family, and had been on the streets since he was eleven. His mother, a woman he referred to as Roberta, had met her end on the banks of the muddy La Plata River in a seedy outlying barrio of Buenos Aires, leaving the boy destitute.

His account claimed he was without friends, and even if he'd managed to cultivate acquaintances no one would remember him. He'd learned early on that moving frequently from place to place was prerequisite to staying alive. His plea to the court included no claims to an official residence, no assets except the recent inheritance, and he possessed no records of his birth or schooling.

The law firm's presentation to the court included payment receipts from a reputable private investigator the law firm had hired to locate Gomez at the time the firm received the estate's letter of direction and retainer. The investigator's report outlined locating Mr. Gomez living under a bridge in an outlying Buenos Aries borough and included a record of his birth-certificate search in the archives of the Federal Civil Registry.

The private investigator's report contained a certified copy of a contracted genealogical search by the firm of Estudio Batres & Franzese, an unsuccessful attempt to locate evidence of a male birth by a Roberta Gomez thirty-five to thirty-eight years ago.

The judge overseeing specialized administrative cases issued a closed-door ruling, absolving Jose Gomez for past legal infractions due to his indigent lifestyle and directing the Registry of Civil

Status to issue a substitute birth certificate and National Identity Document in the care of the law firm. The cost had been ten thousand U.S. dollars wrapped in a plastic bag, buried in the contents of a box of Kellogg's Frosted Flakes and delivered to the judge at his home as part of his weekly grocery order.

Jose Gomez would be officially 37 years old on February 17th, two days from now, and today he would claim his right to the trust and start a new life: obtain a driver's license, open a bank account, establish credit worthiness, easily pass the standard examination for a secondary schooling certificate, and attend college. He was still young. The one million dollar trust account provided a life annuity, and the monthly payments to Gomez would begin immediately. All that was required of him was to move to a new city, grow a beard, act within normal social mores, obey the local laws, and avoid any contact with persons from his past.

***

As Parnevik sat in the law offices waiting for O'Farrell and Alvarez to initial and sign the documentation, his mind roamed over the possibilities of his transformation adventure, his final gambit. Thoughts of working again in neglected fields of his expertise surged to the forefront. He'd always been interested in fluid dynamics. It was, in fact, what had led him into creating nanites at Pharmco that could move through the body. Alvarez had the educational background in several engineering disciplines and a clean resumé. Albuquerque had a rich assortment of hi-tech companies and major university graduate programs in multiple engineering fields. The university was processing his application.

In the meantime, Parnevik would invest some time slipping into Alvarez's identity—maybe redecorate his small condomini-um—make contact with his usual day-to-day routine, and lightly engage with his past acquaintances—set the stage for traveling most of the year.

"Are there any questions, Mister Gomez?" O'Farrell said to Alvarez, smiling.

"Mister Campbell, if you please," the lawyer said, severing Parnevik's reverie.

O'Farrell had spent many hours with Arturo Alvarez, introducing the offering, candidly outlining knowledge gathered about his past life, careful not to cause animosity, and defining the opportunities as well as the covenants the agreement offered.

"Mister Gomez, as you know, Mister Campbell is executing the agreement through a power of attorney granted by a business person who will remain anonymous. That person's efforts in the background are responsible for your new identity and good fortune." O'Farrell slid the copies of the five-page agreement across the table for Campbell to sign. "This will conclude the meeting."

Parnevik was observing Alvarez. He was suddenly looking a little nervous, perhaps locked in last-minute disbelief.

"Why me?" Alvarez cast a blank stare at Campbell.

"You don't need to know," Gregory Campbell said gently, feeling camaraderie for the first time in memory. Two fresh lives were about to begin, vibrant lives without social or financial limitations, lives that didn't require conformity, accountable to no one as long as society's laws were observed.

Alvarez seemed to relax, leaning out from his chair at the head of the table. "You know...? Well, of course you don't, but I always wanted to be an interior designer," he said as he watched Campbell's pen race through the three copies of the agreement. He settled into the comfortable folds of the chair, eyes glazed, a far-away look on his face, possibly acknowledging the reality: he was Jose Gomez.

"Just one more item." Michael O'Farrell stood to face Gomez. "This agreement is verbal—a last favor requested by the benefactor of this arrangement."

"What can I do?" Gomez said, jarred from his meandering mind.

"For the next week, you will reside at the Marriott Plaza in luxury accommodations overlooking the historic Plaza San Martin in the popular *Retiro District*. You are free to begin planning your new life—and await notification and directions from Mister Campbell. You will be flying to Miami, Florida—a last time as Arturo Alvarez. As Jose Gomez, you will stay two nights at a nice hotel that will be booked in advance. The purpose of your trip is to explore interest in purchasing a condominium overlooking Biscayne Bay. Mister Campbell will call on you to deliver up your Alvarez passport. As Gomez, you will report to the Argentine Consulate and claim the loss of your passport. The Consulate will arrange for a duplicate and a letter of explanation for airport immigration authorities. Then, as Gomez, you will return to Buenos Aires and the continuation of your new life—no questions asked.

 One Hundred Ten

Georgia Tech: Day Two

SHORTLY AFTER MIDNIGHT, accompanied by FBI agent Ed Furlow and the humbled and disgruntled Dr. Sarcorcee—who'd been pulled earlier in the evening from his jail cell for his second visit with the lie detector—DSO Field Commander, Christine Johnson, entered the nano research center. Her objective was to ascertain the status of the FBI quarantine, take still pictures, video the replication scene, and acquire a first-hand feel for the predicament.

By 2:00 a.m., DARPA had copies of the photographs and video, an audio of Sarcorcee's detailed explanation of what had taken place in the laboratory's Clean Room, and a containment-status update.

The stasis condition had materially changed: the basement floor of the research center was buckling, and the building appeared to be slowly imploding, indicating the replication process had somehow begun anew, going to depth.

Dr. Sarcorcee believed small imperfections in the two-foot-thick cement floor of the laboratory were yielding to the process. The replicating nanites were searching for carbon-based material. Well aware of the worst-case scenario put forth by a host of capable scientists over the years, he speculated the process was not taking place exponentially because of the lack of electricity, but he had no idea what would happen if it found an unlimited electrical supply.

FBI personnel clad in orange protective suits and wearing gasmasks completed the quarantine of the Nanotechnology Research Center during the early morning hours. The FBI sealed off the building with yellow tape and posted plain-clothes agents around the perimeter.

All through the night, utilizing invasive phone calls and re-quired Internet briefings, DARPA had commandeered and vetted a team of nano-scientists, placing their lives on hold and garnering agreements to rally together in confronting the potential disaster looming in the Georgia Tech laboratory. They were due to arrive in Atlanta, along with a plethora of requested equipment and supplies, over the next twelve hours to assess the situation and come up with a containment solution before a nightmare scenario unfolded.

 One Hundred Eleven

Atlanta FBI Headquarters

IT WAS FOUR in the morning when Agent Christine Johnson returned from Georgia Tech. Doctor Sarcorcee was escorted back to the Fulton County jailhouse to await formal charges. Earlier in the evening, the group had observed Dr. Sarcorcee sweat through his second lie-detector test and interrogation concerning the lab accident. His fate would more than likely remain in limbo while the disaster continued to define itself and the government decided how best to classify and prosecute his travesties. He could end up spending time at Guantanamo Bay, without explanation, suffering abrogation of his rights as a citizen.

Titus Smythe had retired with Edmond shortly after the Sarcorcee interrogation. Severely drained of energy, they had headed back to Emma's waiting arms and warm beds.

Mallory and McKenzie had remained behind in the FBI's conference room while Ms. Johnson went about her business at Georgia Tech. They witnessed its transformation into an emergency operations hub designed to confront an eminent terrorist attack. Ms. Johnson's minute-by-minute reports from Georgia Tech had periodically squawked from speakers in the room.

With a fresh cup of coffee in hand, Ms. Johnson took a seat at the smaller conference-room table opposite Mallory and Agent McKenzie.

"We can't just sit back and do nothing," Mallory said, standing and slapping her hip.

McKenzie had seen her exhibit the habit many times during their graduate school years. They were both in need of rest, their patience frayed. Ms. Johnson's eyes were hollowed and bloodshot, but she leaned back in her chair without reacting.

The room was jammed with communications machinery and mostly unshaven male FBI agents scurrying about in ultra-serious mode. Ms. Johnson reached to gather up several folders on the table. "Let's go back to Furlow's office to discuss."

Ms. Johnson was first out the door, detouring on the way to the break room, picking out something sweet to tide her over and encouraging Mallory and McKenzie to replenish.

Arranged around a sturdy wooden coffee table, McKenzie sat in one of two comfortable cloth couches with Mallory and Ms. Johnson occupying the other. He was shaking his head between bites of an éclair. "It doesn't look like we're going to find Parnevik, does it?"

"Parnevik is the number two DARPA priority now," Ms. Johnson monotoned. "Number one is the potential catastrophic event." Her facial features were etched in despondency. "We've got Doctor Safford, Pharmco's CEO, on his way here. He wouldn't talk to me earlier over the phone when I pressed him for progress details on Pharmco's DOD contract. I was thinking he might have held on to some secrets that could help the situation. Anyway, he was afraid of violating the company's security covenants with the DOD and insisted on face-to-face, seeing our credentials, bringing his security director, and recording the conversation.... He'll be recorded all right. I've got Curtis

Mayborne, the Director of DARPA, waiting on Skype. After that, I've been told to play host to a group of scientists coming in over the next twelve hours. It will be mayhem getting them billeted and focused on brainstorming containment solutions."

"We must be able to do something." Mallory sat frowning, arms crossed.

"Look, you guys, I'm still in charge, but I truly expect that to change shortly. With national security involved, it's really a Homeland Security, FBI, and DARPA direct responsibility. It's getting out of my league. You might also be interested to know that the President will be briefed first thing this morning." She looked at her watch. It was 5:45 a.m. "A little over two hours from now."

"Christine," McKenzie said. "I suggest we give Edwin a try in Miami. Phelps says he's capable of picking up a trail as long as it's not more than two days old."

"I'm ahead of you. An FBI plane is waiting for you at the airport. You might even be able to catch an hour's nap on board. In the meantime, I'll get the Miami office to preview the boarding tapes for every flight that left there after noon yesterday. They'll identify and run down anyone meeting the parameters of Parnevik's body type. We'll look at everybody. You can review the tapes yourselves when you arrive. I'll have you met. Maybe we'll get lucky."

 # One Hundred Twelve

The Oval Office

AT THE CONCLUSION of the President's morning intelligence briefing, he directed Curtis Mayborne, the head of DARPA, and John Lindsay, Deputy FBI Director, to adjourn to the Oval Office. The President and his chief of staff, Peter Costanzo, listened patiently as the two outlined the sordid story leading up to potential calamity waiting in the sealed-off Georgia Tech Laboratory.

"You say the process is no longer in stasis," the President reiterated, "and is slowly dissolving away the cement floor of the Georgia Tech Research Center. And, the bottom line is we don't know what's going to happen if it can't be stopped before it gets access to the raw materials that fuel the reaction—but what *could* happen might wipe out the planet!" The President's eyes were open wide. "Is that the essence?"

"That's the gist of it, sir," Mayborne said.

"*And*, the North Koreans have kidnapped an American citizen on U.S. soil—at a wrestling match in Nebraska—thinking, as you contend, that he is the recalcitrant scientist responsible for the nanotechnology at the heart of a secret DOD contract…a DARPA deal with the Atlanta research company he worked for."

"Yes, sir." John Lindsey nodded. "George Randle was impersonating Parnevik, evidently doing his bidding, demonstrating the live effects of his product."

The President rose from his favorite Victorian chair, frowning and pensive, hands on hips stretching. It was his standard way of beginning to absorb and dissect a situation. He straggled to the service bar along one wall of the grand room; it was sufficiently stocked to last through his morning meetings. He tinkered with the kettle of hot water and poured out a cup.

The American people recently elected this successful executive because he was well known for confronting problems head-on, and because he wouldn't bring political or diplomatic baggage to the table. He pledged to stabilize the nation's economy, equalize the tax burden, stimulate business activity, rid government operations of inefficiencies, repair the country's infrastructure, and forge a powerful foreign policy of actions based on supporting human rights, promoting peace, and bringing the fight on terrorism into full public disclosure.

He dipped the tea bag several times, squishing it with a spoon against the side of the cup, amazed at having to confront such improbable events in the first weeks of his administration.

The silence in the room was palpable. A long half-minute later, he turned away from the service bar with his steaming cup, the beginnings of a smile spreading over his face. "Gentlemen, I think we can deal with these issues," he said, re-seating and crossing his legs. "In fact, we may have been given a serendipitous opportunity as regards this Randle character's situation.... Peter," he said, peering at his chief of staff sitting alone on an opposing couch, the rosewood table at the center of the gathering, "ask the Secretary of State to return to the White House as soon as she can—and to bring the Chinese ambassador. We'll begin a dance with the North

Koreans that I believe will garner their complete attention—and finally bring some semblance of logic to their future diplomacy."

The chief stood and took a few steps away from the grouping, turning his back to make the call.

"As for the Georgia Tech dilemma, a nano-experiment is out of control threatening a possible catastrophe…and you're telling me the only person in the world who has the actual expertise to shut it down—and the cause of this hapless fairytale—has eluded all attempts at apprehension by this nation's highly trained personnel and hi-tech resources—and he's doing this by using disguises and fake IDs?"

The President had attempted to keep his tone from entering the facetious range. "That is astounding to me…. But that being the case, may I suggest we use a little common sense and entice him to voluntarily turn himself in…provide a service to his country in its time of dire need. How does that set with you gentlemen?"

The chief of staff returned to his seat, nodding to the President.

"What did you have in mind, Mister President?" John Lindsay tried not to squirm in his seat, leaning out from his position on the other divan next to the DARPA director.

"I sense you men can't see the trees through the forest. I've been there too, and I know what it feels like. I'm suggesting that we assume the worst-case scenario." He glared at DARPA's Curtis Mayborne. "The scientists you are rounding up to confront this problem will come up empty-handed. Our first priority should be to offer this demented Parnevik amnesty—a free pass—no charges for crimes committed, a story recognizing his scientific contribution to DOD research through Pharmco Corp…a medal for heroism for God's sake—*if* he can put a stop to the replication process. What actually happens afterwards is up to us to concoct for the good of the country."

"Mister President," Mayborne ventured, "with all due respect, sir, we don't know where he is or how to contact—"

Lindsay suddenly stood. "The Genovese had an encrypted email system in place. Parnevik doesn't know we've moved that family out of his business realm. In their present circumstances, I'm sure the Genovese would cooperate."

"Excellent," the President said. "Get with the Justice Department on the best way to contact them—nothing in writing—no evidence of collusion. We need Parnevik here yesterday." He turned toward the chief of staff. "Pete, work with Lindsay on this—and I want to stay directly in the loop. Keep me informed personally. No one else for now. Maybe we can keep this away from Congress if we can quickly put a lid on it...and God knows this can't get out to the media."

"Mister President," Mayborne said, "a further note here. The DARPA Special Agent heading up our investigation through the Atlanta FBI Office called in earlier this morning. The Georgia Tech campus newspaper came out last night. The student editor summarized the "strange situation" that had been unfolding for the last two days. She described the quarantine by saying there seemed to be professional guards posted around the building twenty-four hours a day, and the building was sinking into its foundation. CNN caught wind of it and requested an interview with the Georgia Tech Chancellor."

"That's just great.... Okay, that forces us into a corner. It's time for Homeland Security to shut down all media coverage under the blanket of national security. No interviews, no coverage on site, nothing except a vanilla announcement of an accident...a chemical accident—something wholly believable but not associated with terrorism. Pete, you work out the details with Homeland

Security. And again, keep me informed. I want to know what you come up with before it goes live—and this needs to happen now. Call CNN direct and put a stopper on that interview until we work out the announcement."

***

After his guests departed, the President moved to sit in the big straight-backed chair he'd used so many times in intimate press interviews. He was reviewing the elements of discussion, his tea long gone bitter and cold. He'd have to brief the Congressional Committee on Foreign Relations in secret after he met with the secretary of state and decided what to do about North Korea.

Suddenly startled by a spark of insight, he stood away from the chair, momentarily facing the camel-colored leather sofas in the conversation pit. Then he paced in a circle around the furniture grouping along the perimeter of the wheat, cream and blue-colored oval rug embroidered with the presidential seal.... The media could be asked to provide a public service announcement, an appeal seeking the advice of Corey Parnevik, an expert in the kind of accident cleanup needed at Georgia Tech...direct him to enter a prepared website for information on the type of assistance the government required and the terms of his participation. Signing in with the answers to several personal questions would open his private access to the information. It could work. And it could go live today. *Parnevik certainly will be watching television.*

The President stopped at the communications screen embedded in the wall next to a massive grandfather clock at the side of his working desk. He punched in a four-character code.

"Pete, I'm sorry to run you down in midstream, but I need a minute."

 # One Hundred Thirteen

Chinese Ambassador

THE PRESIDENT SPENT two hours brainstorming with the chief of staff prior to the arrival of the secretary of state and the Chinese ambassador. Both were skillful at hard-core negotiations, having worked together over many years at the helm of the second largest corporation in the United States.

***

The President attempted to be conversational and non-confronting, building the scenario slowly, brick by brick. The ambassador sat quietly with his interpreter, shaking his head and periodically grinning, allowing his eyes to wander around the ornate Oval Office. "You have heard a summary of the dark and heinous acts perpetrated on American soil and watched edited tapes of Mister Hwang Jang, a high-ranking North Korean intelligence officer, posing as a pharmaceutical representative in collusion with our citizen, Mister George Randle. And then the airport video footage of Randle's subsequent abduction aboard a Chinese commercial charter flight from Atlanta to Pyongyang just two days ago. Mister Ambassador, I take it you understand what we've laid out here?"

"Yes, Mister President, I will speak with our government on this matter. Please be assured I was unaware of these events."

"Mister Ambassador, I am requesting that you facilitate an immediate face-to-face meeting between Secretary of State Kelly and the new Korean leader. I believe Kim Young Oon is currently being referred to as the cherubic naïf."

The Chinese ambassador displayed no sign of offense, his face inscrutably cast in stone. Written assurances had guaranteed a secure and unrecorded meeting, and candid was the agreed caveat.

"At their convenience, of course," the President added, expressionless. "Sometime in the next twenty-four hours."

"Mister President, why don't you go through your surrogate channels at the Swedish Embassy in Pyongyang?" the Chinese ambassador asked glibly.

"In this way, Mister Ambassador, the North Koreans will know that their perceived ally is subtly in favor of this secret summit."

"But what could the North Koreans hope to gain by the loss of face generated from caving in to a summons from the United States?"

"Mister Ambassador, let me put it in three parts. And please accept the generalities. The first is that we are prepared to sit down with your people, the South Koreans, the North—and any other nation that wants to observe—to end the Korean War. The second is we are prepared to guarantee the building of a North Korean infrastructure—after successful reunification with the South—and see to it the present North Korean leaders are granted immunity from prosecution. Third, no loss of face should occur since the negotiations will be held in secret. All we ask is for George Randle's immediate return to the U.S. without fanfare and a firm time for the meeting with our secretary of state. The meeting can be initiated by the North Koreans on any basis they choose to soothe their egos."

"And if they refuse, Mister President?"

"Then, Mister Ambassador, the proof of the covert incursion into U.S. territory and kidnapping of a U.S. citizen will go public. Consequences to North Korea will be immediate and severe…meaning, Mister Ambassador, that twenty-one pre-selected, military and political targets will be taken out in an instant."

"You wouldn't dare to even conceive of such a ludicrous idea," the Ambassador said, almost snarling. "Your country has no such capabilities within reach."

"Mister Ambassador, you need to watch the skies. At 6:00 p.m. today, Eastern Standard Time, have your observation knowhow focus on the orbital debris packet referred to as "Bundle 1109.""

Five minutes later, a distraught Chinese Ambassador was escorted from the Oval Office by a covey of secret service agents, leaving the President, his chief of staff, and the secretary of state alone.

"You don't expect them to respond favorably, do you?" Secretary Kelly said.

"Yes, I do. This Parnevik is no dummy. He programmed his nanite samples to self-destruct if subject to experimentation. When the North Koreans find out they have nothing, they'll return what they have. And by now, they must have figured out that Randle isn't Parnevik and is of no value. It will cost them nothing to come to the negotiating table."

"Then why the threats?"

"We want them to be good boys from now on, *without losing face*—and, we want them at the negotiating table for real. The demonstration will force them to realize all their military planning and posturing is obsolete…and I think it might be an opportune time to open confidential discussion with the Chinese on becoming a partner in the maturation of our plans for a moon base."

The Chief of Staff bolted upright out of the leather sofa. "You aren't suggesting—"

"Of course not! But I do believe it can be an ongoing ploy in seeking cooperation on a multitude of issues. And, as we know all too well, discussions often lead nowhere. The old carrot-and-stick gambit will help."

 One Hundred Fourteen

Miami, Florida: Next Day

AT THE MIAMI International Airport, Smythe gave Edwin a fresh dose of Parnevik's winter jacket, and the faithful hound led them on a chaotic chase, paying visits to multiple ticket counters and departure gates. Airport security and TSA personnel hadn't been properly briefed and were unprepared for the security risks created by the gaping crowds that formed whenever the group stopped for more than a minute at a time.

Charging down one concourse after another, the hound dog finally ended the chaos. His whining terminated twenty feet from the entrance to a pizza kiosk in the airport food court where he walked in a tight circle, chasing his tail. Four or five turns and he lay down, sprawled out, panting and sneezing.

"It's the garlic." Smythe stroked the hound's hindquarter. "He can't help it. He's such a good dog."

Mallory and McKenzie just stood stoically, looking down over the faithful hound as Smythe pulled out a bottle of water and a bowl from his shoulder bag.

"We better check in," McKenzie said. "Maybe Christine has had better luck with the departure tapes."

Mallory shuffled next to Smythe as he was stooping to fill the bowl. "So this means Parnevik got wise."

"Not necessarily. It could be accidental, but we know he was here. I'm so sorry, Miss Mallory. And look. Edwin knows. He's almost cowering. You're a good old boy, my friend. Here." Smythe gave the dog a bone treat.

A crowd had gathered, and the TSA had recovered a semblance of organization, forming a cordon around the scene. "I'll call her." Mallory yanked her sat-phone off her knapsack. "We better get a move-on," she said, noticing the onlookers. "I'll meet you back at the FBI plane."

***

Thirty minutes later, the group was airborne and comfortably seated in the plane's customized lounge, hungrily gorging on premade sandwiches washed down with fresh coffee and juices. Edwin was sound asleep, curled up at Smythe's feet.

Mallory had come aboard the plane stone-faced and taken a seat away from the others. McKenzie was familiar with the behavior. It meant she had reached some threshold, a mental limit, and was clammed up, trying to sort it out.

McKenzie clued Smythe in and they stayed out of her space. She'd tell them what was bothering her in her own time.

It took a good fifteen minutes before she came out of isolation to satiate her hunger. Wolfing down a sandwich and finishing off a Powerade, she sauntered over to McKenzie and Smythe and related what Christine Johnson had told her on the call back at the airport.

"What else did she say?" McKenzie quizzed.

"Georgia Power is on-site and systematically cutting power to nearby buildings. The research center foundation is crumbling. The replication process is consuming the ground beneath, and fingers of sinking soil are creeping out toward other buildings. She says the only redeeming fact is that so far the process is slow. It looks like the whole campus will have to be evacuated. The FBI has taken control of the security at the downtown Marriott where the scientists are arriving and gathering to brainstorm."

"Anything on the departure tapes?" McKenzie asked.

"Nothing. There were seventeen flights to check. Anybody remotely similar to Parnevik's body type was clean. I told her Edwin verified he was at the airport—but all we could deduce was if he didn't take a flight out, he's gone somewhere else. She's at a dead end—but…Christine said the President has come up with a plan and a cover story. The government is going to announce an accident to the press and the issuance of a public service plea through the television media for Parnevik to turn himself in." Mallory's mouth curled and she raised her hands palms up. "They're going to offer him amnesty after all the killing. I can't believe it," she said, gritting her teeth and shaking, unable to continue.

"That's outrageous," Smythe said.

McKenzie draped an arm around Mallory's shoulders. "Mal, the process has to be stopped. It's a good idea. Parnevik is probably the only person who can do it. We just have to pray that he'll take the deal—whatever they're offering. I can't help but believe in the end he'll get what he deserves. Right now the President has to stop a potential disaster."

"I know. I know."

 One Hundred Fifteen

Buenos Aires, Argentina

WITH THE ALVAREZ and Gomez legalities laid to rest, Parnevik spent most of the following day morphing into the stream of Alvarez's daily life. The agreement had required detailed descriptions of Alvarez's humble routines, and Parnevik had eagerly practiced disguising his appearance and visiting the places the man frequented. No one he encountered took any undue notice, not even the manager of the condominium complex where he lived and performed odd jobs to help make ends meet.

The man's life had slowly deteriorated during the last two years after completing drug rehabilitation and experiencing endless rejections seeking gainful employment. By the time Parnevik's Argentine private investigator discovered Arturo Alvarez, he'd depleted the severance stipend he'd received from his previous employer and was destitute, bordering on suicidal.

The PI earned a handsome fee. Alvarez turned out to be the perfect fit, devoid of male or female friendships bringing concern or solace to his predicaments, only a few cursory acquaintances. As so frequently happens in life, when a person hits the skids, presumed friends are nowhere to be found.

The end of the day found Parnevik meticulously cleaning every square inch of Alvarez's condominium and washing the sheets and towels left behind at a Laundromat next to a small grocery store two blocks away. He'd changed around the interior to suit his tastes and purchased a leather recliner from a nearby specialty store. He was relaxed and at ease in the small unit. It was middle class and melted into the bland fabric of nondescript condo complexes on the south side of Buenos Aires. He actually felt cozy in the Spartan space, like a kid's hideout.

Lounging in the new recliner, he appreciated the basics Alvarez had in place: Internet access, cable TV, cell phone service, even a small Fiat car housed in a one-car garage. The purchase of a laptop computer to use in conjunction with the new identity completed the utility of the condo. He was now Arturo Alvarez, newly wealthy and affluent, and he felt a stirring of excitement at the prospects of becoming a more social animal, a different human being with an exciting life ahead.

It was 7:00 p.m. The refrigerator was stocked, and he'd made himself his favorite snack: thin rye crackers with cheddar/horseradish spread and an ice-cold glass of fruity, Argentine Sauvignon Blanc. It was a pleasant surprise finding the local grocery had such an adequate selection of upscale products.

He turned on the TV, making a mental note to inform the condo association that from now on he would be randomly in residence, having contracted a consulting job outside the city. He flipped through the station menu to CNN. All the major U.S. stations were live and in English. He reclined in the comfortable leather chair, sipping from a long-stemmed glass.

Suddenly, what was being reported sent shock waves rifling down his spine, and he felt as if he'd absorbed a punch in the chest. The CNN anchor was in the middle of reciting a summary of the President's briefing an hour earlier. Parnevik slammed the recliner down, grappled with the remote, and hit the record button.

There had been a chemical spill at a Georgia Tech research center in Atlanta. Reactions of experimental chemicals to atmospheric exposure had caused a quarantine over half the university campus…. *Sarcoree.* It had happened. He'd warned the smug dwarf, but the unmistakable body language had been there: the coy smiles of satisfaction, the eyes slightly unfocused, and his attention intermittent. That dumb, egotistical idiot had tried to create inventory.

At the end of the cursory report, it was apparent the media had been fed an excellent cover story, but then the anchor went on, reading a public service announcement requested by the Department of Homeland Security. Parnevik placed his wine glass on a side table, stretched forward in the recliner, clutched the remote, and turned up the volume. What he heard caused a different kind of shockwave to his nervous system, and it brought on a fit of nausea. He switched channels and muted the TV, knowing the recording would continue. He needed the mantra. *Chim chiminey. Chim chiminey. Chim chim cher-ee! A sweep is as lucky as lucky can be.*

Several moments went by in the still of the room. His pulse slowed, *chim chim cher-ee*, stability and control returning. He poured himself a fresh, cold glass of wine and repositioned the recliner. With a clear head, he punched the remote to where he had left off in the announcement. The government was requesting his assistance, referring to him as an anonymous, senior researcher, out of reach on an extended expedition in the Amazon jungle. He had to give the government credit. They knew he was the only one with the expertise to stop the replication process, *but how bad could it be?* The taped announcement, obviously spliced into the program, directed him—as if he were watching—to a website for more information. He slipped off the recliner, scurried to the small desk in the dining room, and opened his laptop, forcing back a wave of anxiety...*Chim chim cher-ee. They must be desperate.*

Waiting for his operating system to load, his curiosity was building. The only way to find out what was happening was to go to the website. He opened the Firefox browser but abruptly took his hands off the keyboard. *That might not be such a good idea.* The government geeks could easily trace visitors to their website. He couldn't let anything compromise his location. *What to do?*

He returned to the recliner and changed the channel. The NBC nightly news was just beginning. He needed to hear the whole story again from a different media service.

It wasn't materially different. He turned off the TV and leaned back in the recliner.... Then it hit him. It fit perfectly into the drama of his play. He still had to close the Gregory Campbell loop he'd opened going to Buenos Aires for the shoot at the law firm.

Campbell couldn't return to Atlanta from his Panama City beach house until he was notified. Parnevik's master plan called for completion of his business with Campbell by returning to the U.S. and snail-mailing Campbell's properly stamped passport. He'd call him, describe the job at the Argentine law firm, and give him O'Farrell's contact information. Gregory could carry on his life as if he'd just completed the assignment in Argentina. No need to make physical contact with him, but it was too important to trust the Argentine mail service with delivery of the passport, and calling him from Argentina would leave an out-of-sync trail.

Parnevik reined in the flurry of thoughts, and in the quiet solitude he allowed his eyes to roam over the compact living room. He was calm and back in control. God, how he loved that feeling.

He literally sprang off the recliner and darted back to his laptop to make flight reservations. He'd return to Miami on the overnight flight as the Rastafarian, make contact with Campbell, mail his passport, and use the airport Wi-Fi to get up on the government website. Then on to Caracas.

Carrying garlic cloves should keep the dog at bay if somehow it might be waiting in Miami, and *Chim chim cher-ee* for the diligent and gifted Dickerson Phelps. It would be exhilarating to again fake out his pursuers. He felt strangely more alive and whole than at any other time in memory.

 One Hundred Sixteen

Atlanta: The Process

ONE WAY OR another, something decisive and permanent had to happen quickly. The process had come out of dormancy inside the nano research center and breached the grounds to two adjacent buildings, which were succumbing to the same pattern of implosion.

Engineers from the Georgia Power Company had severed electricity to the Georgia Tech campus, but they hypothesized the process must be tapping some of the more deeply buried lines transmitting power to other parts of the city. They were working on a total containment plan, but it would take time.

The roofs of the affected buildings had collapsed. From the air, it looked as if they'd been bombed out. Pillows of dark gray goop were flowing at a steady pace along the halls and basements of the buildings, randomly absorbing elements from the interior structures in a frenzied continuation of the replication process.

Vents were opening up over the nearby campus grounds in the wakes of the moving underground tentacles, spewing out rancid gases like volcanic fumaroles. The process was picking up speed, and six-foot wide appendages of sinking ground were headed east off-campus toward a major electrical hub fourteen hundred meters on the other side of the I-75/85 expressway. At the rate of progress, and assuming the eight-lane road would only momentarily impede their movements, consensus was if the process wasn't brought to a halt, it could be as little as twenty-four hours before the hub was breached and the world would find out how a worst-case scenario would play out.

Ever since movement had concentrated toward the hub, Georgia Power engineers had been working feverishly to cut the hub out of the power grid and shut down electricity to the buildings between the campus and the hub, but nothing like this had ever entered their terrorist contingency planning. Multiple, high-voltage lines from both underground and overhead fed the hub. How long it would take to do the job was undeterminable.

 # One Hundred Seventeen

The Oval Office

SPRAWLED OUT ON one of the plush couches in the Oval Office, the President had been drifting in and out of disturbing visions ever since the DSO's Dr. Blanton and his own chief of staff finished the latest briefing an hour ago.

He was unable to even doze, jerking to a sitting position in reaction to a gentle knock at the door. It was 6:15 a.m., and he was still fully dressed, tie and suit coat draped over the back of a chair, sleeves rolled up. "Come on in," he said hoarsely, standing, stretching, and making his way to the sink next to the coffeemaker.

Peter Costanzo slipped inside. "Sorry to disturb you, Mister President." The chief of staff had dark hollows under his eyes, and his gray pinstriped suit was hanging in wrinkles. "Parnevik logged into the website ten minutes ago from the Wi-Fi at Miami International. Miss Johnson thinks he may not have left the Miami area and may have learned how to mask himself from that tracking dog and the paranormal detective."

The President was wiping his face with a hot washcloth, still shaky from the decision he'd made to reveal the moon base and its capabilities to the Chinese ambassador.

The heat was reviving, bringing his mind back to razor edge. His thoughts moved on. With the report of the electrical hub cut-off and the sector evacuation and power shutdowns underway, he'd have to bring his staff current after the morning briefing and come up with a story to keep the media at bay. "Do we know what he looks like—not that it matters," he said sharply.

"Miss Johnson and the FBI are reviewing the Miami airport's general security tapes, but she thinks it's unlikely to be productive. He was blatantly using a computer at a Delta airline comp-lounge when he accessed the website. He knows he'll be traced to the airport. She thinks he's acting too confidently not to have a foolproof plan to avoid apprehension."

"I'd say she's probably right…. Sorry to bite your head off, Pete. Fresh coffee is two minutes away, and I'll get some food in here for us." He headed for the intercom on his desk. "At least Georgia Power was able to close off the hub. Anything else from Doctor Blanton or Miss Johnson on the effects?"

"I'm afraid it's more bad news."

The President turned away from the intercom.

"As you know, last night, observers on the ground reported the thing had slowed down. The nano expert at Georgia Tech—the idiot who started this whole mess—said it might have reached a point of stasis because the process wasn't finding sufficient raw materials. But Johnson's last call a few minutes ago informed that it is moving now—the scientists think it's tapping some of the deeper electrical cables. Tentacles burrowed under the Interstate I-75/85 roadbed and have caved the highway. The road's been shut down. She said it looked like a major tentacle was heading north, away from the hub toward the MARTA tunnel on the other side of the interstate. It runs under Peachtree Street, Atlanta's main drag, about a half-mile away. MARTA can be shut down, but the flowing goop could use the system to quickly move to other electrical centers in the city, many of which are located along MARTA routes."

"This is escalating, and nobody has a real handle on it." The President ordered breakfast and shut off the intercom. "So, we still have a calamitous situation," he said, bite returning to his tone.

"Yes, sir, and Johnson said the process has gathered a second focal point of movement off-campus to the west. There's another hub a mile away."

The President shrugged, aware his chief of staff was still standing. "I apologize, Pete. Please sit down and take a load off. I know damn well you pulled an all-nighter. Exactly what did Parnevik say?"

"He said he knew what happened and thinks he can fix it. He confirmed the replication process needed a constant supply of electrical power and the lack of it was holding back the likelihood of a catastrophic event. He also thought the force field would work, but it would be impossible to set up in time if the outbreak reached a significant electrical source. In his opinion, if that happened, the wasting of the environment would grow too big too fast. Very fast. He said he'd help with the force field design and calibration for differing scenarios, but if they *were* able to put together the equipment, it would likely have to be used from the air, and anything electrical for miles around would get fried. His responses on the website were logical and well thought out. I think he's sincere."

"I think it's fair to say all madmen believe in their sincerity." The President grimaced as he poured out two cups of strong brew and delivered a serving tray to the glass coffee table. He curled up at the end of a couch and scrutinized his disheveled friend. "What's the rest of it, Peter?"

"He wants our offer of complete immunity and repair of his reputation in an airtight package negotiated through a reputable law firm before he'll reveal his proposed solution for terminating the process. He's holding us for ransom."

"Incredible!" The President glanced at the grandfather clock in the corner of the room. He made it a point to dress impeccably and be on time for morning briefings. "All the brain power gathered in Atlanta couldn't come up with anything," he lamented, standing in disgust and shuffling in slippers to a closet. He snatched out a fresh suit and clean shirt and hung them on an ornate hall tree. "We have to do it, Peter, even though the situation is just plain unbelievable." The President roughly stepping out of his suit pants, stood there, and stripped down to skivvies.

"Agent Johnson is on standby at the Marriott via Skype if you need face-to-face." The chief rose from the conversation pit and flipped on the HD TV.

"I don't want to chitchat. She'll let us know if anything changes. What else?"

"There are a couple of other problems, Mister President."

The President turned around in his shorts, raising his eyebrows.

"Heavy thunderstorms are predicted for the Atlanta Metro Area over the next two days, starting this afternoon."

"That's just ducky," he snarled, arms flailing away, pushing into a fresh tee shirt. "Nothing we can do about God's will except pray. And the other?"

"Parnevik said he may be out of touch for about twelve hours, and all communications are to be through our website— and we're not allowed to make changes to the site. He said he'd know and the deal would be off."

"Twelve hours at a time like this.… I won't ask why," the President scowled. "What the hell does he think this is, some kind of consulting service?"

"Sir, he's got us and he knows it."

"I know that. Don't remind me. But I'm sure as hell not going to tell that to the politicians in congress—he's smart, but we'll get him in the end. In the meantime, post it that we agree and we'll get it done. Twelve hours is plenty of time. At least this process thing hasn't gone ballistic yet—we can always back away from Parnevik if the situation resolves itself. You wake up the powers that be at King and Spaulding and help them draft something Parnevik will agree to—and get it up on the website. But make sure he understands he has to fix this now before we're forced to evacuate the whole damn city—and tell him he needs to advise Georgia Power on the force field backup." The President finished buttoning his shirt and belting his suit pants. "All we can do now is wait out the next twelve hours." The President took a close look at himself in the hall tree mirror. "I guess I'm ready," he muttered. "It'll be hard to look passive, but I'll do it. You invited the heads of the Congressional Intelligence Committees?"

"Yes, sir."

"Let's hold a special staff meeting directly after the morning briefing, and add the heads of the intelligence agencies—a video conference so the media doesn't get wind of it. I need to bring them totally up to speed—and have the EPA Director standing by. For the time being, I think we continue to let the EPA shoulder the burden with the media. So far, we've been lucky. It's bizarre that even with the evacuation of Georgia Tech and I-75/85 closed down, the hard-core conservative media haven't been able to put together the usual panel of credible pundits on national TV. You'd think they'd love to rail over the possibilities—and tell Agent Johnson she's responsible for keeping a list of anyone having knowledge of what's been happening. If we survive this situation, it will be a nightmare to clean up."

 One Hundred Eighteen

Caracas, Venezuela: Same Day

PARNEVIK USED THE Miami airport Wi-Fi to vent his demands on the government website and make reservations to Caracas.

Shortly after 8:00 a.m., he met with Arturo Alvarez at his Miami hotel, collected his passport, and sent him off to the Argentine consulate to claim the loss of his Jose Gomez passport and apply for a duplicate.

Alvarez had been calm and businesslike. Parnevik was relieved and wished him, as Gomez, a safe trip back to Argentina.

One more task remained before Arturo Alvarez's Caracas flight. Parnevik took a cab to the nearest Walgreens Drugstore, leaving twenty minutes later with a bottle of over-the-counter, local anesthetic; a tube of antibiotic cream; insulin injection needles; a small, nurse's instrument kit; Band Aids; and a bag of empty pill casings.

Returning to the Miami airport's VIP lounge, he locked himself and his duffle bag in a private shower stall, stripped off his khaki Docksiders, opened his personal ditty bag, and removed his sample case.

He always traveled with a sample case of his work in the event a need for a demonstration arose. It contained small, airtight plastic vials of *Amor*, the pink candy tablets; green oblongs of *Bliss*;

red *Fuerte* pellets; and *Delirium* accreted in shapes resembling white rice. He'd tested *Delirium* some two years ago, resulting in the deaths of several guinea pigs. Since then, he'd re-calibrated the stimulation level, achieving satisfactory results and creating inventory.

In a two-inch square area along his upper right thigh—like a medical surgeon performing minor, outpatient surgery—Parnevik injected anesthesia under the epidermal layer. While the surface area numbed, he filled a pill casing with *Delirium* rice grains and cut two Band-Aids into butterfly bandages.

He waited five minutes, disinfected the scalpel, and prodded the site with his thumb until he was satisfied. Then he opened a one-inch incision and squeezed the capsule under the skin layers. Wiping the wound clean, he swathed it with antiseptic cream; brought the skin taut; applied the butterfly bandages, covering them with gauze; and secured the dressing with waterproof tape. The body would not react to the plastic casing.

***

Arturo Alvarez arrived in Caracas at 3:15 p.m. and took a taxi to *Centro Sambil*, a high-end massive shopping mall, and purchased several throwaway cell phones. On the way to the luxurious Hotel Centro Lido, in the heart of the city and near East Park and the Plaza Altamira, he booked a junior suite.

The plaza area contained a plethora of high-rise condominiums, upscale stores and eateries, and he was positive the park would be a perfect spot to relax in anonymity and access any number of unsecured Wi-Fi sites from nearby apartments, businesses, and residences.

During the flight, he'd reviewed his Miami inputs on the government website and was satisfied with his choice of methodology to handle the trade of a clean slate in return for his assistance. But he realized it was much too dangerous to fully trust the U.S. government. The offer of immunity from prosecution and professional redemption had been unexpected and was a powerful inducement to cooperation, but he would have to be vigilant and keep his options open, even though his decision to use Caracas as a safe base of operations in dealing with the U.S. government seemed solid.

He hurriedly checked into the hotel and retired to the suite to get settled. He was anxious to conduct his first sortie into East Park to ascertain Wi-Fi options.

As he loaded a few items into his backpack, his mind automatically reviewed the situation: the path looked clear of major obstacles. He'd be able to stay hidden in Caracas while he communicated, moving with impunity to different, unsecured Wi-Fi sites. Even if by some chance they traced his use of the government website to Caracas, it would be impossible to quickly mount an operation to apprehend him; especially considering the Venezuelan government's anti-Americanism.

If he decided to assist with the Georgia Tech debacle, afterward, he would return to his home in Albuquerque via Caracas-Dallas connections.

He'd made up his mind to seek medical and mental help for his afflictions. His recent research indicated new technological advancements may be available to effectively deal with his condition. The notion that he could be successfully treated ran his mind into overdrive: he'd start looking for a position commensurate with Alvarez's engineering education, something to get a foothold—he'd paid handsomely for the purging of Alvarez's Argentine work history and possession conviction. His resumé was clean.... Maybe he'd qualify for an assistantship at the University of New Mexico. If he found a position, he'd be able to stay in the states for at least seven years. He could start on an advanced degree—build a new career, maybe apply for citizenship. Things were looking up.

***

A variety of hardy tropical trees densely populated the East Park landscape. Pigeons were everywhere, and the scent of their droppings hung heavily in the still, moist-laden air.

Parnevik roamed over the entire extent of the park, checking out different locations with his laptop for unsecured Wi-Fi connections and signal strengths. There were many choices.

The park was sparsely populated just after *siesta* hours. He selected an empty bench seat embedded fifteen feet off the main walkway, next to a bronze statue of a horse-mounted warrior.

Connecting to a randomly selected Wi-Fi signal, he Skyped his geek, hacker acquaintance in Idaho, who confirmed the government website had been hastily organized and lacked sophistication. A quick wire transfer of funds ensured notification should the government attempt to modify its website.

Next, Parnevik took a taxi to the *Ministerio de la Produccion y el Comercio* to register Arturo Alvarez as a VIP interested in establishing an engineering consulting firm in Caracas. He would be meeting with a local pharmaceutical company to investigate potential joint-venture projects in nanotechnology. His business would be legitimate.

There were benefits derived from being up-front with the Venezuelan authorities. In requesting guidance from the ministry in making contacts and finding his way around the city, he was positive the government would assign him an intelligence officer—a convenient personal bodyguard. The Venezuelans were always looking for ways to play intermediary in new business dealings, with an eye toward appropriate bribes.

He retraced his route from the ministry back to East Park. His timing was impeccable. It had been a little over twelve hours. It was time to determine if the U.S. had met his demands.

It was the beginning of the rush hour, and the park remained nearly deserted. He headed for the large circular fountain in the middle of the park, lessening the noise from the streets. Settling on a worn bench near a large circular fountain, pigeons soon collected at his feet, waiting for tidbits.

He chose a Wi-Fi connection and key stroked his way into the government website, *atlantachemicalspill.gov. How clever.* The document drafts were all there. As he perused them, the tightness across his shoulders dissipated and he slowly relaxed. They had given him all he had asked for: the repatriation agreement, if you could call it that, was concise and clear. His citizenship was not in jeopardy. He would receive the Presidential Medal of Freedom, the highest U.S. civilian award. That was unexpected—*such obvious subterfuge.* His assets would be released from levies and his banking and credit reinstated. Pharmco was waiting for him to return to his responsibilities. He would be granted immunity from prosecution, all past records expunged. There was a draft of a media release espousing his credentials and citing his unselfish offer of assistance in attempting to neutralize the chemical spill.

Parnevik leaned back against the bench, thinking. The next step was to execute the agreement, verifying his signature with the answers to questions only he possessed.

The website directed him to complete a form detailing instructions for Doctor Sarcorcee and entering a dissertation to Georgia Power outlining everything he knew about how to develop plans for the force field. The good doctor and the Georgia Power engineers were standing by to communicate with him using a chat form to field questions and answers—if he gave permission for addition of the capability to the website.

So, all he had to do was execute the agreement, and major media would receive the government's press release. He set the laptop on the bench and stood up to stretch. His throat was dry from the mental excitement. *Chim chim cher-ee.* He'd prepared the instructions for Sarcorcee and a summary for Georgia Power of what he knew from experience testing the Driscoll force field. He was capable of proceeding, but he suddenly realized the whole methodology was flawed, and he shuddered as chills ran across his shoulders.

Once the government got what they wanted, they could easily whitewash the whole thing: erase his inputs on the website, refute the existence of any agreement—the absence of a paper trail. No, the deal was still too sticky, too many what-ifs, too much risk…. But if the media release—with a few twigs he would provide— went out before he signed and included the key elements of the agreement in non-inflammatory language—it could work…. And the law firm that drafted the agreement needed to acknowledge its role and certify its validity and execution by the government.

He paced around the bench and then wandered to the wrought-iron fence surrounding the fountain, invited by the calming sounds of water spewing from the fountain orifices and splashing into a large pool filled with Japanese goldfish.

It was happening so fast. He would have preferred more time to let all the pieces settle so he could dissect and analyze them again, but that luxury wasn't available. They wanted the replication stopped before a catastrophe took place—So, if he got those changes, he would sign…. It was alluring. He'd become a national hero, respected. His peers would be envious. He'd be invited to speak at conferences, and he'd be encouraged to pursue his research dreams.

His mind churned through the scenario again as he gazed at the streams of water shooting out from the fountain. Then movement at the opposite side of the fountain distracted him. Through the sun-soaked mist hanging over the fountain pond, a tall, thin man dressed in a dark suit entered the fountain's stone perimeter walkway. He had a newspaper in his hand and began waving it in the air. Parnevik's reaction was alarm, but it quickly dissipated. Evidently, his Bureau-of-Commerce guide had arrived. He must have been followed when he left the ministry.

"*Bienvenido*, my friend," the man said, tipping his hat as he approached. He held out his hand. "*Señor* Alvarez, my name is Philippe. I've been assigned by the Commerce Bureau to assist you during your visit. We are pleased to welcome new business interests in our country."

Phillipe gave Parnevik a cell phone number and politely asked him to call at the beginning of each day to discuss his planned itinerary. He explained he would offer suggestions if appropriate and answer any questions during those calls, but he was directed to remain in the background as Parnevik moved around the city.

The whole exchange took a mere five minutes. The man was scraggly-looking. His suit coat was imperfectly tailored and didn't cover the pattern of a concealed weapon. Just showing up unannounced was probably standard in this country's operating procedures.

This was perfect, Parnevik thought. Returning to his bench, a new surge of confidence quickened his step. He signed into the government website on a different Wi-Fi connection and entered his additional demands.

Habit caused Parnevik to check his personal email. There was one from the Genovese Family, directing him to enter his account on their protected server. His fingers flew over the keys, trepidation mounting. Why did he always react as if pending doom were around every corner? He held up...*chim chim cher-ee*.

His head started pounding as he read the message. In four sentences, they'd severed all business ties, no explanation…. The Feds must have found a way to break the mafia. If they could do that, it was stupid to think he could compete in their game.

Deflated with the abrupt insight, he felt devoid of emotions. He had allowed the situation to convolute, and the pleasant park surroundings suddenly felt like a trap closing in around him. He fumbled in a pants pocket for his meds and threw back a dose, swallowing the three pills dry. He'd lost control.

He waited, head in his hands. As always, his head cleared, the tightness and pounding remitted. He took a deep breath. The park was again a peaceful place. A breeze stirred the trees. The fountain sprayed out its medicinal voice. But, the fact remained: things had become too complicated. What made him so sure the Feds wouldn't come for him? His assumptions may have been naive. He hadn't taken sufficient time to research this move, and he hadn't felt this much danger lurking close at hand since eluding his pursuers in France.

He briskly walked out of the park and headed for his hotel with the intention of adding another layer of precaution from his store of contingency plans. He sidetracked inside a McDonalds, booted up his laptop, and typed in a message on the government's website. He needed to set a time limit on this little game. He gave them until his midnight sign-in to comply with his previously stated demands. If they did so, he'd execute the agreement and give the assistance he'd promised. Then he would disappear.

 One Hundred Nineteen

The White House: Same Day

MINUTES PRIOR TO the President's morning briefing, Ms. Johnson informed him the replication event had for the most part come to another point of balance, or stasis, presumably reacting to Georgia Power's shut-down of the electrical hub east of the Georgia Tech campus and the first of the block-sector blackouts.

Later in the morning, after the video meeting with his staff and the heads of the intelligence agencies, the President's press secretary issued a statement to an irate media, announcing a briefing by the EPA director at 5:00 p.m. The President had decided to stick with the government's story of the chemical spill, blaming it for the electrical shutdowns.

***

Late afternoon found the President in his study down the west hall from the Oval Office. He preferred the intimacy of the study to take care of the endless daily paperwork. He sat stiffly in an executive chair behind his working desk, unable to finish the routine tasks, knowing the chief of staff was down the hall in his office glued to a monitor lit up with the government's website, waiting for Parnevik to respond to the draft documents.

He pushed out of the chair and headed for Costanzo's office. Entering the hallway, the posted Secret Service agent greeted him, and he saw Peter Costanzo racing toward him down the passage-way, carrying his open laptop.

As they came together, Costanzo blurted, "He said he'll do it, but he has more demands."

"Of course he does," the President scoffed. "Come on in." The President led the way back into the study, scrambled to his executive chair, and motioned Costanzo to a leather seat next to the desk. "He's predictable…smart." The President waited for the chief to position the laptop so he could review Parnevik's inputs.

"Where is he?" the President asked after a quick scan. He looked up at Costanzo from the laptop. The chief's face was scrunched up. "You don't look like you've changed your clothes since yesterday. Get a shower and—"

"Caracas." The chief ignored his friend's empathy.

"Nice choice—how did we find that out?"

"He's been logging in from unsecure Wi-Fi connections with his own laptop."

"So, he had to have taken a flight from Miami. Do we have anyone on it?"

"I informed Miss Johnson a few minutes ago."

"That's a pretty brazen move. He seems to think we can't get to him if we want to."

"It's definitely out of character," the chief said as the President finished skimming Parnevik's diatribe. "He's prepared to execute the agreement, but only after we give the media a redraft-ed press release that includes acknowledgement of the agreement by the law firm, highlights the key points of exoneration in—as he states—non-inflammatory language—and provides believable rationale for the immunity from prosecution—past and future events included. He wants it released up front."

"I see that, Peter." The President leaned back in his chair, cupping his hands behind his head. "Well, I don't think we mind admitting to an agreement or coming up with a plausible story justifying the immunity and holding him harmless etcetera—as long as it's clear for national security purposes we don't announce specifics of the agreement…. It's logical to have an agreement," the President mumbled. "After all, we'll be acting on his advice." The President slammed his fist down on the desktop. "He thinks he's a damn consultant for crap sake…this is how government is supposed to work. Right?"

"You already *know* what I'm thinking. This is the first time he's been located. We need to take him in Caracas. This is already a mess. After he does what we've asked, we back up and wipe the slate clean. He'll just be another piece of debris to dispose of. We construct one more explanatory fairytale to the public…. The only question is how valuable are relations with Venezuela? Are we prepared to get caught trying to grab this guy?"

"What relations?" The President sneered. "If we can do it in Pakistan, we can do it in Venezuela. We've publically identified him as a serious threat to national security and labeled him a terrorist—I agree we have to get him—and before he sells himself to the highest bidder. We may not get another chance. He's betting we don't come after him there—work on it."

"I'm ahead of you, Mister President. We have a team in preparation. I informed Miss Johnson he was in Caracas and gave her a heads-up I was sending a team to Atlanta for her to brief. She'll require the assistance of Mallory Driscoll and the DEA Agent, McKenzie."

"They're still in the loop?"

"Yes, sir, they're extremely vested. The Driscoll woman and Agent McKenzie are familiar with Parnevik and how he operates." The chief looked at his watch. "You have about eight hours to change your mind before the team reaches Venezuelan air space."

The chief jerked his attention to the laptop. "He's making another entry."

Two heads were riveted in front of the laptop, like teenagers playing a video game. "Well, I'm not surprised," the President said, "but I *am* surprised he didn't say so sooner.... We have to comply. Even though it appears we've stopped the replication thing in its tracks, we need to make sure we have a plan if it comes alive."

The two men stared at each other. The President said, "He's given us until his midnight check-in. Let's get on it." The President stood and moved out of his chair. "Tell the team it's a go as soon as they're briefed. I get the feeling this guy will want to bolt."

 **One Hundred Twenty**

Atlanta, Georgia: Same Day

THE FBI G-5 landed in rainy Atlanta just after 2:30 p.m. Everyone had napped on the way back from Miami, including Edwin. Charging down Interstate 75/85 in the kennel van, headed for Emma's house to switch vehicles, silence and dejection set the mood.

Smythe, in the back with Edwin, would be returning the game hound dog to his Kentucky home as soon as he paid his respects to Emma for her care and hospitality. He was now convinced both of their special abilities for tracking Parnevik had been compromised. Lately, he'd only been able to sense fleeting pictures of Parnevik, short spikes of emotion, but not enough to get a feel for his personal disposition or location.

While in the air, Ms. Johnson had brought them current on the status of the replication process, the gathering of scientists at the Marriott, and Parnevik's communications with the government website from Caracas. She'd directed them to report to the FBI office. They were to be part of a special ops briefing. Smythe dropped them off and bid them good luck.

"I can't believe he had the gall to show back up in Miami, and probably right under our noses," Mallory said as McKenzie held the door into the FBI's street entrance. "Now he's in Caracas, bargaining with the government—the President's involved. Unbelievable."

"Cool it, Mal. Admit it. We're making progress. The scientists—"

"He's a psycho," she railed. "He left that egotistical wimp, Sarcorcee, with the tools of destruction—and on purpose. He's probably off gloating somewhere, proud of the situation like it was a large-scale experiment. He doesn't care what happens or how many people die."

***

The briefing was over in thirty minutes. McKenzie explained to Mallory that for this kind of mission, a Seal or Delta team would be employed. It was difficult for her to envision how seven highly trained soldiers could accomplish covert missions with such little preparation. McKenzie explained that their job was to be prepared for any scenario under short notice, anywhere in the world.

Ms. Johnson had led the briefing, summarizing the situation as it had developed over the last two months and then bringing the team to an operation's map laid out on a screen table. It displayed the outskirts of Caracas and blow-ups of several residential corridors. She skirted back and forth with a pointer, explaining what was known about the team's potential access routes and the locations of Parnevik's recent Wi-Fi contacts with the government's website.

Mallory and McKenzie painted a profile of the Parnevik personality and described his abilities to deceive and alter his appearance. Ms. Johnson made it clear the team would be dealing with a slippery, conniving lunatic who wouldn't hesitate to inflict bodily harm to save himself.

Just before the session wrapped up, and without being obvious, Mallory poked McKenzie in the ribs and whispered, "Can you get some pictures of the maps without them seeing? I left my phone in my bag." She thumbed the table where they'd been seated.

"Yeah. I've got a lapel lens. It's standard issue, but—"

Mallory canted her head, lips tight.

"All right."

The team departed at 4:30 p.m. from the old Air Force-Lockheed runway in the Atlanta suburb of Marietta. The mission was to locate Parnevik and take him alive—they knew where he was and so did Mallory and McKenzie.

7:00 p.m. found Mallory and McKenzie sitting next to Christine Johnson at the large oval conference table in Banquet Room B of the downtown Marriott Hotel. For the last fourteen hours, the scientists had occupied the room, unsuccessfully deliberating ways to neutralize the Georgia Tech disaster. They were now taking a break for dinner. Marriott banquet staff had freshly cleaned out the room, and FBI personnel had vetted it for the third time today.

"I asked you here because you deserve to watch this thing unfold," Ms. Johnson said.

The hum of the air conditioning system had momentarily ceased, causing Ms. Johnson's words to reverberate in the silence of the empty room. "An hour ago Parnevik issued an ultimatum. He's not going to help the situation unless there's an up-front public announcement lauding his willingness to volunteer assistance and holding him harmless of any wrong doing. He won't sign the agreement with the government or tell us what to do until then. He's given the government until midnight—the next time he's due to check into the website. The Justice Department is drafting the announcement, and if Parnevik agrees, it should go live sometime in the early morning. So, we wait."

"Do you think they'll really go into Venezuela and try and grab him?" Mallory's tone was curt, her face lined. She noticed Ms. Johnson looked drawn from the ordeal of the last three days and felt a tug of empathy.

"The first priority is to get him to lead us out of this mess. If that takes place—and this is just me—I think it would be a stretch for the President to authorize it. If Venezuela discovered our agents inside their country, it would be very bad political news, especially if they were unsuccessful. The team could get captured or killed—I think they'll flounder around talking about it, and the window of opportunity will evaporate…but then again you never know. And Parnevik's not stupid. He's proven more than just resilient. He has his contingency plans. He spit in everyone's face by returning to Miami to make contact and then right in our faces flew off to Caracas as who knows who." Ms. Johnson threw up her hands.

Mallory sank down in her chair, a blank expression on her face. "I'm not going to see this guy come to justice, am I?"

"Don't get down, Mal," McKenzie said. "Let's hope we get to step one first. We wait to see what he does."

"Mallory," Ms. Johnson said, "all of that said, you never know what the President is likely to do—what the whole risk assessment picture is—we went and got Bin Laden."

Mallory suddenly stood up. "The big deal is the real possibility we piss off Venezuela because we execute a covert operation, successful or not, on their sovereign oily soil—and the risk of casualties. Right?" Her hands were on her hips and her eyes blazed.

McKenzie glanced up at her. "So?"

"I think I have an idea, but we have to leave right now."

 One Hundred Twenty-one

Downtown Marriott

CHRISTINE JOHNSON SAT at the conference room table, waiting for the remainder of the scientists to return from their dinner break. Though tuckered out, she had a smile on her face. *Mallory Driscoll. What a package.* She and McKenzie were headed for the White House.

Dr. Stanford, Pharmco's CEO, had just entered the room, distributing stapled packets of letter-size sheets. When the last scientist had taken his seat, he took to the podium. "I apologize for not being present during your earlier discussions. There was little time to put a full presentation together, but this outlines the basics of what is known of how to control a replication process."

Christine hastily read the material. Papers rustled as the scientists scanned their copies.

Dr. Sanford waited patiently. "Unfortunately," he finally continued, "it has only been successful in computer simulations." His tone was apologetic. "The electromagnetic force field concept applies a charge equally in three dimensions over a calibrated area. You'll find a listing of the area size versus the electrical requirement on the *calibration page*. Theoretically, the field doesn't allow electrical activity inside a defined space. Quite frankly, ladies and gentlemen, the equipment necessary, if we should decide on this route, would be considerable and growing with the size of the problem at hand. The time to assemble and test—"

"Dr. Sanford," the Penn State scientist addressed, "I'm inferring here that no standard operating procedures have been published...due, as you have explained here, to the *secret nature* of your company's government contracts. How is it that you are so sure it works?"

"In short, sir, the director of our nano-research efforts, Corey Parnevik, worked with one of our senior computer scientists—who, as you may be aware, died in a tragic accident just seven weeks ago in Las Vegas. They were configuring an electromagnetic field that would shut down a replication process—if it got out of control. We deemed the development of the capability as a critical failsafe in justifying an attempt to produce nanite inventory on a significant scale." Dr. Sanford was becoming defensive. "Previous to this, Parnevik accomplished replications on his own, without backup measures, to produce the limited inventory needed for the company's developmental testing—and yes, in retrospect this was poor judgment on our part.

"At the time of Mister Parnevik's disappearance, the FDA had just approved testing of two commercial products on swine and chimpanzee populations. This would have required significant inventory, and he had been directed to submit a definitive paper on his replication process...so, as far as the electromagnetic field is concerned, we have very little to work with except the original experimental configuration and the results of simulations."

Dr. David Blanton, Director of DARPA's Defense Sciences Office (DSO), abruptly rose and took the floor. "Thank you for your patriotism, Doctor Sanford," he said, furrows etched across his forehead. He paused briefly, scanning the conference table. "The result of the last many hours has been the failure by this group to come up with anything substantive toward solving the dilemma."

Christine sat, arms crossed, wondering if Blanton was in the throes of trying to figure out what he was going to say to the President.

"Ladies and gentlemen, if we can't come up with an immediate scientific solution to our problem, we will be forced to continue what has so far contained the reaction to its present pattern of expansion—keeping it away from major electrical sources. Georgia Power has informed me that within several hours it will be able to cut the electrical hub off on the other side of I-75/85. It is also preparing for a sector-by-sector shutdown of electricity in the metropolitan area, beginning as early as 5:00 a.m. tomorrow. If necessary, it will coordinate its efforts with the National Guard in implementing evacuation of the population. A map of the sectors and schedule of proposed electrical shut-offs are contained in your packets.

"If we are not able to resolve this situation prior to 4:00 a.m., the President has directed me to notify the White House and the director of Homeland Security and present myself at his morning briefing." Dr. Blanton glanced over the forlorn faces. "It's a national security emergency, so he'll be the one to give direction from here on.

"Now, as regards the possible use of the force field alternative, Dr. Sanford, you will work with Georgia Power to design a plan for creating force fields to confront possible replication growth scenarios. We need a viable contingency plan. I suggest you arrange for an extended stay here and report immediately to Conference Room C on the third floor. Senior staff and engineers from Georgia Power have set up a command post there for the upcoming power shutdowns if needed. They have the equipment and expertise to fill your needs." Blanton looked at his watch. "I want a status report in five hours, outlining specifically what is entailed and when an attempt can be ready."

 One Hundred Twenty-two

The Oval Office

FRESH FROM A shower and quick change of clothes, the chief knocked on the open door as he entered the office. The air in the room was stale as if an all-night session had just ended. The stewards had laid out a late-night dinner on the glass table at the center of the conversation pit.

The President had a bounce in his step as he poured out two glasses of his favorite cabernet and took a seat at the table. He'd taken a half-hour power nap and a shower of his own and was dressed in casual khaki slacks and a short-sleeve fishing shirt. "With this replication process at a standstill, and Georgia Power designing the means to kill it permanently, we need to concentrate on dealing with Parnevik—dig in. The Swedish meat balls are great." The President voraciously helped himself. "Tomas makes the bread from scratch."

"They're on the way. ETA landfall is just after midnight." The chief spooned out the savory creation from the serving dish and slabbed butter onto a French roll. "It's fifteen miles to Caracas—say another hour. All the unsecure Wi-Fi sites have been located and plotted within five hundred meters of his past usage pattern. The team has that info. They'll get into Caracas—all civilian clothes—and blend in well before daylight. If we're lucky, when he makes his 4:00 a.m. check-in, they'll be prepared to grab him—and if not, we'll have another backup at eight."

"State still doesn't like it." The President took a draw from his glass of wine.

"Nobody in his right mind likes covert intervention. But we can't get cold feet now, Mister President."

"I'd feel a whole hell of a lot better if we could pinpoint his location. We don't know where he's staying—somewhere around that park. He could bolt on us, and the mission goes bust with the possibility of our team getting caught in the extraction."

"He's not going anywhere. Part of the deal was going to the website on a schedule in case we needed more advice. He said he would. He won't risk his glorious redemption."

"He's hardly trustworthy. He's an insane, ruthless, cold-blooded killer…. I'm still uncomfortable with this."

Unexpectedly, the chief backed away from his meal. "I have a suggestion."

"What?"

Prior to the midnight check-in, we post that questions are arising and we need him to check in every two hours instead of four. We could get a tighter fix on his Internet access pattern. And that should eliminate the possibility that he'll take off on us. Of course, that's assuming all goes well with Parnevik at midnight on the public announcement,

"That's good, Peter. That's real good…. But I should notify the congressional leaders before the insertion goes down. It's not like going for Bin Laden."

"Screw the Congress. This guy can destroy the world."

The President kept chewing.

"Oh, I almost forgot," the chief said. "Mallory Driscoll and the DEA Agent, McKenzie, have flown in from Atlanta. They have a plan they think is important to share with you." The Chief scooted back to his meal. He'd never seen the President this indecisive.

"That's what the phones and video links are for. It's nine-thirty."

"They have a *plan*, Mister President. I thought it a good idea for you to meet them. They're the ones who've been sweating in the trenches with this. The Driscoll girl's sister was killed by this maniac. She and her DEA agent friend went after Parnevik in the beginning. It's what got this whole thing started."

"Okay, okay," the President said gruffly. "I know the story. Where are they now?"

"Waiting in the Roosevelt Room."

The President looked askew at Costanzo. "What's this plan?"

"The woman wouldn't tell me and McKenzie doesn't know."

The President put down his fork and wiped his face, tossing the napkin on the couch as he rose. "Well, let's get on with it. Ask them in. There's plenty of food. We'll see if they're hungry."

 One Hundred Twenty-three

The Scheme

MALLORY AND MCKENZIE were dressed every bit like Friday night at the local pub. The two presidential visitors made quick work of the delicious food, the stewards serving them with deft courtesy.

The pleasantries over and the table cleared, Mallory was anxious to take advantage of the informality so easily exuded by the casually attired President and the warm greetings that had at once put everyone at ease.

"Peter, show them Parnevik's latest entries on the website so we're all on the same page." The President stood away from the table and motioned everyone to the cluster of couches making up the conversation pit.

The chief brought the website up from his laptop onto a sixty-inch TV monitor, signed in, and efficiently reviewed the last eighteen hours, scrolling through the pages of entries.

"So, the nanites will stop replicating if they're given a command from a certain radio frequency?" Mallory's eyes were wide open. "It seems so simple. Why didn't Dr. Sarcorcee know to do it?"

The chief turned off the TV. "Parnevik obviously neglected to tell him that activating a replication process also required a termination instruction."

"So, as we understand it," the President cut in, "the challenge is to develop a powerful enough radio transmitter to cover the infected area—about twenty square blocks. The good news is that the process hasn't gone to great depth or we'd be seeing more ground caving in."

"If Parnevik comes up with a simple program modification," the chief said, "Doctor Sarcorcee says he can be ready, at the latest, mid-day tomorrow."

"And if it doesn't work, Georgia Power uses Reagan Driscoll's force field?" McKenzie asked.

"It's not really a force field," the chief said. "It's a constant burst of a highly charged magnetic field. And we are waiting for Parnevik to fine-tune directions to Georgia Power. No matter what, the application will have to be applied from a hovering cargo helicopter or a low-flying airplane. The equipment array is being assembled in a hanger at Lockheed Martin's Marietta airstrip."

"I get it," Mallory said. "If Parnevik is checking the website periodically to answer questions, then you'll know exactly where he is. Do I assume correctly that the team we briefed is on the ground, waiting for you to identify his location?"

The President smiled. The attractive lady attorney held nothing back. "We were just talking about that when I discovered you were here. There are issues—"

"I'm sure there are, Mister President." Mallory stood from her seat on the couch. "And I'll bet not getting caught is the key one," she said, hands on hips. "I'm sure Congress and the media are still in the dark regarding our little chemical spill. So, those must be the other issues—but let me ask you this. What if Venezuela's new president gave you permission to get Parnevik?"

The President was still smiling. "Hardly likely, young lady."

The chief rose from his seat, showing irritation. "Miss Driscoll, we're on a short fuse here. This visit was a courtesy. Parnevik is due to check the website at midnight and hopefully submit his inputs. We're requesting he check in every two hours after that. We're trying to see to it he'll hang around Caracas. And we've got the team moving into positions around Parnevik's previous pattern of Wi-Fi usage. We're busy. Now—"

"You're just going to ignore me?" Mallory lips were pursed.

The chief was startled. "I apologize, Miss Driscoll, but we don't have time for concocted conjecture—"

"You think I'm some kind of ignoramus. I came here with a plan."

"I'm sure you did, Miss Driscoll—"

"That bastard is not going to get away this time." Mallory shifted her gaze to the President.

"Peter, let her have her say," the President said, still holding on to his smile.

McKenzie sank as deep as he could get into the back of the leather couch next to where Mallory had been sitting, silent as a manikin, waiting to be summarily dismissed.

"I'll trade you, Mister President. If what I tell you is viable—doable—you give me an accommodation, a favor, no questions asked."

"Continue, Miss Driscoll, and please sit down—you too, Peter. But kindly be brief."

McKenzie repositioned into an attentive posture.

Mallory had developed and refined her thoughts on the FBI's G-5 flight to D.C. and made a few inquiries through the plane's satellite phone system. One call was to a prop and movie set service in Washington, D.C., requesting two Venezuelan military police uniforms to be waiting for her at the FBI's special docking gate at Andrews Air Force Base. She'd refused to reveal her ideas to McKenzie because she said she didn't want to waste time having to persuade him.

"Okay. Here goes the short version. A paralegal friend of mine in Chicago met Ramona Madararo, one of President Madararo's daughters, on a church retreat in Venezuela last summer. They were part of a group of volunteers from many different churches, coming from several countries and committed to building a hospital in a small jungle village. Ramona and my friend grew very close. The daughter was a strict Roman Catholic, and she and her sister talked their father into buying the pre-fab units for the hospital and allowing the volunteers to come in and build it. Anyway, the two sisters want desperately to go to college in the U.S., but the State Department won't give them permission. The president loves those girls. He'll do anything for them. I had my friend make contact with Ramona. She got all excited with my idea and said she thought it would work and she'd talk to her father."

"Get to it, Miss Driscoll." The President took a quick peek at his watch.

"My friend got back to me on the flight here. It's all set. All you have to do is call him up. Be cordial—like you always are—paint a cozy, humanistic picture citing the girls' friendship, etcetera, and offer the girls visas and entry into the colleges of their choice in return for looking the other way while you run down a rogue terrorist in Caracas." Mallory was grinning ear to ear.

"Not bad. In fact, it's incredible—something so simple." The President's brow was furrowed, eyes flickering. "What do you think, Peter?"

"It's off the wall, but we can't lose anything by trying. No Congress, no media announcements, just a quiet extraction—"

"Get with Mallory on the details and work up some sweet narrative I can use to butter up this Nicolas Madararo." The President checked his watch again. "Maybe we can get this done without having to wake him from a sound sleep."

"We'll go to my office, Miss Driscoll." The chief stood.

The President looked over at McKenzie as Mallory and the chief left the room. "You could have told us this without wasting the time coming to D.C. We'd have responded."

"She wouldn't tell me, Mister President. She's very stubborn—and headstrong."

"Really? You could have *fooled* me."

***

An hour later, the President had coffee and sandwiches brought in, and the chief and Mallory returned. Anxiety was palpable, everyone spread out around the coffee table, watching the President scan over the notes the chief had prepared. An unannounced, late-night call by the President of the United States to an unfriendly head of state, a government despised by most of the western world, would be a first.

"Well," the President said, clearing his throat and breaking out in a resolute smirk. "Let's get on with this."

The chief picked up the old-style red phone on the glass table and gave instruction to the operator to connect the call.

***

Five minutes later, the phone rang and President Madararo picked it up.

"Mister President, I hope I am not disturbing you.... I understand you are beginning to recapture the hearts of your people. It appears Mister Chavez chose the right man for the job." The President's eyebrows rose as he slanted the receiver away from his face and glanced at the chief. The chief was looking away, mouth askew.

Ten minutes of pleasantries went by. "Yes, sir. You will have all the paperwork delivered to your offices by our ambassador sometime late in the day tomorrow.... No, sir. The business there will last twenty-four hours at most...no violence is expected. Our personnel will be out of your country by this time tomorrow.... Yes, sir. Understand. No weapons...perhaps we can break the ice on other issues at your convenience, Mister President.... Yes, sir. I also wish you well and a pleasant late evening." The President cradled the phone back on its receiver. "Well, who would believe? That went very smoothly. He was overjoyed. Good work, young lady—hell, you all deserve medals, but that's probably out of the question—but the sentiment is real. It was a strange call."

The President turned his attention to the chief. "Okay. Peter, we have an hour or so before Parnevik signs in. You draft the post alerting him to the new check-ins for questions. Hopefully, he stays inside his Internet access pattern and goes for the media release. If your time estimate is reliable, the team should be set up by the 4:00 a.m. check-in."

"What's with the no weapons, Mister President?" the chief asked.

"He just didn't want any possibility of violence from an inadvertent confrontation with locals. Tell the team to take the XK dart guns. If it comes to an argument of words, we only agreed not to bring in assault-type weapons."

"Mister President, I'm happy it's working out," Mallory interrupted. "But the favor?"

The President and the chief looked over at Mallory sitting attentively across from them, back straight, arms crossed.

"You understand I have a vested interest in seeing to it that this bastard gets what he deserves.... We've all put a lot into this,

Mister President. I want to be there." She nodded at McKenzie. "Him too."

The President craned his head toward the chief.

Constanzo grimaced, shrugging.

"I don't suppose you'd mind parachuting in—I'm sorry." The President chuckled, eyelids fluttering. "Please forgive me."

Mallory started laughing, and McKenzie was unsuccessful holding back his own burst.

"Miss Driscoll, you'll never make it in time," the President said, back in control.

"Come on, Mister President, your military planes can fly at Mach II."

A pregnant moment elapsed. He faced the chief. "Peter, you'll have to get hold of President Madararo for a place to land," he said, straight-faced.

"And, we'll need to be armed just like the team we'll be joining," Mallory said sternly.

The President turned to McKenzie.

"We know the operation, Mister President," McKenzie said.

"Are you familiar with the XK CO2 Demobilizer?"

"Yes sir, the DEA has them. I'm qualified on it."

The President stood and faced the chief. "See that Agent McKenzie is issued a unit—one." He turned back to Mallory. "You're something else, woman."

***

Thirty minutes later, the President and the chief sat alone in the Oval Office, waiting for Parnevik's midnight sign-in. Mallory and McKenzie were on their way to Andrews Air Force Base ten miles southeast of Washington D.C.

"Why'd you cave in to the lady?" the chief asked.

"She had to be convinced she was being included."

"I'll have people there to meet them when they land and see to it they stay put."

 One Hundred Twenty-four

Caracas, Venezuela

PARNEVIK LEFT THE Hotel Centro Lido and strolled the East Park perimeter. The early evening air was thick with humidity, and the passing automobiles rounding the park roadway made sloshing sounds on the wet pavement.

A half-an-hour later, satisfied the commerce guide wasn't following him, he registered at a nondescript rooming house three blocks west of Plaza Altamira. It offered three square meals a day as part of its weekly rate. For the time remaining in Caracas, he would keep a low profile and remain vigilant. Worst-case scenario, the rooming house was his safe house.

Two hours later, he had indulged in the evening buffet at the rooming house and cleaned up in the shared lavatory arrangement down the hall from his room. He slipped over to East Park, senses on alert in the quiet of the night, and occupied a solitary bench at the opposite side of the fountain from his last visit.

It was 11:45 p.m. Tension and excitement sent his fingers flying as he logged into the government's website from another randomly selected Wi-Fi connection. He hesitated...*chim chim cher-ee.*

There it was, entered over an hour ago. They'd made decisions quickly. The government was complying. The media release was adequate, and upon his approval, it would immediately be released. He gave it.

As he split the screen on his laptop and opened his CNN app, an epiphany unfolded: no matter how cooperative the government might seem to be, media release or not, he would never come back out in the open. Exoneration was a fantasy.

The CNN program interrupted for a special White House announcement. The glowing words issuing from the lead anchor came across like a practiced part in a play: a brief summary of the laboratory incident at Georgia Tech and then the dramatic accolades to Dr. Corey Parnevik, a national hero about to render harmless the Georgia Tech chemical spill that had decimated the campus and a nearby section of I-75/85. It was all there: the praise, the exoneration, immunity from prosecution, exemption from liability, Pharmco waiting for his return, even possible candidacy for the Medal of Freedom.

Parnevik's face had wrinkled as he listened, emotionally consumed. But, wasn't it just an elaborate smoke screen to appease the media and entrap him with delusion? He could never be sure it was for real.

He was shaking as the bare bones reality made itself clear. He could never go home. He'd always planned for it, but now that it was real he felt alone, an insignificant human being without worthy purpose and the world chasing him. His head spun. *Why have I become such a useless person?* He had all the tools to excel, garner recognition and respect from his peers, but he never allowed anyone inside to commune, fearful of what they'd discover.

He sat on the hard bench, feeling like a shell, devoid of empathy, unhappy, and unfulfilled.... *Damn, chim chim cher-ee.* He couldn't get caught now.... Now, they needed him to check in every two hours. If he didn't, they would disavow. He had to stay with it until the replication process was neutralized—his heroic work confirmed by actions.

He returned to the website and attached files with the instructions to Sarcorcee and the dissertation he'd prepared for Georgia Power. He packed the laptop back in its case and reached for his meds, feeling sorry for himself, tossed about in a sea of desperation and paranoia. His mind settled on his medical condition, his nemesis. It was crystal clear he'd have to fix it if Arturo Alvarez had any chance to carry on a viable life.

# One Hundred Twenty-five

On the Move

THE FBI IMMEDIATELY whisked Sarcorcee from his cell at the Fulton County Courthouse and delivered him to the downtown Atlanta Marriott where Ms. Johnson fed him Parnevik's instructions.

Pharmco's CEO, Dr. Sanford, coordinated with DARPA personnel controlling access to Pharmco's headquarters and labs in organizing Sarcorcee's access to the equipment and containment modules he would need to carry out Parnevik's instructions. FBI agents would guard Sarcorcee 24/7 as he worked.

From their operations center in the Marriott's junior ballroom, Georgia Power engineers were busy digesting Parnevik's recommendations and designing the force field options.

Meanwhile, Mallory Driscoll and Agent McKenzie were in the aft seats of two Falcon HTV-2s at 40,000 feet, somewhere over the Caribbean Sea and about to be refueled.

***

The President and the chief were too keyed up to sleep. The team was an hour away from landing on the Venezuelan shore.

The Secret Service Duty Officer knocked on the Oval Office door. "Mister President, Secret Service."

"Come in, Jim. You want something to eat?" The President waved a hand at the pile of sandwiches on the glass coffee table.

"No, sir," the agent said, quietly entering and standing stiffly in the doorway. "We didn't want a telephone call to jolt you out of a sound sleep so we took a message. It was from Agent Christine Johnson. She said to make you aware the National Weather Service was tracking a powerful group of storm cells due to hit Atlanta in the next hour."

"Oh, hell, that's all we need," the President said. "Thanks, Jim—and have some fresh coffee brewed up. We'll plug in from here."

Peter Costanzo tuned the TV to *The Weather Channel* as the Secret Service agent closed the door.

The President punched a speed dial on his cell phone directly to the National Weather Service headquarters in Silver Spring, Maryland.

 One Hundred Twenty-six

Atlanta: 2:30 a.m.

IT WASN'T UNUSUAL for Atlanta to be placed on tornado watches and warnings during the rainy season from late March to October. Mid-February *was* unusual, but in keeping with the El Nino year and the increasingly unpredictable responses of Mother Nature to the cumulative abuses man had inflicted on the planet.

Christine Johnson stood watching the radar monitor at one end of the Marriott banquet room commandeered by the Department of Defense. FBI agents, the commander of the Georgia National Guard, and a representative of Atlanta's Mayoral Office manned their separate communication stations. Ms. Johnson had elected to retain the operations center at the hotel to facilitate face-to-face updates from the Georgia Power engineers working on the next floor.

"I want live input from the weather service," Ms. Johnson barked at one of the FBI agents. "Get them up on Skype."

"Yes, ma'am."

"Ed, how're we coming with the HD feed to the Oval Office?"

Furlow leaned back in his chair at the FBI's communications kiosk and pointed at a pedestal in the center of the room. A large camera similar to ones used by media cinematographers at football games was being assembled. "It's almost ready. Comcast's working on connecting a dedicated feeder line and audio. The President should be able to remotely scan and zoom the room as well as talk to us.

"Good—but this looks bad. Come take a look."

Furlow scooted out of his post and clicked on the speaker button, bringing in the network of observers posted around the perimeter of the replication process, and joined Johnson in front of the weather screen. The six-by-eight-foot, 3D monitor was running the National Weather Service TV station.

"That is one big-ass storm." She wrung her hands. "Or maybe it's just my first time witnessing sophisticated weather imagery."

"At least if we have to start cutting the power grid, it can be attributed to the storm," Furlow said. "Jeez, there's four—five cells coming in from the southwest."

"Miss Johnson," an agent hailed from the FBI's communication station, "I have a senior meteorologist up on Skype. They've just issued tornado warnings along a path ten miles wide, southwest of Marietta to Stone Mountain. Storms are moving northeast at eighteen miles-per-hour—frequent lightning, heavy downpours and large hail. I'll shoot it up in a corner of your monitor."

"Got it," she said. "Double the size…. Good, and let's get some suppressor equipment in here. We don't want any crashes because of the storms."

"Hello, over there," Ms. Johnson said to the late-forties-looking scientist on the screen. "What's the timeline and how bad is it going to be?"

Johnson and Furlow waited through the inevitable two-to-three-second pause. "Agent Johnson, is it? Doctor Rawlings here. I can tell you we have had three funnel-cloud sightings off to the west of Interstate 285, east of Newnan, Georgia. Relatively speaking—compared to dangerous systems of the past—although complex and large, this one is moving so rapidly we don't think there will be catastrophic tornado landings, but the heavy rains, lightning, and hail could cause considerable damage. There are two cells in particular—you can clearly see them on the screen behind me." She briefly moved aside. "Those are the worst. If they don't shift course, they'll be on downtown Atlanta in twenty minutes. That's all I can tell you right now."

"Thank you, Doctor. I apologize, but I have to ask you to keep this connection live. We need minute-to-minute reporting. Do you understand?"

"No problem. The Department of Homeland Security was very clear. It will be myself or Doctor Falkurk." Dr. Rawlings reached up and removed the webcam from the top of her computer monitor and scanned the weather room, zooming in on an elderly man looking up from his projection screen and waving. "He's my boss. We'll be here for the duration."

2:50 a.m.

The banquet room was buzzing with activity, a cacophony of voices carrying on conversations at different levels of intensity. The mood was creepy, unlike combat or a typical law-enforcement operation with familiar parameters.

Marriott banquet staff had finished setting up a buffet line in one corner of the room and were directed to remain in a security cordon in the back service hallway in case they were needed.

Ed Furlow had the communications net live on the room's speaker system so the back-and-forth between the FBI observers in place around the stalled replication process and the command station could be heard by all.

The speakers suddenly crackled. "This is Peters at the Tenth Avenue I-75/85 observation post. It's on us here," he bayed out over the storm's background noise. "No stars in the sky, and the wind is ferocious. I'm guessing fifty-mile-an-hour gusts. All I can see through the downpour is a moving line of lightning. It's coming in quick. Debris is flying around now. Recommend all posts take shelter until this passes."

Ms. Johnson rushed to the mic. "We hear you. No tornados are showing—all posts, we need eyes on the target and the locations of lightning strikes. The patterns on our screens here are too complex to pick out what hits ground and what doesn't. Report what you see."

Each observer confirmed.

"Peters, you still with us?"

"Understood.... I'll head for the backup just down the street. Should have a front-seat view about halfway up the IBM building. I've got infrared zoomers, but the rain—now we've got hail. I'll call in when I get set inside the building. Peters, out."

"Ed, we need to have a helicopter standing by to video an assessment of the aftermath at first light—piped directly to the White House. Can you handle that?"

"Already arranged. Atlanta PD has the gear and a bird tied down on top of their downtown headquarters building. You say the word."

"Somebody get me Doctor Sarcorcee on the line at Pharmco," Ms. Johnson shouted toward the communication kiosks. "Ed, I have a bad feeling about this. Can you check in upstairs with Georgia Power? I want an update on when the backup at Lockheed will be ready to go."

"Okay—and the President's live." He pointed at a section of the monitor coming into focus.

3:00 a.m.

"Peters, say again. You're breaking up."

"I said it looks like a hurricane. Lightning everywhere. I went through Hurricane Andrew in Miami in '92."

"Paint me a better picture, Peters," Ms. Johnson said, grimacing, bile collecting in her stomach.

"I'm at a window on the sixth floor looking out to the southwest. The building is swaying and there's a rumbling sound that's not thunder. Thunder and lightning bolts are going off like heavy artillery. Every time there's lightning, I get a look down on the Georgia Tech campus and along the I-75/85 corridor. The ground is rising in mounds about ten feet high, rolling and swarming out in tentacle forms twenty to thirty feet wide. Some of the campus buildings I can see are just a mass of caved-in debris. There's a sea of moving gray stuff running along the Interstate like a river, eating up the border walls and overflowing into the surrounding residential areas. Everything is shaking like an earthquake. And there's a horrific smell, like putrefied bodies."

3:05 a.m.

Ed Furlow shouted at the kiosk monitoring CNN News, "Larry, get CNN on a monitor next to the weather screen. They just took off in their helicopter," he said to Johnson. "Got to be crazy. It's still pitch black out there."

"They've been told to stay away." Ms. Johnson slapped her thigh with an open palm.

"Doesn't seem to matter," Furlow said. "It's stupid. They won't be able to get a decent assessment until the storm's over and it's daylight."

Ms. Johnson plopped down in a chair in front of the monitor, dejected, as CNN manifested in its own square space. "All anyone can really do now is pray…" She suddenly jumped out of the seat. "But if they're trying to film, let's order them to feed us live. Hook it up on another screen next to the 3-D monitor so the President has a bird's-eye view—and where's Sarcorcee—?"

"The agents with him having him coming out of the lab," Furlow said. He's going through sanitation—"

"Get him over here ASAP! The President is going to want to hear what he has to say." She looked up at the big clock in one corner of the weather channel screen. Less than an hour before the 4:00 a.m. rendezvous with Parnevik. "Ed, we're all set for Parnevik's sign-in. Right?"

"We built a computer station dedicated to the website on the other side of the room. The Georgia Power engineers and Sarcorcee can have it out with him on chat-ware."

"Mister President." Ms. Johnson faced the camera in the center of the room "The right-hand screen on the big monitor next to the National Weather Center Skype window will be a direct feed from a CNN helicopter that just took off. We don't know what they're doing, but we'll see what they see."

"Good job, Miss Johnson. I heard, and I'll try not to burst in on you. You have enough distractions. Good luck."

 One Hundred Twenty-seven

Caracas

MALLORY AND MCKENZIE made it to Andrews Air Force Base via presidential limousine. The base sentries had been alerted to open the base PX to facilitate picking up personal items. McKenzie also procured a set of two-way radios, all of which they added to their shoulder bags.

After a quick stop at the base armory, the limo and escort vehicle headed for one of the squadron hangars. In the chilly night air, the roar of the waiting planes increased as they approached. The jets were fired up, ready to take off.

A little under three hours later, two Falcon HTV-2s landed at La Carlota Military Airbase west of Caracas.

3:00 a.m.

One behind the other, the two jets entered a camouflaged hangar. The Venezuelan military police had cordoned off the area to provide security for the airplanes during refueling and preparations for a quick take off.

The hangar doors quickly slid closed. Mallory and McKenzie climbed out of the back seat cockpits with their shoulder bags and slid down the wings to portable steps. Three military officers met them at ground level. Without any common courtesies, the one-star general in the middle said in broken English, "I've been directed to see to your needs. A comfortable room has been prepared for you during this unusual incident, which we are told is not happening." The general appeared to be irritated; perhaps he was not used to duties in the darkness of early morning. "If you need anything, these officers will assist you." The general nodded to each.

"Gentlemen, I need to make a stop in the restroom," Mallory said, glowering.

"Me too," McKenzie chimed. "Point the way."

"Facilities are over there." The general waved a hand toward the far side of the hangar under a floor of offices accessed by a catwalk. Mallory watched him mumble something to the major and sergeant escort and turn abruptly, marching in the direction of the two HTV-2s. He'd probably never seen aircraft like these up close and live.

Mallory and McKenzie shouldered their bags and strode away in step. "I've never been so scared in my life," Mallory said, "but I didn't puke. The pilot was a nice guy. He kept it tame."

"I had a ride once with an aviation buddy when I was in the Marine Corps. He gave me the works, so it wasn't so stressful for me." McKenzie smiled.

"So nothing scares you?

"I didn't say that."

***

Five minutes later, they had changed clothes. Mallory wore the military police uniform of a senior sergeant. McKenzie was a lieutenant colonel, and they calmly walked out the building's administrative exit under the floor of offices.

"This one will do." McKenzie headed in a direct line for the nearest military police vehicle.

"I hope you remember how to do this," Mallory said, keeping pace.

"I wasn't always a good teenager. We used to take joy rides. Don't worry. Some things you never forget, like riding a bicycle."

The vehicle was unlocked as expected, and the two piled in as if they owned it. McKenzie pulled out needle-nosed pliers from his shoulder bag and made quick work of the wiring. Pulling away from the hangar and out the front gate, they received salutes from the guards.

"You better tell them we're on our way," McKenzie said, paying attention to the signs to downtown Caracas.

"Nice of the chief to let us have a satellite phone—and the frequencies and call signs." Mallory grinned mischievously. "He neglected to add the battery—must have wanted to make sure we wouldn't use it. On the plane ride, I switched out the battery from the satellite phone Miss Johnson gave us. Here goes. Beta Six, Petticoat Leader here. What's your twenty?"

The radio crackled, and Mallory turned down the volume. "Beta Six here," a stern voice answered. "Ah, didn't know you were aboard…ah, Petticoat Leader."

3:10 a.m.

Parnevik was unable to sleep between his sign-ins, pacing the third-floor hotel room and looking at his watch every few minutes. The whole ordeal was taking a toll. Lack of rest and obsessive reviewing of what had so far transpired eroded his efforts at a balanced disposition. He had decreased the time interval between medications, but it wasn't enough to reach the level of calm he wanted.

With the lights off, Parnevik scanned the area from an open window. This early in the morning, the air was heavy and damp, the streets empty and silent. Looking across Francisco Avenue into East Park, nothing stirred. High-posted lights scattered throughout the park cast weak and eerie shadows through the trees and foliage.

He packed his Alvarez IDs into his laptop briefcase just in case. He quietly crept down the stairs, crossed the vestibule in front of the vacant front desk, and used his room key to exit the premises.

As he walked across the street and into the park, he kept telling himself there was nothing to worry about. But he felt tentative. The dark and stillness seemed a fantasy, ramping his senses into high alert. He'd make the 4:00 a.m. check-in and no more. Arturo Alvarez would be on his way to Albuquerque.

He took the familiar path leading to the fountain, listening for unnatural sounds and alert to any movement. Why was he so wary? His feelings were the same as the times he'd almost fallen into the hands of his pursuers in France and again in Miami.

He scanned each intersecting path as he walked along. Suddenly, as he crossed over the main park walkway, he spotted movement across the street from the park, in the shadows of an apartment entrance façade. He pulled to the side against a tree. It looked like Philippi, the commercial guide assigned to assist him. He was talking to a hard-looking man, bulky, baseball cap, short-sleeved charcoal shirt, black pants.

Something wasn't right. Dozens of scenarios rifled through his brain. *Could they be looking for me?* Had they been to his hotel room? Maybe the Venezuelans discovered the U.S government was after him, and he'd become a political pawn.

What to do? He was perspiring profusely. He had to relax. Take a deep breath, *chim chim cher-ee*. Rationalize. He was safe as long as he could get back to the rooming house. No one knew he was there. He'd paid cash and signed in without showing identification.

He stayed concealed in the shadows and continued to observe. The two men parted, and Philippi hunched his shoulders and turned the corner out of sight up a side street. The park foliage cut off the other man's movements. A car door slammed, and a vehicle entered the main street and drove past the apartment building, seemingly in no hurry.

3:40 a.m.

"I have contact," Beta One whispered in "Group" mode. "A guy with a briefcase. I think he may have spotted you."

"Okay, maybe no harm done," Beta Six came back. "Give me a heads-up where he's going. He's still got fifteen minutes or so to make the sign-in. I'll pass the word to close the perimeter when he finally settles. Six standing by."

***

Parnevik gathered himself. There was no way to know who the other man was or what he was up to. He'd taken off briskly in the direction of Hotel Centre Lido. Maybe Philippi had compromised his hotel location. Bribes were common. He'd have to assume someone would be waiting at his hotel. He needed to make a decision now.

3:45 a.m.

McKenzie parked the military police vehicle in an underground parking garage serving the Altamira Plaza near East Park, where it wouldn't be noticed.

"He's going to meet us on the roof of a five-story apartment building called The Villas." Mallory pushed the Standby button on the satellite phone. "Let's go. We passed it. It's only two blocks down the way we came."

Perfectly situated, The Villas overlooked East Park. The two walked casually, taking up the role of two police officers on an uneventful late-night patrol.

"Let me try it," Mallory whispered.

"Mal, you don't need—"

"Now. I want to know how to use it."

McKenzie pulled the XK out of his bag, shaking his head. "It's ready to fire. You just flip the safety—the red button. It's a semi-automatic."

Mallory took the pistol, pushed off the safety, and fired it from the waist at a palm tree twenty feet in front of them. The pssssst of the CO2 was brief; there was little recoil. "That was easy," she said, handing back the weapon.

Their Venezuelan military police uniforms gained them entrance into the apartment building and a maintenance key for the rooftop door. The moment the door creaked open, they were confronted by a voice. "You need to ditch the uniforms."

"Nice to meet you, too," Mallory spat.

"Sorry, no names. Call me Beta Six. What about the clothes?"

"We can change back to the clothes we flew in with," McKenzie said.

"Hustle up. I'll be waiting next to the air-conditioning units. We've got a bite in the park. Has to be our guy." A beefy-looking man in a gray shirt and black pants moved into view at the head of the rooftop stairwell and then disappeared.

Mallory looked at McKenzie.

"What?"

"You change up there." Mallory waved up the stairwell.

Mallory and McKenzie bent over, keeping clear of being patterned against the city lights, and made their way around the air vents and antennae on the roof to a major grouping of air-conditioning units.

"Better," Beta Six whispered as they gathered behind a shed next to the units. The air was still and sultry, and fortunately the machinery was quiet in the cool of the night.

"What's going on?" Mallory asked.

"Keep it down, Miss. We thought you were going to monitor from the airfield."

"I know that's what you thought, Beta Six. But we're not monitors, and we have permission to be here on the scene. Now, what gives?"

"Since you left the States, the CIA traced the target. He registered down the street at Hotel Centro Lido. Two of our guys took a look. He's still registered, but he wasn't in his room. They said it looked like he was coming back—his personal items were where you'd expect them to be. One of the team is watching the hotel."

"What about the bite you said you had in the park?" McKenzie whispered.

"He's being watched." Beta Six flipped a lid on his wrist-watch. "If it's him, he's got ten minutes to find a place to sign in. The team will let me know. They all have infrared night-vision capabilities."

"Did you have any problems getting here and setting up?" Mallory asked. Beta Six seemed to have accepted their presence.

"None to speak of. The bus ride from the coast to the city was a little rough, but we lucked out. There weren't any other passengers. We had to give the bus driver a little nap when we got off. As far as the Venezuelan authorities are concerned, we have their promise to stay out of our defined working area 'till sun-up. We need to be gone by then. While we wait, take a look at the terrain schematic." Beta Six bent on one knee and scanned a flashlight beam over a plasticized drawing of the park's main features.

Mallory and McKenzie huddled down on their knees to follow.

"We had two hours to recon the park, and all the possible Wi-Fi origination points are plotted here—they're the ones with signals powerful enough to give this guy access from anywhere in the park. It looks like he's going to keep within his past pattern. The shaded arcs are estimates of the best coverage. The team is spread out where they can observe the most likely spots the target would use to set up." Beta Six pointed a finger at four small circles.

"I want you to be aware," Mallory put in, remembering to whisper, "he could look different than the picture you have."

"Not an issue. Anyone in the park after 4:00 a.m. with a laptop we're going to grab."

3:55 a.m.

Swiftly but warily, Parnevik approached the bench next to the fountain where he'd previously signed-in. A sense of relief had seeped into his consciousness after deciding on an exit strategy.

This time he'd climb the maintenance ladder at the back of the fountain and transact his business with the government from there, keeping a close eye on all the arterial paths leading to the fountain. If he detected the slightest sign of suspicious movement or noise, he'd scale the fence at the back of the fountain and circuitously return to the rooming house.

With great care, Parnevik climbed over the spiked gate barring access to the maintenance ladder and cautiously ascended step-by-step, briefcase slung across his back. A common lawn chair was set out of sight, next to a locked shed with an overhang, perhaps a spot for workers to take an on-the-job snooze out of the sun.

Peering through the darkness, he was perfectly hidden. The weak lantern-styled lampposts gave off just enough illumination up the pathways leading to the fountain. The fountain wasn't operating, making the silence complete—no sounds from birds, animals, or human traffic, but clouds of mist were rising from the pond and surrealistically dissipating into whirling strings moved about by fickle air currents.

He pulled the chair to a location in the shadows of the shed where he could keep a vigilant eye. Checking his watch, a cold shiver ran down his back. He'd neglected to pocket it. The LED display read 4:05 a.m. He stripped it off his wrist and stuffed it in a shirt pocket.

It was appropriate to make them wait, he mused, booting up his laptop. Suddenly, he realized he'd have to conduct his dealings behind the shed to avoid the light from the screen giving his position away.

4:05 a.m.

"I have him in range," Beta Three whispered. "He's on top of the fountain."

"Standby, Three." Beta Six clicked the com button three times in rapid succession. "Team, reconfigure a perimeter around the fountain just in case. Stay silent and out of sight. Beta One, move outside the park and take up a position at the rear of the fountain in case he bolts. We have to let him finish his business before we tag him. D.C. will give me the word. Standby."

Beta Six placed his satellite phone in a loop on his belt and turned to Mallory. "All we can do is wait it out, Petticoat Leader." Beta Six was smiling for the first time. The three stood, looking over the deathly still park, Beta Six scanning with night vision binoculars.

"What will you do when you get him?" McKenzie asked.

"If I knew, I wouldn't be at liberty to tell you. D.C. has the call. There are several options on the board."

"I want to be there," Mallory spat. "Whatever happens to him, I need to be there."

"Settle down. It's not going to happen." Beta Six continued scanning the park.

Mallory grabbed McKenzie's arm, pulled him to the side at the back of the air-conditioners, and whispered in his ear. "I got us here to participate, not to sit it out on top of a building."

"We can't do anything. For shit sake, Mallory, let them do their job."

Mallory shoved at McKenzie's arm. "Not me." She reached for his shoulder bag. "Give me that XK gun or come with me. We know where the fountain is."

The air-conditioning units hummed to life.

"Mallory, you can't do this."

She came close to his face and looked him square in the eyes, features stern. "Now! I'll go alone," she hissed. "I brought my Walther." She ducked down and headed across the rooftop, taking care not to disturb the gravel while avoiding the antennae and breathing pipes.

McKenzie threw up his arms, grit his teeth, ducked down, and traipsed after her.

4:20 a.m.

Fifteen minutes was all it required to dispatch Sarcorcee's sordid questions and correct the naive technical assumptions from the Georgia Power engineers. Parnevik shut down his laptop and moved the chair back to his previous vantage point.

He had to laugh at the absurdity of the situation. The nanites were feeding off the lightning bolts and destroying the landscape, and in the face of the storms the National Guard was conducting a citywide evacuation. He wished he was there to witness the havoc.

The only productive scientific information this event would provide was that an uncontrolled replication wouldn't turn the planet into a glob of grey goo. Its need for electricity was the control. If Sarcorcee couldn't get the radio signals to penetrate far enough and deep enough with the equipment he'd have to muster to program a stop to the process, then without juice the process would come to a halt on its own, giving Georgia Power a shot at killing it. Or Sarcorcee could restructure his equipment and go after it piece by piece at depth. It was their problem now.

Parnevik's thoughts held no remorse as he took a moment sitting back in the chair, aware of the cooling effect of evaporating perspiration across his forehead. Visualizing the panic and devastation in Atlanta gave him a sense of satisfaction, and he didn't like that. He knew it was not a normal response to the situation. He renewed his inner pledge to seek mental health guidance and up-to-date medical analysis when he reached his new home. Part of him wanted to be just like everyone else: caring about others, making friends, laughing, loving.

He started packing the laptop in his briefcase, surveying the surroundings one last time. He froze. He'd inadvertently pushed the power button. The laptop screen blinked. He shut it down. He froze again. A couple was approaching the fountain.

"There it is," Mallory whispered. The fountain was shrouded in foggy mist.

"I saw a flash of light at the top," McKenzie whispered back, "so he's there."

"Okay. Put your arms around me big time—start kissing me. Head for the bench at the railing."

He put his right arm around her waist and kissed her cheek.

"Come on. More robust, and grab at my ass. Show some passion," she giggled. "Don't whisper. We're lovers late at night in a deserted park. We're going to look like we're going do it on that bench."

"Beta Six, Three here. There's a couple making out and walking toward the fountain."

"I know. Everyone standby and move to take out the target. The two civilians we inherited decided to get involved. I don't know what they have up their sleeves, but they evidently know where the target is."

***

Parnevik watched them take a seat on a bench at the fountain railing opposite his position. The man's hands were creeping down the female's skirt, and the woman was straddling the man, facing the fountain pool. She started removing her blouse, and they were kissing and groping each other.

Parnevik took his attention from the scene, somewhat relieved by its normalcy. He shouldered his briefcase and slipped around the shed to quietly take the ladder steps down to ground level.

"I'm sensing you're liking this," Mallory whispered, giggling anew. "I see him. He's moving to a ladder. I've got a good angle. Hold still." She reached into McKenzie's bag, brought out the XK, and leveled it against the top of the fountain railing.

"Mal, you'd better let me do it. I'm the marksman, remember?"

"Quiet…steady."

Parnevik grabbed hold of the ladder rail and slapped his upper arm, cursing at not having brought insect repellent. The spot stung, and he rolled up his sleeve to examine the bite. His fingers felt the stinger still protruding from his skin and a circle of swelling. Then it registered.

Reflexively, he staggered out of sight at the other side of the shed, ripped his Alvarez IDs to shreds, and tossed the pieces into the fountain pool. His eyelids felt heavy. He slid down the side of the shed. His sight faded to a single focal point, and then there was only the black of night.

4:25 a.m.

"Somebody got him," came a crackled announcement.

"Are you sure?" Beta Six replied.

"Absolutely. I'm hundred yards away. I saw him fall. What's next?"

"Wait, One. Who got him?" Beta Six's knuckles were white, holding the satellite phone close to his ear.

"Not me," the others came back.

Beta Six had his suspicions. Three clicks. "Team, all close in. Collect the cargo as planned. Extraction at the back of fountain. Three and One, bring the vehicles to the fence at the rear of the fountain. On the way, pick me up in front of The Villas. Six out." The team had prepped two vehicles parked on the street over night, presumably belonging to local residents.

The team leader had been given instruction: if under duress, cooperate with them, but do everything in his power short of physical restraint to keep the civilians away from Parnevik. It looked like that wasn't going to happen.

Beta Six scampered across the roof, entering and locking the top-floor access door. He jogged down the hallway and slipped into the elevator. It shuddered to a stop, and the doors clattered open. The attendant sat behind his control console—no reaction, his back to him, arms folded, feet up, either watching a small television set or asleep. The lobby was deserted. The muted sound of dialog from the TV cut into the silence.

He passed the guard and pushed out the glass doors just as two, non-descript four-door sedans pulled up to the curb. Beta Six got in the back of the first vehicle. The other was empty except for the driver.

Beta Six pulled out his satellite phone. Three clicks. "We're doing a circle check around the park. ETA your location in five minutes. Any cargo problems?"

"Just waiting for you. We collected the civilians. The cargo is wrapped. Five out."

When the two cars pulled up to the locked entry gate behind the fountain, the five team members, all dressed like college kids, were holding another man up between them, arms around each other, like they'd been partying all night.

Mallory and Agent McKenzie were standing next to the group. Mallory was transfixed on Parnevik's lolling face.

Beta Six got out of the car, walked to the group, and put a hand on her shoulder. "I know you wanted to face this guy, maybe even take a swing at him, but he's very asleep and will be for at least another six hours—I gather you or McKenzie took the shot—but for the record, we took him down. Agreed?"

"You watch our backs." Mallory said. "We watch yours. That's the way it works, right?"

"Understood. We need to concentrate on getting the hell out of here. The sun will be up in another forty minutes and our visas expire."

"How do we do that?" McKenzie asked.

"I'll let you know in a minute." He turned away from the group and took a few steps, pulling out his satellite phone. After a few gestures and garbled conversation, he returned. "Let's get going, "he said to the team. "It's Locus. I'll pick up Beta Two at the hotel." He motioned Mallory and McKenzie to follow him to the first vehicle.

The rest of the team climbed into the other car with Parnevik, and the two vehicles drove smoothly away.

"I told you we had options," Beta Six said. "Luckily, the first one is the best. A nice State Department 737 is parked at the diplomatic terminal at Simón Bolívar International Airport. It's twenty minutes. The trip home should be in style for all the passengers except one." He flipped open the case on his watch. We'll land at Andrews Air Force Base around 1:00 p.m. The President plans on being there to greet us."

"I don't think so," Mallory said from the back seat and slid her hand into McKenzie's, looked into his eyes, smiling. "I need a bath and a change of clothes."

"What are you saying, Miss?"

"We'll stay over. We can use Parnevik's suite." Mallory squeezed McKenzie's hand. "You can drop us off. We'll fly back tomorrow...commercial."

 One Hundred Twenty-eight

Atlanta: 5:05 a.m.

THE BELL 206L4, Long Ranger IV helicopter evolved from the legendary 206B-3. It combined a remarkable mix of power, room, and range. Innovative doors and a spacious cabin made the Long Ranger IV ideal for emergency services and law enforcement.

Rising off the Atlanta PD headquarters building in pitch dark, heavy cloud cover cut all the light from the heavens, and the penetrating sweep of the halogen searchlights glared back at the occupants through the moisture-laden air. The stink of ozone had saturated the atmosphere, and the violent storm cells were still lighting up the northeastern Atlanta suburbs, pummeling the ground with hail and drenching rain as they streaked along at nearly twenty miles-per-hour.

With the storms passing, only a light rain was falling in downtown Atlanta, but the rampaging replication process had engulfed over a square mile of the city. From the Georgia Tech campus, just north of downtown, to Piedmont Avenue to the east, the landscape was full of imploded buildings and rivers of solidified grey lava. The ground trembled as the advancing tentacles moved street by street, block by block, pursuing their fading source of life and leaving utter devastation in their wake.

***

"This is Doctor Sarcorcee. We're on our way to the forward-advancing tentacles."

"Wish you luck," Ms. Johnson said. "Keep this channel open and turn up the volume so you can talk us through what you're doing and what you're seeing. Turn the speaker on and attach the phone to something stable."

"This had better work," Ms. Johnson said, eyeing Ed Furlow.

"I don't get a feeling of confidence or competence from Sarcorcee," Furlow said. "His eyes dart around like a caged rat. When this is over, I hope he gets his due."

"If he pulls it off, he'll probably get a medal," Ms. Johnson snapped. "While we wait, let's get some fresh coffee in here."

"You know, it's still hard to fathom Sarcorcee being so naïve not knowning how to terminate the process." Furlow hailed the lone banquet waiter tending the buffet.

"My bet is Parnevik didn't tell him on purpose. The bastard wanted to see what would happen."

One Hundred Twenty-nine

Oval Office: 6:30 a.m.

THE PRESIDENT AND the chief of staff had survived on caffeine. It had been an excruciating ordeal. They both needed sound sleep. It was the second day and night sequestered in the Oval Office.

"The team's ETA at Andrews is 1:07 p.m.," the chief said, pacing the room and sipping a hot cup of tea.

"Great job...and no loose ends. Admirable. Team Five, was it?"

"Yes, sir."

"I want to meet them on the QT. Let's have them debriefed at Andrews later this afternoon. I'll go over on Marine One at the end of the session. Nothing out of the ordinary. Make up something to keep the press away."

"Yes, sir. What about Driscoll and Agent McKenzie?"

"The team leader said they were a pain in the butt. I'll bet he was beside himself, but at least they were there when Parnevik was taken down. He handled it well—I guess we send them back to Atlanta. Christine Johnson should handle all the personnel debriefings of anyone possessing even a smidgen of truth about the real events."

"I'll take care of it. Justice can provide personnel—You should probably have Driscoll and McKenzie over here as soon as they land, Mister President. I called them at the hotel in Caracas and asked them to fly into National. They deserve to know what transpired."

"That's a good idea, Pete. See to it."

"And Parnevik?"

"Put him in the brig at Andrews for now. Give orders to keep his face covered. I don't want any chance of him being recognized. For God's sake, Pete, we've got to keep this tight. And we'll have to figure out how to deal with Congress. We can't have this thing independently investigated. Get with Justice and see what's legal...executive privilege, national security. We have to be ready when the squawking begins."

***

At 5:30 a.m., Homeland Security had entered CNN Headquarters and confiscated the audio and visual records of their two flights over the affected area. Shortly thereafter, all media were directed to cease live reporting anywhere near the devastation on grounds of public safety.

The Georgia National Guard cordoned off the affected areas on the ground, and the FAA issued aircraft no-fly zones. The rampaging tentacular masses were slowing down as Georgia Power executed its grid shutdown.

***

"Mister President, it looks like CNN's latest assessment." The chief turned up the television.

This is Mariel Brinkman bringing you the latest update on Atlanta's devastation from a reactive chemical spill. As we speak, dozens of Department of Homeland Security helicopters are overflying the scene like locusts in a corn field. Initial estimates of damage are seven to ten billion dollars.

From our earlier visuals, at least nineteen multi-story buildings were decimated, including such landmarks as the IBM Tower, Colony Square, and the

Atlanta Federal Reserve along Peachtree Street. Up and down the avenues for over a mile east of Georgia Tech, residential communities are unrecognizable, covered with a grey syrup-like material.

At least nine major tentacles of destruction are continuing to move the carnage northeast towards the fading storm system, but at a slower pace. Since the chemical spill started moving and the National Guard declared a citywide evacuation late last night, text phone reports and on-the-spot videos have been pouring into the CNN newsroom, many of which are now posted on the CNN website. Eyewitnesses reported many residents in the paths of destruction elected to stay bottled up in their homes. Tens if not hundreds are feared lost.

At 6:00 a.m. this morning, much of the city was placed under quarantine out of concern for public safety. At the request of Homeland Security, the news media will no longer bring you up-to-the-minute live coverage of this event as it unfolds here in Atlanta. Hourly information releases have been scheduled by Homeland Security officials direct from Washington, D.C., the first at 7:00 a.m. this morning. We will bring those releases live.

For now, we can only wait and hope that questions about the chemical spill, and what appeared to be its synergistic reaction to the passing of this morning's storm system, will be addressed. What kind of chemical spill could be causing this disaster? Or are the authorities keeping the public away from the truth? Will Congress call for a special investigation? Until later, this is Marilee Brinkman reporting from CNN Headquarters in Atlanta.

6:50 a.m.

"The Director of Homeland Security is coming in on Skype." The chief brought the program to full screen. "They're about ready to go live with the first media update."

"Greetings, Mister President." The confident voice of Dorothy Novak filled the room. "We've worked up the first media release with your press secretary. Joel is a pleasure to work with— Mister President, for your information only, the efforts by Doctor

Sarcorcee to halt the event have failed. The radio signal was unable to penetrate to the depths required. Superficially, there was surface reaction as the helicopter made its passes over the area. It seemed to slow movement, but the process quickly regained momentum. But there *is* good news. The process is slowing on its own. Sarcorcee believes it's running out of fuel. Atlanta's power grid is now totally shut down. Unless there's another storm, we think we may have a hiatus. The National Weather Bureau, if you don't know already, says it should be good weather for the next two days. Georgia Power will begin the electromagnetic saturation of the affected area around 11:00 this morning. We should be able to tell if it is succeeding if the mounds and tentacles formed begin to collapse. We'll keep you posted."

"Good news, Dorothy. Keep up the first-rate work, and make sure you send a mountain of support personnel to Atlanta for Special Agent Johnson's cleanup job. You're the lead on this."

"Yes, sir. I'll look after it personally."

"Mister President, what do you want to do with Parnevik?" the chief asked. "We need to move him from Andrews."

The President unbuttoned his wrinkled white shirt and pursed his lips. "We fly him incognito to Nellis the fastest way possible. The only appropriate place for him is a maximum-security facility. I don't want him to wake up until he's there and secured. At a minimum, he owes the country the rest of his life. His knowledge has to be kept secret.... He becomes a non-person with no one the wiser, and we keep him on the most wanted terrorist list— make up a story he turned down offering assistance and reiterating his theft of sensitive intellectual property from a top secret government research project." The President turned away and headed for the restroom. "I'm hitting the hay, Pete. I suggest you do the same. Pass the word for Driscoll and McKenzie to be met and report here when their plane lands. Gutsy moving into Parnevik's hotel suite. But I can't fault them for taking a well-deserved break. I guess they turned into a couple."

Arming out of his shirt, the President turned around and took a close look at his bedraggled chief of staff. "You look like hell, my friend. I order you to sleep—in fact, use one of the pullouts here. I'll get a couple of hours and then work with Joel on a speech for tonight or tomorrow morning—sum up and show we've been on top of this from the beginning—announce a broad commitment of reconstruction working with the insurance industry." The President yawned, bracing his hands on his hips and stretching his back.

7:00 a.m.

Homeland Security officials released the first video taken from the air in daylight, covering three square miles of destruction. It looked like a giant spider with long, fat legs grasping the landscape, throbbing and squirming, spreading and branching, steam venting from openings like the fumaroles of a volcano—an insatiable, breathing animal consuming everything in its path, leveling and rendering the accoutrements of civilization into solidifying masses of grey gunk.

The last words of the Homeland Security spokesperson indicated the spreading of the spill reaction appeared to be slowing down in response to neutralization techniques devised by a scientific group recently called in to advise.

 One Hundred Thirty

Atlanta: 11:25 a.m.

ACCORDING TO HOMELAND Security's 11:00 a.m. information release, the process had become static. An ever-present, naturally occurring electrical current within the ground was presumed to be sustaining the reaction, but it appeared to be insufficient to facilitate further growth. However, the situation could change if electrical sources were introduced; hence, the present good weather was holding the beast at bay.

A lone C-130 lumbered down the runway at Lockheed's Marietta facility, taking off smoothly without attracting undue attention. This was Lockheed Martin's refurbishing plant for old, workhorse C-130s, and frequent flights in and out took place daily.

With broad authority from Homeland Security, Georgia Power scientists and engineers had been jerry-rigging equipment inside the airplane for the past fifty-six hours. Computer simulations had led to the final design configuration.

They'd borrowed the most powerful electromagnet in the world, the 45-Thybrid Bitter-superconductor, from the U.S. National High Magnetic Field Laboratory in Tallahassee, Florida. From as far away as Toronto, Canada, four portable 120-volt power units, a giant electromagnetic yoke, microprocessors to prevent voltage spiking, and huge coils of copper cable were requisitioned.

In essence, the equipment was designed to produce a localized electromagnetic storm, not unlike those caused by corona mass ejections—solar flares from our sun. In theory, if sufficiently severe, such blasts could destroy the power grids on earth and literally every piece of electricity-based equipment.

Parnevik's theory for stopping the replication process hinged on killing off all electricity to the nanites. When their rechargeable nano-batteries ran dry, the nanites would become inert, unable to replicate or function in any way. The artificial electromagnetic storm would neutralize the static ground electricity. The remains would be piles of crystalline sugars and solid, rocky-gray waste.

The plane was loaded with enough fuel to go over the devastated area three times. From a height of five hundred feet, the powerful magnetic-field output could be focused at ground level into a beam about a hundred yards wide.

As the C-130 cruised toward the target area and leveled out, the technicians powered up the equipment. The unexpected intensity of the whining produced in the confined space of the cargo hold was excruciating. The technicians scrambled to find makeshift earplugs.

Cameras with direct satellite links to the White House, Homeland Security Headquarters, and the Marriott operations center in downtown Atlanta were tested, and the beam was energized and focused at ground level for the first time a half mile west of the Georgia Tech campus. At one-hundred-yard, overlapping swaths, the plane would have to make fifty-seven runs to cover the target area. The plan was to repeat the coverage until ground units verified all electrical energy had been neutralized.

**

The 3:00 p.m. statement by Homeland Security brought good news to the media as well as millions around the world glued to their television screens. It included a fifteen-minute, high-definition video of a swath in the middle of the C-130's second full run over the target. Edited and slowed down, it clearly pictured the ground heaving in great waves and then collapsing, accompanied by massive releases of gas, dust, and flying debris as the plane covered the run at a hundred and forty-five miles per hour.

 One Hundred Thirty-one

White House: Next Day

THE SECRET SERVICE was given instructions to separate Mallory and Agent McKenzie the moment they exited the limousine at the White House North Portico, escorting the woman to the East Wing where the President could deal with her one-on-one.

Agent McKenzie was delivered to the small, private dining room next to the Oval Office where Peter Costanzo was waiting to set him at ease, field his reactions to the ordeal, and get a candid handle on his short-term intentions.

From his encounters with Ms. Driscoll, the President realized he needed to be prepared and undistracted when he confronted her. A serving tray containing hot tea, flatbread, and fruit preserves had been organized by the stewards in a cozy corner of the visitor's foyer in the East Wing. The President was hoping the thoughtful presentation would soften her inevitable demands. The plan was for her to stew in the opulence of the private setting until he was ready to meet with her in the press briefing room.

The President strode down the long corridor connecting the First Family residence to the East Wing, his mind playing over the scenarios of the last few days. He had to admit the woman had panache, and she was smart as a whip. She would have been a solid candidate to join the White House staff had she possessed the ability to compartmentalize her emotions. Well, he couldn't fix that, but at least he could attempt to see to it she experienced enough closure to get on with whatever she wanted to do with her life.

***

Five minutes had gone by. Mallory was seated in a chair next to the President in front of the same ornate table where the press secretary issued press briefings and where the great man often addressed the media and the nation over issues of global importance. The specially prepared delicacies and liquid refreshments had not accomplished their pacification purpose.

"Mallory," the President said, "I know you want to face off with Parnevik—I can't let you do that. You'll have to accept my judgment and my word he will never be allowed to mingle in any way within society. Trust me. His life is over. He will forever be classified as a terrorist, whereabouts unknown."

"Sir, two months ago that maniac was responsible for my sister jumping off the thirty-second story of a Las Vegas hotel. You're telling me that after all this hard work, all this time we've invested, all the destruction and killing, and this animal is not going to suffer."

"I understand your dissatisfaction, but if you will take a contemplative moment and focus on how much your country is grateful to you and Agent McKenzie, I believe your anger will subside. Your dedication in helping apprehend this mental case was beyond commendable. A national disaster was prevented through your actions. And the Venezuelan gambit was brilliant, possibly breaking the diplomatic ice with an arrogant dictator and opening up doors to settling future issues." The President had placed his arm on Mallory's shoulder, and their eyes were locked in a piercing contest of wills.

The tide started turning, neither releasing eye contact. Their faces softened. Mallory's pervasive scowl melted, and she let out a breath. She had a life to live and her country was in her debt.

"That was long overdue, young lady."

"Yes, sir, perhaps it was," she said without rancor. She reached for her teacup resting on a corner of the famous table.

***

Two Secret Service agents escorted Mallory and the President the short distance from the pressroom to the Oval Office, joining the chief and Agent McKenzie. At their entry, the two rose from a seemingly relaxed conversation from opposing couches.

The President smiled, observing congeniality written across their faces. "Hello, Agent McKenzie." The President offered his hand. "I trust the chief didn't grill you too roughly."

"No, sir. We leveled with each other. Let's just say I have a new appreciation for the actions taken."

"Good, good," the President said on his way to the coffeepot staged in its usual place. "Coffee, Miss Driscoll?"

"No, sir. Thank you."

"Peter, I trust you haven't let the cat out of the bag?"

"No, sir. It wasn't my place."

"Relax, Peter, I'm being facetious." The President turned toward the conversation pit, sipping his coffee, peering over the top of the cup, a twinkle in his eyes. He waved Mallory to the comfortable leather couches. "Before I begin, I need confirmation for the record that none of the last two months ever occurred."

"We understand," McKenzie said.

Mallory nodded as she slid into the couch next to him.

"Very well. I have a little surprise for the two of you. I know medals can't stem your grieving," he said softly, "but first let me ask about the dog—and Mister Phelps, isn't it? What happened to them? They deserve recognition."

"I can field that one, sir," Mallory said. "Mister Phelps and Edwin are on their way back to Kentucky. Phelps is bringing the hound dog back to his home kennel."

"Well, when he returns to that lake in North Georgia, we'll have a little something for him as well—now, getting back to what I was saying. Under our laws, as a known and proven terrorist, all of Mister Parnevik's assets have been frozen and are in the process of being liquidated and eased out of his Lichtenstein bank. The final amount is around eleven million dollars and will be divided between the two of you and Mister Phelps. What do you say to that?"

***

A half an hour later, Mallory and McKenzie clacked down the White House halls between two Secret Service agents.

"You *know* how mad I am," Mallory whispered, "but please don't think it's directed at you—but, you know, I still can't help loving the President. Even the chief of staff cared about us. You could feel it—but didn't he just bribe us? I'm not voting for him next time," she said. "I should have demanded—"

"Mal, you have to let it go. Any false moves, and you and I will find ourselves someplace in suspended animation. You did good. You're rich."

"So are you." She glanced sideways at him, frowning like a scamp.

A White House limo was waiting at the arches to take them to Reagan National and a first-class flight to Atlanta. Their last duties were to help Ms. Johnson with her event-vetting operation. But they knew better. They would also be debriefed and required to sign off on a pile of government disclaimers, their daily lives monitored for some undeterminable time into the future.

"Remember how he looked when the team piled him in the backseat of the car?" Mallory asked as the limo doors closed. "Head down, no expression, mouth hanging open, scrawny, weak facial features, wimpy, sad excuse for a human being."

"Mal, it's over."

 Epilogues

Ryan McKenzie

SOME SIX WEEKS after assisting Agent Christine Johnson in the interview and disclaimer process, McKenzie responded to an invitation to visit Chicago. Mallory was proud of her new offices, wanted to show him the town and introduce him to Jane Cobb, her law partner.

McKenzie had been busy in Miami with personal research, snapping back into the DEA's routine and finding a larger trawler, but the invitation brought back the warm feelings lit during a magnificent 24 hours of unabashed intimacy back in Caracas.

McKenzie arrived on a Thursday morning, taking a room at the Westin Hotel on the Chicago River and intended to spend the weekend.

The firm of Driscoll & Cobb was humming with business. They had taken on four convicted prisoners as clients and were consumed with the research necessary to lay compelling grounds for reopening their cases. The firm now employed two paralegals and two assistants. It appeared the partnership was off and running.

He hit it off with Jane, impressed with her dedication to seeking elusive truth and justice. Her sincere sweetness was refreshing, and her casual wit kept him amused. The passion the two women displayed for their work heightened McKenzie's interest. They were making a difference, something he cherished.

With financial security a non-issue, both he and Mallory had been at ease sharing enthusiasm for the future in multiple directions, but the opportunity to get one-on-one over the details never materialized. Unfortunately, late Saturday afternoon McKenzie received a call from Miami. He had to catch the next flight back to take care of DEA business. Some of his research had struck an urgency chord. The Saturday night he and Mallory had set aside for just the two of them would have to wait. It was an emotional parting, and McKenzie didn't even have a chance to discuss what he'd been up to in Miami.

***

McKenzie had taken his sweet time scouring the southeast for the ideal vessel. He'd also given a lot of thought to what he wanted to do with the rest of his life. He was bored with the DEA.

He finally located a ship nestled in the caring hands of a Sarasota couple in their early 80s. They'd had their pleasure with the twelve-year-old boat, and begrudgingly it was time to adjust their lives to the lesser hardships of landlubbers.

She was a fifty-three-foot Marine Trader, an oceangoing trawler with dual cockpits, a twelve-by-sixteen-foot enclosed sundeck, two staterooms with adjoining head and shower, and a double bunk-bed compartment. McKenzie christened her *The Shard.*

After two months of re-fitting, the ship sported all the latest navigation equipment, including a long-range radar unit that automatically warned of approaching vessels or aircraft up to a distance of sixty miles. The all-teak interior was pristine and polished, and the boat was virtually self-sufficient: a desalinization water-purifier; solar panels; a bank of eight, deep-cycle gel batteries; a 3000-watt inverter; and major appliances operating on 12 volts, 120 volts, or propane. A state-of-the-art security system based on motion detectors protected the ship, and secret compartments had been crafted to house an assortment of weaponry and survival gear. He'd stocked the boat with freeze-dried and dehydrated staples sufficient for two years.

The final project required moving *The Shard* to the working docks in Fort Lauderdale. The aft swim platform underwent a conversion to span eight by fourteen feet. It supported a hydraulic, cantilevered section for his Avon jet-boat tender. Returning to its slip at the Rickenbacker Marina on Key Biscayne, *The Shard* was the envy of McKenzie's seafaring cronies.

As McKenzie's obsession preparing the boat for every conceivable scenario played out, a pool of pent-up curiosity had surfaced, and he'd started spending time looking into the modus operandi Mallory and Jane were using in Chicago, uncovering potentially innocent persons serving time in prison. It wasn't difficult to discern a list of high-visibility candidates from old media coverage. Over the years, Miami had accumulated a long and varied history of heinous crimes.

The time he was putting into the endeavor slowly increased; he'd become hooked. In several cases, his research of trial records revealed glaring errors in legal procedures that should have been reconciled during the trials. The revelations got his dander up, but the infractions weren't sufficient on their own to justify reopening a case. But with the new forensic technologies of today, if the evidentiary record contained items lending themselves to re-analysis, new evidence might be uncovered to justify filing to reopen a case.

In two of the cases piquing his interest, McKenzie began to believe in the possibility of innocence. In both situations, a wealth of forensic evidence had not been brought before the court due to the lack of analytical techniques and recognized expertise.

McKenzie found himself at the brink of making a decision. The final hurdle to pursue or not to pursue would be whether loved ones believed in the innocence of the convicted; why they believed; and would he, she, or they be willing to invest the financial resources in an attempt to gather grounds for reopening a case. Should he approach family members and perhaps become embroiled, or should he back off?

McKenzie had planned *The Shard's* maiden voyage with an old seafaring salt, who had lived aboard a thirty-foot sailboat anchored off Coconut Grove for the last twelve years. All his buddies and cohorts at the Rickenbacker Marina were aware of his departure date. The ship was ready and waiting, and Cuba and the Bahamas were calling.

It was a wrenching decision, but he decided to postpone the voyage and go all in. Without letting Mallory and Jane know what he'd been up to, he had taken the next step with the two promising cases and contacted the family members. The wife of one of the incarcerated males responded favorably and was interested in talking to him.

Two weeks had passed since his last visit to Chicago, and here he was landing at O'Hare early on a Friday morning with Mallory waiting for him somewhere out in the airport lobby. He'd excitedly come clean over a long Skype contact: he had his first client and needed her advice. She was shocked, but her face immediately lit up, and she asked him a hundred questions.

He picked her out from two hundred feet away, standing hands on hips in the middle of the exit concourse. She was dressed in a beige jumpsuit and looked like a college preppie, long caramel curls held tight against her face by a White Sox baseball cap and hanging down both shoulders.

Ten yards away, he started to tremble and his forehead felt flush. He wasn't sure he could speak. From fifteen feet, he saw wet streaks running down her face, and he was suddenly overwhelmed with fleeting images, recalling silky skin, smiles, cooing, gentle movements, the well-being of lingering oneness.

McKenzie took both her hands.

She dropped hers to retrieve a handkerchief from her suit pocket and blew her nose, dabbing at her face. Then, like a chameleon, she looked up into his face and said, "Before we get into it, Mrs. Leonard needs our help."

Walking side by side down the concourse, Mallory explained that after Titus Smythe returned Edwin to his people in Kentucky, he hadn't surrendered control back to Professor VonMitton. All this time, she hadn't been able to cajole or trick him into submission and didn't know what to do.

"Rymac, she's at her wit's end. Smythe is driving her crazy, and she's in constant fear of losing the professor permanently." Mallory abruptly halted and held out a number ten envelope with a Delta Airlines logo on the front.

McKenzie stopped and stood in front of her with a dazed look on his face. "Let's move to the side, Mal." He shuffled to the concourse wall and dropped his backpack. "You could have told me about this in advance."

"I just got off the phone with her two hours ago." She leaned against the wall and placed a hand on McKenzie's arm. "You were en route…. It would have been nice to have the sat-phones."

McKenzie peeled an airline ticket out of the envelope and grimaced. "Gee, we have twenty minutes to kill," he said facetiously. The Chicago visit had morphed into a turnaround.

"Okay. Get it over with if you're gonna be pissed."

McKenzie took a good look at her flushed face. She was beautiful—clear skin, high cheekbones, expressive, long thin lips—but she was always on the move. You never knew where the next ball was coming from. "Sorry," he sighed, "I guess I had a lot of pent-up anticipation and excitement. What with the interest in the cases and all, and then your offer—What do we know?"

"Nothing more except she's got Smythe believing we're coming just to see *him*. It seems he slipped on a wet spot in the kitchen a couple of days ago and sprained his wrist in the fall. Poor Mrs. Leonard kowtows to his wishes. Evidently, he's become very sure of himself and dictatorial. He's been watching her like a hawk ever since she tried the usual method of retrieving the professor."

"The spiked toddy?"

"Right. He was wise to it and wouldn't drink or eat anything unless he made it himself. Mrs. Leonard said she feels like a servant. In fact, he's given her a celebration menu for our arrival dinner. He's going to play chef. But at least he's convinced the visit is all for him. Mrs. Leonard and I have a plan."

"Tell me."

Professor Barrius VonMitton

They landed at Atlanta's Hartsfield International at 2:30 p.m., rented a Toyota FJ Cruiser, and at 5:15 they were walking up the gravel pathway to the big country house on Lake Rabun. Late spring was everywhere: magnificent magnolias, flowering dogwoods, cherry blossoms, the greening hardwoods, and cool pine-scented air.

The last time they laid eyes on Smythe was three months ago at the debriefings in Atlanta with Agent Johnson. Part of the agreement prepared by the Justice Department required Smythe to notify the FBI in Atlanta if he wanted to leave the State of Georgia.

Mrs. Leonard was processed as well, and it had been clear even then that she was out of sorts dealing with Smythe, though she voiced confidence she could re-establish control given time. It hadn't transpired. Smythe had been in charge too long to be subservient again, and Mrs. Leonard was now a virtual prisoner to his whims and fancies.

During the flight to Atlanta and the drive into North Georgia, McKenzie brought Mallory up to speed on his outside DEA endeavors in Miami, and Mallory outlined the plan to replay the toddy gambit but with a twist. Smythe loved his hot buttered rum by the fire before dinner, as had the professor.

"The place looks the same." Mallory climbed the stone steps to the screened-in porch. It wrapped around the summer house and was cantilevered out over the clear green waters of Lake Rabun.

"I smell lamb," McKenzie replied, a step behind. "I'll bet it's a stew. I detect potatoes and veggies."

Mrs. Leonard greeted them as they opened the porch doors. She smiled, but there was a measure of worn-out sadness in her eyes.

Mallory embraced the older lady and then backed away, holding Mrs. Leonard's shoulders. "It's so nice to be here again in this beautiful place."

"We missed you." McKenzie gripped her hand.

"We better go inside and pay respects to the master of the house," Mrs. Leonard said, "before he thinks he's being ignored."

Mallory and McKenzie dropped their duffle bags inside the doorway and watched Mrs. Leonard add wood to the huge stone hearth, coaxing it to blazing, and then slipping off to the kitchen.

Titus Smythe sat in the leather loveseat closest to the heat, clad in a dark-blue, velour smoking jacket and matching slippers, reading a journal, evidently oblivious to Mrs. Leonard or the entry of the two visitors.

"Well, how have you been, Titus, or is it Dickerson Phelps?" Mallory quipped, leading the way to the comfy couches around the fireplace.

"Oh," he said, craning in her direction, "I do apologize. My concentration these days seems to be singular. Come in." He saved his place with a bookmarker, placed the magazine on the coffee table in front of him, and rose. "Ah, and Agent McKenzie. It's so nice to see you both again."

"How's the hand?" Mallory took a seat next to Smythe as he sat back down.

"I'll check on Mrs. Leonard." McKenzie strolled toward the kitchen. "Sure smells good."

"It hurts and throbs so," Smythe complained. "I do hope VonMitton understands. He can stay at rest while my wrist heals."

"I'm sure he does," she said gracefully. "After all, you were quite the hero." She changed the subject. "And I understand you're to meet with the President."

"Yes. I assume Mrs. Leonard told you," Smythe snickered. "I wish she would stay out of my personal affairs."

"Actually, it was the President's chief of staff. Ryan and I will be there as well in recognition of *our* contributions. I think it's wonderful for you…the award and attention…unselfishly volunteering your abilities over the years to law enforcement. I understand you're the first civilian to be honored with the FBI Medal for Meritorious Achievement."

"Yes, it will be quite an event for Dickerson Phelps. I'm afraid my real name must remain in the shadows, so to speak."

"Toddies, if you please," McKenzie announced, carrying a silver serving tray and trailing Mrs. Leonard bearing a plate of crackers and fresh, white sturgeon caviar.

McKenzie placed the uniquely designed country cups of hot buttered milk around the cherry-wood coffee table.

"Titus, would you do the honors and pour the rum?" Mrs. Leonard asked as she turned her back and headed to the kitchen.

"I'd be pleased."

"Don't make mine too strong," Mallory said, scooting off the couch and squeaking in her running shoes across the planked floor toward the restroom.

Smythe stood and reached across the table for a glass decanter filled with honey-colored, light rum. He went around the table and dispensed an equal measure in each cup, easing up on Mallory's. "Agent McKenzie, if you wouldn't mind, that's my favorite cup." Smythe pointed a finger at the cup in front of Mrs. Leonard's seat. Let's just switch it out if you would."

McKenzie mechanically did as he was asked.

"Thank you," Smythe said, exchanging cups and regaining a cross-legged position in the corner of the couch. He smelled the aroma and took a sip. "Absolutely an aphrodisiac in my book."

The ruse had been carefully staged. A double dose of sedative had been added to all the cups in anticipation of his due diligence.

Mallory returned and they called Mrs. Leonard to join them in a toast. Several minutes went by before Mrs. Leonard scurried out of the kitchen, a towel draped over the shoulder strap of her cooking smock. She took a seat next to McKenzie and picked up her cup, eying Smythe at the same time.

They all raised their cups. "To a nice reunion," Mallory declared, and they pretended to sip their toddies.

Perhaps three minutes of small talk elapsed before Smythe closed his eyes. His head found a soft resting place against the folds of the couch back.

"I think we should have our dinner," Mrs. Leonard said, placing her toddy cup on the serving tray. Mister Smythe should be out for about two hours. Now we have to see if it's been enough to break his control."

"What do you mean?" Mallory glanced at Smythe slumped in the corner of the couch.

"The sedative we use doesn't really put him to sleep. He's just immobile. We think he retains some perception of consciousness. As it wears off, the professor has always been able to come to the fore. He's told me in past episodes he's aware of waiting and is able to impose his will. We'll just have to see."

"Will he remember what Smythe has been doing these last months?" McKenzie asked.

"Most of it, if past experience prevails. But do let's have a pleasant repast. I have some background to share before the professor returns—or the other master. We'll have to be prepared for both possibilities."

The country dinner was indeed tasty: lamb stew in the English tradition with dried plums, a crisp garden salad tossed in a raspberry vinaigrette, and tapioca pudding for dessert. In between courses, Mrs. Leonard shared the research she and Professor VonMitton had compiled over the years.

The times when Titus was in control, Mrs. Leonard had grilled him on his background. As a full picture emerged, and when the professor regained the operating helm, he invested his time putting the pieces together. Titus Smythe was indeed a real person. He grew up outside of Edinburgh, Scotland and never married. He was a loner. He possessed PhDs in chemical engineering and microbiology and was an actual professor himself at Edinburgh University until October 6, 1982, when his recollections abruptly terminated while at a conference in London. His only other memories were those of his forays as Dickerson Phelps.

As time went on, Smythe's perception of his dilemma became a dichotomous conundrum. On the one hand, he knew the physical body wasn't his, and on the other, he'd grown to despise the real owner and was reticent to acknowledge the professor's presence. Lately, he'd gone as far as to suggest to Mrs. Leonard that he was capable of carrying on the professor's work, that no one need be the wiser. At that point, Mrs. Leonard had called on Mallory for help.

"What happened in 1982?" Mallory placed her napkin neatly over her dessert plate. They had feasted at the heavy, wooden dining table where they could keep an eye on Smythe and enjoy the crackling fire.

"Most mysterious," Mrs. Leonard said, casting glances between the two listeners. "Even Titus admitted it disregarded every scientific principle. Professor VonMitton and Titus were attending the same neurological symposium in London. A hit-and-run car accident took place in front of the conference building. It so happened that Professor VonMitton witnessed the accident. He'd rushed to aid the victim, but it was too late. The man had expired. In the professor's signed statement, he claimed he didn't remember any other details and drew a blank in attempting to describe what happened after he realized the man was dead. The next thing he remembered was walking into the conference about a half hour late, a little shaken up but no worse for wear.

"The dead man was later identified as a professor of micro-neurology at Edinburgh University. His name was Titus Smythe. And he was well known for his gift of seeing part of a person's recent past through sensing their intense emotions."

"Incredible," McKenzie said.

"So, what did—"

"Patience, Miss Mallory." Mrs. Leonard smiled for the first time that evening. "The professor took a trip to London just this last June. Back when the accident took place, there was a bank with an ATM across from the conference building. The London police had made a copy of the camera footage as part of the accident investigation and eventual identification of the hit-and-run driver. They allowed the professor to examine the tape. It showed a stream of light connecting the dying man to Professor VonMitton. It was only a split second and ignored by the police as just a flaw in the recording. That's all of it."

"That's unbelievable," McKenzie exclaimed. "Outside of the people in this room, no one would believe a story like that, except maybe Christine Johnson. What are you going to do now?"

"We've come up with a plan."

"Who's 'we'?" McKenzie frowned.

"Who else? Mallory and I."

Mckenzie turned and glared at Mallory. "Why didn't you let me in on this, Mal?" McKenzie already knew the answer. It was Mallory's modus operandi not to taint the evidence with hearsay.

"I wanted you to hear the story firsthand from Mrs. Leonard."

"Okay. I'll bite." McKenzie cast his attention back to Mrs. Leonard, who was fixated on Smythe still slumbering next to the fireplace.

Returning her attention to McKenzie, she was wide-eyed and looked conspiratorial. "If the professor comes back in control, he's going to go public and seek help from his many scientific friends at Emory University. If Titus shows up, we'll threaten him with a full FBI investigation into his false Dickerson Phelps identity and possible complicity in the missing person of one Professor VonMitton. The professor put the Phelps, investigator ID together by himself. It would easily break down under scrutiny, and there's no way Titus would be able to convince anyone he's the professor."

"Mrs. Leonard," Professor VonMitton called out, bent over, holding his head in his hands. "He's after me."

The three raced to the professor's side. "What can we do?" Mrs. Leonard croaked.

"Are you all right?" Mallory blurted.

The look on Professor VonMitton's face was forlorn. "It worked, but it's not the same. He's gotten too powerful."

"We were afraid this would happen," Mrs. Leonard said.

"It's worse than we imagined. We'll need to come to the arrangement we've prepared," the professor said, looking up at Mrs. Leonard. "Now don't let's get upset," he said. Lines of heavy sadness filled her face, and tears were building. "Let me collect myself. I should be able to stave him off until I've used up my energy reserves. But I can tell you one thing. It's terribly good to be back."

"Do you remember anything?" McKenzie gently asked.

"It was fleeting. Events seem compressed, but I realized Smythe was on the hunt again—the dog, the airports, the calamity at Georgia Tech—But of the time gone by since he's been here in this house, I have little recollection. He's learned to dominate my consciousness. It felt like being bottled up in a container. Horrible."

"What is this arrangement you mentioned?" Mallory asked, slipping next to the professor and taking his hand. He responded with a squeeze and an attempt at a smile.

"Give me a few moments," he said. "And perhaps some hot tea would help. Mrs. Leonard, if you don't mind, the dandelion root—and do stoke the fire, Ryan. Let's get some gaiety back in this reunion."

The professor clearly needed some space. Mallory followed after Mrs. Leonard, and McKenzie added more wood to the fire and reorganized the grate.

"With your permission, Mrs. Leonard, let me begin with a brief summation."

"Of course, Professor."

"Very well." VonMitton sipped his tea, fire crackling, everyone silent. "When we—Mrs. Leonard and myself—discovered the evidence of the melding and Titus Smythe's background, it became obvious two lives were at stake in this situation. Two valuable lives. Over time, it also became obvious that Smythe was progressively becoming stronger. Prior to this last time I let him come forth, we sensed he would not easily return to the status quo. It was bound to happen. And now, even if I could control him for a brief period, I could easily forget to take the medications that assist me in that effort, or lose the bottle, perhaps receive a poorly measured dosage, or the meds could go bad. Or I could take a fall and become unconscious. Any number of scenarios would allow him to regain control without my permission."

The professor turned toward the fireplace, seeming to bathe in its medicinal warmth, and then twisted back, stony resolve etched across his tired face. "We realized he was becoming the dominant personality, and a bargain of sorts would have to be struck before he was able to take over permanently. Neither of us relished the thought of legally pursuing Titus through public exposure. It would be a nightmare, counterproductive, and who could know how he would react? The man is capable of disappearing into the ether."

For a moment, except for the crackling fire, total silence filled the massive living room. Tongues of flame cast linear shadows of the huge timber joists and rafters against the V-shaped, wooden ceiling.

"I had vehemently disagreed with any bargain," Mrs. Leonard put in, "and I still do. He's too dangerous. He's oblivious to harm. He's selfish, obsessive, and devious."

"Ah yes, but it came down to what about his gift?" the professor stated.

"What about your research?" Mrs. Leonard came back.

"We've been over this, and it's been decided, dear woman."

"Okay, we get it," Mallory piped up. "What's the deal?"

"It's really in your hands—the three of you. I admit we've consorted a tiny bit in having you visit. We planned it out conceptually, as I said, some time ago. We offer—you offer Smythe control on a schedule of one week on and one off—except leeway is to be given if his gift calls him to provide assistance. We believe he will consent. If he does not, we are hoping you will agree in shifts to stay with me and monitor my state of consciousness, diligently watching for signs Smythe is breaking through. Mrs. Leonard will explain the medications and dosages to be used in different scenarios. In any case, we all go together to my neurological friends at Emory University and try to figure out how to deal with the situation permanently.

"Now, if he agrees, we want the two of you to act as guardians of the relationship. If Smythe doesn't live up to his end, Mrs. Leonard will not make the weekly control call you'll set up between you, and the guardians will rush in. Mallory, to further ensure compliance, I have given your law firm irrevocable power of attorney over my assets. Smythe can be separated from access, and theoretically it would be unlikely he'd be able to fend for himself using his present Phelps identity."

Mallory looked forlornly at her mentor, past memories flying across her mental screen. "Worst case, how do we keep him sedated if he takes over and won't cooperate?"

"Mrs. Leonard has become proficient with guns used to immobilize wild animals and will be ready to use one she keeps hidden—even from me." The professor nodded at Mrs. Leonard, and she rolled her eyes and pursed her lips.

***

The event unfolded the next morning. The professor and Mrs. Leonard were exhausted, the professor having experienced fitful efforts at sleep, fending off Smythe's attempts to gain control, all under Mrs. Leonard's watchful eye.

Gathered around the dining room table for breakfast, the professor allowed Titus Smythe to regain control. Mrs. Leonard had assigned the gun to Agent McKenzie, and it rested in his lap. But to everyone's surprise, once the arrangement was explained, Smythe was pleased to agree, mentioning, as he put it, "It's a burden off my shoulders. Maybe we can all be friends."

Mallory and McKenzie were jubilant. Non-stop discourse filled the two-and-a-half-hour drive to Hartsfield International, reviewing the last four months and reveling in a profound sense of well-being that the Lake Rabun duo had been successfully put to rest.

As they settled payment at the rental car booth, McKenzie's stomach tightened. They were about to say goodbye and go their separate ways. He had to return to work at the DEA in the morning.

Mallory lingered, putting her credit card back in her shoulder bag. "Anything you want to say? I've got to rush to make my flight."

"I'm good—"

"You're impossible," she said, glaring up at him. "So will you join us? You'll be the Miami Branch."

"McKenzie warily smiled. "You mean Driscoll, Cobb & McKenzie?"

"What else?"

"It has a nice ring to it."

"I certainly agree."

"Should I give notice at the DEA?"

"It's your decision…. We'll be able to confer together."

"On my boat."

Area 51: Six Months Later

Wherever Parnevik went, cameras watched 24/7. As part of his daily regimen, two armed guards were always at his side, escorting him any time he moved within the vast Area 51 complex. And no matter how redundant it seemed, each time he entered a room, including the restroom, he was searched and scanned.

Ninety percent of every workday he spent in his laboratory, perfecting *Fuerte* for DARPA. As part of a scientifically managed diet, he was forced to ingest supplemental vitamins and minerals. Every other day, a blood test led to rebalancing his medications to eliminate any possibility of depression and paranoia. Weekly MRIs and bone scans were standard to reveal any disease before it could get a foothold. Minimum performance levels were required in a variety of daily exercises. Except for his operations supervisor, his primary physician was the only person allowed to interact with him. He consumed his meals in a corner of the cafeteria in total silence, sitting between two mute guards.

***

"How are we feeling today, Mister Parnevik? You're such a lucky man: full room and board, no worries, no distractions, just dedication to your country, and full psychiatric support for your anti-social tendencies."

Parnevik's eyelids fluttered as the mental fog cleared. The knockout medication he'd been given allowed the doctor to work through the elements of his weekly examination unencumbered by a lack of cooperation. He quickly became aware of the IV and realized where he was. It was always a shock to awaken to the metallic smell of purified, super-dry air that fed his underground prison.

Mustering control of his senses and reining in the automatic tendency to struggle against his bonds, he was intent on not giving satisfaction to this demented swine by reacting to his abusive remarks; it would only set off a tirade of physical torture—bodily damage undetectable to casual observation. Today, he could not afford an injury.

"You passed with flying colors." The doctor continued talking to Parnevik as if he were unconscious, standing next to the gurney and shuffling X-ray prints, comparing them to screens on his laptop.

The medical ward was a sterile enclosure of three-foot-thick, sealed walls two hundred feet below ground. It consisted of several, self-contained, full-service operating rooms, an outpatient clinic, and multiple experimental labs. The ward was one of twenty-six rectangular units branching off a central corridor and housing a mini-rail line with electric vehicles transporting people, supplies, and equipment.

"The X-rays were certainly interesting. You see these two little knobs on the top of your pancreas? They regulate what you call your manufactured life." The doctor smiled demonically. "Pity, without them and artificial adrenaline you'd succumb to a state of permanent paranoia. And without your dopamine dampeners, the synapses in your brain would fry, bringing your mind to an absolute halt. I wonder what that would feel like, Mister Parnevik?"

The little man was talking to himself, circling the wheeled stretcher, clad in a clinician's white coat, latex gloves, a stethoscope, and oval-shaped wire-rimmed glasses. Sprigs of light red hair grew sparsely in unruly tuffs on his shiny pate. "I hate you," he burst out, teeth clenched. Phlegm spewed onto the floor. He raised the clipboard he was holding and slammed it down flat against the sidebars of the gurney. "I know you can hear me, you pitiful scum. Just remember, I can make your life unbearable, excruciatingly painful with a small adjustment to your medications. I only wish the Hippocratic Oath didn't apply in your case. To do you harm would be my pleasure."

***

The time had finally come. He'd patiently waited, every spare moment dedicated to absorbing the routines of the facility and memorizing the structural layout. After lunch would be perfect. His medication was freshly balanced, and he was scheduled for an hour in the aboveground exercise yard, alone, to complete his required regimen under the scrutiny of the armed guards at staffing posts along an elevated catwalk. Like any other day, after his exercises, they would allow him to roam around the fenced pen until his hour was up.

Early on, he'd discovered the water distribution layout under the outdoor exercise field by discolorations in the sandy soil. The pipes perspired, branching off a central conduit connected to a large, aboveground water tank supplying the base a hundred meters outside the fences. The branches terminated at Area 51's many innocuous outbuildings, and a major artery led to the belowground complex. A water fountain and shower stalls occupied the far side of the exercise area, tapping into the main water conduit.

Parnevik put in an extra-strenuous workout on the equipment in the yard, finishing off with a vigorous jog around the inside perimeter. Ten minutes remained in the session. He shuffled toward the shower unit, hands on hips, breathing hard and sweating profusely. Several times he'd almost coughed out the wad of plastic he held with his tongue against an inside cheek.

Open shelving contained stacks of fresh towels and standard, green cotton uniforms worn by the medical and scientific staff. The guards paid little attention as he entered the male side of the double-ended structure, taking with him a towel and a change of clothes. He stripped off his dirty, wet uniform and removed a granite shard from a pocket; he'd long ago found the sharp rock amongst the gravel in the exercise yard and buried it next to the bench press.

Out of sight, he showered and steadied himself, repeating his mantra: *Chim chiminey. Chim chiminey. Chim chim cher-ee! A sweep is as lucky as lucky can be.*

He inhaled slow deep breaths as he dried off and took a seat on the bench for the disabled. Carefully, he cut a three-inch incision down the midline of his right *quadriceps femoris*. His heart was pounding anew, and excitement surfaced that he hadn't experienced in half a year of suffering.

He tingled and felt no pain as adrenaline seeped into his bloodstream. Squeezing around the edges of the crude slit, he coaxed the oval pill casing. It popped out from under a layer of fatty tissue, slithering to rest in the palm of his hand. Sufficient *Delirium* nanite packets were encased in the one pill to infect a major city. He set the capsule on a dry spot next to him on the bench, stripped off pieces of his towel, and fashioned a bandage to stop the blood from leaking through his fresh uniform.

What he had to do now was gain control of the delivery vector. The water fountain was the answer. A connector of copper tubing was spliced into the main water conduit, but the water was under pressure from the force generated by the height of the water in the storage tank. Hypothetically, he'd solved the problem: the capsule could be delivered by inserting the four-foot length of joined straws he'd fashioned together in the cafeteria restroom after his lunch. He'd held it wadded up in his mouth since then.

654   M A R S H A L L   C H A M B E R L A I N

The tricky part was quick removal of the water fountain spig-ot, and, against the water pressure, stuffing the straw chain down the copper connector. Over many previous trips to the exercise shower, Parnevik had practiced removing the faucet and working with straw chains.

If he took too long, the guards would get curious and come for him; or they may notice the pool of water accumulating on the ground from the released water source. But he was ready.

He punctured the capsule, exposing the miniature rice pack-ets, and stuffed it into one end of the straw chain. Twisting the spigot free, he quickly jammed the chain of straws down the connector. Taking a deep breath, he blew on the end to stiffen the chain and move the packet along.

It worked. He felt a tug on the other end of the straw chain. The rushing water running through the main conduit was pulling at the chain. He gave the straw a hefty burst. The current would do the rest. The nanite bundles would melt into tens of millions of little packeted warriors. When ingested, human stomach acid would dissolve the packet's protective coating, freeing the nanites to follow their body map programs.

He retrieved the straw, checked to ensure the pill had been expelled, twisted the spigot back in place, and walked out of the shower room toward the yard entrance, carrying his dirty clothes and what remained of the towel. *Chim chim cher-ee!*

Now it was a waiting game. Parnevik envisioned it might take up to twenty-four hours for nearly everyone on the base to become infected. He couldn't wait for that to happen. The effects would only last around six hours, so he would have to make his moves when chaos was rampant and before the unaffected realized something was drastically wrong. If his timing was off, Area 51 would be quickly inundated with special ops teams from Nellis AFB, and the base quarantined.

Back in his laboratory, he was frenzied in anticipation and unable to concentrate on his work, piddling around with test tubes, syringes, and his centrifuge equipment to convince his guards he was productively on task. He didn't have a watch, but after six months of exposure to the base routine he guessed it was dinnertime. He had to summon every ounce of calm he could muster to appear natural if the evening's endeavor was to succeed.

***

He didn't bother going through the line. The evening meal consisted of a can of Diet Coke and two Twinkies. His stomach was rolling. By the time he was escorted back to his cell, he'd had adequate opportunity to observe dozens of people, their body language, and snippets of conversation. He recognized symptoms beginning to manifest. One of the guards in his transport entourage noticeably fumbled with the keys locking his cell door. It was happening.

Parnevik remained rooted to his cell door's peep-slit, keeping an eye on the guard station down the hall in the middle of the cellblock; he was not the only guest in this section. There were two guards, and it was about 8:00 p.m. and time for their relief. He had to pick the right moment.

A few minutes later, he saw the relief guards approaching from the other end of the hall where the elevator terminated. They were gesturing back and forth, and their gait appeared gangly, unmilitary. One of the two guards staffing the guard station had his head down on the table. The other one rose unsteadily as the relief arrived. Parnevik could hear pieces of the disjointed conversation. "Are you feeling weird?" one of the relief guards asked with a supercilious grin on his face.

"I can't seem to concentrate," the guard being relieved said as he steadied himself against the wall.

"Hey, you," Parnevik yelled through the slit. "I need help."

"I'll go," the same guard said, pushing off the wall. "You guys get Freddie moving. He was feeling dizzy. Maybe it's something he had for dinner."

This was the true test. He'd designed *Delirium* to cause a subject to lose not only his sense of balance but also his ability to easily put two and two together, making him susceptible to suggestion.

The guard left the station and was having trouble navigating, using the corridor walls to keep from stumbling. The relief guards were poking at Freddie and at the same time having trouble maintaining their own balance.

It was time. Parnevik scurried around the cell, stripping the pillowcase off the bed pillow and stuffing it with an extra uniform: a makeshift travel bag.

"Paa, Parni...." The guard was having trouble positioning in front of the peep-slit.

"Let me out of here!" Parnevik demanded with authority. "Didn't you hear the P.A.? You're supposed to take me to my doctor's appointment."

"No...okay." He fumbled the ring of keys at his belt. "We can do that."

The door opened and Parnevik motioned the guard inside. "You look beat," he said as the guard staggered. "You can rest a minute here." He helped the guard into the one chair in the cell. "We're going to play a game. You take your clothes off and put mine on."

"Okay."

Except for the grunts and scuffling sounds from the guards attempting to remain upright, the hallway was as silent as a graveyard. And then, one after the other, they slouched against the wall and slid down into sitting positions, heads bowed, chins on their chests, arms flailed out on the floor, mouths hanging open.

Parnevik hadn't counted on sleep as the general result of the combined actions the nanites were presenting to the brain. A blessing. On his way to the elevator, he relieved the guards of a Taser, a nightstick, a watch, and a radio linked into the base security frequency.

At the elevator, he turned on the radio. The voices he heard weren't using proper communications protocol. Conversations were disjointed and confused. One lieutenant colonel was shouting commands to subordinates who didn't understand or didn't recognize him. So, there was at least one person unaffected. There would be others, but before they could assess the situation and call for help, Parnevik planned to be long gone. The base would soon succumb to paralyzing pandemonium.

He entered the elevator and checked his new watch, spirits soaring, grinning like a Cheshire cat. It was 8:45 p.m. He pushed the button to the mess hall cafeteria two floors up from the basement cellblock. The cafeteria was silent, waiting for the 4:00 a.m. breakfast shift. Next to the kitchen a dumbwaiter leading up to the laundry. Parnevik hoisted himself by hand up the dumb-waiter, quietly rolled back the exit doors, and soundlessly climbed out into the deserted laundry. A guard was hunched over a small administrative table along the wall next to the loading platform doors.

***

At 9:00 p.m. every evening, a service truck arrived from Las Vegas, the nearest city with laundry service providers. Area 51 used the same catering, provisioning, and laundry services contracted for Nellis Air Force Base. The truck was waiting at the loading dock for a guard to slide open the heavy, steel double doors and assist in the exchange of clean for dirty.

The Mexican driver was unaware of what lay below ground. As always, the two-hour drive had been pure drudgery, much of it on poorly maintained dirt roads, and his only companion was the sound of the truck's faulty air-conditioning system. He was tired of looking at his watch and muttered a few Spanish cuss words. He'd been there since 8:45, just in case he could hurry the process and get home in time to see his wife and kids before bedtime.

It had been twenty minutes since he'd used the speaker system to let the laundry know he was there, but finally the heavy steel door rolled away, and a guard dragged out the first bin full of dirty laundry. The driver got out of the truck, opened the rear doors, and the routine began: he rolled empty bins into the building's holding area, and the guard rolled bins of dirty laundry into the truck.

As the guard was rolling in the last bin, the driver noticed he was new. "I'll give you a hand," the driver said, meaning to establish friendly rapport. The guard mumbled something, and they both pushed the remaining full bin inside.

The Mexican man turned to say something to the guard, but a blast from a Taser gun dropped him to the floor, withering, gasping in pain, every nerve in his body on fire. He was conscious but unable to move.

Parnevik stretched the driver out flat and stripped off his uniform. The pants fit him fine, but the company shirt was too tight. No time for details. He placed the baseball hat with the company logo the right way on his head and put on the driver's sunglasses. Hoisting him by his underarms, he slung the man's body over his shoulder and dragged him to an empty linen bin inside the building. In one deft move, he flipped him into the bin with a thump.

Parnevid drove slowly up to the control post, observing a guards having difficulty making it out of the bulletproof shack and attempting the usual overhead waving signal to stop for the sign-out procedure. All Parnevik had to do was sign the log presented, add the date and time, and he was on his way. He pulled to a stop in front of the gate and waited for the guard, who was struggling, supporting himself hand over hand along the side of the truck to get to the driver's window and present the log.

The guard managed to steady himself on the open window frame with one hand and shove the logbook at the driver with the other. "What's that over there?" He suddenly pointed back in the direction the truck had approached, facial features slackening, eyes wide. "A fairy lady," he giggled.

Parnevik looked back where the guard was pointing. "Yeah, weird. Where is everyone this evening?" he asked in Spanish.

The guard released his grip on the window frame and lost his balance, crumpling to the ground, a silly expression on his face. Parnevik hesitantly got out of the truck, pretending to assist the man. "*Necesito ayuda aqui*," he said loudly, but there was no response from inside the guard shack.

Parnevik cautiously walked the twenty feet to the doorway and peeked inside, expecting there would be several more guards posted here. There were three; two were sprawled in chairs, and one was slumped at a computer station, mumbling incoherently. Parnevik frisked the guards for cash and IDs and opened lockers at the rear of the guard station. He came away with some civilian clothes that would work, two cell phones, and a small tote bag to boot. Perfect.

A metal control box screwed into the side of the shack's doorjamb housed the control switch for the gate. He opened it, hopped back into the truck, and drove away. He clicked the radio on…nothing but static.

***

On the outskirts of Las Vegas, Parnevik parked the delivery truck behind a convenience store and scurried into the back to change-out the laundry company shirt for a black, Under Armour, short-sleeve, collared pullover. The off-brand khaki dungarees he'd taken from the Mexican driver were adequate. A pair of gray running shoes, white sport socks, and a UNLV cap completed the fitting. He used one of the stolen cell phones to Google information on the city's various transportation systems and arrival/departure schedules.

He drove a mile and a half to a Walmart Superstore, parked the truck in the middle of the lot, and headed inside to purchase a cheap backpack, a ditty bag, and a few personal items: a watch, better sunglasses, bathroom necessities, a mirror, and makeup items if he needed to modify his facial features.

A cab ride delivered him to a Racetrack truck stop on the highway to Albuquerque. He spent an hour watching the news in the trucker's lounge and befriended a truck driver, whom he talked into giving him a lift.

Trouble had been reported at Area 51. A laundry van had run through the guard gate on the way out of the base after completing its daily delivery. There were no injuries, the driver was in custody, and the van reportedly recovered. The incident was attributed to a faulty accelerator pedal. The media report made Parnevik shake his head.

***

Parnevik gave the trucker all the cash he'd taken from the gate guards and bid him a safe haul onto Phoenix. He'd been dropped off at the storage company where he'd stashed his Panamera Turbo S Executive model.

The following day, Arturo Alvarez rose from a sound sleep for the first time in his mesa-top hacienda eleven miles outside of Albuquerque. Parnevik retrieved the set of IDs he'd hidden in the house months ago and adeptly transformed himself into the respectable Argentine engineer. He had many stops to make today: setting up interviews for entrance into New Mexico University's Graduate School of Engineering, introducing himself to the dean, completing the patient in-take process at the Lovelace Medical Center, and gathering the items on several large shopping lists at grocery, do-it-yourself, and computer stores.

Tomorrow he'd get out letters of introduction and resumés to local engineering firms he'd pre-screened. Alvarez's travel visa was good for another six months; he was confident it could be converted to a student visa as soon as he was accepted for graduate work. If his research was correct, his future employer would facilitate any work visa extensions and sponsor him in applying for U.S. citizenship.

The last stops for the day were interviews with three of the state's most prominent plastic surgeons. Shivers ran down his spine as he pressed the Porsche's ignition button, preparing to depart from the Home Depot parking lot. He leaned back in the soft Corinthian leather, smelling the newness, letting the engine warm up, mind meandering. After all, it would be counterproductive to have to make himself up daily. A fresh start was a fresh start.

Women were going to like Arturo Alvarez.

CNN: Eighteen Months Later

Today the FDA announced positive testing results on a future line of mild stimulants produced by the Pharmco Corporation of Atlanta, Georgia. Two recreational products called Amor and Bliss successfully passed vigorous, stage-four trials. Pharmco sources tell us the FDA is drafting distribution regulations, requiring purchasers to register, setting usage limits, and mandating chip implants to monitor potential user abuse. The pharmacy operations of major drug store chains will act, under contract with the FDA, as distribution centers, and products are expected to be available in the next few months.

In a short statement issued by the White House, the President's press secretary stated that the new products should put an end to drug trafficking as we know it.

Dear Reader,

I hope you enjoyed *The Apothecary*. I have to tell you, I really love the characters of Mallory, Agent McKenzie, the split personality of Professory VonMitton and Dickerson Smythe—and even the decadent Corey Parnevik.. Many readers have written me asking, "What's next?" Well, stay tuned because all the characters in the first two books of the Ancestor Series of adventure thrillers are returning in the final book.

I've received countless letters from fans thanking me for *The Apothecary*, citing their opinions about the characters and the twists in the story. I love feedback, and candidly, you motivate me to explore new thriller ideas and stick to a writing schedule. So, I encourage you to tell me what you liked, what you loved, even what you didn't care for. I want to hear from you; you can write to me at author@gracepublishing.org, or you can keep up to date with my works, activities, and peruse book trailers at my website: www.marshallchamberlain.com.

Finally, I need to ask a favor. If you're so inclined, I'd appreciate a review of *The Apothecary* on Amazon or Barnes and Nobel. I learn a lot from your feedback.

Thank you so much for reading *The Apothecary* and in that way spending time with me.

In Gratitude,

Marshall Chamberlain

Coming Soon

Book III in the Ancestor Series

of Adventure-thrillers

The Ancestors: Resolution

By Marshall Chamberlain

Excerpt

 One

The Graduate Students

A SHALLOW CAVE they'd converted for use as their campsite was down some fifty meters from the highly eroded edge of an extinct volcano, keeping them out of the windblown dust, secure and protected from the elements. Subject to the weather, an Indonesian Park Service helicopter was scheduled to pluck them from their nest in the morning, the first leg on the journey home.

Sitting at a field table under the cave overhang serving as a front porch, the two were dirty, smelly, and drawn past their tolerance levels for each other.

"I just didn't send it," Linda said.

In Alex's view, she never did anything you asked her to do. She might do it in her own sweet time, or she might not. She was just sitting there smiling, a dirty-faced, spoiled little mole, eyes wide-open like she was about to eat a big piece of birthday cake. She was a perfect clone of her prune-mouthed mother. "Why? I was counting on you to do it like you said you would. This is the third time we've missed reporting. Don't you think Shalard might be getting pissed off?"

"It's your job to do the e-mail, not mine," she said, looking away, lips pursed and tight, teeth showing.

"You know it would have been bloody better if we'd never been thrown together here," he pressed. "You're going to cost me a grade in this course."

"Bugger off," she said, chewing on a pencil eraser, pretending contemplation.

Their summer vacation, compliments of the Cambridge University Graduate School Program, was six weeks of climbing around the craggy slopes of Mt. Agung, a crusty volcanic rim of eroded gray lava and basalts over ten-thousand feet in elevation, thirty-five miles from Bali's capital of Denpasar. Summer field sessions, collecting rock samples at volcanoes along the *Rim of Fire*, had been taking place for twenty-five years as part of Professor Ivan Shalard's pet research project.

The required, mountaintop field experience was a tragic ordeal for them both. They saw their world through narrow slits of selfish, parochial pride, the product of English upper-crust isolation. Volcanology had appeared adventurous and romantic.

Alex ignored her and stood up from the field table, kicking his wooden folding chair in a heap against the side of the rocky overhang. "It doesn't look good again," he lamented, observing the clouds forming below and billowing up the mountainside. "We're never going to get off this piece-of-shit rock. The helicopter won't come if there's any bad weather."

Linda put her pencil down on the table and turned in his direction. "When was the last time you tried to make contact with the satellite?" Her dingy brown hair hung in disarray down her face. A tall skinny girl, she carried a permanent facial expression of amiability, but underneath a manipulative personality lurked, tenacious and grasping like a moray eel. Bright, self-consumed and assured, she could turn warm and reflective in an instant, appearing filled with genuine caring and affection.

"Half an hour ago, when the clouds started to thicken. Nothing worked. I still can't believe you dropped the radio."

"It's not the radio, Mister electronic whiz. You keep missing the satellite."

"Well, *I* think it is. All it does is spit static—and the weather's not my fault. Maybe the helicopter will come in anyway," he said, changing the subject. "Stout and bangers. I can taste them already." He smirked, picked up the collapsed chair, and sat back down at the table, thinking about which girlfriend he'd call first.

"Yeah, but I hope this fiasco doesn't hold up my dissertation," she snapped, reaching for the stick she always carried around, propped against a boulder next to the field-table. She started tapping on the tabletop. "My parents are going to have a cat if I don't get my degree with the rest of the class. I can just hear them now, worried about what the Duke and Lady Kathleen will think, arguing about what kind of sickness they could say I caught in Bali—excuses for embarrassment."

Linda glared at him, slouched in the chair, wearing that stupid baseball hat, fidgeting in his pants pocket for a cigarette. It was his fault they couldn't communicate. The satellite was his problem, weather or not. What a prig, just like his bloody prince father. She turned her eyes away in disgust.

Alex hadn't seen her examining him as he lit up and leaned the chair against the cave rock. "Linda, I'm in the same predicament. You know that," he lied. "My family will have a fit if it takes any more time. They're already planning the announcements and making it into a reunion.... Even the queen may be coming."

For a moment, Alex's mind drifted among images of lofty royalty, and then he abruptly leveled the chair and stood up. "I'm gonna take a leak. Keep trying the radio, and watch the satellite monitor. It should be coming into range soon."

The only son of Alexander T. Townsend, the Prince of Wales, Alex was short, ferret-looking, quick to mock, and forever carrying an aura of self-proclaimed competence underlain by contempt for anything unassociated with power or wealth. He was prone to blowing off steam in short bursts and recovering quickly, believing he possessed prowess in self-control.

Twenty minutes later, he returned in an incessant drizzle, scampering under the overhang, stripping off his wet shirt, agitated and excited. Tossing the tarp-rigged cover to the cave-opening aside, he entered and began going through one of the gear lockers.

"What are you doing now?" Linda asked, stretched out on her cot and putting aside the paperback she was reading. "It's going to rain cats and dogs as usual," she added. "How about helping me get more dry wood in here and stoke the fire? It'll be cold again tonight."

"I found something—ah, here's what I want." Alex strapped on a geologist's tool belt and changed from sneakers to climbing boots. "Come take a look." He grabbed a rain suit and a coil of nylon rope.

"I'm not interested. All I want to do is go home. Help me with the wood. The downpour will be here any minute."

"Do it yourself," Alex exploded, tossed back the tarp, and scurried up the mountain trail. He thrust on the rain parka as he went, slipping up the rocky grade, plying over his righteous frustrations. Adding up the tally, he started justifying in his head: she was a klutz. She'd managed to break most of the equipment. He'd busted the stove, but she'd already trashed the control knob. The bitch let their tea blow away on the second day. The sleeping bags were full of fungus because she hadn't aired them out—her job. She wouldn't even go downwind to take a crap. Everyday it rained like hell. The dust and sulfur were tearing up his lungs, and his eyes wouldn't stop burning. Mornings he had to go five hundred feet down and five hundred feet up, just to fill six, little quart water carriers—his job. The pathetic packaged food was WWII rations; it gave him the constant runs. At least there weren't any bugs, and it was the last week. It would be good to get back to civilization and no more Linda Jan Berkshire.

***

The rain came in wind-blown torrents, and the dark clouds cut off most of the sunlight. Gusts tore at her rain suit, and she held on tightly to her hood-strings as she made her way up the trail, trying not to take a fall on the wet rocks. "Alex, where are you?" she yelled for the fourth time. She was almost at the volcano's rim. It felt like shouting in a closet. The pouring rain absorbed her words. The pelting downpour had beaten the trail dust into flotsam mud, streaming and bubbling along the sides of the trail.

He was purposely ignoring her, her mind snapped out. Why was she bothering, trudging around in the rain and muck? He was probably trying to get out of fixing dinner.

"Over here."

She could barely hear him off the trail to the right. What was he doing over there? There were just big craggy exposures of underlying country rock where time had eroded away the lava, nothing of interest.

She picked her way through the rocks and boulders, using her stick for balance, coming upon him kneeling, scraping, and digging with his pickaxe around the base of a large smooth outcrop that seemed to protrude from the host granite. It was an interesting formation, a sort of big mushroom without a stalk, sticking up about eight feet above ground level, a granitic intrusion probably created by wind and rain erosion.

The rain was abating as she approached, and the clouds were quickly breaking up and dissipating, leaving rays of sunlight glistening off the wet rock facets along the saturated mountainside. "What are you doing? I'm hungry. It's your turn. I still couldn't reach anybody. Probably because of the rain—or maybe the satellite's still out of range."

"Just button up for a minute and come here." Alex stood. "Watch and listen." He tapped the pick at the base of the outcrop and then moved up an inch or so at a time until he was almost at the top.

The rain stopped, and the dark storm clouds were receding down the mountainside, leaving it steaming and the air fresh smelling.

Linda was getting out of her rain suit and wasn't paying attention to him. "What's the big deal? Let's go eat."

"Didn't you see it?"

"See what? Let's go."

"Just shut up and come over here."

Linda shrugged and shuffled next to him, peeved, not wanting to have to start another fire herself, open the cans, and make something edible out of the field rations. It was his turn. "What?" she squealed.

"Watch." Alex repeated the tapping from the base. When he got near the top of the outcrop, the tapping sound stopped, and the tip of the pick seemed to sink into the rock. "Well?" he said, staring her in the face.

"Well, what?"

"You're not even curious. You're such a prig. Watch this." He put down the pickaxe, jumped up, and took handholds on the smooth rock face. His fingers had disappeared. Look at my hands."

"How'd you do that?" Linda's eyes were wide open.

"There's a lip up there you can't see." He dropped back down. "Listen, I came off the trail to take a piss. I was looking around, and the weird shape of this rock got my attention. I noticed the rain wasn't flowing off its top like you'd expect. From where I was, up there," Alex pointed, "it looked circular, so I came down and checked it out."

"And?"

"When I got here, it didn't look so unusual, but I couldn't see the top. I don't know why, but I threw a rock up to see what would happen. It didn't roll back down. I walked around it and kept throwing rocks. Nothing came down. So I piled up some boulders and tried to get to the top. That's when I found the lip. The top of the outcrop isn't real. It's invisible—must be a big hole."

About the Author

 Marshall focuses his adventure in life around principles that define him as an above average man. He is absorbed with his passions, no time for pets, lawns, plants, puttering around or companion compromises. He completed a master's degree in Resource Development at Michigan State University and received a graduate degree in International Management from the Thunderbird School near Phoenix, AZ.

He served as an officer in the U.S. Marine Corps and spent many years in investment banking, venture capital, and even a stint as a professional waiter. He is obsessed with preparedness, survival and independence. This combination of traits and an unconditional openness to life have led him to all manner of personal adventures and the authoring of the *Ancestor Series* of adventure-thrillers and other works. Chamberlain's primary worldview is simple but profound—"I'm in awe of the magnificence of this world."

He's lived on Estero Island, better known as Fort Myers Beach, in a little house he calls the "Writing Rock" for some seventeen years—but more recently dedicated to the motor-home life. To discover more about Marshall, his works, and what's coming next, visit,

www.MarshallChamberlain.com.
Write to him: *Marshall@MarshallChamberlain.com.*

Made in United States
Orlando, FL
11 April 2022

16702587R00378